# THE ANUBIS PLAGUE

ZAHRA KANE ARCHEOLOGICAL THRILLERS
BOOK ONE

MATT JAMES

NICK THACKER

*For our combined readership.*
*Thank you for your support.*

# PROLOGUE

**The Catskill Mountains, New York** | 20 Years Ago

Located approximately 100 miles northwest of New York City, the Catskill Mountains were the favorite vacation spot for the Kane family. Every summer, they'd take a week and camp at Bear Spring Mountain, something they all lived for. Even the children, like their parents, loved the outdoors.

Zahra Amelia Kane had always dreamt of becoming exactly like her parents. George and Hanan were famous in the world of archaeology and history. It was a subject that Zahra and her younger brother adored, though lately, Baahir had become enthralled — obsessed even — with Ancient Egypt. No one could blame him.

Hanan Kane's ancestry dated back generations, and was wholly Egyptian. Half of her blood flowed through Zahra and Baahir's veins. Their father was of English and Irish descent and had been born and raised in Long Island, New York. It was there, at the Museum of Natural History in Manhattan, that George and Hanan had first met. They had said many times that it had been love at first sight. Hanan had been stateside, studying abroad at New York University. As luck would have it, she and George would later be rostered in the same archaeology class.

From then on, the two never left the other's side — much to the chagrin of Hanan's family back in Egypt. They had not been thrilled that she had fallen in love with a boisterous *American*. But she didn't care. The two married the day after they graduated from NYU, and Hanan Hassan became Hanan Kane.

Their camping trip in the Catskills had come to an end, and now they were on the drive home. The entire week had been a fantastic experience for them all, mostly because they had been able to spend it together with no distractions. The Kanes had traveled the world together, but it was still hard to have *just* family time. Their work took them all over, yet they consistently refused anything to do with Egypt, which was odd considering their heritage. Baahir had become increasingly resentful towards his parents, even at such a young age. He *loved* Egypt, and George and Hanan had always quickly refused any, and all, jobs there.

*Probably has something to do with Mom's family,* Zahra thought, rolling her eyes. The twelve-year-old was a clone of her mother in many ways. She sported the same striking eyes and a thick mop of identical black, perfectly straight hair. The Kane siblings both had their mother's skin tone, too.

"You're very lucky," George had once joked.

"Why is that?" Zahra asked, sitting on the floor of the living room.

He grinned. "Because you don't turn into a lobster when you get too much sun."

Hanan had laughed from somewhere in the kitchen. "Why do you think I always carry around butter and lemons?"

The memory made Zahra smile. The conversation had come after a boy in school had commented on her skin color...

In a not-so-friendly way.

Zahra had punched the kid in the nose after the snide remark. Growing up in New York around the same time as the attack on the World Trade Center was difficult for anyone of Middle Eastern descent. Since then, Zahra and Baahir had been homeschooled.

But it wasn't all bad. That decision had opened up their parents' travel schedule. They became free to go wherever they wanted — *whenever* they wanted. Prior to that point in time, George and Hanan had turned down big opportunities because of their children.

While Zahra looked like her mother on the outside, she was one hundred percent her father her the inside. George was exactly how Hanan's family had described him. He was a boisterous American. Tall, handsome, more than a little cocky. But in private, he was a sweet and loving human being. He adored his wife and children. Few got to see George like that. Zahra loved *both* sides of her father's personality. He was tough as nails when he had to be, and soft and kind when the time came. George had grown up a scrappy, poor kid on the streets of New York. And more than a little of that feistiness had stayed with him as the years passed.

As they drove out of the Catskills, Zahra leaned around her mother's seat and spied the two lovebirds clasping hands. Her father drove with his free hand, a dangerous game under normal circumstances. The Catskills featured many narrow, winding mountain roads, but George had a lot of experience navigating them. This had been their fifteenth trip together here — Zahra's twelfth and Baahir's tenth. So far, since the kids were born, the Kanes had never missed a summer on Bear Spring Mountain.

"You okay, kiddo?" George asked, spying Zahra's glum face.

She nodded. "Yeah, I'm just sad we have to go home."

He nodded. "Me too, kiddo. Me too. But look at it this way, in a couple weeks, we'll be in Japan! Isn't that cool!"

"How 'bout you, champ?"

Zahra looked over at her brother. He didn't reply.

"Baahir?" George asked. "Earth to Baahir..."

Hanan turned around to look at her second born. "He's still mad at us, aren't you?"

Baahir leaned away from his mom and peered out the passenger side window. He had been giving everyone the silent treatment for the last two days, ever since George announced that they would be going to Japan for their next trip — not Egypt, as Baahir had hoped.

"Come on, Baahir," Hanan cooed. "Who's my handsome boy?"

No reaction.

"Baahir. Wha — "

"Honey?"

Hanan glanced over at her husband. His eyes were glued onto his overhead rearview mirror. Mrs. Kane must have sensed something was wrong, because her demeanor instantly changed from a loving, playful mother, to a hardened, protective survivor. Her eyes narrowed, and she brought her attention to the back window of the SUV.

Her face fell, and she practically dove back into her seat as George picked up the speed.

"How did they find us?" George asked.

Zahra was confused. "Who found us?"

George reached a hand for his wife's leg and gripped it hard. Then, he reapplied both of his hands to the steering wheel and sped up even more. Zahra was too short to see what was behind them. She tried to look but couldn't see anything. The only way she'd be able to see something was if she unbuckled her seatbelt — and she wasn't about to do that. Not only would she get scolded for doing so, but she'd also be thrown out of her seat given how aggressive her father was driving.

Whatever was behind them, it had frightened both her mom and dad. Her father had made some enemies over the years, but that was mostly with envious colleagues.

*Nothing life-threatening...* She didn't know of anyone who would want to hurt him.

Then again, she was twelve.

George suddenly sideswiped something considerable in size, sending them fishtailing around a bend. He quickly got their vehicle under control and didn't let up on the speed, much to the dismay of his wife.

"Slow down, George!"

"No," he replied. His jaw was tight, and his eyes were locked onto the road.

They took another winding turn at breakneck speed and, once more, ground against something. Zahra guessed that it had been the safety railing lining the near-vertical drop to their right.

"Dammit, George, I said — "

"And I said, no!" he shouted, cutting her off. Zahra had never heard her dad yell at her mom like that before. "I won't let them harm you."

*So, it's not Dad that they're after,* she thought.

Zahra was about to inquire as to who would want to hurt her saint of a mother. Hanan was, in every way, the perfect woman. Stunning and kind, but also tough as nails when she had to be. As far as Zahra knew, she had never wronged a single person in her life. But her mother's past was an enigma to her and Baahir.

Their SUV was suddenly rammed from behind. It took George everything he had in him to keep control of it. Everyone screamed as they were hit again. This time, they slid across the road and hit the safety railing. To her left, Zahra witnessed a massive black Suburban slam into the driver's side of their vehicle and pin them in place against the barrier. The cry of shrieking metal was agonizing, as was the sound of her mother's cries. She reached back and gripped both of her weeping children's hands.

Zahra hadn't even realized that she had been crying. They all were — except for George. He was an emotional man, but was currently too focused on keeping them on the road to be bothered with such things.

"Daddy!" Zahra shouted. The driver behind them yanked on the wheel, sped up, and hit them again.

George tried to brake, but they were then hit by a *second* vehicle. It had come out of nowhere.

This one sent them careening through the guardrail and over the edge.

Zahra felt her stomach turn as their car flipped over on its side.

...and then kept rolling.

She held on to her seatbelt strap and the handle above her window as the Kanes' vehicle barrel-rolled down the steep grade of earth.

Zahra didn't know how many times they had rolled by the time they stopped. She shook her head, hearing a high-pitched whine emanating from somewhere inside her brain, shocked that she was still conscious.

And now she wished she wasn't.

She could hear her father's wails, even over the sound of the ringing in her head.

"*Hanan*!" he shouted, bleeding from a cut to his forehead. From her vantage point, all Zahra could see was her dad's face. He was turned toward her mother. He shook her. "Hanan. Wake up. We need to — "

The tears in George's eyes started to fall. "Hanan?" He shook her again.

Zahra watched as her mom's head flopped to the side. She wasn't moving. Zahra tried to unbuckle her seatbelt and help her father but couldn't. It had jammed during the wreck.

She leaned around her mom's headrest but still couldn't see much of anything... except blood.

Lots and lots of blood.

**The British Museum,** London, England | 5 Years Ago

Zahra was working late at the museum. She was new to the job, and wanted to make a good impression on those around her — mainly a young Brit named Dina, a woman Zahra knew would become a close friend. She waited outside the museum lobby's door for Zahra now that their shift had ended.

Though the two women were polar opposites of one another, they had hit it off the first time they'd shared a shift. Zahra enjoyed getting her hands dirty, rarely ever dressing up to attract the attention of the opposite sex.

Dina, on the other hand, *loved* doing anything that would attract the opposite sex. Actually, Zahra couldn't be sure it was just the *opposite* sex Dina was trying to attract.

"I'm just living my best life," she'd told her once.

The blonde with the short, styled pink haircut savored the feeling of people ogling her from afar. That same sort of attention made Zahra, a naturally beautiful woman in her own right, uncomfortable. Even now, with no makeup on, and sporting a thick, winter coat, Zahra was a head-turner.

"Goodnight, Bernie!" Dina called, waving back toward the front doors as they closed. A slight, gray-haired man in his sixties returned the gesture, then speedily flicked the deadbolt. Zahra was about to wave goodbye, but Bernie had already stepped away from the door.

*No doubt, returning to his desk to finish his movie,* Zahra thought. She had caught the man watching the 1968 Steve McQueen classic, *The Thomas Crown Affair*. She personally preferred Pierce Brosnan's 1999 portrayal.

Zahra smiled. "Do you find it funny that Bernie is watching a movie about an elaborate museum heist while he's working in a museum?"

Dina snorted, smiling wide. "Who wouldn't find that funny?"

The midwinter evening was brisk and the air wet. Not cold enough to snow, it teased with sporadic rain. Zahra preferred the heat — humid or not. For whatever reason, she had never developed a positive rapport with the cold. The temperature didn't seem to bother Dina, though. She had grown up here — a true Englishwoman, through and through. Zahra had spent a large percentage of her childhood in the milder climates of the U.S., as well as the blistering heat of Egypt.

The pair descended the steps down the front entrance, stopping on the sidewalk outside the museum.

"See you in the morning?" Zahra asked.

Dina yawned. "Unfortunately, yes. Which means I'll actually have to go to bed at a decent time."

"Tell me about it." Zahra gave her a tired smile. She checked her watch and cringed.

"Share a cab?" Dina had asked.

Zahra didn't answer right away. She liked Dina, but she wasn't one to have too many close friendships. She was a loner outside of work, and always had been. She would have kept their relationship purely professional if it were up to her. It wasn't that she didn't *like* Dina. It was just... the way she was.

"Come on, Z. You live out near me, right? Plus," she pulled out a black, flat object from her purse, "I have something to keep us warm."

Dina's nickname for her — 'Z' — amused Zahra since she had only recently started digging into the history of *The Lost City of Z*. An expedition was already in the works, though Zahra had no idea when — or if — she'd receive the approval from the museum. It would be an expensive undertaking, but her new bosses were excited about the possibilities, and it looked like it might go ahead.

*Let's hope for the best.*

"Is that a flask?" Zahra asked, eyeing the object.

Dina unscrewed the top and grinned. "Sure is. Got some nice stuff in it too."

Zahra sighed and shrugged, holding out her hand out. "What is it?"

"Bourbon. Something called *Eagle Rare*, I think. My uncle brought it back from America for me."

Dina unscrewed the cap as the two headed out, turning down Great Russell Street. They walked and talked for a few minutes, sipping on the warming, high-octane booze. For good measure, Dina had slipped the flask back into her purse as they approached the intersection at Bloomsbury Street. They quickly crossed under the flashing signal.

Once safely across the road, Dina redrew the flask. The streets were utterly empty. It being late on a Tuesday night probably had something to do with it. There was no one around to reprimand them for drinking in public. It was just Zahra and Dina.

"Well, 'ello," a voice called out from the shadows.

And *them*.

The two women stopped and spun toward the Cockney voice.

A pair of large men had somehow snuck up right behind them. Zahra guessed they had more than likely come down Bloomsbury Street just as she and Dina had hurried across the road. The two women hadn't seen them coming, apparently too lost in their conversation... and their bourbon.

The men were only ten feet from Zahra and Dina now. Both strangers looked to be heavily intoxicated, perhaps even on drugs. Their eyes were dark with heavy bags underneath them. Regardless of their current mental state, they didn't look like they wanted to casually exchange pleasantries. These guys wanted to forcibly exchange something else.

*Like bodily fluids.*

Dina clutched Zahra's left bicep. She was of slight build, petite, and Zahra knew she wasn't athletic. The worst fight she had ever been in was probably with herself over which article of clothing to wear on a Friday night out.

Unlike her friend, however, Zahra had no fear of these two. She had dealt with far more challenging odds in her life than a pair of overstimulated, voracious sex hounds.

Zahra leaned in close to Dina and whispered. "Whatever happens, stay behind me."

"Huh?" Dina was confused. "What do you — "

Zahra gave her a stern look and then slipped out of her grip. "Hey, boys," Zahra said, tossing back her shoulder-length hair. She buried her piercing eyes into the bald man on her left. He was the biggest of the two, and the one she would focus on first if things got dicey.

The bald guy spoke up first. "What are you two lovely ladies, like yourselves, doin' out at this hour?"

Every word was stilted, leaned on. He was definitely drunk, or at least well on his way.

Zahra held up the open flask, ready to play along. *Goad him in,* she thought. She let loose a giggle and a fake hiccup. "Getting... gettin' tipsy. Want some?"

The left side of Baldy's mouth curled into a small smile. He shrugged and stepped forward. "'on't mind if I do. Gerald, by the way." He tipped his head toward his partner. "An' this is Mickey. What about you?"

He reached forward. Instead of going for the flask, though, Gerald bypassed it and sensually rubbed on Zahra's shoulder with a clammy, cold palm. Mickey's eyes latched onto the intimate gesture, and he swallowed. His face twitched with a disgusting, frenzied delight.

If Zahra didn't know any better, this guy was about to do something terrible.

*And something he'll regret*, Zahra thought.

"She's Julie, and I'm Mar — "

Zahra cut herself off while she had them focusing on her words, then she forced Gerald away with a double-palm-strike to his chest. Without looking, she splashed the bourbon into Mickey's face with a flick of her wrist. She followed that with a snap kick into Gerald's crotch, dropping the man to his knees.

With him somewhat incapacitated, she turned her attention to Mickey, who was shrieking and rubbing the alcohol deeper into his bloodshot eyeballs.

Knowing that he wasn't an immediate threat, she allowed Mickey to blindly swipe at the air. She'd focus on Gerald instead. He was still on his knees, holding his privates tightly with both his hands.

*Time to teach you boys a lesson.*

"How do you want it?" she asked confidently, standing tall with her hands on her hips.

Gerald growled from his knees. "*Fuck* off, you twa —! "

She didn't let him finish. Zahra stepped in close and drove her right knee into his unprotected face. The single blow rocked him back, and he fell to the sidewalk in an unconscious, bloody heap. The impact had broken the man's nose.

Zahra was half-tempted to leave Mickey be, but she also wanted to continue her lesson in *civility*. She waited for Mickey to get himself into position, and then silently snuck up behind him. Zahra kicked-out the back of his left knee. The strike stumbled Mickey, but he still needed a little bit of a push. She took two steps and leaped into the air, delivering a stiff front kick into the middle of Mickey's shoulder blades. The impact threw the man forward, driving him headfirst into the post of a nearby metal streetlamp. With a resounding *gong*, Mickey went down like a ton of bricks, flopping onto his back in the gutter.

*Where he belongs.*

Breathing hard from the cold air but not the short-lived altercation, Zahra picked up the empty flask, then handed it back to Dina. The blonde was shellshocked by what she had just witnessed. She couldn't take her eyes off the carnage.

Zahra waved her hand in front of her friend's eyes. "Earth to Dina..."

The Brit blinked. "Wh — ," she stuttered, still staring at Gerald, "*what* did you say you did in the army?"

Zahra shrugged and pulled her hair into a ponytail. "I was a linguist. Why?"

# CHAPTER 2
# ABBAS

**Mena House Golf Course, Giza, Egypt** | Present Day

Emergency lights flashed in intermittent patterns, giving Abbas Faez a headache that rivaled the discomfort of a full-blown migraine. It was getting late, nearly ten o'clock, and it had been raining off and on since the sun had gone down. The weather was an anomaly and gave him the chills. He attempted to blink away the pain and pressure pushing on the back of his eyes but failed to achieve the bliss he desperately sought.

The tall, thickly built construction boss snarled at the incoming headlights. Their illumination sent the beast into a near rampage. He lifted one of his calloused hands, and he blocked out the pair of lights the best he could. But the damage was done. He sighed, breathing hard out through his nose. The man — the *expert* — that had just arrived wasn't to blame for Abbas' condition. Dehydration and a lack of sleep were at fault here. Abbas drank too much for his own good — and not water.

The newcomer climbed out of his well-maintained silver SUV, and he quickly popped an umbrella, not that the device did much to protect the man from the elements. His bottom half was immediately doused by a combination of the deluge and the sharp gusts. Abbas was beginning to think the gods of old had cursed this job. A week before, a sinkhole had opened up beneath the southern corner of a picturesque nine-hole golf course, swallowing a chunk of the eighth green, as well the bordering road, Othman Ibn Effan. Once Abbas and his people had cleared a large portion of the earth and rock, a second, more significant section of land had fallen in, taking a backhoe and its operator with it.

Even a man of Abbas' rough background and character understood the historical importance of their find. They had spotted the discovery after rescuing the backhoe's operator from being buried alive. Abbas' team had been working through the night to clear debris until they had come across something that ground their efforts to a halt.

"Hello," the expert said, holding out his hand, "My name is Dr. Hassan. I'm an Egyptologist with the Ministry of Antiquities. I'm here to take a look at your 'significant discovery.'"

That was the term Abbas had used to describe what he had found, though he had said it in a much less condescending way. For that reason, he decided not to shake the man's hand. He simply tipped his head back and muttered. "Follow me."

He didn't have the time or patience for pleasantries, especially with a person who carried himself in the way that Hassan did. All people like Hassan cared about was their job — in this case, to build a golf course. That was a bust, now that they had found something of historical significance — Abbas knew that immediately. This would not be the first time people had been stopped from doing their jobs in the name of history. He knew that the find below their feet would take months, perhaps *years*, to properly sift through and catalog.

The last time something like this happened was five years ago. That discovery had been nothing more than a hole in the ground that some thief had crawled into — and died in — 2,500 years prior.

It had caused a mild panic amongst Egyptologists and archaeologists, but had turned out to be nothing extraordinary.

*This is different,* he thought, visualizing the immense structure. He knew he and his team were done for good here — so was the golf course, more than likely. *This one might be special.*

Abbas led Hassan down off the road. To enter the golf course, one needed to step over a thigh-high, temporary barrier constructed of yellow tape and road cones. Abbas' muddied boots sloshed across a narrow, muddy stream while Hassan avoided it with every ounce of his being. The construction foreman could tell that the *expert* was comfortable operating in a clean and controlled atmosphere, whereas Abbas was more used to conditions such as this.

*Except for the rain,* Abbas thought, choosing his steps wisely. The earth had already been difficult to navigate. Add in the rain, and it made it nearly impossible to do so without losing your footing.

Hassan started to go down but grabbed onto Abbas' arm for support. The larger man allowed the expert to right himself before shrugging out of his grasp. The pair made their way down a switchbacking trail, descending thirty feet before reaching a single large tent. Abbas' crew had set up shop here as the rain came in. Now, it was the only somewhat-dry place within what had quickly become an archaeological excavation instead of a construction site.

Both men shielded their faces from the wind, entering the tent just as the natural phenomena tried to rip the structure away from the ground. Every able-bodied person held onto one of the various supports and rode out the barrage. Even Hassan lent a hand. Abbas was grateful too. His crew was down to barebones numbers since he was forced to shut down the job the night before. Now, the only other people inside the tent other than himself and Dr. Hassan were two of his men and a man who had introduced himself as a government representative. It was this man who had decided to involve the Ministry.

The storm raged for two more minutes, and just as the operations tent was about to finally lose the battle against nature, the outside force calmed down to nothing. Abbas breathed hard, forgetting all about his pulsating head. He patted his men on the shoulders and gave Hassan a curt, thankful nod. The Egyptologist looked shaken, but seemed otherwise fine. Same for the government agent.

Finally comfortable with the state of the tent, Abbas made the introductions.

"Dr. Hassan, this is Fahim Rahal. He represents the government, in some capacity, though he has yet to reveal exactly *what* that capacity is."

"It is a pleasure to meet you," Hassan offered his hand, same as he had done with Abbas. And just as the rough foreman had done, Rahal did not accept the offer.

"Likewise," Rahal said, folding his arms across his chest. "Is it just you?"

Hassan looked around. "It is. I will send for more men if I decide that this so-called 'significant discovery' is worth their time."

A sly smile formed on the agent's face. "It will be."

"What does that mean?" Hassan asked, eyebrows raised.

Rahal glanced at Abbas. "Show him."

Abbas glared at the agent, but he spoke to the Egyptologist. "This way."

Hassan nodded and skirted around the unnerving, government agent.

The front of the tent held twin flaps, which were currently lashed shut. Abbas swiftly untied them and held one of them open for Hassan. He stepped through and saw nothing. Only blackness welcomed them.

"Ghazzi!" Abbas shouted. "Lights!"

A slight, small-statured man came into view and rushed forward with nothing except a flashlight with a dim, yellow bulb. He entered inside the yawning void and disappeared from sight. Seconds passed before the telltale hum of a generator puttered to life.

A series of construction lights ignited, and the "significant discovery" came into full view.

**Mena House Golf Course, Giza, Egypt** | Present Day

Dr. Baahir Hassan stumbled backward, nearly spilling to the unforgiving, rocky ground. Abbas had caught him, holding him aloft while the Egyptologist was lost inside his own head as he attempted to dissect what greeted him. But he couldn't.

It was obviously a tomb entrance, but it was unlike any other tomb entrance he had ever seen or studied. The crypt had been built directly into the wall, similar to Abu Simbel. But instead of the twenty-five-foot-tall figures depicting that of the men or women responsible for it, the figures on either side of the blasted open, five-foot-tall doorway were that of Anubis, the jackal-headed god of the afterlife.

His initial hypothesis had been that this place was a crypt of some kind. He was wrong, though. Tombs were designed to house bodies. Baahir knew that this place, even without exploring it, held no human remains because of the god it was dedicated to.

"A temple devoted to Anubis?" Baahir asked himself, thinking aloud. "I can't believe it..."

Abbas understood his tone. "You don't sound like you do 'believe it.'"

Baahir shrugged. "There are no records of anything like this." He took his eyes off the relic and looked up at the taller foreman. "This is entirely new to us — to history." He turned back to look at the find and saw something he didn't appreciate. "I see you found a way in."

Abbas scratched his head. "We, um, may have tried to have a look before *he* arrived." The barrel-chested construction worker pointed at the government agent. "Can you blame us?"

Baahir couldn't blame them. Men like this — hard-working blue-collar folks — didn't earn a noteworthy wage. Abbas' crew had done what they thought was right for themselves. They had discovered this place and should get credit for it. But that wasn't at the top of Baahir's list of priorities.

Searching the temple was.

"Have you been inside?" Baahir asked, stepping forward.

Abbas shook his head. "No. We were about to, but then Mr. Rahal showed up and shut us down. The storm rolled in shortly after that. Now, you."

Baahir swallowed hard. Life must have thrown this guy some nasty curveballs lately, and it was easy to tell that he didn't appreciate any of it. For his own good, Baahir would watch what he said to the man.

"I'm sorry you've been troubled by all this." Abbas' severe, stoic glare softened for a split-second. He seemed to appreciate Baahir's apology, even though none of this was his doing. It was all bad luck and bureaucratic protocol. Baahir decided to throw the Abbas a bone. He motioned to the entrance. "If it makes you feel any better, you're about to become a very famous man for finding all of this."

Though there were protocols to follow, this was Egypt. There was plenty of money to be made in situations like this, not by selling the site but by selling *access* to it. While the red tape of bureaucracy stretched around the Ministry of Antiquities and provided everyone there with enough paperwork for the next two years, the locals onsite could manage access to the temple.

For a fee, of course.

It had been a common, age-old tradition. Unless met with a show of force from the Egyptian military, this temple would effectively become a tourist attraction before Baahir's team could even get it marked on a map.

Talk of money seemed to perk Abbas up a bit. He fell in stride with Baahir and turned on his flashlight, directing its beam at the crumbled opening. The Egyptologist added his own light. The top two-thirds of the sealed entrance was missing. Only the bottom portion was still present and intact. Baahir stopped and studied what was left of the blockade.

"Was there any kind of writing or artwork carved into this section?"

Abbas shrugged. "I don't believe so. Why?"

Baahir stood and shook his head. “No reason, though, sometimes the Ancient Egyptians would warn us of what awaited those who entered sacred places like this.”

“Like what?” Abbas asked. He sounded nervous.

“Oh, you know, just your run-of-the-mill curses and boobytraps.”

Abbas paused mid-stride and gawked at the Egyptologist.

Baahir glanced over his shoulder and gave the guy a sly smile. He was kidding, of course. Abbas’ reaction was priceless. He huffed in annoyance and flared his nostrils. Baahir dipped his head inside the quaint doorway. As he lifted his left foot to step over the threshold, he could hear the foreman cursing under his breath in Arabic. What he said wasn’t very nice at all.

Baahir mentally translated the curse, and thought of his reply. *No, Mr. Construction Worker, my mother wasn’t an ill-tempered goat... my mother was a living saint. Until my father killed her.*

Deep down, part of Baahir understood that it wasn’t his father’s fault that his mother had died when he was just a boy. He even recalled her saying that it was her family that had been after them. Still, George should have been able to protect her better than he did. Plainly, Hanan Kane should still be alive today. It was because of Baahir’s love for his mother, and his equally strong disdain for his father that he had changed his last name to her maiden name when he was old enough to do so. Then, on his eighteenth birthday, Baahir left England forever and moved to his mother’s homeland, Egypt. Happily, he had not seen or spoken to his father since. The only person he stayed in regular contact with was his older sister, Zahra.

“Ghazzi!” Abbas bellowed back the other way. “With us!”

The punitive man fell in behind his boss, without so much as a word.

“I’m coming too.”

And so did Mr. Rahal.

Baahir and Abbas gave each other a look of aggravation. Already, the Egyptologist and foreman had seemed to have fashioned a semi-comfortable rapport. Baahir respected the foreman to a degree, and he knew Abbas did not like having the government agent along for the ride.

*Wherever the hell we’re going.*

After two minutes of traveling like old hermits bent over at the waist, Baahir’s flashlight, which had been swinging back and forth from wall to wall, found... nothing. He stopped and knelt, giving his lower back a much-needed respite. There, while inspecting the tunnel exit, he kneaded his spine with the knuckles of his left fist.

"Why did we stop?" Rahal asked.

Baahir shook his head, even more annoyed than before. "You in a hurry to be somewhere? Whatever is here, it has been here for centuries. I think it can wait a little while longer."

Abbas softly chuckled behind Baahir. If there was one single thing the two men had in common, it was their joint contempt for the pushy government agent.

"Dr. Hassan," Rahal countered, "I'm on a tight schedule, and — "

"Well," Baahir interrupted, "I'm not. And as the only person present who's qualified to be here, I will be moving at the pace I see fit." He turned and leaned around Abbas' hulking mass. "You are welcome to go outside and wait if you prefer."

Typically, Baahir was soft-spoken and well-mannered to everyone he met. It was a quality he had inherited from his mother. But when someone stood in the way of him and his work, he tended to erupt and lash out. He blamed it on the other half of his bloodline — his father's half. But, in reality, it stemmed from his unresolved issues with the man. That's what Baahir's therapist had said, anyway. Not everyone deserved his wrath. Those that didn't received a quick apology from him.

Baahir spun and continued forward. Mr. Rahal wouldn't be getting an apology.

Slowly, Baahir leaned into a chamber. It was empty, save for a three-foot-tall altar built of stone near its rear wall. *Definitely not a tomb.* Thankfully, the space was tall enough for them to stand erect. Baahir unfolded himself, instantly forgetting his sore back. The walls of the room were etched from floor-to-ceiling in hieroglyphs and pictographs. He immediately dove into the story — a story Baahir knew well. But when Baahir was halfway through skimming over the text, he realized that it wasn't the same familiar story, after all.

He dragged his light back to the beginning, stopping on the wall to the right of the chamber entrance. He was still missing something.

"What's that?" Abbas asked, pointing his light at a section directly above the doorway.

Baahir added his light and was astonished by what he read.

"It *can't* be..."

"It can't be what?" Rahal asked, not understanding the significance.

As far as Baahir knew, he was the only one who could read the hieroglyphs.

Abbas' voice was low and soft, and he uttered a single word — a name. "Anubis."

Baahir looked up at the construction foreman. Abbas had figured out part of the riddle, but how?

Somewhere between finding the text above the passageway and Baahir deciphering it, Abbas had turned back toward the altar. And Abbas hadn't figured out the Anubis thing by reading the scripts, it had to have been something else. So, Baahir turned to see what Abbas had been looking at — something each of the had missed when they had entered the room. The wall above the altar put the entire story into context. It was easy to understand, even for a child.

"What?"

Apparently, Mr. Rahal *still* didn't get it.

Baahir shivered with excitement and explained. "This — all of this — describes a collection of scrolls that was eventually put together to become the Book of the Dead." He took a deep breath. "The *first* Book of the Dead."

Baahir's eyes opened wider as he stepped forward and inspected the altar. It wasn't an altar at all. It was a chest of some kind — a vault! And as vaults only really existed for one purpose, Baahir was pretty sure he knew what was inside of this one.

*We're inside a temple dedicated to Anubis that features texts highlighting the god and his burial practices and funeral rites.*

"And him?" Rahal aimed his light at a figure looming over the rest of the carvings, as well as the altar and the people inside the tomb. The impossible individual held out his hands as if he was offering something of value to them — to the world.

*Knowledge,* Baahir decided.

But there, between his open hands, was a depiction of a single canopic jar. It reminded him of another one he had seen many times before.

"Isn't it obvious?" Baahir asked rhetorically. He peered up at the jackal-headed being. "That is Anubis..." he took a deep breath as Abbas, Rahal, and even the grizzled laborer, Ghazzi, encircled him, "author of the original Book of the Dead."

**The Pharaoh's Lounge** | Giza, Egypt

Less than a mile south of the Giza Pyramid Complex sat the most luxurious nightlife destination in the entire region. Originally opened as a local watering hole in the mid-seventies, *Seti's Place* had been purchased by a private investment group, torn down, and rebuilt into the spectacle it was today, *The Pharaoh's Lounge.* Only the social elite, or those with enough money, could get in without making a reservation months in advance. Not only were the services and menu impeccable, but so were the second-floor *accommodations.*

Weapons, drugs, women... The Pharaoh's Lounge dealt in them all.

Since re-opening under its new moniker, the establishment had successfully skirted the law with nothing more than an occasional slap on the wrist. *The Pharaoh's Lounge* was mostly untouchable because one of its oldest clients was a ranking member of the Egyptian Parliament. But the business' resounding success wasn't the only thing that interested its owner. Khaliq Ayad used the financial gains to feed his obsession, the ancient mythology of his homeland.

Like his father and grandfather before him, Khaliq believed in a very specific and unusual subject matter that many had laughed off, including other members of his bloodline. In the generations since, his family had formed a coalition of radical extremists — devotees to their cause.

To Khaliq, and those that followed him, Anubis wasn't just the fabled death god of Egypt. He was a real historical figure, a man. He was an archaic scientist who had been ahead of his time. Like Noah and Merlin, Anubis was thought to have been a real person whose myth and legend had been built up and expanded over time, eventually becoming the larger-than-life tale that seemed utterly fictitious.

Khaliq believed there *were* fictional accounts of Anubis, but that all of the stories and myths were based on reality. Long ago, there *was* a man who called himself Anubis.

Still, there was a looming issue. The place where Anubis was said to practice his trade had been lost to time through multiple wars, and famine, and even disinterest. Some of the Ayads had given up on their calling and buried anything to do with Anubis.

But a devout few even claimed to be Anubis' direct descendants.

"Which makes us gods!" Khaliq's grandfather once told him.

The family's deep-seated patriarchal beliefs spanned millennia. Khaliq took it to another level and introduced outsiders with the same hardcore views, recruiting men from all over the Middle East, Northern Africa, and Eastern Europe. He even enlisted the service of a few women. Khaliq had no time for the traditional, sexist practices of the area. The handful of women he had employed were equals to him based on their beliefs, and because they had proven themselves to be the most dangerous of them all, having the ability to hide in plain sight. There were advantages of having female agents planted in places like Egypt. A veiled woman was hardly ever perceived as a threat.

He grinned. Khaliq had put together quite the army. It was an organization that several law enforcement agencies had tried to shut down over the years, but to no avail.

He filled his thick, barreled chest with air and released it slowly. *Let them try.* Khaliq repeated the same exercise several more times before being interrupted.

His cellphone vibrated across the nearby nightstand. He growled and snapped open his intense, dark eyes. Meditation was the only thing that kept him under control and focused. If it were up to Khaliq, he'd march downstairs and slaughter every single one of his patrons. If they weren't directly helping his cause, they were nothing but a speed bump of meat and bone.

Khaliq could be slowed down, but he would *never* be stopped.

The buzzing nuisance was too much to ignore, and he angrily snapped his attention to it. The caller's name intrigued him, and he decided to take a break from his exercises to answer it. Seated in a classic lotus position, Khaliq uncrossed his legs and climbed off his bed, slipping back into his expensive, black silk shirt. He picked up the phone and reflexively ran his other hand over his thick beard and clean-shaven head, discouraged to feel a slight prickle of hair. He'd need to shave the latter before long.

"Speak," Khaliq demanded, his baritone voice booming through the device.

The man on the other end stuttered. *"I...I think you will be happy with the find."*

Khaliq's right eyebrow rose. "Yes?"

He was aware of the construction project, and the discovery that was made there. And it just so happened that Khaliq had a trusted man on the ground to keep an eye on things. Throughout the years, his family had found similar temples all over Egypt, though they had successfully kept the discoveries hidden from the public. Unfortunately, none of the temples they found had provided any additional information other than what they already knew.

"Is it there?" Khaliq asked, forcing himself to stay calm. It had been a lifetime of searching. Could this be it? Had they finally found it?

*"I'm not sure. The museum sent an Egyptologist that moved slower than a festering corpse. But,"* the caller added, teasing something hopeful, *"there are engravings that will... interest you."*

"Engravings?"

*"Yes. They speak of a collection of incantations. Written by Anubis himself."*

Khaliq's whole body tensed. "The scroll? It speaks of the scroll?"

*"I believe that it does,"* the caller replied. *"And it's a glorious sight. You must see it for yourself."*

Khaliq needed to be careful. Just because he had a client involved with the government didn't mean he would remain untouchable. He involved himself with people like the man on the other line to do his dirty work for that reason — the government traded in secrets, power, and control, and so would Khaliq. All the better that he could maintain plausible deniability as well.

"Keep me informed," he ordered. "If anything else arises, be sure to let me know."

"Yes, Khaliq. I am very confident that we will soon have what we seek."

*Then, the world will be mine.*

The thought made the extremist leader beam from ear to ear. If what he believed was, indeed, written within Anubis' scroll, then obtaining the world would be a conceivable conclusion.

# CHAPTER 5
# BAAHIR

**Mena House Golf Course** | Giza, Egypt

It had been nearly an hour since Baahir had first laid eyes on the chamber dedicated to Anubis. But since then, the exploration had ground to a halt. Baahir refused to open the sealed, cube-shaped vault built into the rear wall. In his report, he would call it the *Vault of Anubis*. A discovery such as this deserved Baahir's unpopular method of patience. He would study it and the space encapsulating it for as long as it took before attempting to open it. God forbid he rushed things and damaged what sat inside.

The others came and went while Baahir worked. Most of his work was jotting down notes and hypotheses. Simple orange glowsticks gave him enough light to see by. Abbas had tossed a dozen of them all around the room before exiting and conversing with his superiors back in town. As far as Baahir knew, Mr. Rahal had been on the phone the entire time with his office back in Cairo.

Shuffled footsteps pulled Baahir from his thoughts.

He glanced over his shoulder and saw a hunched figure standing in the doorway. It was Ghazzi, Abbas' man.

"Sorry to have disturbed you," the local apologized, bowing slightly.

Baahir didn't mind the man's presence. "Magnificent, isn't it?"

Ghazzi nodded and took a small step inside. "It truly is a wonder."

The Egyptologist beamed with pride. He enjoyed meeting people from all walks of life, especially those that shared his love of history.

"Come, sit."

Ghazzi nodded and settled in beside Baahir and stared longingly up at the death god. The look in the man's eyes was that of deep understanding. He didn't just appreciate the temple. Ghazzi adored it — same as Baahir. This meant more to him than just being another relic.

"Tell me, Ghazzi, do you think it's possible for Anubis to have actually existed?"

Ghazzi looked surprised to have been asked the question.

"I suppose anything is possible." He shook his head. "But no, I believe that the gods of old are just one part of a grander fantasy."

"And what of all this?" Baahir asked, motioning to the floor-to-ceiling hieroglyphs and pictographs. The questions were more for himself than Ghazzi. It was easier to work things out when conversing with someone other than yourself.

Ghazzi shrugged. "Forgive me, sir, but you are the expert, not me."

Baahir liked Ghazzi. He was polite and honest.

So, Baahir provided his own opinion. "It was common for the kings and pharaohs of Ancient Egypt to believe themselves to be living gods, yes? I think that's what we're seeing here."

"And that?" Ghazzi asked, pointing a gnarled finger at the oversized jar.

Baahir had an idea of what it was, but there had been no historical accounts, just a tall tale from his mother.

"It's Anubis' personal canopic jar."

Ghazzi's eyes lit up. "Really?"

Baahir shrugged, and his mind wandered. "That's what my mother told me, anyway..."

"Your mother?"

Baahir nodded. "She was the real expert on all of this. No one knew more about Anubis than she did."

Ghazzi glanced away, looking like he wanted to say something.

"Yes?" Baahir asked, curious.

"What do you think is in the jar?"

*Oh...* That wasn't something Baahir expected Ghazzi to ask him.

He recalled what his mother told him and, in turn, recited it.

"My mother said that there was a sect of ancient priests that believed that the jar contained Anubis' mortal soul."

The local grinned. "His soul?"

Baahir knew it sounded asinine, but that's what he had been taught. "Yes, his soul. My mother once found papers that spoke of the *Book of the Dead*, describing it as a hellish scroll made of human flesh and penned in human blood. Sadly, the texts were destroyed in a fire long ago."

Baahir felt his chest tighten. The thought of a historical relic such as that being lost forever combined with an image of his mother's beautiful face was too much. He cleared his throat. "It was said that Anubis — through supernatural means — removed his own soul and placed it inside a one-of-a-kind canopic jar constructed of a substance dubbed 'hellstone.' Legend says that the jar was supposed to be the only thing that could contain it."

Ghazzi turned and faced Baahir. "If this is true, no matter how unbelievable it sounds, why would Anubis imprison his own soul?"

Baahir sighed. This was hard for him to repeat. His mother had been so sure of the reason that it scared him. What was strange was that it had never turned away his father. He believed his wife, but Baahir figured that was because he loved her deeply and supported her no matter what and nothing more. Zahra *loved* everything about the folklore. But to her, it was more *cool* than *fascinating*. That was the difference between Baahir and Zahra's viewpoint of history. She was in it for the adventure. Baahir had dedicated his life to the consumption of knowledge.

"Legend says that, in order for Anubis to become a god, he confined his mortal soul, and that, if released, it would unleash a plague upon the world."

Ghazzi's smirk morphed into a full-fledged, gap-toothed, jack-o-lanterned smile. "A plague?"

He didn't believe a single thing that Baahir was telling him, though Ghazzi had graciously allowed him to explain it without interruption or ridicule. Baahir had rarely ever repeated what his mother had believed in for fear of mockery. She had hidden her beliefs from the public, knowing it would have destroyed whatever professional standing she had maintained.

And if people found out that Baahir believed the plague story, *his* reputation would be tarnished.

*Just like a credible historian chasing Atlantis or the Loch Ness Monster.*

Baahir refused to ever become that, no matter how convinced his mother had been.

He tilted his chin up to the god, more specifically, the relic between his hands. "My sister has a jar similar to that, you know."

Ghazzi looked back to the engraving. "She does?"

Baahir nodded. "It's a family heirloom. After our mother died, Zahra begged our father to have it. She cherishes it."

"Zahra?"

"Yeah, she works for the British Museum. She's brilliant, but is also an adrenaline junky. The woman never stops."

"And the jar?"

Baahir shrugged. "Last I saw, it was in her office."

Speaking about the mythos of Anubis and his own family's beliefs spurred something inside of Baahir. He stood with Ghazzi closely in tow. Baahir tipped his head back at the tunnel and spoke.

"Retrieve Abbas and Rahal. We'll need their help if we're going to open this thing and see if we're right."

Ghazzi smiled wide and excitedly headed off. Baahir knew he should call in proper reinforcements, but he wanted to see it through on his own. His mother had believed in all of this myth and legend, and he made it his personal mission in life to either prove her right or invalidate her work.

For better or worse, it would be the closure he needed.

He was a man of *real* history. As much as he loved his mother and respected her convictions, Baahir was a true academic. He had treasured his abbreviated time with her, but he had grown to not always agree with her. This whole story was just too wild — too *outlandish* — to believe.

Baahir valued Occam's razor. *The simplest solution is almost always the best.*

The being who had portrayed himself to be Anubis was most likely just an intelligently gifted human being who had displayed psychopathic behaviors, alleging himself to be divine. He had been a person living in a dark time who possessed an understanding of a deeper knowledge, one that had often been confused with magic and witchcraft over the years.

In this case, the simpletons of the period had feared what would come to be known as *science.*

That's what made the most sense to Baahir anyway.

The fact that there were some people that actually believed that Anubis had been real and, in fact, a god both concerned and terrified him. Then again, all religions seemed odd to Baahir. He was wholly agnostic, even before his mother died. An all-knowing entity that watched over the universe was too farfetched for him to have ever believed in. He could never grasp it. But if there was one thing that had always intrigued him, and gave him hope that it was all true, it was the idea of there being an afterlife.

Because Baahir would give anything to see his mother again.

Ghazzi returned in no time with both Abbas and Rahal. The prospect of opening the vault's lid was too much for either man to ignore.

Baahir stepped up to the front of the stone lid with Abbas on his right and Ghazzi on his left. Agent Rahal was holding Baahir's phone high above them, filming everything the device's light touched. Baahir's heart raced, as he was sure everyone's was. This was history in the making.

"Ready?" Baahir asked, meeting eye to eye with Abbas and Ghazzi.

Both men nodded, sweat pouring down their faces. Baahir's face was likewise drenched. The storm had brought an uncomfortable thickness to the air, and the lack of airflow inside the temple was brutal.

"Okay, Mr. Rahal, make sure you get everything."

The fourth member of their party leaned in close and held the phone directly above the lid. Rahal was so close that he was practically pressed up against Baahir's back. The Egyptologist didn't care, though. He was too focused on the task.

"Up. Slowly."

The three men lifted, getting no movement out of the lid.

"Stop," Baahir directly. They relaxed their grips and reset their stances. "We need more leverage. Try getting lower."

The trio leaned in and, instead of lifting with their fingers, they positioned their palms under the lid's shallow ledge. Now, they'd be able to use more of their bodies than just their arms and backs.

"Okay, let's try again." Baahir let out a long breath. "Up."

As one, they dug in and pushed, driving the cover skyward. Their change in tactics had worked, and the lid slid, grinding stone on stone. It wasn't just any normal lid, either. The architects had made sure that whoever opened it was going to have to work hard for what was inside. No one could come in and simply shove the lid off. Its girth extended the entire depth of the vault itself.

"You're almost there!" Rahal announced, excitement radiating in his voice. "Keep going!"

Baahir was out of breath, and he was becoming lightheaded. Abbas and Ghazzi didn't seem to be fairing as poorly as he was. Then again, they were laborers, familiar with the strain of a hard day's work. Baahir worked hard, but his job kept him mostly behind a desk, not out lifting heavy objects and digging holes. He was in shape, but he had to hit the gym every other day to maintain it.

The trio nearly dropped the lid when it finally came free. Luckily, they each had the wherewithal to hang on.

"Set it down...on the edge of the vault," Baahir said in between gasps.

They did, and for the moment, were free of its weight. Now, with the lid stacked on top of the vault itself, the two objects combined were as tall as Baahir.

"Ready?" Baahir asked, getting nods all around.

The three men reset their grips on the lid. "Up," Baahir said. "Toward me."

With Baahir backpedaling, the three men cleared the open container and eased the weighty lid to the temple floor. Once free of its weight, neither of them waited to catch their breath. The men huddled around the vault, spotting something inside. A two-foot-tall vertically standing tube of black stone greeted them.

*Volcanic rock?*

The object and the setting around it brought him back to his mother's description of the hellstone.

"So dark that it absorbs the light," Baahir mumbled to himself.

Abbas reached for the relic but was stopped.

"Don't!" Baahir warned, grabbing the man's wrist. He was spooked. "We need to be cautious." Abbas looked at him strangely. "Trust me."

Baahir slipped into a pair of latex gloves. Then, he produced a pair of heavy leather gloves and adorned them as well. Within the light, he could just barely see the artifact's surface. It really did seem to swallow whatever light that touched it.

He thought he spotted a set of hieroglyphs engraved into it, and...

*Slow down, Baahir. First, extract the...thing.* He didn't quite know what it was.

Following his own orders, Baahir carefully placed his shaking hands on the object. He imagined his parents standing next to him, instead of his current company, and how proud they would be of him. Baahir tried as hard as he could to shut up his mind. This was the first time he had thought positively of his father in years.

The tube didn't budge. Baahir released his grip and peeked down into the container but didn't see any hindrances. The tube was stuck, locked in place after so many years.

"Help me, will you."

Abbas and Ghazzi wrapped their hands around Baahir's, avoiding direct contact with the artifact. Together, they pulled. Similar to the lid, the tube didn't move an inch. The construction workers knew what to do this time. They leaned in close and squeezed Baahir's hands tighter. The trio put everything they had into it, and, with a trio of growls and a pop, the object came free.

As did Baahir.

He and the tube went flying backward. Baahir tripped and landed on top of the three-foot-tall lid, flipping ass over teakettle to the floor on the other side. The air instantly left his lungs with an audible "Oof!"

He coughed, marveling at the discovery he now possessed. Baahir couldn't believe he had found... what exactly?

"That doesn't look like a scroll," Rahal pointed out.

Baahir sat up and held the tube up for everyone to see. He shook his head. "If I'm correct, I think this is just a protective casing of some kind."

He set the tube down on the lid, using it as an examination table, and moved to a kneeling position. Rahal moved in closer and bathed the workspace in light. It didn't reveal much.

"How come the light doesn't work?" Abbas asked.

"Because," Baahir explained, dipping into his past, "it's hellstone." He looked up at Ghazzi. "We need more light."

Without another word, Ghazzi hurried back down the corridor.

Rahal's focus narrowed onto the artifact, and he stepped toward it with a hungry look on his face. "No!" Baahir snapped. "We'll wait for Ghazzi to return to see if Anubis' scroll is real."

The impatient government agent huffed. “Well, then, I’ll go make sure Mr. Ghazzi doesn’t linger for too long.” Before Baahir or Abbas could argue, Rahal was gone.

# CHAPTER 7
# KHALIQ

**The Pharaoh's Lounge** | Giza, Egypt

Khaliq Ayad's man at the dig site had just notified him that a mysterious artifact relating to the scroll had been found. Even though the scroll itself had not been seen, it was enough to mobilize him and a few of his most faithful men. At worst, if there was no scroll present, he would still possess the black cylindrical object. It would make a fine addition to his Anubian collection. Then, once he translated its inscriptions, he would lock it away and conceal the knowledge it contained. No one but Khaliq could know.

*Which means everyone that has seen it must die.*

He relayed the sentiment to his man on the ground before climbing into one of two blacked-out SUVs. Luckily, neither the Egyptologist nor the government agent had requested additional help from their superiors. Their lapses in judgment had unknowingly aided in Khaliq's efforts. Stealing the artifact was going to be easy.

*How do the Americans say it?* he thought. *Oh, yes.* Khaliq grinned.

"Like taking candy from a baby."

**Mena House Golf Course** | Giza, Egypt

Ghazzi rummaged through the tent, searching for more batteries. The two flashlights he had found weren't going to work. One barely had enough power to create a noticeable difference, and the other was completely dead — probably even broken. He cursed Abbas and the others for hastily packing everything up before the storm. It was usually his job to keep the equipment organized and ready to go, but with everything happening so quickly, the gear had been tossed aside and battered.

He was on edge, scared. He knew something was happening, and he knew his place in all of it. He needed to be ready, to act when the moment was right.

Ghazzi paused his search and listened. He looked behind him, peering through the open flap of the tent, but saw nothing.

At least, he *thought* he saw nothing. The bustling wind and shadows the construction lighting created were making it hard to make out much of anything. To Ghazzi, the darkness looked alive. It didn't help that there was an endless staccato of noise coming from the roof as the rain continually pummeled it, though it had lessened some.

He looked up and sighed. Even if someone was behind him, he wouldn't hear the person coming until it was too late.

A sudden shout called out from behind him. Spooked, the construction worker jumped, grabbing a heavy wrench. He hurled it back towards the tent entrance just as Rahal appeared there.

It almost struck Rahal in the forehead, but the government agent dodged the projectile, turning and diving back through the open flap. Rahal landed hard, rolled onto his back, and glared at him with venom in his eyes as Ghazzi inched outside.

Not another word was exchanged between the two men. Rahal climbed to his feet just as Ghazzi re-entered the tent and backed into a table. His hand slid across its surface and found something familiar. The rectangular object was exactly what he had been looking for. He confirmed as much by glancing down at the box of batteries. With that, he rushed forward and edged around the irate agent. Ghazzi tucked the box and the single operating flashlight under his shirt and made a mad dash for the temple entrance, never once looking back.

He carefully scaled the debris caused by their earlier blasts and ducked his head inside the corridor. If he had been a few inches shorter, Ghazzi could have walked upright. As he walked, he blindly unscrewed the front of the flashlight and exchanged the burned batteries for new ones. Ghazzi was used to working in conditions with low visibility. In truth, he preferred working at night. The harsh Egyptian sun could sap even the strongest man's strength in no time at all.

Ghazzi ignited the flashlight and stepped inside the chamber. He focused its beam on the tube and was taken aback by what he saw. The additional light revealed that the artifact wasn't just some uninteresting vessel for the treasure that laid within. It, too, was a remnant worthy of extreme care.

"Rahal?" Abbas asked, looking past Ghazzi.

The worker shrugged. He didn't want to tell his boss that he had almost killed the man.

"Okay, let's — "

The man in question stepped through. Everyone's attention was on him now — on his clothes, rather.

"Did the weather worsen?" Abbas asked.

Rahal shook his head and snarled. He jabbed a finger at Ghazzi. "This...*rodent*...nearly took my head off with a wrench!"

"It was an accident!" Ghazzi cried, shrinking away from the larger man.

"Like hell it was! You peasant-types are all the same. You — "

"Peasants?" Abbas asked, standing impossibly tall. "We are peasants, now?"

Rahal's face went white. "I..."

"Hey!" Everyone quieted and turned their attention to the only person kneeling. "I don't care what happened between you two. We have a job to do, okay?"

Ghazzi nodded emphatically.

Rahal didn't physically acknowledge Baahir, but nor did he hurl any other insults at Ghazzi.

Abbas glared at the agent for a moment longer before returning his attention to the artifact.

"Mr. Abbas," Baahir said, holding out his phone, "if you would?"

Rahal's eyes bounced back and forth from the Egyptologist to the foreman.

Baahir held up an apologetic hand. "Sorry, I can't risk it getting wet."

Rahal locked his jaw and crossed his arms, none too happy.

"Okay," Baahir said, blowing out a long breath, "here we go."

The chamber was blissfully silent as Baahir got to work. He ditched his thicker work gloves, continuing with only the latex pair he wore beneath them. With the addition of Ghazzi's flashlight, Baahir was able to see that the hellstone tube was, indeed, so much more than just a casing. It, like the chamber's walls, was covered with beautiful artwork. Something about the writing was different, though. The engravings on the walls spoke of Anubis and his teachings, including a collection of them. Baahir had to read the hieroglyphs twice before he realized what was dissimilar.

"First-person perspective?" The implications were mind-blowing. "It's written in first-person! Here, listen..." He glanced back and forth between the tube end and the others as he read. "*Within this vessel is the grandest prize I can offer.*" Baahir nervously swallowed. "*My knowledge.*"

Abbas and Rahal didn't seem to understand, but Ghazzi did. "Then, it's true?"

Baahir nodded, his eyes watering. His joy ended there.

He turned over the tube and found one last line, mentally translating it four times. A wave of dread washed over him. The others noticed the change in his demeanor.

"What's wrong?" Ghazzi asked.

Baahir's hands shook. He couldn't answer.

"Dr. Hassan?" Rahal asked. "What does it say?"

Baahir followed the symbols with his forefinger, carefully reading them aloud. Ancient civilizations were full of doom-and-gloom stories, but this one felt different.

*"And also, the means to abolish my enemies."*

The Egyptologist set the artifact down and stood, and stepped away. He didn't know exactly what Anubis was trying to convey, but he knew he didn't want to be holding it when the truth was revealed. To him, it sounded as if Anubis, the one and only, had devised some kind of weapon.

*And I held it. And it was on my hands...*

Baahir held up his gloved hands and imagined some type of ancient biological weapon eating through the protective layer. His skin would be next.

"Dr. Hassan?" Ghazzi's voice was soft. "It's just a scroll."

Baahir glanced over at the local. "How do you know?"

Ghazzi motioned to the room. "All of this tells me that."

"And the text on the tube?" Baahir felt better simply talking it out.

The other man shrugged. "I'm not sure, but I don't think it's dangerous. That sounds silly, no?"

Baahir smiled. It did sound silly. He put together what he did know and walked back his initial reaction.

"If it's not a weapon, then what could it be?" The question was more to himself than the others. "The evidence suggests that it's our scroll — a scroll filled with Anubis' teachings — his incantations," his eyes lit up, "his experimentations..." Baahir knelt and, again, picked up the tube. "What if it really is the first Book of the Dead, but also contains something else unseen by modern man, like a recipe to create a weapon of some kind."

"An ancient cookbook?" Abbas asked, grinning.

Baahir didn't get to reply. Rahal did.

"There's never been any indication of that."

"And how do you know that?"

"It's my job."

"And what is your job, exactly?" Baahir asked.

"I'm with the Ministry of State of Antiquities, and I assure you that there is nothing — not anywhere — to suggest that a mythological deity created a doomsday device with nothing more than sticks and sand and then hid it down here."

Baahir was going to say something else but held back. There was more to Rahal than it seemed, and Baahir needed to remember that. He, and maybe even his bosses back in Cairo, owned intimate knowledge of the subject matter.

"So," Baahir said, "do I open it?"

It took a second, but all three of his compatriots either shrugged or nodded their heads.

Baahir blew out a long breath. "Okay, here goes nothing."

He examined the tube again and found a razor-thin slit halfway up. If Baahir had to guess, the artifact could be separated there.

*That's a start.*

Baahir gently gripped the two parts and applied a small amount of force. Surprisingly, the pieces began to pull away from one another on the first try. Baahir had expected them to have been locked together with years of grime. Then again, the inside of the vault had been in pristine condition. So had the chamber itself, for that matter.

The grating of volcanic stone was minimal. Once more, Baahir was incredibly surprised by the craftsmanship on display. He had never seen anything like it before. Ancient Egyptians typically used clay pots to seal up their valuables, not cylindrical containers made of ethereal stone.

*Why the change?* Baahir asked himself. He grew more uneasy. Even if it wasn't Anubis who had penned the scroll and then built this elaborate container, why had he chosen to use hellstone?

Baahir was startled when the two halves of the tube came apart, but when they did, he saw *it*, and stopped. Everyone in the chamber held their breath. There, in the bottom half of the tube, was a wound scroll.

But was it their book?

Baahir stood. "I have to get this to the museum."

"What?" Rahal shouted. "You can't — "

"We are not set up to handle precious documents here. The fact that we even found something is amazing, but I won't potentially damage the find because I can't contain my excitement. That would be negligent on my part, even more than me opening the tube here." Saying it out loud put it into perspective. Baahir had already broken several rules for the sake of his need-to-know. He wouldn't be breaking any others.

He pieced the two halves of the vessel back together and headed for the exit. He pushed through Abbas and Ghazzi and ducked into the tunnel. A loud click made him stop. He turned around, staring down the barrel of a pistol.

Mr. Rahal smiled.

"What are you doing?" Baahir asked, hugging the artifact tight.

"He's betraying us," Abbas said, growling. "He's taking the scroll for himself."

Baahir's eyes flashed back to the government agent. "Is that true?"

Rahal relaxed, looking very confident. "Half of that is. I am going to take it, but no, it's not for me."

"Who is it for?" Baahir asked, stepping back.

Rahal laughed. "This isn't the movies, Dr. Hassan. I'm not going to tell you the deeper details of our nefarious plan." He stepped toward the Egyptologist. "But what I *am* going to do is take Anubis' scroll, and if you don't hand it over, I'll shoot you here and now."

Baahir's eyes opened wide. *So, he actually believes it belonged to Anubis!*

"Okay... Okay. Here," Baahir said, holding out the artifact. "As long as no one gets hurt."

Rahal reached out for the tube and greedily ripped it from Baahir's hand. He held it up as if it were the Holy Grail. His eyes were maniacal, though focused. Baahir could tell the man believed in everything they had discussed.

He needed to know. "I thought you said there was no evidence of any of this being true?"

Rahal's attention returned to him, and he leveled the gun at his chest. "I lied. There is evidence, but it's only known to a chosen few."

The gunshot caused Baahir's ears to ring. But other than that, he wasn't hurt. Just as Rahal had pulled the trigger, Abbas and Ghazzi dove for the man's gun hand. In doing so, the shot had gone high and impacted the entryway directly above Baahir's head. The two construction workers struggled to relieve the agent of his pistol. Abbas got one of his meaty hands up and wrapped it around the other man's throat. Rahal responded by dropping the scroll to the chamber floor and clawing at Abbas' face. The tube landed with a clunk and rolled, stopping right in front of Baahir's toes.

He snatched it up and momentarily thought about using the solidly made, stone cylinder as a weapon. But could he really use a priceless artifact in that way?

Another shot rang out.

Baahir flinched and was appalled to see Ghazzi stumble away from the fight, holding his stomach. The local had been shot at point-blank range. Blood poured from the wound, seeping through Ghazzi's clutched hands. He fell to the floor and inched away from Abbas and Rahal, eyes wide and his mouth agape. He was in shock.

"Ghazzi!"

The foreman roared and lifted Rahal off the ground by his armpits, driving him backward into the adjacent wall. Baahir wanted to help, and he knew exactly how. He turned and ran, holding the artifact tight. He needed to get outside and call the police. Luckily, Rahal had handed over Baahir's phone before turning coat.

The world around Baahir rushed by in a blur. His adrenaline levels were off the charts. He used his runner's frame to good use and poured on the speed, aiming for the hill he and Abbas had originally descended. He was so focused on escaping that he didn't realize the rain had slowed to a light drizzle. Once Baahir reached the slope, he pulled out his phone and called the police.

"Hello... my name is Baahir Hassan! There's been... a shooting at the Mena House Golf Course... well... beneath it, and —"

*"Slow down, sir,"* the operator said. *"Where exactly did you say you are?"*

"Beneath the *Mena House Golf Course*!" he shouted. His mind was racing. "A sinkhole... caused by the storm. The construction site!"

*"Okay, Mr. Hassan, I have officers inbound. Find a safe place and wait for help to arrive."*

"Yes, okay," Baahir replied, nodding to no one as he hurried.

*"Do you know the gunman?"*

Baahir turned and looked back down the hill just as a third gunshot startled him. It was much quieter than the others — only a subtle *thump* this time. The underground chamber had acted as an oversized sound suppressor. But Baahir wasn't focused on the repressed discharge. He was thinking about the men who had saved his life.

The emergency operator repeated herself, speaking direct and slow. "*Mr. Hassan, do you know the gunman?*"

Baahir pulled his attention off the excavation, spotting his SUV up ahead. He rushed towards it. "Sorry... Yes. His name is Fahim Rahal."

# CHAPTER 10
# RAHAL

The only sound in the chamber was the whimpering cries of a dying man. Ghazzi's stomach wound would eventually kill him, but it was going to be a slow and agonizing death. The larger man, Abbas, had gone down with a single shot to the back of the head. Rahal had first broken Abbas' nose, and then he swiftly hip tossed the foreman to the ground. It was all over after that.

The agent sat in a catcher's squat, balancing on the balls of his feet. He nonchalantly wiped his sweaty face with a handkerchief while watching Ghazzi suffer. His plan was to interrogate — possibly even torture — Dr. Hassan for information. Rahal and his people knew everything there was to know about Anubis, but Hassan was smart. It couldn't hurt to see if Hassan had said anything of note to add.

Ghazzi had the gall to smile.

"What's so funny?" Rahal asked.

The digger's words were slow and wet. "You seem... to be... missing something."

Rahal's eyes went wide, and he leaped to his feet. He searched the floor, realizing that the scroll was gone.

"Hassan."

Rahal needed to retrieve the artifact at all costs, but getting information was still a necessity. He thought back and realized that Ghazzi had spent some time by the Egyptologist's side.

*I wonder...*

Rahal, once more, squatted in front of Ghazzi and redrew his pistol. "Tell me, Mr. Ghazzi, what did you and Dr. Hassan talk about?"

Baahir couldn't get his breathing under control. He had never been more terrified in his life. A man — a government agent, no less — had turned a gun on him, and tried to kill him. And why? Because he believed that the scroll they had found was actually written by the death god, Anubis.

"Unbelievable."

He was doing what the emergency dispatcher had told him to do. Baahir was currently sitting inside of his locked SUV with the engine running and the lights off. It was the safest place he could think of being. There was nowhere he could go on foot that Rahal couldn't follow.

*Ghazzi...*

Baahir had never witnessed anyone get shot before. Seeing the look in the injured man's eyes was something Baahir would never forget.

What about Abbas?

Baahir closed his eyes, allowing the tears to fall freely. He clenched his hands around the steering wheel and squeezed as hard as he could. So much violence, and for what? He couldn't believe that people still acted like this in the modern age, especially toward the acquisition of historical relics. Baahir had seen the same kind of radical behavior before, but that was in the form of terrorism. He lived in Egypt, after all.

A bolt of lightning struck somewhere in the distance. In its flash, he saw something — a blurry lump silhouetted against the skyline.

Then, the lump started to shoot at him.

The bullet penetrated his windshield, spiderwebbing the glass. Pieces of it hit Baahir in the face and neck, but nothing large enough to seriously injure him. He felt the flow of blood, and the sting of the small, superficial cuts on his exposed skin.

Baahir threw the SUV into *reverse* and sped away backward toward the entry ramp. More gunshots followed his attempted escape. One obliterated his right headlight. The road was a straight shot behind him and as soon as his tires found it, he screeched to a stop and shifted into *drive*. He used the vehicle's powerful engine to his advantage and floored the pedal as more and more projectiles hit home. The tailgate's window shattered as he pulled away.

"Oh, my god." His voice quaked. Baahir had no idea what to do next. He called the police again and reported what had just happened.

"Okay, Mr. Hassan, I need you to stay calm and — "

More bullets tore into the interior of the vehicle. As a result, Baahir dropped his phone. He didn't know if the operator was still on the other line or not, and he wasn't about to pull over and check. So, Baahir drove faster and came up with a plan of action, rather, he figured out where he was going to go. In his mind's eye, he pictured himself examining the scroll.

"The museum."

There were armed guards stationed at the museum around the clock. He'd be safe there.

*At least, I hope I will.*

**Giza, Egypt**

Agent Rahal sprinted after Hassan's vehicle, peppering it with nine-millimeter ammunition. Soon, the Egyptologist was out of range, speeding away with a squeal of rubber on road. Rahal spied the vehicle jerk around the nearest turn, tires continuing to wail in protest.

More lightning announced the next wave of rain and wind. As they each picked up in intensity, Rahal spun on a dime and marched over to his own car. He should have been more worried about losing the scroll for good, but the Egyptologist was a predictable man. His own interests would trump his safety. Instead of heading for the nearest police department, he'd go somewhere far less secure.

Rahal fell into the driver's seat and shut the door. He sat for a moment to collect his thoughts before calling his superior. The phone rang twice.

*"Yes?"*

"The Egyptologist has the scroll."

Khalid Ayad sighed. Just with that subtle noise, Rahal could tell his boss was not happy. He could feel the man's rage radiating through the phone.

*"This is most disappointing."*

"But I will regain it shortly," he said. "I know where he is going."

*"You do?"*

Rahal grinned. "Yes. He will take it to the museum in Cairo. I'd bet my life on it."

Khaliq's laugh was grating, menacing. "*We will see, Mr. Rahal. We will see...*"

Rahal swallowed. He began to answer, to clarify, but the call was suddenly disconnected.

Baahir made it to Nile Corniche without further incident. His vehicle was decimated and beyond repair. He knew he should have headed straight for a police station, but Baahir was frightened. There wasn't anywhere in the world that he felt more comfortable than the museum. From here, it was a straight shot. He'd properly phone the authorities once he was inside. Speaking of which...

Baahir had dropped his phone some time ago, and he was too focused on not dying to retrieve it. Double-checking his surroundings, Baahir glanced down to the passenger side footwell. Nothing. He leaned into the steering wheel, and finally spotted the device laying facedown. Keeping his eyes on the road, Baahir reached down and to his right, stretching as far as he could without losing control of his SUV.

His fingers grazed it, but he couldn't quite grab it.

"Dammit."

He slowed and pulled off on the side of the road. He unbuckled his seatbelt, giving himself the extra range that he required. *Got it!* The screen was dark. The call between him and the emergency operator had ended when he dropped it. Baahir was about to check his missed calls. A set of headlights approaching him from behind made him freeze in place. Their owner was still a good distance away, but he didn't want to chance that it being Rahal. Baahir's survival at the construction site had been a fluke, and he wasn't about to test his luck again.

Baahir took off, staying far ahead of the pursuing vehicle. He got off at El Tahrir Avenue and headed east toward Tahrir Square. At its center sat, what was typically, a busy traffic circle, though, at the late hour, it was mostly empty. There were only two other cars in the large roundabout. One whizzed by him, heading back the way he had come, and the other one exited the circle and went south.

Once more, Baahir was alone.

He followed the traffic circle around to the north and exited, spying the museum up ahead. It sat majestically against the Cairo sky along the west side of Meret Basha Street. Powerful exterior lighting illuminated its burnt-orange façade. Baahir was so lost in its aura that he didn't notice the fast-moving vehicle quickly approaching from behind him.

Before he could do anything, the car clipped his rear fender and caused him to fishtail out of control. He skidded sideways, but somehow, didn't crash. His tires recaught the pavement and he straightened out, beelining for the museum. It was just up ahead. He could just now make out the main entrance.

As Baahir came up on Kasr Al Nile Street, he was bumped again. This time, he was forced off the road, clipping a concrete telephone pole as he passed. The passenger side window exploded into a million pieces, bathing Baahir in more shrapnel. The bedlam was too much for Baahir to navigate. The SUV flipped onto its side and skidded sideways across the sidewalk in a shriek of protesting metal. Sparks flew, and so did a flurry of nonsensical obscenities. The latter originated from Baahir's shouts as he and the vehicle flipped onto the roof. Baahir braced himself with his hands, gluing them to the ceiling above his head. The vehicle spun and careened into a storefront before finally coming to a stop.

Though groggy and a bit lightheaded, Baahir was still aware enough to unbuckle his seatbelt. He fell to the roof, landing on something that felt like a steel pipe. In the chaos of it all, Baahir's eyes snapped open when he figured out what it was.

*The scroll!*

He wiped away the blood running down the left side of his face and crawled out of the totaled vehicle with the artifact and his cellphone tucked against his chest in his left hand. He pushed aside the sting of the small shards of glass, forcing themselves deeper into his right palm as he moved.

Sirens wailed in the distance, but Baahir had a feeling that the authorities wouldn't get there in time to save his life. So, he ran, aiming for a nearby alleyway. Automatic gunfire pursued Baahir. Bullets pinged all around him, impacting the walls of the surrounding buildings and shattering the business' windows. The barrage made Baahir flinch, and he reflexively closed his eyes and turned his head away. He clipped his shoulder on the alley entrance, clumsily bouncing off it and into the opposite wall. The accidental change of direction had saved his life. A single bullet impacted the wall right where his head should have been.

Baahir didn't stop to thank his lucky stars. He pushed himself off the wall, gathered his footing, and ran as fast as his battered and bruised body would allow him. It was amazing what adrenaline could do.

Baahir, an accomplished collegiate long-distance runner, had never run so fast.

**The British Museum, London, England** | Present Day

Zahra's phone vibrated noisily across her desk, startling her. She snapped her head up, tossing her disheveled hair back over her shoulders. Blinking awake, she smacked her dry, parched lips together, looking for her bottle of water. Not finding it, Zahra groaned and checked the time on her laptop's screen and saw that she had been out cold for nearly thirty minutes. Grant should have been by to find her, but he had been engrossed in his own work all night, same as Zahra.

Grant Upton had recently been assigned to Zahra as her assistant. She didn't want one, yet here he was, at the behest of her superiors. Grant was a spectacled, athletic college kid — an intern — studying archaeology at Oxford under the institute's top professor, Zahra's father, George Kane. The whole thing felt like an attempt by her father to keep an eye on her. Zahra knew her "old man" was aware of her off-the-books excursions, and he worried deeply for her safety.

*Thanks, but no thanks, Dad.*

Currently, Zahra and Grant were sorting through artifacts and photos she had taken while she was down in the Amazon. She had successfully retrieved her pack and the rest of her gear from outside the quaint plunge pool — the same pool she had used to enter the underground realm of *The Lost City of Z*.

The mission, as a whole, had been a bust. While she *had* found the fabled city, she had taken very few photos of anything important. Not that she had the chance... the only artifact she had found was a journal belonging to the late Jack Fawcett.

The museum's restoration department was now doing its best to save the heavily soiled book. Its torn and waterlogged pages were nearly indiscernible by the time she had made it back to London. It was a long shot, but if they could repair even a fraction of the journal's guts, her travels would have been worth it. The Fawcetts were important to the people of England. Anything relating to them would surely draw more visitors to the museum.

Zahra had almost died several times, too — that had to count for something.

She wiped the sleep from her eyes and snagged her phone, and saw that it was Dina who was calling. Zahra checked the time again.

*12:05?* Why in the hell was Dina calling her so late?

Zahra rolled her eyes. She knew why...

"Hey, Dina," she said, yawning as she answered.

*"Z?"* Dina shouted over the phone. *"That you, love?"*

The Brit was yelling at the top of her lungs, speaking over a voluminous, bassy beat. If Zahra had to guess, the woman was at a club and was utterly trashed.

"Yeah, Dina... it's me."

*"Zahra?"* Dina couldn't hear her. *"Zahra, that you?"*

"Dina!" she yelled. "*Yes,* it's me!"

Her outburst got Grant's attention. The younger man poked his shaggy, dirty blonde head through the door into the next room and gave Zahra a questioning look. He removed one of his earbuds from its place, unsure if she had been trying to get his attention or not. Zahra waved at him and focused on the call. Grant replaced the earbud, shrugged, and disappeared back into the darkened room. It was, in essence, a large storage closet that Zahra had given Grant to use as his personal workplace. It wasn't much, but at least he had that. Back when Zahra started, she was forced to share office space with other people and had constantly been searching for her things.

*"Hey, Z."* Dina hiccupped. *"Whatcha doin'?"*

Zahra put the call on speaker and set it down, rubbing her face hard. She didn't have time for this.

"I'm working, Dina."

Dina snorted. *"No, shit, what else is new?"*

Zahra sighed. Dina loved to point out that she had no life outside of work. “Look, Dina, I — ”

*“Come out with us, Z! Have three to five drinks and blow off some steam.”*

The combination of the background music and Dina’s shouts were too much for her. Zahra dipped her head and closed her eyes.

“Sorry, Dina, but I think I’ll pass. It’s already after twelve, and — ”

*“And nothing!”* Dina interrupted. *“It’s Friday, love!”* She giggled. *“Josie — stop! Let go of that... Come have a drink with us, Z!”*

*Us* meant Dina and the person who had grabbed her *something,* Dina’s girlfriend, Josie. They belonged to a scene that Zahra had never enjoyed, and one she had rarely ever partaken in. Zahra was solely focused on her career and her physical training. Her laser focus was a trait she had acquired from her father. Her mother had been on the other side of the spectrum, to a degree. Her mother would have happily laid down whatever she had been doing to be with her family. Her dad had been a wonderful provider, but he sometimes lacked when it came to the “love department.” He was a workaholic to the core — still was to this day.

“Goodnight, Dina!” Zahra yelled, picking up her phone. “See you Monday!”

She ended the call before Dina could say anything else. For a moment, she contemplated hurling the device across the room. Instead, Zahra turned it over and set it facedown so she couldn’t see the screen. Her face fell into her hands.

“Trouble with Dina?”

Zahra paused and spread her fingers open. Grant was, once again, poking his head into her office.

Zahra’s hands fell to her lap. “No. She’s fine. You know Dina...”

Grant frowned. “Yes, I do.”

Shortly after joining the staff, Grant had gone out with Dina and her crew to celebrate his onboarding. For the entire two days following their barhopping expedition in downtown London, Grant looked like he’d been through hell.

Since then, he followed Zahra’s lead and stuck to his work.

*Smart man,* she thought, waking her wireless mouse with a jiggle.

As soon as she got back to work, her phone began vibrating again. If she could have, Zahra would have crushed the mouse in her hand. She squeezed it as hard as she could, gritting her teeth in annoyance. Dina got like this sometimes, and for whatever reason, the only person she ever called was Zahra — on purpose or with her butt cheek.

Zahra sighed. She couldn't get mad at her. Dina was her friend, and she truly was looking out for her well-being. Zahra worked long hours and was constantly traveling on behalf of the museum. No one knew the mental and physical toll Zahra's job took on her better than Dina.

She turned the phone over and hovered her finger over the screen. But she didn't immediately answer it. The name that was displayed was one she didn't expect to see. She hadn't talked to the caller in nearly a year, nor had she seen him in nearly three.

Zahra silently mouthed his named. "Baahir?"

**Cairo, Egypt**

A pair of big, burly SUVs stopped close to where Baahir's vehicle had come to a shrieking halt. But the Egyptologist was already long gone. With the sealed scroll clutched in his bloodied hands, Baahir ran as fast as he could down the narrow alleyway. He took the first right and then put on even more speed, darting across the road toward the rear parking lot of the Cleopatra Hotel.

He had no idea why Agent Rahal was trying to murder him. A find like this shouldn't have been something to kill for. It was a phenomenal, historical discovery, but not one that should cost lives. The only reason he could comprehend it was because of money. Baahir wasn't an expert on the value of black-market antiquities, but he imagined that the first Book of the Dead ever written would fetch a pretty penny.

*Still...*

That didn't feel right. Rahal didn't admit much back at the temple, but what he had relayed spoke volumes. He had said that the scroll wasn't for him. Whoever it was for, Baahir had a feeling that they wanted the scroll for themselves, and not just to acquire it to sell it off to the highest bidder moments later.

They wanted Baahir dead because he was a witness. *That* he was sure of.

Baahir entered the parking lot and pulled out his phone as he ran and, for a moment, thought about calling the police again. Baahir balked at the idea, though. For all he knew, the police were in on it as well, and would lead him directly towards his would-be captors.

Three sets of headlights came zooming around the front of the hotel. Two more vehicles had joined the manhunt. Baahir was at a serious disadvantage. Getting to the museum was now an impossibility. They knew he was headed there and would, no doubt, have someone watching the building closely.

*Shit,* he thought, ducking behind a minivan.

Two of the three automobiles stopped. Five men in total exited the vehicles, speaking in hushed tones. Baahir recognized one of the men as Rahal, the man from the dig site. The other four were total strangers to him...

Except for one.

*It can't be.*

Surely his eyes were playing tricks on him. His memory was usually sharp, but in his current condition, Baahir was having trouble focusing on any one thing. He took a moment to catch his breath and get his bearings. As his mind cleared, he picked up on what was being said between Rahal and the mystery man.

"Where is he?" the bald, bearded man asked.

Rahal threw up his hands in frustration. "I don't *know*. I swear I saw someone come this way."

The larger of the two men stepped up to the other. "Find him, Fahim."

Rahal shrank away. "I will, Khaliq. You can count on me."

*Khaliq.*

The other man's intimidating presence and name jogged Baahir's memory. He recalled a news story about a man named Khaliq Ayad, owner of *The Pharaoh's Lounge* back in Giza. About a year ago, there had been a brutal murder committed in the establishment's parking lot. Baahir hoped the memory wasn't a premonition of what was to come. Khaliq himself had apparently been responsible for the atrocity, but the only witness to the event had died mysteriously mere days before Khaliq was to be tried, and the charges had been thrown out.

*Why are you here now?* Baahir questioned.

Khaliq held a phone up to his ear, and in the illumination of the two vehicles' headlights, Baahir saw a symbol that he knew all too well. Khaliq's right forearm contained a simple tattoo depicting the scales of

Anubis. And there, in the middle of the two scales, was the jackal-headed god.

Buried deep within Baahir's years of research, he had come across the mention of the clandestine organization surrounding the ancient deity. Whenever something incredible was discovered that revolved around the death god, the Scales of Anubis were said to have been involved in some capacity. To this day, most people believed them to be nothing more than a myth — a legend like, Anubis himself.

"Fahim," Khaliq called out.

Rahal paused his advance into the parking lot. "Yes?"

"What of the jar?"

Baahir's ears perked up. *Oh, no!*

"Dr. Hassan said it was with his sister in London."

Khaliq pulled the phone away from his ear. "London? Where *exactly*?"

Baahir didn't know why a man like Khaliq Ayad would find it so interesting that the jar was in London.

"The British Museum."

"And the sister?" Khaliq lifted the phone back to his ear, but his attention was still on Rahal.

The agent turned and stepped into the parking lot. "Her name is Zahra Kane."

Baahir fumbled for his phone and snuck away, heading deeper into the parking lot. The police had just moved into second place in the order of whom he needed to contact.

Zahra needed to be warned.

Baahir tapped a name toward the top of his speed dial and lifted the device to his bloodied temple. He winced and switched ears. He didn't exactly know what injuries he had sustained in the crash. Everything hurt. Each of the individual wounds masked the other injury's severity to a degree. He was definitely bleeding from a cut to his ear and to his right temple. Baahir vaguely recalled the explosion of glass that struck him in the face as his SUV flipped.

The phone rang twice and connected.

*"Baahir?"*

**The British Museum** | London, England

*"Zahra, thank God!"*

She hadn't heard from her brother in eleven months. The tone in his voice concerned her. "What's wrong, Baahir?"

*"Listen to me carefully. I don't have much time."* He grunted, and in between his deep breaths, she heard heavy footfalls. Baahir was on the move, running from something...or someone. *"Do you still have the canopic jar?"*

Zahra's right eyebrow rose. *This* was why he was calling? She turned her head and eyed the heirloom. It sat majestically atop a four-shelf, mahogany bookcase. The jar's placement made it look like one of the gargoyles overlooking the grounds outside Notre-Dame in Paris.

Twenty years ago, George and Hanan Kane had acquired the beautifully carved, black, two-foot-tall jackal-headed object. Ancient Egyptians used similar canopic jars to preserve the embalmed organs of the recently departed. The Kanes' jar was an oddity. It had been carved out of volcanic igneous rock, not limestone, as tradition had dictated. Whoever had made it had also given it a heavy coat of polish.

Other than the impressive craftsmanship, the piece wasn't all that unusual. At the time, it had been a remarkable acquisition, one that Zahra's parents had made together while on vacation in Cairo. They had bought it from, what Hanan had described as, a less-than-reputable street vendor.

But George didn't care. He had been immediately enthralled with it and had happily handed over a wad of Egyptian pounds amounting to one-hundred U.S. dollars.

After Hanan's tragic death, George had given it to his daughter at her request. He agreed, explaining that it was for "safer keeping," but Zahra really knew why he had gifted it to her. The jar reminded him too much of the lost love of his life. Zahra had kept it *because* it reminded her of her mother and her extensive Egyptian heritage.

Zahra grinned. *And yet, Mom married a white guy from Long Island.*

George's love of Ancient Egypt had spilled over into his love of the people of the country. He had spent as much time abroad as possible, but as fate had decided, he wouldn't meet his future spouse in Egypt. Egypt had come to the States to meet him. The young woman had owned a pair of striking eyes — eyes that were eventually handed down to her firstborn, Zahra Amelia.

"Yeah, of course, I still have it," Zahra replied, still eyeing the heirloom. She put the call on speakerphone and brought the device in front of her face.

*"Excellent,"* Baahir replied, wheezing for breath. *"Keep it safe. They know you have it, and they're coming for it."*

"Who — what are you talking about, Baahir?" Zahra asked, confused.

*"I... I found it, Zahra. I found the original* Book of the Dead, *and now they are trying to take it and kill me."*

Zahra's eyes went wide. Though she hadn't talked to her brother in some time, she knew he had become increasingly obsessed with the legend. The fact he believed that he had found it and that someone was currently trying to kill him and take it confirmed that it did, in fact, exist. Baahir was a lot of things, but a liar wasn't one of them. If anything, he was honest to a fault.

"Holy shit, Baahir!" Zahra pushed away from her desk. She stood and paced the room. Grant noticed the commotion from the other room and stepped inside. She paid her colleague no attention, focusing on her brother's words instead. "And our family's jar? How does it figure into this?"

*"The temple — the one we found the scroll in — there was an engraving of it there, alongside Anubis and the story of the scroll. They are connected. These people..."* he sounded winded. *"They believe the same as our mother did."*

Zahra paused her steps and stared through the wall. The myths surrounding the jar and Anubis had always interested Zahra as a kid, but they had only been stories, and nothing more.

*Right?* Zahra thought, unsure.

"What are you saying, Baahir? Are you telling me that hellstone is real — that all the crap Mom spoke about was true?"

Baahir's footfalls fell silent. Zahra guessed that he had paused to catch his breath. The volume of his voice dropped to a whisper.

*"The people trying to kill me think so."* He quickly recounted what had happened since he first arrived on the scene back at the golf course. *"And their leader. He's a man I've heard of... and not in a good way. I believe he's involved with the Scales of Anubis."*

Zahra nearly blurted out a laugh. "Really? The 'Scales of Anubis?'"

*"Yes, Zahra."* He started to run again. *"Our mother knew a lot more about this than we thought."*

"But why?" Zahra asked, confused and concerned. "What was she involved in, Baahir?"

But he didn't answer.

"Baahir?"

*"Shhh,"* Baahir replied, shushing her. *"Hang on a second."*

Grant was now standing opposite her desk, listening intently. Zahra didn't care that he was poking his head in her family's business. His interest in the goings-on was the least of her worries right now.

*"Zahra, I'm starting to think that our mother's death wasn't an accident."*

The statement hit Zahra hard. The accident had been labeled as a simple hit and run by the police. But Zahra specifically remembered the fear in her parents' voices. They had been hunted by someone that wanted them dead.

*Our mother died because of what she knew.* Zahra sighed. *But if that's true, why didn't Dad look into things deeper?*

Zahra and her father needed to have a face-to-face about it.

"Hang on, Baahir. Back it up a little. I thought Mom and Dad bought the jar from a street vendor?"

*"But where did the vendor get it from?"* Baahir countered.

"Or..." Zahra said, "they lied to us about its origin."

*"That is also a possibility."*

Zahra didn't have a real answer. She had assumed that the vendor had made it, or possibly bought it from the person who had built it, though it was also just as likely that the vendor had discovered it, or even stolen it from the person who had. Then, he sold it to the Kanes before he could be implicated in its theft. Now, Zahra's family was squarely in these people's crosshairs — whoever the hell they were.

*The Scales of Anubis? Really?*

*"Dammit!"* Baahir hissed.

"What is it?" Zahra asked, picturing her brother slinking in and out of the shadows. She sat at her desk and closed her eyes, concentrating on the call.

Baahir spoke, his voice incredibly low. *"Another car is blocking the parking lot. Two more men just climbed out. I have to — oh, God."*

"Baahir?"

*"The man — I think he saw me,"* Baahir explained, his voice catching.

"Rahal?" Zahra asked, recalling his name.

*"Yes, him. Look, I don't have much time. Keep the jar safe. Do whatever you have to do. I trust you, Zahra."* He took a deep breath. *"But if you can't protect it... destroy it. They cannot come into possession of it."*

"Baahir?" she asked, waiting for a reply. But none came. She launched back to her feet. Zahra's office chair zoomed across the space and slammed into something with a crash of glass. She held her phone out in front of her face. "Baahir!"

She eyed the screen.

*Call Ended.*

Grant stepped around her desk and reached a gentle hand out for her shoulder. "You okay, Zah — ?"

She tossed her phone on her desk and pushed Grant away, diving for her computer. Zahra's fingers flew over the keyboard with lightning speed. She knew a lot about the shadowy organization that Baahir had mentioned, but she didn't know everything.

As soon as she entered the Google search, the lights in her office, and presumably the entire museum, went out, as did the Wi-Fi. Red emergency lights came to life, basking Zahra and Grant in their eerie, hellish glow.

"What happened?" Grant asked, slinking back.

Zahra looked down at her phone, then back to her now blank computer screen. Her brother's warning was swiftly coming to fruition.

Her eyes shifted to her terrified assistant. "They're here."

"Who's here?" Grant asked. His voice and hands shook.

Zahra faced the office door. "Trouble."

**The British Museum** | London, England

Twenty years ago, Bernie Switzer had described the museum's sizeable remodel as a 'physical violation.' But as time went by, the head of the night guard really did love what the Great Court had become. He presently stood near the center of the yawning room, in front of the cylindrical Reading Room situated there, lost in the wonder above him. On multiple occasions, each and every evening, he could be found just standing in this exact spot, staring up at the ceiling. He couldn't see them, but Bernie pictured the stars shining bright, high overhead. Working nights made it difficult for him to enjoy the burning balls of firelight. He smiled. The 3,312 triangles of glass that made up the ceiling were all the stars he needed.

A sound like sandpaper on stone drew his attention away from the ceiling. He dropped his eyeline and looked left. There was only one thing between him and the western wall.

Originally discovered in Turkey, the Lion of Knidos was a colossal marble statue weighing more than 13,000 pounds. It depicted an powerful, male lion in a resting position, and had been created sometime in the third or fourth century, sourcing marble from the same quarry as was used in the construction of the Parthenon. The beast was situated as such that it was staring longingly through the darkened court...and right at Bernie. The animal's empty eye sockets were eerie in the lowlight. The sight gave the tenured museum employee the chills every time he caught the predator gazing at him in his periphery.

Even though he loved the museum more than anything, Bernie would have rather been back at his station finishing up *The Monuments Men* instead. Now in his mid-sixties, Bernie was having trouble with his feet and knees. They had been bothering him for a number of years, but never as bad as they were now. Bernie feared he'd have to retire soon. He wasn't afraid of losing his job.

Bernie was terrified of boredom.

His father had been the same way. Bernard Switzer Sr. died while on the job at a local lumber mill at the age of seventy-seven. He had been the oldest member of the staff by over a decade and outworked most men thirty years his junior.

Bernie Jr. was twenty-two years older than the next oldest guard employed by the museum. He was proud of that fact, but it also advanced the growing concern of his eventual departure. He knew he couldn't do it forever.

*Thirty-four years...* He thought, shaking his head. *Where has the time gone?*

Bernie had been at the museum for over three decades, watching patrons and co-workers come and go. The second longest-tenured employee was the museum's curator, Ian Freeman. He was a man Bernie avoided at all costs. Luckily, the curator worked mostly days and rarely ever ran into the senior guard. Freeman wasn't an awful person — quite the opposite. His overly bubbly personality was one that just didn't mesh well with Bernie, a man that kept to himself. In fact, the only person that Bernie truly got along with was Zahra.

She was different.

The lights in the Great Court went out, save for a handful of red emergency lights. The lone man was cast into near pitch-black darkness. What was left was a looming, infernal setting. The multitude of figures and full-scale diorama exhibits seemed to come to life all around him. Bernie's heart raced.

He scolded himself. *Quiet your mind, you old fool.*

The grinding sound immediately picked up again. It — everything that was happening — deeply concerned Bernie. He was the only person out right now. His subordinates were "on break" in their office playing cards. It was why Bernie had gone for a walk. Their hooting and hollering had become too much to bear. So, he had paused his movie and left his station to come here.

It had been over a decade since the last incident that had caused Bernie any concern. A trio of crooks had attempted to break into the museum through a roof access, but their efforts had been denied by the building's tough security system.

*An animal?* he asked himself, flicking on his flashlight. He aimed it at the lion but saw nothing out of the ordinary. Still, he needed to confirm that he was still alone. Bernie stepped lightly, creeping up to the statue.

"I swear," he mumbled, "if this is just Josh or Drew pulling a prank, I'll fire their arses tonight!"

Halfway to the lion, the scratching noise stopped, and so did Bernie.

"Hello?" he called out, tracing his light around the creature. "Anyone there?"

Bernie nearly had a heart attack when a figure stepped out from behind the lion and collapsed to the hard floor. "How did you — ?"

"Help..." the voice was female, and she sounded like she was injured. "Please, help me." She reached a hand up and attempted to crawl toward the guard but stopped, favoring her side.

Bernie stepped forward but stopped. There were protocols to follow. He needed to contact Josh and Drew and report his findings. From there, they would contact the authorities.

"Please..." The woman's face fell, and her forehead clunked to the floor. She didn't move.

Bernie rushed to her and knelt, feeling his aching joints protest the quick movements. He gently turned her over and swept her dark hair away from her face. The first thing he noticed was that she was young, maybe in her early thirties. Her skin tone and hair color spoke to a Middle Eastern background, though he didn't hear it in her voice. Her accent, in the few words she had spoken, was undeniably British. This woman reminded him of Zahra in a way, though his co-worker spoke with a brutish American inflection.

The second thing he realized was that he recognized her, though he didn't know from where. Bernie saw hundreds, even thousands, of people a day while wandering the halls, even when he came in a few hours before closing time.

The woman roused and blinked awake. Her eyes were striking, even in the dim red lighting. Bernie held her head in his lap with one hand and reached for his radio with the other.

"Don't," the woman said. Four sets of footsteps closed in around him. Her face transformed from one of terror to one of joy. She smiled wide and held up Drew's keycard. "You've already done enough."

"You!" Bernie cried, standing. He backpedaled into a huge individual, bouncing off him as if he were a small child.

Earlier in the day, just as he and Drew had arrived, a woman had careened into them. The younger night guard had taken an elbow to his ribs, growling at the museum visitor in protest. Bernie had quickly stepped in and dissolved the situation to the point of getting the headstrong Drew to apologize for running into her. But now, Bernie could see that it had been all a ruse to steal the guard's keycard. Whoever these people were, they had then used the card to access the museum unperturbed.

Before Bernie could call for help, someone grabbed him from behind and dragged him around to the other side of the Lion of Knidos. He gazed up at his beloved glass ceiling as something cold and sharp pressed up against his throat. Then, the unidentified assailant yanked the unseen object sideways and dropped Bernie to the floor as he gasped for air.

But none came.

**Cairo, Egypt**

Baahir was surrounded on all sides. The only reason his exact location had yet to be discovered was thanks to the poor lighting inside the hotel's parking lot. It also helped that he was wearing mostly black clothing. The beam of a high-powered flashlight swung his way. He stooped beneath it and scurried under a truck. Voices called out all around him. The men searching for him were confused. Rahal was the loudest of them all. He angrily chastised the others for losing Baahir.

The Egyptologist stayed put and waited. He'd do so all night if it meant his survival. Footsteps approached his position. Baahir ducked his head down and allowed his dark hair to hide his face. But just as quickly as the light came, it went. As the seconds passed, his hunters grew restless.

Baahir lifted his head and spied a lone individual standing perfectly still some thirty feet away. He had yet to join in the search. Baahir figured that it could only be one man, considering who he was dealing with.

*Khaliq Ayad.*

Never in his life had Baahir thought he would be in this position. He had never done anything to warrant *this* kind of attention. Sure, like his mother, he had ruffled a few feathers within the historical community over the years, but besides that, Baahir had been a stand-up guy to everyone he met. His involvement in the golf course dig had been a classic wrong-place-wrong-time scenario. If he had been out of town, or sick, it would have been a coworker running for his or her life and not him.

*Lucky me,* he thought, spotting Rahal stomping by.

The betrayer was the one leading the charge here. He was screaming at everyone to find Baahir, even going as far as threatening the other men with their lives if they failed. If it were anyone else, Baahir would have laughed the claim off as an empty threat. But this was different. Rahal and his boss weren't people to be trifled with. Abbas and Ghazzi's deaths were a perfect example of that. If Agent Rahal was as cold-blooded as recent history would suggest, then a man like Khaliq would surely be just as bad, if not worse, than Satan himself.

Baahir pushed aside the images of his future torture when a set of boots stopped three feet in front of his nose. Luckily for him, the wind was howling through the parking lot. His heavy breaths were masked, but for how long? The man standing before him spoke.

"Anything yet?" It was Rahal.

He received a chorus of disappointing 'nos.' Only then did Khaliq move. He marched his way over to Rahal and Baahir's position. Baahir held his breath and waited to see what would happen.

The thought terrified him. The stories surrounding the Scales of Anubis weren't heartfelt ones. Everyone involved with them was supposedly violent, obsessive, and manic beyond reasoning.

During Baahir's extensive research into the group, he discovered an account by one of their followers after capture describing what the leadership supposed. At this point, there was no reason to think that Khaliq didn't believe the same. The family alleged themselves to be blood relatives — descendants — of Anubis. The organization functioned as if they were the death god's real-life scales of justice, weighing the hearts of mankind against *Ma'at,* truth. From what Baahir knew, the Scales of Anubis found everyone who opposed them and their mission to have "heavy hearts" and therefore be unworthy of entering *Duat,* the underworld.

And Baahir was the next to be judged.

*What about the jar?* Baahir's instructions to Zahra were hasty but warranted. His reasoning was sound. If she destroyed what Khaliq's men sought, then maybe they would leave her alone.

Beams of light ignited all around Baahir. He would have leaped to his feet and run, but he was trapped beneath the truck. Someone reached beneath the automobile and latched onto his jacket's collar, ripping him out from under the vehicle. Baahir and the scroll went rolling, bouncing along the asphalt like a ping-pong ball. He landed flat on his back and hurriedly rolled onto his hand and knees. Baahir climbed to his feet and took off running but collided with an unmovable object. Through strained eyes, he saw that the barrier wasn't one constructed of brick and mortar. It was made of flesh and blood, and it was the last person he wanted to meet up close.

"And where do you think you're going?" Khaliq asked, staring down at him with a carnal smile.

Terrified, Baahir curled his knees and the scroll into his chest. His protection of the artifact didn't go unnoticed. The unarmed boss stood tall and crossed his arms. Baahir recognized the look of a man putting together a plan. Khaliq stepped closer and knelt into a catcher's squat.

"I see that you appreciate the scroll as much as I do."

Baahir didn't say a word. He just tightened his grip around it and waited.

Khaliq's eyes narrowed. "I'll make you a deal, Dr. *Hassan*." The man said Baahir's last name with disdain. Why? "You can come with us and, if you behave, you may participate in what we have planned."

"And what is that?" Baahir asked, voice soft. "What do you have planned?"

"Something that you might just live through."

Khaliq never once broke eye contact.

It didn't matter what it was. If Baahir wanted to see the next sunrise, he was going to have to play ball. Baahir wasn't sure what stunned him more, the fact that the leader of the Scales of Anubis knew who he was, or the fact that he was trying to recruit him into the fold. Baahir's gut — his emotions — told him to shout "No!" and spit in the man's face. But his logical mind overruled him. If Baahir agreed to help, maybe he could delay Khaliq until help arrived? Either way, he needed to know what was going on, and why the group, all of a sudden, wanted to include him.

"Why me?" Baahir asked, speaking softly.

Khaliq stood and reached out a hand. Slowly, timidly, Baahir accepted the offer and was hauled to his feet. "Because, Dr. Hassan," Khaliq replied, squeezing hard, "I need every learned individual I can find. And few have dedicated as much time to the subject as you."

*Just wonderful,* Baahir thought, sighing.

"The Temple of Anubis is on the horizon."

Baahir cocked an eyebrow up. "The 'Temple of Anubis?' We found that already."

"No, you just found the scroll's resting place." He held out his hand and waited for Baahir to take it. "I thank you for that."

"Uh, yeah, no problem." Baahir had never felt so uncomfortable.

When they parted, Khaliq's eyes locked onto the tube in Baahir's hands. "With this, I will find the temple and fulfill my destiny."

"A map?" Baahir was shocked. "You need my help to read a map — written inside the original *Book of the Dead*?"

Khaliq gave him a wicked grin. "Yes, but I also need an insurance policy against your sister, just in case she decides not to cooperate with my people in London. Speaking of which..." He glanced at his watch. "They should be at the museum by now."

Zahra wasn't one to simply roll over when trouble arose. If anything, the tougher and more ruthless the conflict became, the harder she fought back. Whoever had been sent to steal the canopic jar from Zahra was about to get a rude awakening into the woman that she was. Baahir had never seen his sister in action, but he knew what she was capable of. Even now, he was sure that she was devising an effective counterassault.

Rahal's phone rang. The agent answered it, and quietly conversed with the caller. The conversation was short, and he ended the call. "Khaliq, we should go before — "

Khaliq drew his pistol and shot Rahal in the head, dropping him where he stood. The agent's blood splattered in all directions. Some of it reached Baahir. With shaking hands, he wiped away a droplet from his cheek, and returned his attention to Khaliq.

"W — why?" Baahir's voice was barely audible.

Khaliq turned toward him, gun dangling by his leg. "Fahim was no longer of any use to me. Let this be an example of what happens when someone makes themselves expendable."

Baahir knew what he had to do. "I — I'll help you."

Khaliq holstered the weapon. "Smart man. Come, we have much work to do."

"What do we do, Zahra?" Grant asked, his voice shaky. Based on the look on the younger man's face, he wasn't being stealthy. The college kid was terrified, and could barely speak.

Unfortunately, the only answer Zahra could come up with was, "Uh…"

She had no clue. The impending attack on the museum had caught her wholly off guard. She was in a setting that she never thought she'd have to defend, though she'd thought about it before. The fact that the Scales of Anubis had been able to cut the power so effectively told her that they were more than a group of gun-toting thugs. These guys knew exactly what they were doing.

Zahra needed a weapon, but England's strict gun laws prohibited a civilian from owning a pistol. Not that something as *silly* as the law had ever stopped her… She possessed a handful of firearms but kept them in a hidden safe inside her home…along with an array of knives. She perked up at the thought and dove into her desk. Unbeknownst to anyone at the museum, she kept her favorite blade in her office when it wasn't on her person.

"What are you doing?" Grant asked, watching her.

She knelt and buried her arm up to her elbow into the top drawer of her desk-side, metal filing cabinet. Zahra grinned when she felt it. There, at the rear of the cabinet and magnetized to the underside of the lid, was her Seal Pup knife. It had been a gift from a friend who had been in the American military, a retired Navy SEAL. The perfectly balanced, all-black armament was nearly ten inches long from tip to butt. Half of that was its razor-sharp blade, which was partially serrated near the hand guard.

It was a gift that had come with training, as well. She could wield the blade as deftly as any trained operative.

Zahra then opened a box that had been sitting next to her desk for the last week. Its contents had arrived from an obscure address in America, from the name 'Tommy.' She had yet to test out the updated model. *No better time than the present,* she thought. Zahra took comfort in the fact that the sender had promised it would fix the 'issues' she had with the previous iteration. Gripping the new — and hopefully improved — grappling hook tight, Zahra felt its weight in her hand. It was a tad bit heavier than her last one, but not by much.

While she was good with a knife, *this* was her preferred tool of the trade. The grappling hook was sleek and modern, yet built like it would last a lifetime. She had used and abused the previous iteration while searching for *The Lost City of Z,* and this was the replacement, complete with a few tweaks.

She quickly snapped her wrist and opened its four imposing blades, inspecting their agile, yet rugged construction. Zahra nodded, approving of Tommy's design. Following the instructions in his email, she gently pulled on the cable and watched as the blades folded back into place. The grappling hook was now built around a load-bearing, spring-back system. Tommy had included the blueprints in the email, but even after reading them several times, Zahra didn't fully understand them.

*Whatever. As long as it works...*

He had also mentioned that it would only support up to twenty percent more than her current body weight and to not overload it, or it could fail.

"Well," she had said, closing the email, "no more Taco Tuesdays for me."

Zahra attached the hook and its coiled, seventy-foot-long cord to her belt on her left hip. Last, but not least, was Zahra's high-powered handheld flashlight. Adding her trusty Glock to the belt, she would feel ready for anything life could throw at her. Zahra was also wearing her customary all-black attire, though her current clothing wasn't as rugged as her typical outdoors gear. Her outfit included a pair of well-worn jeans and a shirt featuring her favorite band, a Canadian hardcore group named, Counterparts.

Grant cautiously eyed Zahra as she flipped the fixed-blade knife into the air, nonchalantly catching it by its handgrip. The weapon and its sheath buckled onto her belt right next to the grappling hook. "Um, what did you say you did in the army?"

Zahra rolled her eyes. *Why does everyone ask me that?*

"I was a linguist… Now, stay here and keep your mouth shut, or I'll come back here and curse you out in every language I know."

Grant swallowed hard. His Adam's apple visibly rose and fell as he backpedaled into the center of the room. Slowly, Zahra opened the door and peered out into the hallway. She looked left, and then right. Nothing moved. Satisfied that all was clear, Zahra slinked out and whispered back to her assistant.

"Lock the door, and don't open it for anyone besides me." He nodded. She playfully winked. "Be back in a jiff."

The door closed and the lock reengaged with a soft click. Zahra knelt outside her office and peered down the dark hallway. The only illumination was up ahead in the form of a single red emergency light. She stalked forward, staying low. The corridor ended at a set of plain, off-white double doors. These led out into the main hallway of the Lower Floor, where a handful of the administrative areas were stationed as well as the Clore Centre for Education, including a series of lecture halls and classrooms. She gripped one of the two door handles and slowly tried it, twisting it until the partition opened just enough to peek out. Zahra saw nothing of note through the inch-wide gap. The area was deserted, as expected at this time of night.

*Good,* she thought. She took a deep breath and opened it more, sliding through. Zahra helped the door close without a sound and headed right. She would have normally used the elevator to move between floors, but not now. First off, there was no power to call the lift. Secondly, if she used it, and there were, in fact, people trying to break into the museum and harm her and whoever else was there, the elevator car would have been the perfect place for an ambush.

She continued forward and looked up. To either side of the elevator was a long, rectangular gap in the floor above. They each gave way to a beautiful glass roof high overhead that had been designed by Foster and Partners. The two-acre space situated below it was the single largest covered public square in all of Europe, the Queen Elizabeth II Great Court.

Even though Zahra had walked beneath the ceiling hundreds of times, she was still marveled by its majesty. Some days, she would just stare at the pattern of triangles and watch them gleam in the sunlight. She often found Bernie there as well, also staring in reverence.

Zahra silently ascended the right-hand stairs up to the Great Court without conflict. She hurried across a fifteen-foot expanse that, under the current circumstances, felt as wide as the Grand Canyon. Keeping her head down, she took cover behind the black siltstone Obelisk of Nectanebo II, the last native king of Egypt. The five-and-a-half-foot tall relic stood atop a thick pedestal in the southwest corner of the Great Court. She poked her head out and confirmed that she was still alone. Luckily, for her and Grant, the museum didn't publicly post the locations of the offices anywhere. The network of corridors and workspaces were veiled behind simple, unassuming doors.

Directly to the north of her position was the Lion of Knidos. She hated the animal's eyes.

*Or lack thereof.*

Zahra found herself constantly glancing back to its face, half-expecting it to morph into another expression. Rage? Maybe hunger? She imagined the scene as if it were something out of *Jason and the Argonauts* or *Clash of the Titans*. She would have loved to have seen what Ray Harryhausen would have done with the stone beast. It honestly gave her the willies, but it intrigued her too.

Staying low, she bolted straight for the creature. Once there, she pivoted and pointed herself at the nearby information desk. She swiftly moved away but slipped and spilled to the hard floor. Her fall was like a shotgun blast inside the still auditorium-sized room. Caught out in the open, Zahra panicked and backward crab-walked, returning to the concealment the bulky lion gave. She sat and caught her breath, and luckily, heard nothing. It seemed that no one had heard her.

With her back against the heavy base, Zahra reached her left hand out and placed it on the floor, using it to brace herself as she stole a quick look around the statue. When she did, she felt something odd — something wet. Zahra slowly lowered her eyes to the floor and spotted the fluid. Its presence instantly filled her with dread. Even in the low light, Zahra knew what the dark, viscous substance was.

Blood.

Someone was hurt, or worse.

"Shit," she mouthed, lifting her wet fingertips.

Zahra smeared the blood across the floor before wiping some off on her jeans. She got onto her hands and knees and, once more, glanced around the base of the lion, careful not to touch it again. In that second of exposure, she spotted a streak that continued around to the other side of the animal.

*Dammit,* she thought, biting her lower lip.

Death didn't bother Zahra. But in this case, she was confident that she'd recognize the body. The only people here, besides her and Grant, were Bernie and his crew of guards, Josh and Drew.

And one of them was in serious trouble.

With her back against the lion's pedestal, Zahra headed right, in the opposite direction. She made sure the coast was clear before moving out. After confirming that she was still alone, she hurriedly army-crawled to the far side of the lion and nearly screamed in fright as she came nose-to-nose with Bernie. He was on his back, his empty gaze locked onto Zahra's face. The older man's throat had been cut, and he was unmoving, at rest in a pool of his own blood.

Muffled voices echoed throughout the Great Court. Zahra was prone and out in the open. She leaped to her feet and scrambled around Bernie's body, diving headfirst behind the nearby information desk just as a pair of flashlight beams appeared from around the Reading Room. As the speakers neared, Zahra recognized the outline of rifles.

Zahra growled in anger. She refrained from launching into a crazy, rage-fueled assault. She'd wait for the right opportunity. Then, she'd strike.

# CHAPTER 20
# GRANT

Grant Upton was *this close* to pissing down his leg. Never had the young man been so afraid. His life was literally in the balance based on what Zahra had told him. Now, he was alone, vulnerable. He was stuck in the very same room that housed the wanted canopic jar. This was the last place Grant wanted to be, but he knew he would not stand a chance out there without Zahra.

Grant had become smitten with his superior ever since the day he had met her. At first, he had even thought about asking her out on a date. The ten-year age difference between them didn't bother him. If anything, it made him want her more. Plus, Zahra looked more like a college student than someone in her early thirties. No one could have guessed she already had so much life experience under her belt.

But Grant had balked at the notion. He was terrified of rejection and losing, not only a close confidant and an irreplaceable mentor, but also his job. Plus, her father was his professor and could flunk him on a whim. Grant loved what he was doing, and he was hoping to be hired on permanently after he graduated next summer. He needed Zahra's recommendation for that to happen.

He turned away from the black canopic jar and attempted to get his frayed nerves under control. He had been staring at the artifact for some time, trying to figure out how it was the center of everything going on.

*Why you?* he asked.

With nothing better to do, Grant spun and made his way over to it. He clasped his clammy hands behind his back and leaned in close, inspecting the intricate engravings. He knew a multitude of Egyptian hieroglyphs, but not all of them. In this case, he could understand most of what the writing said, but not all of it.

"It more or less says: 'the soul of the... of the god-king Anubis... it, um, resides within.'" He stood straighter. "Well, *that* puts it plainly."

He turned away from the jar but stopped and flashed back to it. Going against his better judgment, he picked it up and held it up to his face. Grant reread the inscription. He looked up at the blank wall, lost in thought. "The god-*king* Anubis? The hell?"

Anubis had never a king. That would imply that he had been human. A god, sure. But not a *king*. Grant had spent hundreds of working hours near the artifact but had never gotten close enough to notice the inscriptions. And even if he had noticed the glyphs, it wouldn't have mattered. It was preposterous to think any of it was true.

He glanced at the office door. *Until now.*

If a secretive ancient society was going through all this trouble to acquire the jar, then maybe the mythos surrounding it were true? At the very least, they believed it was.

Grant snickered at the disillusion. But the ridiculousness of it didn't make the intruders any less dangerous. It didn't matter what was true. All that did matter was what they believed.

And it was only a matter of time before they came here to take it.

He cautiously rotated the jar and examined its lid. There was a layer of grime jammed between it and the rim. The sight reminded him of something Zahra had once said. Her parents had never let her open it, and even today, Zahra had yet to open the artifact.

*Dumb superstitions...*

Grant gripped Anubis's head by its base and pulled, applying consistent, gentle pressure. After adding a touch more effort, the lid came free.

A horrible stench erupted from within, slapping Grant hard in the face. The smell reminded him of a wet, rotting rat. He reeled back in disgust, nearly dropping the family treasure.

Grant gagged and reeled backward. He took a moment to calm himself before continuing his examination of the object. His actions amused him. He wasn't typically this jumpy. Then again, he'd never been in a life-or-death situation before.

"And now... you are *free*," he jokingly announced, picturing Anubis' Casper-like ghost zooming around the room.

But the humor was suddenly gone, and the thought of an ancient demigod floating around the room with him made the hair on his arms stand up straight. Shaken, Grant replaced the lid.

A soft *clunk* somewhere out in the hallway spurred Grant into returning the heirloom to its dedicated spot. A second sound hurried him back into his portion of the dark office. Grant sank down next to his desk and sat against the wall out of direct eyesight of the door. He tucked his knees into his chest and shivered. Grant was going to take Zahra's instructions to heart and not open the door for anyone unless it was her.

*Or maybe Bernie.*

rifles pointed nonchalantly at the floor. They spoke softly to one another before being interrupted by the squawk of a radio.

The voice on the other end hollered in angry Arabic. The man to Zahra's left hurriedly replied, stating that they had yet to see anyone besides the "old man." The guy who initiated the call screamed for these two to pick up their pace and keep searching.

"Yes, sir!" he replied, clipping his walkie onto his belt.

With that, the two intruders sped up their hunt. Based on the frustration and urgency in the caller's voice, Zahra gathered that the team here had yet to find her office. It was one of the first times she was thankful for the museum director's paranoia. Openly labeling the office rooms would have screwed them royally tonight.

The pair swung up their rifles, using their barrel-mounted lights to guide the way. Each one swept it side to side, stopping every now and again to check nearby doors, most of which were locked. A gunshot rang out as one of the men obliterated the deadbolt with a single round. Zahra laughed inwardly. He had just wasted a bullet on the lock to the Great Court's mop room.

*Boy, is Charlie gonna be pissed!*

Benjamin "Charlie" Porter was the clean-up crew's supervisor. And no, Zahra had no idea why he preferred to go by Charlie and not Benjamin — or even Ben. She never asked, and based on what her co-workers had told her, he wouldn't tell, not even with half a bottle of Jameson in his system. And honestly, Zahra didn't really care, so she left the matter alone. There were plenty of other things to focus on in her day-to-day life.

*Like not dying,* she thought, smiling as the two intruders split up.

One of them continued forward. The other stopped and headed back in the direction they had come. She quietly watched them move about. When one of them entered through the archway leading to the east wing, Zahra knew who her first target would be.

Thing One swung right, passing between Zahra's position inside the information desk and the Reading Room. She duck-walked to the opposite side of the oval workstation and decided on a course of action. She could try to bullrush him but doubted she could get close enough without being heard. She didn't possess a long-distance weapon of any kind. This was where her Glock would have come in handy. If she was going to successfully subdue the gunman, she'd have to do it up close and personal.

*Unless...*

Zahra looked over her right shoulder and identified something that might just close the gap between her and her target. Back toward the front doors was a stand-alone diorama dedicated to the tribes of Africa, specifically the Maasai of Kenya. At its center was the wax figure of a native man holding an authentic spear that had actually been used to hunt and kill lions. Zahra knew from personal experience that the spade-shaped tip was still plenty sharp. If used properly, the spear could do some serious damage.

Slipping from cover, Zahra stayed low and moved heel to toe. She reached the display in seconds and carefully mounted it to retrieve the weapon. Pulling it free of the native's grasp wasn't as easy as she figured it would be. Zahra applied some force, and it finally came free — and with a price. The mannequin's wrist snapped in half, alerting Thing One to her presence. Zahra gripped the Maasai spear and froze out of fear of being gunned down.

But oddly, nothing happened.

The intruder's weapon light swung her way but didn't linger.

*Uh...* Then, it hit her. *He thinks I'm part of the exhibit!*

So, Zahra played the part and stood as still as a statue. She was facing the wrong direction and couldn't see him. So, she used her other senses, and waited to hear him step away. When he did, she made her move. Zahra turned and leaped from the knee-high podium. As soon as she landed, Zahra launched the spear into the air like an Olympic javelin thrower. She'd done a bit of it back in college, but never competitively. It was mostly her wanting to see how far she could throw the 'long, pointy thing.'

The flexible shaft exited her hand in what she hoped was the perfect toss.

But Zahra didn't stop there. She sprinted *toward* the guy with the rifle, watching the spear reach its peak. Saying a quick prayer to the Maasai god, she witnessed the projectile drop like a bomb, and head straight for her quarry. Thing One turned just as the spear struck home, impaling him in the meat of his left shoulder. The impact sent him sprawling to the floor, but unfortunately, he didn't drop his weapon. Zahra was still too far away to do much else. So, she did the only other thing she could think of.

It took him a minute, but Thing One sat up, crying out in pain. The delay gave Zahra time to unbuckle her grappling hook. She kept its head closed and gave the line enough slack to get in a few overhead twirls, mentally gauging the distance to her target. Not wasting any more time, she released the hook and cringed when the infant-sized metal object smashed into the bridge of Thing One's nose.

He was out cold — possibly even dead. Zahra didn't care what his current state was, alive or not. She hauled in her line and slid to a stop at his feet. Zahra immediately began to drag the much heavier gunman back toward the information desk. Her plan was to relieve him of his rifle once they arrived, but she didn't get the chance. Thing Two came running back into the Great Court, chasing Zahra away from his compatriot. Apparently, her attack hadn't gone unnoticed.

She released Thing One's ankles and bolted in the opposite direction, heading around to the western side of the room. Bullets whizzed through the air all around her. A few of the stray rounds impacted several of the museum's priceless artifacts, including the backside of the Lion of Knidos. One of the bullets smacked the marble bust of Julius Caesar right in the forehead. The loud *crack* of the impact caused her to flinch and stumble, but she kept moving. She instinctively covered her head with her hands and practically dove through the entrance to the first room she came across.

# CHAPTER 22
# ZAHRA

The wing to the west of the Great Court held her favorite collection, that of Ancient Egypt. She knew its contents better than anyone, even rivaling the knowledge of the museum's curator. Zahra loved engaging in exhaustive debates with the man, and not because she wanted to prove him wrong. It was rare that anyone employed by the museum could hold a proper conversation with Zahra when it pertained to the specific subject matter.

Room 4 held one of the single greatest archaeological discoveries on record, the Rosetta Stone. The granodiorite stele contained three versions of the Decree of Memphis. The trilingual stone slab was the first of its kind ever discovered to include Ancient Egyptian and Demotic script alongside a third, widely known language, Ancient Greek. Because of the slight similarities between the three languages, the stone had been the key to unlocking the Ancient Egyptian language.

It was a priceless piece of history, and Zahra often found herself consumed by its significance, staring at it whenever she happened by the exhibit.

She veered around the left side of the display and ducked behind it just as a volley of automatic gunfire struck it half-a-dozen times. Luckily, the eleven-millimeter-thick reinforced glass ate the rounds without a problem.

But the shooter wasn't finished.

Additional gunfire completely decimated the protective case as well as the priceless artifact within.

The intruder hesitated as his gun jammed, which provided Zahra the opportunity to move. Bolting right, Zahra peered over her shoulder in time to spot several chunks of the Rosetta Stone fall free and crash to the floor.

The senseless destruction angered her.

Bernie's murder enraged her.

The northern hall was split in two with a bevy of beautiful pieces running down the middle of it. Additional displays sat against each wall as well. A visitor could spend hours inside the British Museum and never leave Room 4 — and she had seen many who did just that.

Zahra spun around abruptly to see what her attacker was doing.

Her ankle rolled as payment. Zahra went down awkwardly, sliding for five feet on her side before scampering on all fours behind one of the largest pieces of the entire Egyptian collection. She flattened her back against the base of the colossal statue of King Rameses II. The upper half of the carving was remarkable. Zahra wished its lower half had survived the ravages of time. It would have been a majestic sight to behold considering it had been carved from a single block of two-colored granite.

Zahra held her breath and listened.

There, buried beneath her heavy breaths, was a single set of footfalls. The gunman, Thing Two, was still on the prowl. Zahra stood and tested her ankle. It didn't hurt as much as it just felt weak. In time, it would be fine and be back to normal. The problem with that was that she didn't have that kind of time.

*I need to hide*, she thought, looking around. *There!*

It wasn't her first choice, but Zahra found a place to lay low. She limped forward and vaulted over a waist-high, ram-sphinx sculpture. She went against museum rules and planted her hands on its back, going airborne. A second later, Zahra disappeared from view inside the sarcophagus of Nectanebo II. The sarcophagus had belonged to the same man as the black obelisk back in the Great Court. The one thing she could take solace in was that the coffin had never been used to house the dead. Nectanebo II had fled to Nubia following the Persian invasion of 343 B.C.

Zahra rolled onto her side and cringed when her flashlight dug into her side. She tore it free of its holster and peered through one of a handful of holes drilled along the sarcophagus' base. They had been used to drain water once the coffin had been converted into an elegant bath for its new owner.

*Huh, I guess it did hold bodies, after all.*

Thirty agonizing seconds passed before Zahra spotted a pair of black, military-style boots. Thing Two stepped carefully, but the hard floors and high ceilings made it impossible for him to fully hide his steps. Quietly, Zahra gripped the handle of her knife and unsheathed it, biting her lip as she did.

The gunman's toes turned her way, and he stepped forward. If she was discovered, Zahra would become a permanent addition to the exhibit, and it'd be her blood, not the waters of the river Nile, draining through the holes at the base of the sarcophagus.

She pulled her mind away from the image of her lying dead inside a 2,000-year-old stone casket. The gunman took two more steps toward her position. But then, he turned back the way he came and spoke.

"No sign of her here."

A radio crackled to life. "Keep looking, Ehsan. And do not call me back until you have her!" This time, the caller's voice was female.

Thing Two grumbled. "Yes, Ifza."

*Ifza?* Zahra asked herself. *So, their leader is a woman named Ifza?"*

This was Zahra's chance. With the assailant distracted, she heaved her flashlight high into the air, aiming for the end of the room. When it landed, Thing Two — Ehsan — spun.

That's when Zahra made her move. She jumped to her feet and plunged the blade of her SOG knife deep into the meat of Ehsan's right shoulder. For good measure, Zahra twisted it around before ripping it free. The injury caused the man to drop his rifle and his walkie-talkie and reel back in surprise and agony. He stumbled and fell, clutching the wound with his opposite hand. The injury wasn't life threatening, however, it left him unable to shoot Zahra in the back while she got away.

Zahra thought about pressing the attack, but quickly decided against it. Instead, she hurried for Room 4's northern exit and the staircase beyond.

her training or conditioning, it was her knowledge of the labyrinthian museum.

The wide, low-angled stairs were deeply set, making them simple to casually traverse in large groups. The design didn't make it easy for Zahra to sprint up them, however. Taking the steps two at a time was practically impossible. She was never able to get into a comfortable rhythm. Her strides became jerky and awkward, causing her ankle to hurt worse.

She rounded the first landing and kept going, heading up to the third floor. Just beyond it was Room 59 and the collection celebrating Ancient Levant, a region comprising modern-day Israel, Jordan, Syria, and Lebanon, among other Eastern Mediterranean countries. Following the flow of the floor to the east, Zahra would eventually pass through rooms containing exhibits featuring different eras of Mesopotamia.

She barely made it inside Room 59 before a figure stepped into view further ahead. In the dim emergency lights, Zahra spotted a long rectangular object in his rising hands.

*Shit!*

Moving on pure adrenaline and instinct, Zahra unclipped her new grappling hook and swiftly snapped open its hooked head. She hung it on the banister and planted her left hand atop it, and jumped just as Thing Three opened up with his rifle. This wasn't exactly the way she had planned to test Tommy's new design. Her calloused hands managed against the fifty-foot drop, but they burned like mad. Any more, and the skin would tear.

Zahra looked down to spot her landing. She did so just in time too. Ehsan appeared directly beneath her, and looked up, obviously confused by the rappelling cord's initial appearance. The timing couldn't have been better... Zahra lashed out with a strong kick and caught the bleeding murderer in the face, spilling him to the floor as she landed.

Tommy's new design worked like a charm.

At the same time Zahra touched down, she looked up to see the spring-loaded hook disengage, now free of her weight. The device fell harmlessly back to earth.

She heard a shout from the other gunman.

He had just swung his legs over the banister in an attempt to pursue Zahra. Tommy's warning replayed in her head.

*It will only support about ten percent more than your current body weight.*

Zahra turned away from the edge as the assailant landed with a slap and a crack.

"That makes three," Zahra muttered, catching her breath. She had no idea how many of them there were. She knew there was at least one more, the leader of the group, Ifza. "No way I'm that lucky."

This time, Zahra was given the opportunity to disarm Ehsan, relieving him of his weapon, a Russian-made Kalashnikov assault rifle. The select-fire AK-103 featured its signature "banana mag" that held thirty rounds. Zahra guessed there was about half of that available after the man's destructive salvo back at the Rosetta Stone. Still, it was better than nothing.

She released the magazine and confirmed the round count. *Sixteen left.*

Zahra slammed the magazine back home, mumbling to herself. "Now I have a machine gun. Ho, ho, ho..."

She shouldered the AK and got moving, going straight rather than heading right and returning to Room 4. The commotion she and Ehsan had created would surely bring unwanted attention. In a blur, Zahra made it to Room 24 and its massive Easter Island head — a Mo'ai — without conflict. The stunning stone monument sat dead center in the middle of the *Living and Dying* gallery.

*A decent place to die, I guess.*

# CHAPTER 24
# GRANT

A soft knock at the door caused Grant to stand bolt upright. His bladder tingled, threatening to release its payload then and there. Until now, Grant hadn't heard a peep out of anyone or anything. The underground office space was typically silent, naturally soundproofed by the tons of concrete surrounding it. A voice followed the third knock, but its owner was speaking in too hushed a tone for him to understand what was being said.

Grant tiptoed closer, stopping within two feet of the door. He was under strict orders not to open the door for anyone besides Zahra. The voice picked up again. The speaker was female. Grant reached for the deadbolt. Just before his shaky fingers met it, the woman, Zahra or not, shouted loudly.

"Open the door. It's me!"

The lady's voice sounded a touch different than Zahra's did. It was lower and laced with gravel. Maybe he was overthinking it. She could just be out of breath or thirsty...or hurt.

He decided to stay quiet. The woman's long, drawn-out inhalations caused him great concern. If it was Zahra, and he kept her from safety because of his fear, he'd never forgive himself.

"Please, open the door! They're coming!"

Grant couldn't wait anymore. He needed to help his boss. "Okay, Zahra, I'm here."

He gripped the deadbolt's latch with his thumb and forefinger and snapped it left. The door lock disengaged. Just as quickly as it did, the door was opened and thrown into his face. The impact dropped Grant to the floor. He held his nose with one hand and groped a nearby counter with the other, attempting to arrest his fall. A miasma of papers, snacks, and tools spilled to the floor around him. Grant felt liquid run from his nostrils into his open mouth. The impact had broken his nose.

He scurried backward as a woman — not Zahra — entered. She resembled his superior in a way, though. The newcomer, likewise, sported jet-black hair and striking eyes. This woman, however, also owned a series of scars that ran vertically just outside her left eye, starting within her eyebrow. Other than the blemish, she was just as attractive as Zahra.

"Who — who are you?" Grant stuttered, spitting plasma from his mouth.

The well-built woman's eyes bore holes into Grant's soul. They were much more intense than the ones belonging to his boss. These oozed with rage, whereas Zahra's emitted confidence with an underlying dose of mischief.

The 'other Zahra' finally broke her laser-like focus when she noticed something directly above Grant. He followed her gaze and saw it.

The Kane's canopic jar.

Grant launched to his feet and seized it. He held it high over his head and did his best to portray someone poised to destroy it. He failed miserably. Grant visibly shook with fright. The woman saw straight through his act.

"What will you do?" she asked, glancing up at the jar. "Will you destroy your friend's most-valued possession?"

Her English was remarkable, though it was laced with a Middle Eastern inflection. *No,* Grant thought, *not Middle Eastern. She's Egyptian.*

*Who are these people in relation to Zahra's family?* Grant wondered.

He narrowed his eyes. "How do you know she values it like that? For all you know, she purchased it at a jumble sale."

The attacker's eyebrows knit. "I know the Kanes well enough to know that isn't true."

It begged the question again.

"Who are you?"

The woman relaxed. "I am Ifza Ayad."

Grant's jaw hit the floor. He swallowed. "Ayad?" He had overheard the between Zahra and her brother. They had mentioned the name.

Ifza nodded. "Yes. Khaliq Ayad is my brother."

Dozens of unfinished thoughts bounced around inside Grant's skull. He didn't know what to do next. But he knew one thing for certain. Zahra would rather destroy her jar than have it fall into the hands of these terrorists. Her brother had said to do just that.

Grant lifted it higher. As he did, Ifza drew a pistol from somewhere behind her back. She leveled it at Grant's chest but didn't pull the trigger. The young man froze. Never in his life had Grant had a gun pointed in his direction before. The act weakened his legs, turning them to jelly.

Ifza smiled when he lowered the jar. "Smart man." Grant didn't understand. She explained. "That," she said, pointing at the jar, "is the only reason you are still alive."

"W — why is that?"

Ifza did something Grant didn't expect. She lowered the pistol and returned it to the back of the pants.

"Because, if you destroy it, there will be no reason to keep you alive."

Just then, two burly men entered the room. This pair held intimidating rifles in their hands, and they had them trained on Grant's midsection. Being a bit of a gamer, Grant recognized the weapons as variants of the famous AK-47.

Ifza stepped closer. "You and the jar are coming with us. You will be our insurance policy against any retaliation from Ms. Kane — same as her brother."

"That won't stop her. She won't stop until she gets what she wants."

Ifza took another step closer. Now, she was within arm's reach of Grant. "So are we."

With no other choice, Grant lowered the jar. "You promise not to kill me?" He handed over the artifact. "Not yet, anyway?"

Ifza grinned and took a step away. Her boot came down on something crunchy. She looked down and lifted her right foot, spotting a smashed cracker. Its box lay next to it.

"Gluten-free, huh?" she asked.

He nodded. "Celiac."

"Interesting." She shouted something in Arabic, and her men charged forward and apprehended Grant. "*Very* interesting."

# CHAPTER 25
# ZAHRA

The thick rubber bottoms of Zahra's sneakers squeaked as she ground to a halt. She silently stood in place and listened, hearing something out of place in the ultra-quiet air. Zahra could just barely hear muffled voices. She closed her eyes and gauged their exact location.

*Front door,* she thought.

Zahra took off running, desperately trying to keep her footfalls quiet. She headed west around the back of the Reading Room, slowing when she reached the entrance to the western wing.

Room 4 was an utter disaster. Her heart broke to see what was left of the Rosetta Stone. The relic's protective case had stood up to the initial barrage of gunfire. Regrettably, the second wave had done it in. A handful of rounds had made their way through, striking the priceless artifact with one nauseating gut punch after another.

And Zahra currently possessed the weapon responsible.

With tears forming in her eyes, she turned away from the awful sight. The murmur of voices started up again and interrupted her intensifying emotions. Currently, she felt loss. The Rosetta Stone was incredibly important to the world, as well as to Zahra's ancestors back in Egypt. The fact that it was damaged as badly as it was while in England wasn't going to sit well with the Egyptian people. It could be argued that if it had been in Cairo that it would have avoided any harm.

There had already been millions of dollars in damage tonight, and Zahra doubted it was going to end there.

She hurried forward, circumventing the Lion of Knidos and the body laying beneath it. She still couldn't believe that Bernie had been murdered. Zahra's eyes flicked to the lump in the floor, then back to the front doors. She ducked back inside the information desk and got to one knee, lining up a massive man in the sights of her pilfered rifle. He had just appeared from the floor below her, ascending the same staircase she had used earlier. The violent intruders had, it seemed, located the offices belowground.

*Which means...*

Grant appeared next, as did a woman that looked remarkably like Zahra. It took the *real* Zahra aback. Lastly, another armed goon brought up the rear. The big guy stepped aside and allowed the others to pass. The woman now led the pack, guiding Grant and the other man toward the front doors. The mountain stayed put next to the Obelisk of Nectanebo II and surveyed the area.

Zahra didn't know what to do next, apart from stalling these people until the authorities arrived. Then again, she didn't even know if they had been alerted yet. And who was around to call them? Were Drew and Josh still alive, or had they also shared Bernie's fate?

The thought sickened Zahra.

Against her better judgment, she stood and stepped out, aiming her AK-103 at the woman.

"Stop!"

Everyone turned their attention to Zahra. The big guy left his post over by the obelisk and joined the others, walking confidently even with an armed adversary in his presence. It was plain to see that he didn't fear being gunned down. None of them raised their hands in surrender.

The leader stepped away from Grant and her man.

She smiled. "Zahra Kane, I presume?"

Zahra recalled her name from the radio conversation she had overheard earlier.

"And you must be Ifza."

Grant attempted to rip free of the gunman's grip but was unsuccessful. "She's Khaliq's sister, Zahra!"

The aggressor shoved Grant in the shoulder and then drove the stock of his rifle into his lower back. Grant cried out in pain and fell to his knees, grabbing at the injury. Zahra took a step forward but stopped when Grant's assailant swung his rifle around on him.

Zahra gave the gunman a long look before turning her attention to her assistant. "You okay?"

Grant winced but nodded. "Yeah, I'm alright." His face soured. "I'm sorry, Zahra, but they got your mother's jar."

Both of Ifza's men wore matching backpacks. If Zahra had to guess, the mountain-of-a-man was the one who was carrying.

The news of the theft was bad, but at least Grant was still alive. "It's fine. As long as you're safe." Zahra looked at Ifza. "You have what you came for. Leave him and go."

Ifza chuckled softly. "You are in no position to make any demands."

"Okay, then..." Zahra said, lowering her rifle to the floor. She stepped away from it. "Can you at least tell me what you're going to do with him — my brother too?"

The woman's fiery eyes ignited. The corners of her mouth turned upward into a manic smile. "You really don't know, do you?"

"Know what?"

Ifza laughed. "You've been lied to your entire life, and *this* is how you find out?" She gave Zahra a faux frown. "Poor thing."

Zahra had no idea what Ifza was talking about. She couldn't put her family history in front of Grant's safety. So, she repeated her question. "What are you going to do with Grant and my brother?"

"You'll see."

Ifza shouted in a language that even Zahra didn't understand. It sounded like a form of Ancient Egyptian. Something was abnormal in it, though. The inflections were different, like American English versus British English. Accents changed from region to region.

It also could be similar to the tribes of the Amazon or the Congo. Isolated cultures developed their own language over time. Was that what this was?

It was an interesting concept.

The big guy slipped out of his pack and handed it to Ifza while the man with the rifle spun and headed for the door. Ifza took Grant by the arm and pulled him back a little as the mountain stomped toward Zahra. She leaned back toward her discarded AK but didn't get far.

Ifza drew a pistol and jammed it into Grant's temple. "Don't even think about it." The big man kept coming. "This is Odai. The man you killed," Ifza's eyes darted to the person Zahra had impaled with the African spear, "was his brother."

*Oh, shit.*

Zahra unsheathed her SOG knife and took a step back. Odai pulled a blade twice that size out from a holster on his right thigh. The extra-large Bowie knife looked comfortable in his hand. The two must have been old friends.

Zahra held up her much smaller blade and laughed at the ridiculousness of the situation.

She looked around for something better and saw an artifact that she recognized. Thirty feet behind her was a weapon she had already used earlier that night. She sheathed her knife and turned, and ran for it. Her actions confused the behemoth, pausing him in his tracks. In one motion, Zahra slid to one knee, snagged the bloodied Maasai hunting spear, and popped back up to her feet. She brandished the imposing weapon as if she was expertly trained with it — which she wasn't. It's not as if Zahra was pretending to be Okoye, General of Wakanda's Dora Milaje.

Odai growled, staring at her between the African tribesman's legs. The diorama was now equidistance between the two combatants. If it were possible, he now looked even angrier than before. Zahra understood why too. She glanced right, to a pair of feet protruding from inside the information desk. Then, she focused on the spear tip — the plasma that coated it.

The blood belonged to Odai's brother.

Instead of simply shooting Zahra where she stood, the mountain was going to make her suffer. He wanted to kill her with his bare hands.

Zahra couldn't let that happen.

She charged.

# CHAPTER 26
# ZAHRA

Zahra made it to the Maasai exhibit first. She leaped onto its raised platform and swung the spear in a long upward arc. Odai blocked it with the blade of his enormous Bowie knife, absorbing a large portion of the kinetic energy with his thick body.

But it did knock him off balance.

Zahra used that moment to press the attack. She went airborne, once again, and launched a strong kick into Odai's chest. He staggered away, unsure. Zahra doubted he had ever fought a woman with Zahra's skill or ferocity before. His culture subjugated the opposite sex to the point of treating them like animals.

Odai regained his composure and got his boots back underneath him. He swung his Bowie knife in a long, powerful downward arc. Zahra had only just gotten her own feet set before having to block it, using her spear like a bow staff.

Donatello would have been proud.

An ear-splitting *clang* reverberated throughout the Great Court, as well as in Zahra's ears. She cringed but kept her focus on Odai and not on her personal discomfort.

Still, it hurt like hell.

The big guy moved impossibly fast. Zahra dodged his attacks but was driven directly into the platform. She rolled backward, losing a few strands of hair as she mounted the exhibit once again. Odai's next attack had come *that* close.

On one knee, Zahra jabbed at Odai's face and was delighted to see it connect with his left cheek. He reeled back and snarled but didn't grab for the wound. He never lost concentration and promptly retaliated. The beast's pain tolerance was as impressive as his physical stature. He attempted to swipe it across Zahra's throat, but luckily, she wasn't there.

Her spear was.

Their weapons met with a skull-pummeling *clang*. This time, it was too loud for either of them to ignore, and both Zahra and Odai responded and grimaced. She wasn't sure what Odai was feeling, but Zahra's ears rang worse than getting kicked in the head by a mule.

Or so she thought.

She shook the cobwebs loose and shoved the blunt end of her weapon into Odai's chest, pushing him back as she dismounted the platform. Back on level ground, Zahra was taken aback by how much taller he was than her. Six inches, at least. It didn't matter, though. If her life had taught her anything, Zahra was similar to a cannonball made entirely from ill-tempered wolverines.

The elder Kane sibling was a lot to handle, even in her compact, unassuming package. She enjoyed using her stature and looks to her advantage when at all possible. But now wasn't one of those times. Odai wasn't about to show her any mercy, regardless of the fact that she was an attractive damsel in distress — mostly because he was the one causing the distress.

Zahra and Odai sized each other up while regaining whatever strength they had left. Both were drenched in sweat and gasping for air.

"I like your knife," Zahra said, speaking Arabic, trying to delay the inevitable. "It looks really sharp."

Odai relaxed and looked over his blade. "Yes, it will make quick work of you," he grinned, "same as the old man."

It was Zahra's turn to growl like a feral, bloodthirsty Chupacabra. She rushed the beefy man, and poked and slashed at every part of his body. Every two or three attacks, she made contact. Most of the injuries were superficial at most, but even the smallest of wounds could weaken your opponent if there were enough of them.

It was a classic *death by a thousand cuts* scenario.

"*Bastard*!" Zahra shrieked, jamming the spear tip into the meat of

Odai's right pectoral muscle. She smiled like a wild huntress and twisted the blade in deeper. "Oh, look, just like your shish kebab brother."

This was the first time she had seen a change in emotion on the man's face. Until now, he had exhibited pure rage — nothing more. He had originally possessed the embodiment of vengeance. Presently, he had an expression of uncertainty plastered across his face.

Zahra savored the moment.

Odai shook off the injuries, charged her position, and hacked and slashed at her uncontrollably. Zahra took the defensive and blocked every swing and stab, but she was quickly running out of real-estate.

The Maasai diorama came up fast behind her, so much so that she didn't have the wherewithal to roll atop it this time. Odai leaped forward and pinned her lower back against the raised platform, using his prodigious upper body strength against Zahra's lither frame.

She wasn't entirely out of options, though. She did what any woman in her situation would do: Zahra kicked her attacker in the testicles as hard as she could.

She imagined every lady's self-defense instructor clapping enthusiastically.

Odai's reaction was instantaneous. He clutched his wounded manhood with one hand and backed away, parrying Zahra's attacks with the other. Her blade sliced Odai's right wrist, opening a fairly deep cut. The injury made him transfer the weapon to his left, offhand. This was Zahra's moment. If she could capitalize on it, she might still be able to rescue Grant.

Odai brought the Bowie knife down on Zahra's head. She just barely got her Maasai spear up in time. The force of Odai's attack bounced the staff off her forehead, dazing her a bit. Zahra stumbled away.

Her response to the shot to the head saved her life.

As she fell back, Odai's Bowie knife passed just beneath her chin. If she had been standing still, her throat would have been cut. Zahra gathered herself and went on the defensive, once more. She concentrated her efforts on blocking Odai's blade and nothing else, zeroing in on it with extra emphasis. Even though her opponent held a serious physical advantage, Zahra was still holding her own. Plus, Odai was tiring. Every successive attack was more sluggish and wilder than the previous.

Odai leaned into the next one, giving Zahra an idea. On his next strike, she would allow Odai to get in close.

The mountain practically leaped out of his shoes, bringing his blade down on...nothing. Zahra ducked under the attack, turning the giant around in the process. Now, his back was to the African exhibit. But that didn't stop him. He hacked at Zahra's face again. She quickly transformed into an overtired child and became what every parent's sore back dreaded: Deadweight. Zahra dropped to the floor and brought up her spear. Instead of using the staff to deflect Odai's slash, she went on the offensive and thrust the blade of the Maasai spear into the bigger man's stomach just beneath where his belly button should be.

Ifza's enforcer dropped his Bowie knife and clutched the mortal wound with both of his hands. He bore holes into Zahra before his legs went out, and he collapsed in on himself. Remembering that Odai wasn't the only threat in the room, Zahra climbed to her feet, gripping her spear tight. But there was no one there.

"Zahra!"

She looked left and found Grant, Ifza, and the other gunman huddled together behind a pillar. Before she could contemplate why they had gone into hiding, the world in front of her turned into that of pure light. Zahra was tossed backward by an immense heatwave. Her battered and bruised body slammed into, and through, the wax Maasai tribesman.

She lost the spear at the same time she lost consciousness.

## CHAPTER 27
# GRANT

Grant was rushed outside. He fought against his captors, trying desperately to run back inside the ruined entrance. He couldn't believe what had just happened.

The British Museum had just been bombed by terrorists.

But Grant couldn't break free. He shouted Zahra's name over and over again, praying that she had somehow survived the explosion. And what if Zahra was alive? She'd surely follow Grant and the others outdoors only to be gunned down moments later.

The trio of himself, Ifza, and her man, Tahsin, hurried down the steps as the front entryway continued to fall apart. Fires raged, spreading quickly.

And there was still no sign of Zahra.

No movement at all.

The prospect of her being dead broke something in Grant. Tears fell as he was shoved inside a waiting van. He all but fell into the bench bolted to the inner wall of the driver's side. Tahsin sat across from Grant, scowling deeply. Ifza slid into the front passenger seat. Without further instruction, the driver floored the pedal, spinning the tires. When they grabbed the road, the vehicle took off like a rocket.

Grant's face fell into his grimy hands.

It finally hit him. He had just been abducted by a band of murderers.

Ifza spoke softly, conversing with the driver before pulling out a cellphone. Grant had no idea what was being said. He didn't understand the language being used but recognized it as a form of Arabic. That made him feel even more alone.

His ears perked up. Two words, however, did stand out. He kept his face buried in his hands and listened.

*Anubis* and *Khaliq*.

She was either talking to her brother, or about him.

"*Mae alsalama*," Ifza said, ending the call.

She got up and switched spots with Tahsin. Ifza sat across from Grant, mimicking her man's deep scowl. She didn't speak. It took him a second to realize that she wasn't actually staring at him. Ifza was staring through him, lost in thought.

"Something on your mind?" Grant asked.

Ifza blinked and straightened her posture, but she didn't answer him.

Grant sighed. "Can you at least tell me where we're going?"

"I think you already know," Ifza replied, sitting back against the inside wall of the van. She closed her eyes, ending the discussion.

*Right,* Grant thought, picturing a landscape of desert and pyramids.

He was going to Egypt.

# CHAPTER 28
# ZAHRA

Zahra felt good. She dreamt of being tucked in for the night as a child on a cold winter night back in Long Island. The layer of blankets and quilts kept her toasty warm. Zahra loved a comfortable blanket. It didn't matter how hot it was. She had always needed one to fall asleep.

*Mmm,* she moaned, smiling in her sleep. The warmth was nice, comforting.

Except, she wasn't a kid anymore, and she wasn't back in New York with her brother and parents. The last thing she remembered was a flash of light and a shockwave that knocked her off her feet and out of consciousness. The soothing warmness wasn't coming from her blankets either. It was coming from a fire — and not a crackling fireplace or firepit, but *actual* fire.

*Wake up!*

Zahra jerked into an upright position. Her head throbbed, and her vision was severely blurred. She knew she had suffered a head injury. She needed to take it easy before she either passed out or vomited all over herself, and then passed out. The room spun, and the roof swirled with red, orange, and yellow lights.

She closed her eyes and kneaded her forehead with her palms, pausing the therapeutic massage shortly after starting it. The lighting inside the museum was all wrong. It flickered as if it were lit by flames. Zahra kept her face covered but opened her fingers far enough apart to see that she was in deep shit.

Zahra lowered her hands and blinked against the heat. "Oh. My. God."

She followed the burning ceiling down to the gaping hole in the building where the front doors should have been. The explosion... The Scales of Anubis had set off a bomb. It's what had sent Zahra into La-La Land, and it's what had caused the damage she now found herself gawking at.

The revelation helped clear Zahra's thoughts. She scooted forward on her butt and dismounted the platform containing the remains of the quartered Maasai tribesman. Zahra had smashed through the man and sent his arms and legs in different directions.

*Smart move,* she thought.

The bombing would make the heist look more like a *typical* terrorist attack rather than a robbery — not that anyone, outside a chosen few, would know what was stolen. The Kane family canopic jar wasn't museum property. Only a couple of people even knew of its existence.

Multiple murders had also occurred, along with a kidnapping. And forget the irreplaceable destruction caused by the blast. She looked around the Great Court and spotted a dozen-plus invaluable artifacts either in pieces, or on fire.

*Or both.*

Zahra knew she needed to get out while she still could. So far, the ceiling had held up, though quite a few of the triangles had cracked or flat-out shattered. Regardless, Zahra didn't know how long it would be until the rest of them came down. She shambled forward, avoiding the pooled blood that encompassed the freshest body. Odai had died where he had fallen. Zahra circled around his corpse and headed for the front of the room. The heavy doors had been peeled open like a banana. Steel, glass, and concrete and marble rubble were strewn about, covering nearly all of the floor. It was an obstacle course that Zahra wasn't prepared for, and one she would have never imagined tackling.

*I can't believe this happened,* she thought, understanding one thing.

It was her fault. If the jar hadn't been on the premises, then the museum would have been spared.

*Bernie too.*

She tried to look back toward the old man but couldn't see through the billowing, abusive miasma. Zahra tucked her nose and mouth into the crook of her right elbow and coughed. The air was getting more unbreathable as she closed in on the entrance. She pushed forward, squinting against the sting of the intense heat and smoke.

The gift shop and diner stationed just inside the front doors were now nonexistent. Their wares, like some of the historical pieces behind her, were unrecognizable.

Tears streaked down her filthy cheeks. Zahra had no idea what she looked like, nor did she care. She was alive — that was better than everyone still in here could boast. Stepping through the ruined entryway, she said a prayer, thanking whoever was listening for allowing her to survive the heinous attack.

As soon as Zahra left the high temperature of the fiery museum and was struck by the cool breeze swirling about outside, her mind swirled, and she fell to her knees.

Zahra collapsed atop the front steps. Her forward momentum caused her to roll down them like a limp, beat-to-hell Raggedy Ann doll. She flopped onto the sidewalk, landing face-up on her back. She was so out of it that even the nip of the autumn air didn't stir her.

But the wail of faraway sirens did.

As she had just done inside the museum, Zahra snapped awake and sat up. She only made it halfway up before she was run over by a wave of nauseating vertigo. There was too much pain to move, and the world was still spinning way too fast to try.

The sirens grew louder, and they had multiplied significantly in a short time. Zahra could have just as easily stayed put and sought medical attention, but she didn't — she couldn't. Police would question her and delay her ability to respond to the attack. Baahir and Grant didn't have that kind of time, and if her brother's assessment of the situation was accurate, the entire world was at stake.

*Get. Your ass. Moving.*

Slowly, carefully, Zahra pushed herself to her feet. She wobbled and headed west, following the sidewalk to the corner of Great Russell and Bloomsbury. Just as she turned north, she glanced back to see the first of several police cars arrive on the scene. Zahra hurried around the corner, feeling a little like Dr. Richard Kimble.

She knew she should have at least clued in the authorities as to who was responsible for the blast, but she couldn't. If the Ayads found out it was Zahra who ratted them out, then Baahir and Grant would be goners.

Emergency vehicles weren't too far behind the police.

Zahra kept her head down and fast-walked up Bloomsbury Street. Her car wasn't too much further ahead. Some nights, Zahra and Dina, and even Grant, would walk home. None of them lived all that far away from work.

Suddenly, another wave of dizziness propelled Zahra to the ground. She tripped on nothing and went down hard. Hacking deeply, Zahra was unable to catch her breath. Instead, she crawled out of sight and slumped into a row of shrubs. Even if she did get to her car, it wouldn't be safe for her to drive.

Zahra sighed. There was only one person close enough to the museum that would come to her aid at this time. Pulling out her phone, she dialed the number.

*"Z? You okay, love?*

"Hey — um, no, I'm not okay."

She heard rustling on the other end. *"What's wrong, Zahra?"*

A police car whizzed by Zahra's cover.

"I need your help."

**The Pharaoh's Lounge** | Giza, Egypt

Even given the early morning hour, *The Pharaoh's Lounge* was hopping. People from all walks of life were enjoying the atmosphere. While on the surface, the patrons didn't look like they had much in common, they did in one way. Money. Everyone here was extremely wealthy, and by the looks of it, not all of them had made their fortune legitimately. Baahir recognized a number of faces. Two local politicians, one famous television star from London, and a Grammy Award-winning singer from America. The cornucopia of higher-ups was currently gracing Baahir with their presence in the upstairs private bar.

Khaliq Ayad's private bar.

The fact that these particular people were granted permission to be here told Baahir all he needed to know about them.

They were all scum.

*And they were all members of the Scales of Anubis,* he thought, shocked by the revelation. Khaliq had recruited far outside those typically associated with violent, zealot-filled organizations. Only half of the people here were even locals! That's what scared Baahir the most. Khaliq's group spanned more than just specific pockets in Egypt. What started out as an ancient society centering around a singular bloodline had morphed into a global, serpentine entity.

He could almost hear Khaliq as he gave his pitch to join his group.

*Think of it as a business opportunity you can ill-afford to miss!*

"Dr. Hassan." Baahir was thrust out of his daydream and found Khaliq standing over him. "Are you comfortable?"

Considering the events of the last few hours, yes, Baahir was very comfortable. He had been looked after — fed superb, award-winning cuisine, was clothed in an exquisite suit, and his injuries had been treated with the utmost of care. Whatever Khaliq had in store for him, he wanted the Egyptologist to be healthy for it. The plush leather chair Baahir now sat in probably cost more than Baahir had accrued in the last month. Everything inside The Pharaoh's Lounge — forget the treasures within the private bar — was expensive and immaculate. Even the exclusive upstairs retreat held at least a dozen pieces that any museum on planet Earth would have loved to have had on hand.

Khaliq wasn't just some maniacal madman. He was also a person of good taste.

"You should count yourself lucky, Dr. Hassan," Khaliq had said upon entering the private bar.

"And why's that?" Baahir replied.

Khaliq spun and looked at him. "Because most men in my position don't treat people in your position with such care."

It was true. In this part of the world, extremists weren't exactly known for their hospitality. So, Baahir kept his mouth shut, and he waited.

But he had to know.

"Why are you going out of your way to take care of me?" It was an honest question. And, as expected, Khaliq gave Baahir an honest answer.

"Because I need you at your best for the next part of my plan to work."

"The map?"

Khaliq didn't answer. He simply tipped his head to a hallway that was guarded by a pair of thickly built men. None of the other people had ventured that way. Even a simpleton could tell that it was off limits.

"Come with me."

Baahir was led through the bearish duo. Neither one of them gave Khaliq or Baahir the time of day. Their solitary focus was on the other people lounging about, not the boss and his personal *guest*.

The twelve-foot-wide hallway held all sorts of artwork, from paintings to marble busts to historical artifacts. Baahir couldn't tell if the pieces were originals, or not. He suspected they were authentic, considering who their owner was.

A strip of thick glass was set into the middle of the flooring. Khaliq passed directly over it without fear of it breaking. It overlooked the center of the *Pharoah's Lounge's* main room. From here, Khaliq would be able to keep a watch on his flock. The two men passed a handful of doors on the way to the end of the hall. Baahir figured that the doors led to lavish suites. Why wouldn't they? Khaliq led him to the end of the corridor, to a single, heavy looking wooden door.

"Dr. Hassan?"

Baahir turned and brought his attention up from the glass floor and spied Khaliq standing in front of the single door. Whatever was behind it would be the culmination of the exquisite ingress.

*Guards and all,* Baahir thought, glancing back at the pair of coated men.

When Baahir caught up with Khaliq, the extremist pressed his thumb against a small black square set into the door where a handle might have been. A weighty clunk announced the disengagement of a locking mechanism. Baahir wasn't sure what to expect next. Based on the collection behind him, and the Book of Dead now being in Khaliq's possession, Baahir guessed there'd be some sort of research laboratory or an impressively stocked library on the other side.

The door opened.

"Oh." Baahir was saddened to see nothing more than another suite, though it did hold additional treasures.

Khaliq laughed. "Don't sound so disappointed, Dr. Hassan. Come."

The Scales of Anubis leader continued across the luxurious space, one Baahir guessed belonged to Khaliq Ayad himself. He spotted a second door and saw that it, too, owned a similar thumb pad. The precautions being taken screamed more than just being her to keep Khaliq safe.

*He's hiding something.*

This time, Khaliq reached out and gently pressed his entire hand against the pad. The result was instantaneous. And, instead of the door swinging open on a silent hinge, it slid sideways to reveal a quaint elevator.

"Going down?" Baahir asked eyebrow raised.

Khaliq didn't reply. He stepped inside the lift and turned back toward the Egyptologist. Baahir entered with extreme caution, passing over the narrow threshold one step at a time. He turned in time to witness the door close. Then, the cramped, metal coffin-like box descended for what Baahir guessed was five or six stories. Khaliq must have registered the confusion Baahir was feeling, so he spoke.

"Shortly after acquiring this place," Khaliq explained, "we discovered a system of naturally formed caverns directly beneath it, though there had been rumors of their existence. For our cause to come to be, I knew we would need something more than just some hole-in-the-wall base of operations. That's where my father, and his father before him, had failed. And with the help of a few loyal, very wealthy benefactors, we built this..."

The elevator stopped, and the door slid open.

Baahir gazed at the scene beyond. "Woah."

At the bottom of an ancient staircase was a workshop bustling with activity. Baahir descended a single stone step and stopped. It took everything within him to avert his eyes away from the basement laboratory. However, the stairs were a wonder in themselves.

"What... how?" he asked, unable to form a coherent question.

Khaliq shrugged. "We do not know. As we dug and cleared rubble, we discovered more. No one knows what this place was originally designed for, but I thought it was as fitting of a location as any for my research center."

**London, England**

Other than a few souvenirs from her past exploits, Zahra Kane's house was sterile and simple. It wasn't at all like her father's place, like the home she had grown up in. Here, her concrete floors were covered with gray, snap-in faux wood, and the walls were white with black trim.

It was modern, spotless, and boring.

Zahra's reasoning for the lack of personality in her house was simple: she was never *home*.

Usually, Dina had a retort whenever she stepped into the model home-quality space.

But today, Dina didn't say anything. They entered as one, Dina helping her friend along. Zahra didn't really need the help, but she was too tired to voice her annoyance. She knew Dina was just being nice. If their roles had been reversed, Zahra would have done the same thing for her.

She led Zahra to the square kitchen table.

Zahra cringed as she sat. "Usually, it's me who's getting you home safe after a wild night."

The Brit went to the kitchen and opened Zahra's freezer. "Yes, well, let's just say I owe you one."

Zahra snickered. "More like thirty."

Dina sat next to her and gently placed a bag of frozen peas against Zahra's face, fully covering her left eye and cheek. It, like most of Zahra, was banged up and a bit raw. The cold "compress" felt amazing against Zahra's tender skin. She reacted to its touch by slumping forward onto the table and resting her head against the peas like a pillow.

"Ah..." Zahra moaned, patting Dina's hand. "Thank you."

Dina was already up to speed on what had happened. Everything. Zahra had explained it all at warp speed on the car ride over to her place. Baahir, Grant, the jar, the attack... Zahra had spilled the beans.

"How are you feeling?" Dina asked.

Zahra snorted, head still down on the table. "Like shit."

Without another word, Dina got up and headed back into the kitchen. Zahra didn't see what she was doing, but she could hear the woman rummaging through a cabinet that was wholly dedicated to alcohol.

"Ah, yes. This'll do just fine."

"What'll do just fine?" Zahra asked, keeping her head down.

Dina rejoined her at the table and set down a glass. "This."

Zahra lifted her head and saw that there were *two* glasses. "Let me guess? Eagle Rare?"

Dina picked up her lowball and softly clinked Zahra's glass. They were both healthy pours, something both women needed, all things considered. The archaeologist worked up the strength to sit up, clumsily fingering the glass before getting a good grip on it. Together, both ladies took a solid sip, relishing in the bourbon's warmth as it made its way down their throats and chests.

"Oh, yes," Zahra said, wincing as she smiled, "this'll do just fine."

They stayed at the kitchen table while they drank. Once both women were finished, they moved across the living space to Zahra's bedroom. The master, like the rest of the quaint home, was nothing spectacular. Her bed was pushed up against the right-hand wall with a TV mounted across from it.

"How are you doing, Z, really?"

"Fine, *mom*," Zahra replied. She gave her close friend an appreciative smile and sat on the bed. She looked around her room. "Finally got me in bed, huh?"

Now, it was Dina's turn to roll her eyes. "What's your next move?"

Zahra glanced at her closet. Dina knew her well enough to know that she wasn't going to back down and give up. There was more to do than just curl up and go into hiding. But first, Zahra needed to reboot and recharge.

She gingerly got to her feet. "Help me with my clothes, will ya?"

There was no joke about Dina finally getting to see Zahra in the buff.

The pair worked together to get Zahra undressed and into the shower. The water was boiling and felt incredible on Zahra's abused physique and psyche. Both needed a reset in the worse way. Apparently, Dina did too. She had left Zahra alone to clean up before re-entering the bathroom, carrying another pour of bourbon.

Once Zahra was bathed, she got redressed, replacing her soiled, and slightly singed, clothing with a fresh set. The only thing she kept was her sneakers. New jeans — black, of course — and a fresh top. Color? Duh, black. It featured a very-recognizable logo on it. The vintage *Jurassic Park* shirt wasn't falsely aged, as was the current style. This particular t-shirt was as old as the original film.

Lastly, Zahra threw on a leather jacket that was just as worn as her shirt. When she was fully dressed and comfortable, she opened her closet. Inside of it was...nothing out of the ordinary. An assortment of seasonal garbs hung from hangers. Outdoorsy gear was tossed about in an unorganized manner on the floor. Compared to the rest of the home, it was out of sorts.

It was also on purpose.

Zahra dug through the mess until she hit the floor. When she did, she pushed on the rear portion of it, right where it met the wall. With enough pressure, the two-by-two section of false floor popped free to reveal a hidden compartment full of *things* she wasn't technically supposed to own. Out came a black JanSport, already packed with everything she'd need for the next phase of her journey. Zahra was always prepared for the worst. She added her knife, flashlight, and grappling hook to it. They had come in handy tonight.

What she could have really used was a gun.

Zahra removed the Glock 19 from her pack and checked it over, making sure the light mounted below the barrel still worked. It did. *Good,* she thought, knowing Dina was watching her intently, but she didn't care. Zahra trusted the Brit with her life.

"Expecting more trouble?" Dina asked.

Zahra peered over her shoulder. "Yeah. In my experience, this is about the time where things get ugly."

Dina's eyes opened wide. "Worse than tonight?"

Zahra returned her attention to her gear. She sighed. "Yeah, Dina, much worse."

The two women stayed at Zahra's place for the rest of the night. Dina had called her girlfriend and explained that Zahra needed some looking after following a 'rough night out.'

Zahra wanted to immediately get moving, but Dina successfully talked her out of it, and Zahra hadn't been able to put up much of a fight — a testament to just how banged-up Zahra was. And at her core, Zahra knew Dina was right. She'd be of no use to anyone half-asleep and sore as hell. So, Zahra climbed into bed in her fresh clothes and closed her eyes. Dina curled up next to her to keep an eye on her.

*That* part of Dina's lie was the truth.

"You don't have to sleep here," Zahra said.

"Well, your couch is lumpy as shit."

Zahra was asleep before she could laugh.

Surprisingly, the walls and ceiling were still natural. The only additions to the cavern, besides the equipment and workspaces on the floor, were lights and air ducts that hung between randomly formed stalactites. The ducts weren't part of a cooling system. Their purpose was to ventilate impurities out of the air. The space felt cool and dry thanks, in part, to the ambient temperature that existed beneath the surface of the world.

*Fifty-five degrees Fahrenheit, give or take.*

He quickly descended the steps, uncaring if Khaliq had followed him or not. Baahir was too absorbed in the extremist's underground headquarters to care. He felt like he was in a Bond movie, and Khaliq was his Goldfinger or Hugo Drax. Thanks to their father's incessant need to have one playing at all hours of the day, Baahir and Zahra had been obsessed with old-school spy flicks when they were younger.

Men and women of all nationalities moved about, paying Baahir very little attention. They were too busy with their work to worry about Khaliq's plus-one. It gave Baahir the impression that he wasn't the first stranger to walk amongst them.

The Egyptologist buzzed by examination tables featuring all kinds of trinkets and doodads. Each individual tool had its specific purpose. But they didn't concern Baahir. At the center of the rectangular cavern was a space dedicated to something important — Baahir could feel it in his bones. Plus, the human presence was the densest there.

*Is that a glass table?*

He scooted around a squat man that was pulling along a rolling dry-erase board that featured crude sketches and short-hand notes. One of the quips caught his eye. It spoke of the Book of the Dead.

The scientist came to a stop where Baahir was headed, jabbing at the board with a single, pudgy digit. He was shouting in Arabic about a new passage they had apparently found within the Anubian scroll. Baahir rushed over. His presence caused those gathered around the table to stir and part like the Red Sea.

"He's the one who found it," one man whispered.

"That's him," another added.

Baahir slowed when he saw what it was that held their attention. There, pressed between a sheet of glass and the glass tabletop like a sandwich, was his scroll. It was gently backlit from beneath while also being mildly lit from above via a fluorescent light ballast. In Baahir's absence, it had been relieved of its protective stone tube and rolled out for all to see. Thankfully, Khaliq had people on his team that knew how to properly handle fragile documents, though Baahir would have preferred the work be done in a sealed-off, dust-free examination room. The lack of one bothered him greatly.

The Egyptologist wheeled around on Khaliq. "You're examining a once-in-lifetime discovery in a cave?" His hands were on his head. He was infuriated. "This is abhorrent!" He looked around. "Hardly anyone is even wearing gloves! Do you have any idea how destructive the oils in our skin are?" Baahir was breathing hard. He needed to catch his breath.

Baahir pushed through the crowd, even bumping Khaliq as he moved. He stopped in front of the dry-erase board and closed his eyes. He placed his hands on his head and took deep breaths.

It didn't help. Hardly feeling calmer than he had been before, Baahir opened his eyes and stopped breathing altogether.

Before him on the dry-erase board wasn't a map, as he thought there would be, but jumbled directions were pointing to a place in the middle of nowhere, far west of Giza. It wasn't much, but given enough time, Baahir knew Khaliq would find it.

To the left of the location was something that made Baahir's stomach sink.

It took him a moment to understand what was written there. Not hieroglyphics — not Egyptian of any sort.

It was a chemical equation.

He was no chemist — he couldn't read the equation clearly. But it was obvious what it must be. It *had* to be.

He was staring at a chemical compound. A recipe.

And it was missing a component, judging by the blank, underlined space to the right.

Baahir knew exactly what would fill that space, as well. It was the same thing these people had been looking for.

To the naked eye, the missing chemical resembled nothing more than a harmless volcanic stone. Baahir knew it well.

*It was the chemical inside the stone itself.*

A corded, landline phone rang somewhere behind Baahir. One of the scientists hurried to answer it, quickly conversing with the caller before holding it out for Khaliq. Baahir stepped away from the dry-erase board and eyed the Scales of Anubis leader. He spoke softly, making it all but impossible for Baahir to snoop. He did hear Khaliq say one thing, though.

"You have it?"

Baahir's skin went cold. The only way for them to have acquired the jar was to have gone through Zahra.

His chest constricted. "No..."

Khaliq finished and turned. "Excuse me?"

"Zahra?" Baahir asked.

The larger man shook his head. "I am sorry. She put up a good fight until the explosion."

"Explosion?"

Khaliq nodded. "And fire."

Baahir stumbled away. His sister, a woman that, until now, seemed indestructible, had been taken out by a goon like this.

He growled. "You son-of-a-bitch. I'll — "

Khaliq stepped toward him. "You'll do what?"

Baahir backed down. There was nothing he could do now. His sister was gone, and he was being held captive by the man responsible for her death.

"Join us, Dr. Hassan."

With tears streaking down his face, Baahir laughed at the ridiculous request.

But Khaliq wasn't joking, and it wasn't a *request*. "Join us... or share her fate."

He didn't have another option. If he denied the man, he'd die here and now. But if he accepted the *invitation* and became involved in Khaliq's heinous plan, could he ever forgive himself? Could he live with the consequences?

He looked between the table and Zahra's murderer, then nodded.

"Wonderful," Khaliq said. He motioned to the back of the cavern. Situated against the wall was a row of cots. "Get some rest. You begin your part of the work at sunrise."

Baahir turned and sauntered off. The tears kept flowing. He didn't care.

He fell onto the first cot he came across and closed his eyes, picturing his sister's mischievous grin. Her face began to fade with the incoming sleep.

*No!* Baahir's eyes snapped open. *No, Zahra is alive.* He sat up and took in his surroundings. He sniffed and wiped his nose with his sleeve.

*Whining and mourning will not change anything,* he knew. *I choose to believe she is* not *dead.*

Baahir would keep his head down and do what he was told.

*She'll be here,* he thought. *She's going to come.*

# CHAPTER 32
# ZAHRA

Just a few miserably short hours later, Zahra climbed out of Dina's Prius, and they said their goodbyes. Zahra was exhausted to the point of staying completely silent on the ride back to the museum.

"Thank you, Dina... really," Zahra said, sticking her head inside the lowered passenger window. She gave her a loving kiss on her cheek and squeezed her hand.

Dina yawned and waved the gratitude off. "No worries, Z. It's not like I'm going into work today anyway."

"Yeah..." Zahra was saddened to hear that the museum was closed indefinitely to both patrons and staff members, though the latter should be returning shortly as long as the damaged portions of the structure were still sound enough. Fortunately, Dina could do a lot of her job from home.

"You going to be okay?"

"We'll see," Zahra replied. "Let me know what happens here, okay? I'm not sure when I'll be back in town. This *situation* might take a while to fix."

Dina's face fell.

"Right, well, see ya later, Dina." Zahra winked and walked away, car keys in hand. For good measure, she tossed them into the air and whiffed when she tried to catch them. The miss was on purpose, of course, and it got a chuckle out of her nervous friend. It made Zahra laugh too.

Dina pulled away but stopped and shouted out her window. "Hey, I forgot to ask! Where you headed now?"

Zahra turned around but kept walking backward. "To find answers."

"Where?"

She paused and sighed. "There's only one person that can help me right now."

"Who?"

"I... " Zahra looked away. It was better than Dina didn't know. "I'll talk to you later. Thanks again."

And with that, Zahra climbed into her nine-year-old, black Toyota 4Runner and pulled away. It wouldn't take Dina a lot to figure out who Zahra was going to see. Zahra's path had been plainly laid out in front of her. There was only one person now who could give her the answers she sought — a man who had hidden them from her for years.

*My entire life*, Zahra thought, feeling her heart rate pick up. She had believed everything Ifza had said inside the museum. Why would the woman have lied to Zahra after going through all the trouble to steal the canopic jar?

*Because it wasn't a lie.*

It would take Zahra an hour to get to her destination, so she'd have to get moving. Every minute wasted was another minute Baahir and Grant, and possibly the world, lost.

Zahra pulled onto Gower Street and picked up the speed, quickly remembering the firearm she had in a bag in her backseat. Zahra snarled, frustrated, and kept it a mile an hour below the posted speed limit. For good measure, she reached behind her and repositioned the backpack to the floor behind her. The casual speed was pure torture for someone who notoriously liked to move fast.

"Dammit!" Zahra was stuck behind a two-door beater. Today was not a day to be late.

She needed to see her father, right away.

**Oxford, England**

It had been months since Zahra had last seen her dad, and she had never visited him while in her current condition. Some of the bruising had subsided since the morning, but a little of it had also come to the surface with gusto. She now sported a subtle black eye. Her left cheek was tender, and she had another headache just starting to poke its ugly ass out. A pair of aviator sunglasses hid some of the injuries. They also helped with the rising brain pain.

George Kane lived in a modest flat less than a quarter of a mile to the south of River Thames. Half a mile north of the river was his place of employment, Oxford University. Zahra hoped she'd catch her father before he left for work. She checked her watch and cursed herself for being so careful on the roads. This was life or death, and she should have been driving like a woman possessed, and not like, well, her dad.

"Easy does it, girl," she mumbled to herself. "Easy does it." Getting stopped by the police would help nobody.

Zahra's brakes squeaked as she pulled over and parked directly in front of her father's home. She had no idea how she was going to open up the conversation with him. What could she possibly say to him to convince him of what was happening? It all sounded so fanciful — even for Zahra.

Her eyes never left the red front door as she gathered her belongings from the floor of her backseat. She opened her door and slung the heavy pack over her shoulder. Like the rest of her body, the joint ached. She surmounted the seven steps up to her father's front door and lifted her fist to knock.

But she didn't — she couldn't.

Zahra was nervous, and a bit scared to see him. The answers she sought would surely crumble her world worse than it already had been. The museum was her livelihood, but this...this was her *life*.

Just as her closed hand descended toward the wooden door, it swung open. Zahra stepped back and nearly fell off the narrow landing at the top of the steps. Her father brought a hand to his chest with his mouth agape. Neither Kane spoke. Both just stood there and recouped themselves.

Zahra opened her mouth to speak, but nothing came out. So, instead, her dad was the first to talk.

He looked her up and down. "Rough night?"

Zahra checked her watch. "Technically, it was a rough morning."

She removed her sunglasses to speak but was stopped by her father's appalled response to the bruising on her face. The sight of his little girl so beat up brought a hand to George's mouth. He was stunned to see her in a state such as this.

He held out his hand. "Why don't you come in."

She gave him a curt nod of thanks and entered. Unlike Zahra's home, her father's house was filled wall-to-wall with historical references and artifacts. George Kane lived and breathed everything to do with the subject. He was a real student of it, and as it was, a teacher of it too.

"Look, Dad, I don't want to make you late." Zahra stepped back toward the door. "I can come back later, and — "

George raised an open hand. "It's okay. Something tells me that this can't wait."

Zahra looked down at her attire and nervously readjusted her backpack. "Can we sit? I'm a bit tired."

He grinned. "You look like hell. Did you have a run-in with someone?"

She snickered. "Yeah, you could say that. There were six of them, I think."

They hung a quick left, entering George's study. Books lined the walls, and where there weren't any bookshelves, there were maps of different countries. They sat in matching brown leather chairs. Zahra carefully set her bag down and relaxed, her tense posture melting away into the coolness of the leather.

George kept his mouth shut and waited for his daughter to speak.

She leaned forward and placed her elbows on her knees. "Tell me about the Scales of Anubis."

He chuckled. "Is this why you drove an hour to see me?"

Zahra's eyes narrowed. "Tell me about Khaliq Ayad." Her father stammered his words, clearly trying to make something up. "Did you know he kidnapped Baahir and stole Mom's canopic jar this morning?"

George's stubbled face went white. "Baahir? Khaliq? He did this to you?"

"No," Zahra replied, shaking her head, "his sister did. She and her men nearly destroyed the museum. It's probably all over the news by now."

"Ifza was there?"

*So, he does know about her.*

Zahra nodded. Her eyes became wet. "They killed Bernie, Dad." She refrained from mentioning the men she had personally killed. As far as her father knew, Zahra had never ended another human's life and she wanted to keep it that way.

George looked like he had gotten punched in the stomach. He knew Bernie well. He reached a hand out and gently placed it atop hers and squeezed. Zahra winced.

"Oh, sorry," he said, softening his grip.

Zahra smiled. "It's okay. Just one of a hundred things that hurt right now."

He didn't add anything. George plucked the remote off the rectangular coffee table and powered on the wall-mounted television. The scene was excruciating to watch. The entrance to the British Museum was a charred, smoking husk of its once beautiful self. Men from what could only be the coroner's office carried out a large black bag on a stretcher.

*Bernie?*

"You were there?" George asked, eyes wide.

"Yep. The bomb threw me halfway across the Great Court."

"Bomb?" George shouted, leaping to his feet. "What the hell is going on in your life these days?"

Zahra stood and met him eye to eye. "I was hoping you could tell me. Dad, I need to know. Ifza said that I didn't know. What don't I know?"

He bit his lip, but nodded, and waved her onward. "Come with me. I'm going to need a lot more coffee. This could take a while."

"What about work?"

He glanced over his shoulder as he stepped out of his office. "I'll call in and tell them the truth."

"The truth?"

He turned around, sporting a sly smile. It was the type of smile that Zahra also used quite frequently. "Yeah, the truth. I'll tell them that I had family drop in unannounced."

*He's not wrong,* Zahra thought, glancing around the main hallway. But she couldn't focus on the historical pieces her father had on display. Something nagged at her. She knew the answer, but she needed to hear it from him.

She slowed, stopping in front of a picture of her and her parents and Baahir from eons ago. "This is bad, isn't it?"

George stepped up next to her, his reflection just visible in the glass of the framed picture. He laid a hand on her shoulder, choosing his words carefully. "Zahra... this is precisely what your mother and I were trying to prevent."

# CHAPTER 34
# ZAHRA

The coffee maker percolated somewhere behind Zahra. She sat at the kitchen island, locked in on the news report. A man around her age stepped into frame and spoke loudly. The commotion behind him was chaotic and noisy.

*"Spencer Tenson here at the British Museum, where authorities have confirmed the grim news. Six fatalities — the causes of which have not been released. I'm told there is one man in custody, though no charges have been immediately filed."*

*Six dead?* Zahra thought, quickly ticking off the men she had encountered. *Guy in the Great Court — spear. Another one in the stairs. Third guy — the mountain — also in the Great Court.* The person they arrested must have been Ehsan, the man she had stabbed in the shoulder with her knife when she was hiding in Nectanebo II's sarcophagus. Then, there was Bernie. *Who are the other two?*

Her face fell into her hands. "Drew and Josh. Shit..." During the raid, Ifza and her men didn't just kill Bernie. They had silenced the entire Night Guard.

"You okay?" Her father sat beside her, placing a steaming mug of coffee in front of her.

"No, Dad, I am not 'okay.'" Her hands fell away, and slapped the marble countertop. "Do I look 'okay?'"

George looked away, eyeing the TV.

Zahra picked up her mug. "I'm sorry."

He nodded but didn't look away from the news report. They sat and watched and listened to the information being provided, which to say, wasn't much. Spencer Tenson tossed out a few theories as to why the museum had been bombed. The most likely scenario Spencer offered, and one Zahra could vouch for, was a terrorist attack.

As they continued to watch, Spencer was handed an index card. He quickly read it to himself before repeating it for the viewers, the Kanes included.

"This just in, two employees of the museum, Zahra Amelia Kane and Grant Lawrence Upton, were not among the deceased and are currently missing from the scene. As of now, they are presumed to be alive." He glanced up at the camera and then back to the card. "When questioned, police said that they are, and I quote, 'not ruling out the pair's involvement.'" Spencer took a deep breath. "Elizabeth, back to you."

George shut off the television and faced his daughter. "Now, you're being hunted by the police. Wonderful..."

Zahra shrugged. "It's nice to be wanted."

*Things just got a lot more complicated,* she thought, draining the rest of her coffee.

"So," she said, setting down her empty mug, "where should we start?"

Her father got up and poured her another helping. "The beginning, I suppose."

He rejoined her and cleared his throat. "Do you remember the story of how your mother and I met?"

"You were classmates at NYU."

"Correct," George said, "but your mother's reasoning for being in America wasn't what it seemed."

Zahra paused mid-sip and gazed at her father. She didn't say anything.

"It wasn't until after I had proposed to her that your mother told me the truth about herself...and her family."

"The car ride. The day she died... You guys were talking about someone finding her."

He nodded. "Yes, well, I'm afraid that mine and your mother's problems have now become yours and Baahir's." He frowned and moved to get up. "This is all my fault." Zahra stopped him with a single gesture. She reached out and closed her hand around his. George squeezed back and relaxed. "I'm sorry, Zahra. I should have done more to protect you two."

"Tell me. I know we can figure this out together."

George smiled. "You sound just like your mother. She always looked for the positives in everything." He let out a long breath. "Speaking of which..."

"What?"

"Your mother's name wasn't really Hanan."

"What? It wasn't?" That was a sickening gut punch. Zahra squeezed her fists together as hard as she could. She was sick of the secrets. She took a deep breath and relaxed, for her father's sake.

"No, it was Kamaria, though I never knew her as that. To me, she was always Hanan. She changed it to Hannan once she was stateside — before we met."

It was plain to see what Zahra's mom had done. "Who was she hiding from?"

"Her family back in Egypt." He sat back and slouched down a little. "A trusted few back home came to her aid. They helped your mother change her name and fake her death. Then, she came here and enrolled at NYU as a student of archaeology. The depth of her knowledge was unbelievable, especially at her age. She knew more about Ancient Egypt than her professor. It enraged him."

Zahra grinned. "Yeah, Mom could do that to people."

"So can you."

Her eyes flicked to her father. The left side of his mouth was curled slightly upward.

"What did she call it, my 'warrior blood?'"

George nodded and laughed. "Yeah, she had it too. Your brother and me, not so much."

The mention of Baahir made George uncomfortable. "Do you know if he's okay?"

Zahra shrugged. "Last I knew, he was being hunted by Khaliq's people down in Cairo after he found Anubis' Book of the Dead."

George launched to his feet, spilling his coffee everywhere in the process. "What? They actually found the Scroll of Anubis?"

She nodded. "That's what he told me, yes."

"Oh, no, no, no. This is bad, Zahra. This is really bad."

She stood and held out both of her hands, trying to calm him down. "Easy, Dad, it's just a scroll."

"You don't get it, Zahra. It's not just a scroll. What your mother told me about it — where it leads — the temple! No, this is awful."

"Dad!" Zahra shouted, getting his attention. "What did Mom tell you?"

They returned to their seats. Zahra cleaned up the mess while George attempted to collect his thoughts.

"Zahra, the scroll, it *is* the original Book of the Dead, and it *was* penned by Anubis."

Zahra snorted a laugh. "Come on, Dad, Anubis? Anubis the Egyptian god? He was a myth, along with all the other ones."

"That may be so. Yes, Anubis, the god of death, was a myth, but Anubis wasn't a god at all, was he?"

"Are you asking me?"

"Anubis was a scientist — a man years ahead of his time. His practices became legendary and were included into the lore of the region."

Zahra looked out the kitchen's square window. "Like what some people think about Merlin, right?"

"Correct. There is no magic, Zahra. There is only science, and depending on the time you lived in..."

"It could be seen as magic — witchcraft, even."

"Correct, again," the professor replied. "Your mother's family was hellbent on proving that Anubis was real and even more fanatical about continuing his work."

"The plague?"

George nodded, making sure his daughter was paying full attention. "It's the same sickness that struck down Egypt in the Bible." Zahra smiled, but it faded almost immediately. Her father wasn't joking. "The Scales of Anubis want to recreate the plague and unleash it upon the world."

"But, Mom, she — "

"Wanted no part of it," George finished, extinguishing some of Zahra's rising anxiety. She couldn't bear to think that her mother was a fanatical killer like Khaliq and his sister, Ifza. "It's why she chose to go to the States. She wanted to learn as much as possible about her country so she could stop what was coming. As you know, knowledge for women isn't all that easy to come by where she's from. There was still so much she didn't know."

"And you were okay with all of this?"

George nodded. "I didn't care. I loved her for who she was. Her family history meant nothing to me. When we found out she was pregnant with you, she broke down and told me everything."

"One thing still doesn't make sense — more than one thing, really?" She collected her thoughts. "What does this have to do with Mom's canopic jar?

I thought you guys bought it from a street vendor outside of Cairo before I was born."

He shook his head. "A lie, I'm afraid. Your mother stole it from her father the night she disappeared. A close friend of hers smuggled it, and her, out of the country an hour later aboard a ship to the UK. Then, she headed to New York."

"And the jar itself?"

"This is going to sound crazy, but —"

Zahra smiled, interrupting him.

"What?"

"*All* of this is crazy, Dad."

"Touché. Your mother's canopic jar is the only evidence of hellstone that has ever been found."

"Hellstone? I remember Mom mentioning that before. I thought it was just a spooky way of describing igneous rock?"

George nodded. "She did, and sort of... Hellstone is believed to be the secret to unlocking Anubis' plague. Something within the rock itself reacts negatively, or positively, depending on what outcome you desire, to heat. I personally believe there's some sort of bacterium that's responsible."

"So, it's not the jar itself. It's just the hellstone they're after?"

"Correct. I even had a colleague of mine back in New York run some tests on it years ago, and it came back as a substance similar to something found inside of a meteor, though he didn't know about the possibility of bacteria."

"Hang on, Dad." She pieced it all together in her head. "You're telling me that I've had this rock in my possession for over a decade, and that it's crawling with tiny microbes from space — from another world." She pointed at the ceiling. "Aliens, Dad. Aliens!"

He grinned, looking very amused. "Not at all. I think that wherever the hellstone came from — an undiscovered cave system, maybe — naturally houses the bacteria. The fact that the rock is from space is just coincidence."

"Oh," Zahra said, feeling a little stupid. She had jumped to the most outlandish explanation first, rather than the most realistic. She glanced out the kitchen window again. Coincidences, chance, luck... They didn't usually get along with Zahra, unless it related to her ability to stay alive.

"You said the scroll leads to somewhere. Where does it lead you, exactly?"

"Supposedly to the Temple of Anubis, a place made entirely of hellstone — the jar's origin."

"Oh, and that's really bad considering the length they went to steal Mom's jar."

"Yes, it's not good news. I doubt Khaliq had enough hellstone to do any real damage. He needs the full quarry to enact his plan."

She pushed her coffee aside and leaned forward. Her hands found her face, and she closed her eyes and rubbed her forehead.

"Oh, there's one more thing."

Zahra paused and parted her fingers enough to see her father. She sighed and leaned back in her chair. "Why do I have a feeling I'm not going to like what you're about to tell me?"

George looked extremely uncomfortable. He knew whatever he was about to reveal would seriously piss off his daughter. "Your mother, her last name wasn't really Hassan."

Zahra took a deep breath and turned, and fully faced her father. "Fine, then, what was it?" she asked through gritted teeth.

"It was," he cleared his throat, "her last name was — "

"Just tell me!"

"It was Ayad, Zahra. Her last name was Ayad."

Zahra didn't verbally respond. She just stood and walked away, placing her hands on the kitchen counter. She looked at her reflection in the window as her father added onto the dogpile of information.

"Her brother was once the leader of the Scales of Anubis."

"Khaliq's father?" Zahra asked, already knowing the answer.

"Yes," he sorrowfully replied. "It also means that Khaliq is — "

Zahra spun, tears freely falling. "It means that psychopath is my cousin!"

# CHAPTER 35
# ZAHRA

Zahra finished rinsing her face off in the guest bathroom. Patting it dry, she glanced up at herself in the mirror and wondered how someone like her could be related to a person as wicked as Khaliq Ayad. Then, there was Ifza. She was part of Zahra's family too.

No, she told herself. Just because they shared the same blood, it didn't make them family. Zahra was nothing like the Ayads.

She took a deep breath and tossed aside the hand towel. Zahra exited the bathroom and rejoined her father in the kitchen. He was still nursing his second cup of coffee, though he didn't look all that interested in it.

Zahra sat. "You okay, Dad?"

He gazed up at her, his eyes wet. "No. How can I be? My son..." he sniffed, "my son is with that madman, and I'm here, safe and sound... and scared."

Zahra reached a hand out, and her father took it. "Look, Dad, I have to go. Baahir needs my help."

"Zahra, no."

She held up a hand. "He has no one else. I'm going to Cairo tonight, but — "

"But what?"

"Do you have any contacts down there you can trust? Maybe someone who knew Mom?"

George was thinking. His eyes were glassy, looking through the wall rather than at it. When his posture changed, and he blinked back into the world here and now, Zahra knew he had thought of someone.

He confirmed as much. "I may know one man. If he's still alive..."

"Who?"

He looked at her. "You know him, Zahra."

"I do?" Zahra tried to remember the people she had met in Cairo over the years, both in her present life and the past. She couldn't pick out anyone that could help in a situation like this.

George revealed the man. "Waleed Badawi."

Zahra snorted. "Uncle Wally? You're kidding me, right?"

She remembered her Uncle Waleed as a crazy son-of-a-bitch, someone her mother never liked to talk about much. By all accounts, he was as intelligent as his half-sister — Zahra's mother, Hanan.

But instead of going into academics or the sciences, Uncle "Wally" had gone into the unofficial business of importing and exporting.

Zahra hadn't even known the man was still alive — her father had fallen out of touch with him shortly after her mother's passing.

"No, I'm not kidding, and he's, um, he's not really your uncle."

She gave an exhausted laugh. "Now, you're going to tell me Grandma and Grandpa weren't really my grandparents, aren't you?"

He shook his head. "No, but Waleed really isn't your uncle. We just had you guys call him uncle to make it easier on you whenever he came stateside to visit."

It made sense. If she and Baahir were conditioned to call the man "Uncle," then it was understandable that the man could be trusted. That was Zahra's assessment, right or wrong.

"And you're sure we can trust him?"

"Absolutely." He wiped his eyes and faced his daughter. "Zahra, Waleed is the man who smuggled your mother out of Egypt all those years ago. If there is one person in Egypt we can trust, it's him."

Zahra stood, knowing what she had to do. "Let's hope he's still around." She pulled out her cellphone and clicked away.

"What are you doing?" George asked.

"Texting a friend — well, an acquaintance — with a plane. I need to get to Cairo, ASAP."

"And this friend can get you to Egypt on a whim — just like that?"

"For the right amount of money, yes." Zahra looked up at him. "Cork hasn't let me down yet."

"Cork? Your pilot-friend's name is Cork?"

She nodded. “It’s a long story.”

George got up and left the kitchen. Zahra could hear him head down the hall and into his bedroom. A minute later, he returned with something.

“Here,” he said, holding out a photo.

Zahra took it and looked it over. It was a picture of her, Baahir, her mom and dad, and Uncle Wally back in New York City. They had posed for the photo somewhere in Central Park, though Zahra was a bit fuzzy as to exactly where.

*The ballfields?*

“If you find Waleed, give him this and tell him everything that’s happened.”

**The Pharaoh's Lounge** | Giza, Egypt

As soon as Baahir had arrived, he quickly took over the entire operation beneath *The Pharaoh's Lounge*. If a priceless artifact was going to be dissected — in a cave, no less — then it was he who was going to do it, much to the chagrin of the old-timers already in place. He didn't care what anyone else said, and Khaliq didn't seem to mind.

"Do it," Khaliq had said, eyeing his people.

Those two words gave Baahir anything he wanted, including a better place to rest. Instead of sharing one of several communal cots, he was given his own, as well as whatever books Khaliq's aboveground men could scrounge up. There was also a computer filled with terabytes of information, but it had no internet connection. Khaliq had made sure that the people working below had no way of contacting the outside world.

Which made Baahir think... *Are all of these people here willingly?*

Maybe, just maybe, when the time was right, he could use that little tidbit to his advantage. He'd also have to ask some questions and discern the radically devoted from those forced into loyalty.

Like him.

And then, there was the status of his sister. Baahir looked up and pictured Zahra coming to his rescue with an army beside her. He saw the stairs, down which she would descend with a group of trained killers, men, and women who could rescue all of them.

He imagined it, a slight smile coming to his face. He *willed* it to be true, but he also couldn't shake the feeling that what Khaliq had told him earlier might be true. That Zahra was not coming to the rescue.

Because Zahra was dead.

His smile vanished. He knew his sister, knew what she was capable of. But he also knew people like Khaliq. And he had been prepared — just looking around this place reminded him of that.

He had been prepared for all of it. And, he had no reason to lie to Baahir. Khaliq had told him that his sister was dead.

Zahra might not be coming at all.

**Oxford Airport** | Kidlington, England

Twenty minutes northwest of Oxford University was the private airport where Zahra would meet her pilot. At first, she hadn't been thrilled that her father had offered to drive her there, but now, she realized how much of a blessing it was since it might be the last time that she ever saw him. The next leg of her journey wasn't going to be easy.

In fact, it was going to be the toughest thing she had ever done.

George parked in a spot just outside a chain-link fence and killed the engine to his silver Lexus LS. He and Zahra sat for a moment in silence, watching small private jets roll up and down the tarmac on the other side. She took a deep breath, nearly gagging on the "new car" smell. Her father had, only recently, purchased the luxury sedan, and it still contained one of the most noxious smells in existence. It was similar to the way Zahra felt about tuna fish and air-fried Brussel sprouts.

*Ugh...*

After two minutes of inaction, George got them moving and climbed out. Zahra opened her door and moved to retrieve her overstuffed backpack from the backseat. Her father beat her to it, though. He threw open the rear driver's side door and lifted the heavy bag with a grunt. Tossing it over his shoulder, he stood and met his daughter's gaze.

She smiled. "Ever the gentleman."

"Unfortunately, I might be the only chivalrous man left."

Zahra rolled her eyes. "At least you're modest."

All joking aside, Zahra was sad to be leaving her father behind. She wished he could have come with her, but she knew it was much too dangerous for him to come along. George Kane was a lot of things, but a man of action, he was not.

*Mom was the fighter.*

A familiar two-engine prop plane whizzed by overhead and descended upon the tarmac. That was Zahra's cue to get going. Cork wasn't a patient person, especially when she was transporting illegal goods, such as Zahra's pistol, among other items over the years. Once the aircraft touched down and refueled, Zahra would board and be off as soon as they were cleared to do so. Luckily, Cork knew Oxford Airport's head of air traffic control. The two had been an item in the past and were still on good terms.

At least in terms of 'hush-hush' operations and booty calls.

George stepped away but stopped. "Aren't we going?"

"Not yet," Zahra replied. "Just wait."

As soon as she had said something, a uniformed man approached them on the other side of the fence.

"Ms. Kane?"

Zahra stepped up. "Yes?"

"Head to the gate further down the fence, and I'll let you in."

The Kanes followed the controller's instructions and marched left. Zahra could see a side gate up ahead, and they arrived just as the airport employee unlocked it and swung it inward.

"My supervisor says you're some kind of VIP. We usually don't do this kind of thing, you know."

"Really?" Zahra replied, feigning ignorance. "I had no idea." In reality, this wasn't her first rodeo, and it made her question how many ports Cork had lovers in.

"No, we don't." *Timmy Sunshine* was a very pleasant individual.

Zahra stepped through the open gate but stopped when her father didn't follow. "Walk me out, will ya?"

His face lit up, and he quickly caught up with her. The Kanes followed Timbo out onto the tarmac just as an antiquated Cessna 337 Super Skymaster stopped. Zahra loved the distinctiveness of Cork's aircraft. Where most twin-engine planes had their props mounted one on each wing, the Cessna was of a completely different design.

One engine was mounted on the nose, and another on the back of the fuselage — on its ass — between the duo of booms holding the tail assemblies. The push-pull configuration produced a unique sound and was always a head turner to the novice aircraft enthusiast.

Especially when the plane looked like a hunk of shit.

George slowed when Zahra moved toward the off-white junker. It featured a weathered, angry octopus on its nose and the words *Puss E. Galore* on its flank. "Hang on," he said, pointing to the plane, "that's what you're getting on?"

Zahra stopped and turned. "What? It hasn't killed me yet."

Cork could be seen moving around within the plane through the row of circular windows that dotted each side of the stubby fuselage. Zahra couldn't wait for her father to approve her mode of transportation, and she headed away. George hurriedly caught up with Zahra, walking stride in stride with her.

"Don't do this, Zahra!" he pleaded. "That thing has to be fifty years old."

"Sixty, actually, but Cork keeps it in good shape."

"Zahra, please, don't do this."

She spun on a dime and held up a hand. "Dad, stop!" He did, and Zahra felt bad for chastising him in front of Timbo. She backpedaled, calming her voice. "This is how we're doing it, regardless of your approval, okay?"

*Besides,* she thought, *it's not like there's a better idea.*

He glanced over at the plane and swallowed. "I... I trust you."

"Good." She leaned in and hugged him. "I'll stay in touch."

"Please do. And tell Baahir that I'm sorry, will you?"

Zahra smiled, but she didn't reply. Her attention wasn't on her father anymore. She was looking past him, back toward the parking lot. A pair of blacked-out Audi S6 sedans pulled up next to her father's Lexus, and a pair of ornery-looking men climbed out of each vehicle. Zahra was relieved to see that Timbo had shut, and presumably locked, the gate after escorting the Kanes through.

Zahra's eyes snapped to her father and then back to the newcomers. She snatched his wrist and pulled. "Sorry, Dad. Change of plans."

"What?"

"You're coming with."

His eyes widened, and he fought against her firm grip. "I'm not getting on that thing! I can't go to Cairo!"

"Too bad!" she shouted, causing him to twitch. She extended a finger back the way they had come. "It's either this or death by firing squad."

He saw the men approaching them, and Zahra could see the confusion on his face. Two of the men were already checking out his car, while the two others were shielding their eyes from the sun and peering through the chain link fencing, looking for... them.

Zahra made eye contact with one of the men. "Dammit... come on, Dad!" She watched the guy alert his comrades, and the foursome charged for the main building.

The Kanes sprinted across the last thirty feet of tarmac, leaving Timbo in the dust. They practically leaped into the waiting Cessna and scuttled through the tight confines of the plane and into the first seats they could find. Typically, there should have been eight seats inside the cabin, situated in four rows of two. As of now, there were only four. The first two sections had been torn free to allow for more cargo space.

The Kanes fell into the *new* front row, sitting across the narrow aisle from one another. They swiftly buckled in, keeping watch on the doors leading from the main building to the tarmac.

"Cork!" Zahra yelled, spying movement in the cockpit. "Get us airborne — now!"

"Yeah, yeah, hold onto your cocks!"

Zahra had grown numb to Cork's choice of words, but her father was about to get a crash course into the woman's personality. Cork wasn't what most people would call *refined*.

A muscular mass of flesh squeezed out of the cockpit and stood hunched beneath the low ceiling in front of the Kanes. Zahra didn't pay the brash, African American Brit with a buzzcut and nose ring any attention. She was too focused on her father. His reaction was priceless.

"George Kane, meet Cork."

Cork looked him up and down and then glanced at Zahra. "He single?"

George leaned closer to Zahra. "She knows I can hear her, right?"

Zahra bypassed the pilot's inquiry and pointed out the window. "We really gotta go."

The enormous woman turned and peered through the glass partition. She snorted back a laugh just as the foursome pushed through onto the tarmac. "That's it, just the four of 'em?" She looked over her shoulder. "We've been in tougher scrums than this." Cork reached for the door. "Might be a nice warmup, eh?"

"She's not joking, is she?" George asked.

Zahra shook her head. "No, she isn't, *and* no, she isn't going anywhere, right?"

The pilot grumbled. "Killjoy." Cork gave the advancing men one last look before reinserting herself into the cockpit. Her chair squeaked when she sat, protesting against her mass. "Alright, you two, hold on to your arses. Up we go." She leaned around her chair and looked back into the hold. "Oi, new guy!" George glanced from Zahra to Cork. "Don't get sick in my plane. That's fine Corinthian leather you're sitting on."

George looked between his legs at the gigantic tear in the worn pleather chair.

There was nothing *fine* about it.

Cork throttled up the twin engines and pulled the Cessna away from the main building. It always surprised Zahra how smooth the *Puss E. Galore* moved. While the outside looked like a shitheap, the parts that mattered were finely tuned and well-maintained...sort of. George didn't seem to notice any of the good that the flying machine offered. He was white-knuckling the armrests, eyes closed, teeth chattering. That, or he was praying to God not to die.

*Probably both.*

"What about fuel?" George asked, holding back his breakfast.

"Don't worry about it!" Cork called back. "We should have plenty."

"Should?"

Cork didn't elaborate. The Cessna made it out onto the runway and without too much time wasted, she was given the all-clear from the tower, and they took off like a rocket. The rear engine spurted a bit, increasing George's already atmospheric level anxiety. But just as quick as it sounded like it was dying, the engine kicked back into gear and roared in unison with its nose-mounted sibling. In seconds, they were airborne, and at the moment, safe.

Zahra laughed and patted her father's shoulder. She could feel the tension in it.

"Hey," she said softly. "We're fine."

George opened his eyes and looked around. Seeing that they hadn't crashed into a fireball of metal and gas, he took a deep breath and released his death grip on the armrests.

"You know," he said, swallowing, "I've never hated flying until now."

"Oi!" Cork shouted from up front. "It wasn't *that* bad!"

George gave Zahra an apologetic look, then spoke up. "I'm sorry. I'm just not used to flying in such an — " Cork glared at him in her small rearview mirror, "antiquated machine." He gave her a false smile. "It's a very impressive plane."

Zahra held back a laugh.

"So..." George's voice was low. His eyes darted to the cockpit. "How did you two meet?"

"Back in the army. Cork, as you'd expect, was a pilot — helicopters back then. After I retired, I found out that Cork also retired and had started doing private charters."

"And the Cessna?"

Zahra grinned. "Hey, Cork, tell my dad how you acquired your bird!"

"I won it!" Cork replied, laughing. "I bet some cocksure bloat fish that I could beat him in blackjack. If he won, he could have his way with me. Anything he wanted. *Anything* at all. I'm open for anything as long as it doesn't involve the Cupid Shuffle."

Zahra had never seen her father so uncomfortable, and her smile widened.

"But if I won," Cork continued, patting the dashboard, "*I* get his wings. Then, when he tried to back out of the deal, I beat him within an inch of his life until he signed it over to me."

George's face went white. "That's interesting..."

Zahra took over the story. "This was back in the service too. She even ripped the cork out of her whiskey bottle and jammed down the pour guy's throat."

Her father nodded. "Hence the name."

"Yep, her real name is — "

"Oi, Zahra! Shut your hole!"

Now, it was Zahra's turn to shrink back. If there was one thing that Cork didn't appreciate, it was someone calling her by her birth name.

Zahra leaned in close and shared a hushed giggle with her father. "It's Gwendolyn."

"What did you say?" Cork asked, turning and glaring at her.

"Nothing! My dad just asked me, um, 'when do we land?'" Zahra's big-eyed expression got a chortle out of her compatriot.

"Good cover." George congratulated her with a sly smirk.

Zahra's expression darkened. "Seriously, though, don't say it out loud. She *will* throw you out of her plane — "

George stopped himself.

"...and she won't land it first."

**Barcelona, Spain**

As reliable as Cork's Cessna was, its diminutive fuel tank and slow-as-molasses cruise speed made getting to Cairo "in a hurry" impossible. Cork never pushed her plane either, no matter the situation. Even in the face of life or death, like now, splashing down in the Mediterranean was much worse, especially to someone like Cork. The *Puss E. Galore* was her life, and she'd protect the aircraft as if it were her child. Unfortunately, it meant the Scales of Anubis, and Grant, would get to Egypt far in advance of them.

Zahra checked her watch. *They're probably already there.* That fact deflated her a little.

The stopover wasn't all that bad. Zahra and George were short on provisions and in need of a few things. At least Zahra had her gear with her. She had planned on being gone for days on end. Her father hadn't been prepared to travel. Zahra had literally dragged him onto the Cessna with only what he was wearing.

Cork set down in a remote airfield on the outskirts of Barcelona. While she went over her plane and gassed-up, the Kanes took a taxi into town for a supply run. Zahra slipped her Glock into the waistband of her jeans, hiding it beneath her black shirt and jacket.

"I am Francisco. Where would you like to go?" the cabbie asked in Spanish.

"Anywhere close by with clothes and food," Zahra replied, slipping into her third language in the last twelve hours. The feat earned an impressed look from her father.

"That has always amazed me."

"What has?" Zahra asked.

"The way you can just flip the switch and speak an entirely different language on command with no difficulty."

Zahra shrugged. "Languages have always been easy for me."

"Must be a Godsend when you're in the field."

"Definitely," she agreed, yawning.

The four-plus hours of flight time in the slow-moving, cramped aircraft was hitting her hard. The small amount of sleep she had gotten after the night she had endured at the museum was killing her. Her head was pounding behind her sunglasses, and she needed coffee in the worst way. She wasn't jetlagged per se, but she sure as hell felt like it.

"So..." George said, clearing his throat, "is this how you always travel?"

"No, usually the museum takes care of me."

"Then why trust a person like Cork?"

Zahra glanced at him. "She's around when I need to move quickly and stay off the books."

"Off the books?"

Zahra nodded. "The museum isn't interested in everything I find. But there are other parties out there that are."

George's face dropped. "You work with black-market antiquities dealers?"

Zahra snorted out a laugh. "God, no, Dad! Geez... But I do know a few private collectors who will buy almost anything I bring back with me."

"And then sell it on the black market!"

It was a gray area that Zahra lived in — that even fewer people knew she partook in. "What they do with it is their own business. I get paid and turn that money into jaunts like this." She motioned around her. "Believe it or not, archaeology doesn't pay all that well, Dad."

George let out a tired laugh. "Yeah, tell me about it. Speaking of which, do you have enough to finance all this?"

She tried to hide her smile. "I have a little bit saved, yes."

"What is 'a little bit?'"

Zahra found something else to look at and faced away from her prying parent. "Let's just say that we won't have any problems any time soon."

Zahra had put together quite the savings account. It wasn't enough to retire on at her age, but she was well-off enough to never have to worry about going broke. This trip, however, felt like it could push that statement to the test. There was no way this was going to be a fast, in-and-out kind of mission. Even now, based on their current flight plan, they still had another stop between Barcelona and Cairo. Cork was going to need to get some shuteye down the road too. Having a dreary pilot wouldn't benefit anyone.

Twelve minutes into their taxi ride, the Kanes unloaded outside of a strip mall. There found everything from a small café to a laundromat to an electronics store to a supply outlet. The cabbie had done his job perfectly and brought them to a smorgasbord of useful places.

They climbed out. "Hey, Francisco," Zahra said, leaning down toward the driver's side window.

"Please," he said with a shit-eating grin, switching to adequate English, "call me, Frankie."

Zahra leaned in close, never once losing contact with the man's eyes. "Okay, Frankie, I'll make you a deal." She tossed her hair for good measure. "Wait for us here, and I'll give you an extra fifty bucks. I promise we won't be long."

Frankie's grin turned into a beaming smile. "For you, *senorita*, I'll do it for forty-five."

Zahra stood and gave the cabbie a playful wink. She turned and gave the cabbie a chance to ogle her ass before she was met with the disapproving gaze of her father. She had never seen the man look so sick, even aboard the Cessna.

"What was all that about?" he asked, following Zahra to the café.

"*That*, what?" she asked. George crossed his arms and gave her the most dad look ever. It worked. Zahra melted under his laser-like gaze. "It was nothing, just a successful negotiation to retain our driver for the duration of our stay."

George rolled his eyes. "You were flirting with him for a favor."

"Of which, I'm paying him for. It's a win-win for both of us. The fewer people that know we're here, the better off we'll be. It would be foolish to think that Khaliq doesn't have eyes and ears everywhere."

Her father's serious demeanor cracked. He agreed with his daughter. George opened the café's front door and glanced back at the cabbie, who was still eyeing his little girl's butt. "I still don't like it..."

Zahra snickered. "I never said you had to li — " She was hit with a blast of perfuming espresso, and she instantly forgot everything she was about to say.

It was exactly what she needed. Her father too. George looked terrible and ready for a nap. There'd be plenty of time to sleep on the Cessna if he could calm himself down enough to do so. Zahra could sleep through anything. It was a gift of hers, and it paid off when she was out in the wilds.

"Two *cortados*, please." Zahra hadn't enjoyed a traditionally made cortado in years. The woman behind the register motioned to Zahra's bruised face, asking who did that to her. Zahra waved the lady off. "I'm fine, believe me, I don't look nearly as bad as he does." Zahra raised her bruised knuckles. That got a wide smile out of the stranger.

The barista gave Zahra a basket of delicious-looking churro bites, on the house, to go along with their espresso drinks. Zahra felt like she was in heaven, and based on the way her father stared longingly at the churros, so did he.

The Kanes sat quietly and enjoyed themselves. It had been a long time since the two of them had done something like this together. Not the defying death part, but the traveling the world part. Zahra and George used to go on thrill-seeking escapades all the time between them moving to England and Zahra joining the army. Baahir had come along because he was forced to do so. Zahra never saw it as a chore, like her brother. She truly loved the adventurous lifestyle.

The next time someone spoke up, it was George, and he asked his daughter something unexpected. "Why do you work for the museum?" Zahra opened her mouth to answer but didn't. Her father took her silence as permission to press her. "You're obviously smitten with this part of the job, and I can tell you're good at it, based on the things you've told me."

Zahra still didn't have an answer as to why, but it was becoming more apparent that she might have to do without the museum. It was, more than likely, going to be closed for the foreseeable future. Zahra would need to go about things a little differently now. She'd need to look out for herself more than ever, with nothing to go home to besides her friends and family.

Neither roster was all that deep, either. She could count the people she loved and trusted on one hand.

*Let's see,* she thought, staring out the front windows of the café, *there's Dad and Dina, and I guess Cork. Baahir doesn't really count since he lives in Egypt. Who else? Hmmm...*

There was no one else. Zahra could disappear forever, and there would only be two or three people in all of England that would personally miss her. It was becoming more and more clear that she really could live on the move, if she wanted, and not feel guilty about it. The sound of George's espresso cup clicking down on the table brought Zahra out of her internal evaluation.

She stood. "Ready?"

He nodded and wiped the churro dust from his lips with his napkin.

"Thank you!" Zahra waved to the barista. "Everything was wonderful."

The older woman waved back and wished them good fortune on their impending endeavors. Zahra could definitely use a healthy dose of luck right about now. Currently, life was less-than-ideal, but it was nowhere near as bad it was about to get if the Scales of Anubis got their way. Once they touched down in Cairo, Zahra wouldn't stop until Baahir and Grant were safe, and Khaliq's genocidal plan was dead in the water.

**Unknown**

The burlap sack caused his sweaty scalp to itch intensely, and the covering reeked of something he couldn't place, and it was making him ill. There was an almost barnyard-like quality to the odor, but he didn't know if the stink was originating from the sack, or the place he had been led to. The last few hours had been the most trying in his young life, but they had gone by in a blur. He still couldn't fully process what was happening.

Grant had been kidnapped by a group of violent zealots and then moved out of country somewhere. From the moment he had exited the SUV at an airfield he had never seen before, to boarding a private jet, Grant had been wearing the rotten sack over his head. There was no way of telling where he had been taken except that he had been flown out of the UK.

The outside temperature was presently much warmer than in London, and the ground was sandy and radiated the same heat as the air. The time aboard the aircraft clued him into his present location as did his present company. He was in Egypt somewhere. Grant had made that trek once before. A direct flight from London to Cairo was about five hours of total flight time.

His captors had mentioned Zahra several times — how she had killed a handful of their men with little trouble — and with no gun. Unknown to those around him, Grant understood enough Arabic to get around. Zahra's reputation as a woman who could get the job done was plain to see. She was more than just an archeologist. Grant was confident in his assessment of her. She had shown him that — shown these people that.

Her abilities were what Grant was holding out hope for.

She stood atop the Great Pyramid in Giza and witnessed a shambling, zombie-like horde closing in on her position. She had no idea how she had gotten to the peak of Khufu's tomb. It didn't matter. All she knew was that there was a voice in head laughing at her predicament, and then *zoom*, here she was.

Zahra spun, gauging her escape, but she saw none. The swarm surrounded her on all sides and was nearly halfway up the pyramid's four sides. And the most horrifying element of this moment was the zombie-like crowd and those who were leading the charge.

Dina, Grant, Cork, and her brother and father.

*Dina? How did she get here?* It made no sense. None of it did. The contagion was supposed to resemble the same one that God used in the Old Testament. People died because of it. The firstborn of every family had been targeted in the event unless they smeared the blood of a lamb above their doorway. If they followed God's instructions, the Angel of Death would *pass over* their homes and leave them be.

*That's not this,* she thought, thinking hard.

The world around her shook, and she fell forward and nearly rolled down to meet her makers. Zahra climbed back up to the perch, breathing hard.

The people beneath her toes, to an extent, looked alive, but they also resembled that of the living dead. Their blank expressions, and unblinking eyes, sent a chill down Zahra's sweaty, sun-stricken neck.

The stone below her rumbled and fell apart. Zahra was cast into a pit of utter darkness, screaming and thrashing like mad until her father woke her.

*It was just a dream*, she thought, realizing that a part of it was real. But the rumbling of the ground beneath the earth wasn't that of the earth. It was Cork's plane.

The pilot called back to them. "We, uh, may have a slight problem!" It was the first time Zahra had ever heard uncertainty in Cork's voice. If she was concerned about something regarding her bird, then everyone aboard was in serious trouble.

Not a second after the thought had crossed Zahra's mind did the rear engine cut out. There was a pop followed closely by a sputter. Then, nothing at all. The Cessna dropped. The sudden altitude change caused Zahra's ass to lift off her seat in a moment of weightlessness, similar to how astronauts trained.

Cork leaned into view and turned around just in time to see Zahra land awkwardly back in her seat. "You may want to buckle up."

Zahra wanted nothing more than to counter with a "No, shit, Sherlock," but she didn't. Her eyes were glued to the landscape off on the horizon.

"Are we going to make it?" George asked, once again gripping his armrests so hard that his knuckles turned white.

Cork called back. "Too early to tell, but you can bet your arse I'm going to try!"

# CHAPTER 42
# ZAHRA

**Levanzo, Italy**

Zahra gritted her teeth as the mechanical failure-induced turbulence rattled her fillings. She wanted to help Cork but didn't know what she could do. Zahra was a lot of things, but a pilot wasn't one of them. She understood the systems responsible but had no real flight experience aside from sitting up front and watching.

*Better than nothing, I suppose.*

Zahra went to unbuckle, much to the dismay of her father. George looked at her like she was nuts, and maybe she was... She was a person that was never comfortable sitting idly by and doing nothing in the face of danger. Call it a flaw of hers. It's why she loved fieldwork, even back when she was in the army. It's why she had trained so hard. She wanted to be combat-ready.

George reached across the narrow aisle and grabbed her left hand, halting her exodus. "Are you crazy?" he shouted, squeezing hard. "This," he motioned around the cabin, "is not a fight you can help with!"

"I can try." Zahra pulled her hand free.

"The hell you will!" Cork yelled. "Stay in your seat until I tell you to do otherwise!"

Zahra was going to argue but was, once more, defeated by the pilot.

"Sorry, Zahra, but my plane, my rules."

The headstrong archaeologist wasn't one to be put in her place all that often. She didn't like the feeling of being scolded like a school kid. Zahra was always the boss on trips like this. However, she respected Cork. So, she did as the captain ordered and kept her ass planted and buckled into her seat.

And she was glad she had stayed put.

The *Puss E. Galore* lost altitude again as it approached the ever-growing landmass. They were headed toward an island, one that Zahra wasn't familiar with.

"What is that?" she asked.

"Levanzo!" Cork called back. "It's an island to the west of Sicily!"

"Can we land there?" George asked.

Cork laughed. "Doesn't matter if we *can* — we *are*!"

Zahra saw pockets of low buildings dotted here and there. It wasn't much, but at least Levanzo was inhabited.

A humming sound filled the cabin interior, freaking George out even more.

"Easy, Dad, it's just the landing gear coming down," Zahra explained, grabbing his shoulder and clutching his jacket. She didn't let go until their *airstrip* appeared.

George lifted a finger and pointed. "Is that a road?"

"And our runway!" Cork replied, powering down the lone functioning engine a little more. With their airspeed decreased, the Cessna descended quickly. At this rate, they'd touch down any second.

By Zahra's estimate, they were directly over the southern tip of the island. The road led straight for a port, from what she could tell. It was hard for Zahra to make out exactly where they were headed with all the bouncing and shaking. Any more of it, and she'd repaint the ceiling with her vomit.

"Cork!" Zahra yelled. "Any day now!"

"Almost there..." Cork relayed. The wheels caught asphalt. "Got it!"

But the road wasn't empty.

One after another, drivers blared their horns and swerved out of the way to miss the Cessna. Cork tried her damnedest to avoid them too, but the plane didn't have the same maneuverability as the vehicles. She kept the fuselage lined up with the central yellow lines of the four-lane road and mumbled incoherently to herself.

After the tenth car horn, Cork was able to stop the plane just as they were about to enter the gate to the port. A local — the guard — stumbled out of his shack and looked the Cessna up and down. He sprinted over to the driver's side and waved at Cork. She slid open her window, breathing heavily.

The guard was shouting at her in Italian.

"Oi, Luigi, I don't speak Italian!

Zahra unbuckled and squeezed into the cockpit. She leaned over Cork and quickly conversed with the guard.

"*Grazie!*" Zahra shouted, thanking the man, and waving him off. The guard hustled back into this shack and picked up a phone.

"What'd he say?" Cork asked.

Zahra plopped down in the front passenger seat, sweating. "He said that we can't park here. We're blocking access to the port."

Cork was confused. "That's it?"

"No," Zahra replied, "I explained what happened and that we are in need of some help. He went to call his cousin, who, from what I gather, is a pilot. He does helicopter tours of the area."

"Oh, well, that was awfully lovely of him." Zahra got up, but Cork grabbed her wrist. "One last thing..."

"No, Cork, I don't know if he's single."

returned. He rolled over, facing away from the rising commotion. It wasn't until he heard the voices that Baahir became curious as to who exactly the guests were.

*Ugh, fine.*

He rolled back over and stood, yawning. Baahir lifted his hands high over his head and paused mid-stretch. Across the cave, he spotted an unfamiliar woman, and two burly men led a hooded figure down the steps. This was the first time he had seen anyone treated like this since his own arrival.

*How long has it been already?* It was hard to tell the time. There were no clocks and no windows—no sunrises and no sunsets.

The others gave the newcomers a wide berth. Baahir didn't. He marched straight for them, stopping in the empty space between his cowering coworkers and the bottom of the stone steps. The hooded man was on his knees, panting beneath the filthy burlap sack.

The woman could only be one person. "Ifza Ayad, I presume."

She glared at him, but her expression softened after seeing it was Baahir who had greeted her. It was obvious that Baahir's actions were out of place. Everyone here was terrified of Khaliq's sister. Baahir was too, but he had nothing else to fear from her. He was already in hell, working for Satan himself.

She stepped toward him and held out her hand. "It's a pleasure to meet you, Dr. Hassan." Baahir didn't accept the handshake. Ifza lowered her hand. "I have someone I would like you to meet." She looked over her shoulder. "Get him up."

Her henchmen pulled the prisoner to his feet, and one of them roughly removed the cloak from his head. Baahir was expecting to see someone he knew. He had never met this man before.

"Baahir Hassan, meet Grant Upton." Grant collapsed to the floor. "He used to work closely with — "

"Zahra," Baahir said. He knew Grant by name only. His sister had mentioned him several times over texts and emails. He was a rising star in their world, from what Zahra had said. She had been very impressed by him.

The younger man was, understandably, afraid of the situation he found himself in. It was also plain to see that he was sleep deprived and dehydrated — possibly feverish. Even in the cool, ambient temperature of the cave, he was slathered in sweat.

"He's sick," Baahir said, kneeling in front of him. "What did you do to him?"

"Nothing, but I suspect he is reacting negatively to the sack."

"The sack? What's so special about a sack?"

Ifza gave Baahir a look that said she knew something he didn't. "It used to hold flour." Before Baahir could question the oddness of the sack's usage, as well as its relation to its prior contents, Ifza continued. "Mr. Upton is being prepared. We need him at his weakest for what we have planned."

"And what's that?" Baahir asked. Grant clawed at him, mumbling softly to himself.

Baahir leaned in close enough to hear.

"Alive..." Grant whispered, coughing hard. "Zahra is alive..."

Grant then fell face first into the hard floor, unconscious. He allowed Ifza's men to pick his sister's assistant up and drag him away. The news of

Zahra's survival was glorious, but he needed to maintain his position of servitude until he knew more. No one else seemed to have heard Grant. The young man had used his last ounce of strength to deliver Baahir some much-needed good news.

"You didn't answer my question," Baahir said, standing.

"My apologies, Dr. Hassan." Ifza feigned forgiveness with a lax bow of her head. "What did you want to know?"

"What is it that you have planned for him?"

Ifza kept her subservient posture but looked up at him with a wide, predatory smile. "He is to be our latest patient. Hopefully, he'll last longer than the others."

*The others?*

She stood. "Thanks to you and your sister," Ifza held out her hand behind her, "...and your father, and your dear, *dear* mother."

That was the second time that Baahir's family had been brought up with disdain. There was definitely history here, but he had no idea what it was. One of the men unslung a backpack and unzipped it. He reached inside and pulled out what Baahir had been dreading to see.

"This," Ifza said, examining the large, black canopic jar, "I thank you for this. Had your family destroyed it years ago, none of this would have come to pass."

Baahir looked over his shoulder, spying the light table at the center of the cave. The extended portion of Anubis' scroll mentioned something about the hellstone being the key to unlocking the plague. He didn't understand the science behind it. Since Baahir had arrived on the scene, the team here had only been responsible for research and translation. He knew they were looking for a temple, but other than that, he wasn't sure of anything else.

Regardless of what was really happening, Grant, and everyone else in the Scales of Anubis' way, would be doomed.

It begged the question.

Why didn't Baahir's mother turn the jar to dust if she, ultimately, knew what it would be used for?

**Levanzo, Italy**

So far, the people of Levanzo had been nothing but gracious. Even the chief of police was a gentleman. When he and his partner showed up, they quickly put in a call for a tow truck to haul the plane to the ferry guard's cousin's house. As it were, the tow truck belonged to the cousin, and pilot, Vincenzo. He was a man of many hats, apparently. Only one of the motorists had complained about being run off the road, and even he had left without much more than a fist shake.

"This is the most excitement we've seen in months," Chief Stefano explained.

Zahra grinned. "Well, then, I'm happy to have been of service to you and your people."

"Yes, thank you." Stefano let out a boisterous laugh. "Your Italian," he said, switching to English, "it is impressive."

"*Grazie*," Zahra replied. "I couldn't not learn the 'real' language of love."

Stefano smiled and waved the tow truck over as it pulled in. "*Signorina* Kane, this is Vincenzo Barone. He is, like you say, a Swiss Army knife. He does it all!"

Vincenzo tipped his cap to the police chief. "*Grazie*, Stefano. Thank you kindly."

The versatile local backed his truck up to the Cessna and climbed out. He and the much taller Cork went over the best way to rig the tow cable and then speedily went about attaching it. Zahra and George stood off to the side and watched the boats come in and out of port. Gathered around their feet were the trio's belongings. Neither of the Kanes spoke again until Cork prompted them.

"You ready?"

Zahra spun. "Yeah. So, what do we do for tonight?"

Cork pointed at the mechanic. "Vincenzo says there's a place down the road that can put you two up for the night."

"Just us?" Zahra asked. "You aren't coming?"

She shook her head. "No, I'm going to help him with my plane. No one knows my bird better than me." She flicked her eyebrows. "But he did mention that he has a rollout at his place if I do want to get some sleep."

Zahra wasn't exactly sure if the local had meant it in the way that Cork was hoping, but she wasn't going to be the one to burst the woman's bubble. All four people piled into Vincenzo's heavy-duty, four-door tow truck. It was just like the models that were used to transport disabled big rigs on the highways.

The first thing they did was drop the Cessna off at his shop. It was only a ten-minute drive from the port, north across the island's interior. Vincenzo and Cork unhooked the plane from the vehicle's winch and climbed back inside. After another short drive, they arrived at a charming cottage right smack on the water.

"Sofia will be by in the morning to see you," Vincenzo explained. "Key is under the mat."

Zahra didn't know what to say. The people of Levanzo were incredibly trusting to outsiders, operating in a very old-fashioned manner. Nowhere in England, or even the United States, would anyone allow you to just waltz into their place unannounced and without payment, or at least an ID. For all Sofia knew, she could be harboring fugitives.

And Zahra sort of, *technically*, was.

"*Grazie*, Vincenzo. And please, whatever you can do to get our plane operational would be much appreciated."

He glanced over at Cork, and then back to Zahra. "Based on what Cork here has told me about her plane, I don't see why the two of us can't get it back in the air by morning." He waved. "Goodnight, *Signorina*." Then, he tipped his ballcap at George. "*Signor*."

George waved back and looked at his daughter. Both were dumbfounded. "Remind me to come back here again when all this is over."

Zahra nodded. "Same here. This place is..."

"Unusual?"

She laughed. "I was going to say, unbelievable, but yes, *unusual* works too."

Just as Vincenzo had said, the key to the front door was under the front doormat. Zahra still couldn't fathom the trust the people here had in one another, let alone with complete strangers. Based what she had seen from the aircraft earlier, Levanzo was a very small island. It couldn't have more than three or four hundred year-round inhabitants. Were all of them as welcoming as Stefano and Vincenzo? Even the port guard had been kind and understanding.

George did the honors and keyed open the front door. The quaint cottage was impeccably well-maintained. Everything inside was modern, though, not brand-new. The decor was a nice mix of colors, mostly those of the sea. Zahra counted four shades of blue in the kitchen alone. It had been built into the right-hand corner of the great room, just inside the door. The central living space was a high-ceilinged, twenty-by-twenty square with a spiral staircase in the corner that looked like it led up to a loft. But that's not what Zahra was focused on. She was lost in the view the living room's balcony offered of the Mediterranean.

"Wow."

George saw it too. Both father and daughter were instantly transported to another world. Together, they just stood there and allowed the cool, calming breeze to caress their achy, exhausted bodies through the already open French doors. Zahra had no idea what it would cost to stay here for even one night, but whatever it was, it was worth every single penny.

She reached out and took her father's hand and squeezed it. "We definitely need to come back."

# CHAPTER 45
# ZAHRA

**Levanzo, Italy**

Zahra hadn't slept that well in months, and to be honest, she felt terrible about it. Somewhere in Egypt, her brother and Grant were being held captive by a band of lunatics who were trying to reproduce the Biblical plague — a plague, as it were, that was created by ancestors of the group behind it all.

*My ancestors...*

As much as she'd like to distance herself from these people, Zahra was a part of it. Ayad blood flowed through Zahra's veins, just as her blood flowed through them. They were family, for better or worse.

*Worse, much, much worse.* Nothing about this was "for the better."

Zahra stretched and sat up, wearing a pair of gym shorts and a sports bra. She had spent the night in the loft above the living room and had the space to herself. Her father had insisted that she take the bed since she had had the rougher go of it lately. She swung her feet over the side of the bed and went to stand but stopped. On the nightstand holding her sunglasses was a pamphlet. Curious, Zahra picked it up and saw it for what it was.

*It's a brochure of the island.*

There wasn't much — just locations to take photos and explore and places to eat. The Grotta del Genovese also contained Neolithic cave paintings.

*On an island in the Mediterranean Sea?*

Zahra guessed that there would be more information as to how cave paintings came to be on Levanzo. At the moment, it didn't really matter, though. She presumed that the independent landmasses making up the island chain were connected at one point. There was also a shipwreck of a Roman cargo vessel off the eastern shore in the waters of Cala Minnola that had made recent waves in the historical community, though Zahra hadn't looked into it any deeper than what she read in the headlines. Levanzo wasn't a sprawling, luxurious getaway. It was a place to relax and recharge, and Zahra had done just that.

The floorboards creaked under her weight as she stood. Her knees and back, not to mention her feet, were sore as hell. She stepped lightly, unsure of whether her father was still asleep or not.

He wasn't.

She leaned over the railing of the loft and saw that the couch was already empty and put back together, exactly the way they had found it the evening before. Her father was sitting quietly at a small table out on the balcony. He clutched a coffee mug in both his hands. Even from here, Zahra could feel the chilly morning breeze coming in off the water.

Zahra dug through her bag and found a clean shirt, tossing it on before carefully making her way down the tight, spiraling staircase. The metal beneath her bare feet was cool and felt great pressed up against her aching soles. The discomfort reminded her that she needed a new pair of boots.

*And a foot massage.*

The ball of her right foot struck the wooden floor of the living room.

"There's more coffee in the kitchen," her father called out, never once looking at her.

"Thanks," she replied. "How is it?"

"Eh..." He waggled his left hand. "Not as good as the view, that's for sure."

Zahra would soon find out. So far, it smelled incredible. She could only imagine how good it would taste. She greedily poured a heavy helping into a mug that had been waiting for her. Slowly, Zahra lifted it to her lips and took the smallest of sips. It was hot, but not too hot.

And it tasted amazing.

"Dad," she said, laughing, "this stuff is great. How can you say it's not as good as the..." Zahra stopped and stared. "Oh."

As good as the coffee was, the view was infinitely better. The sun was still low in the sky, and the traffic on the crystal-clear water was minimal. Zahra spotted a couple of sailboats and a ferry off in the distance, and nothing else. The sea was unbelievably flat, and a pristine shade of blue that Zahra couldn't recall ever seeing in such a large body of water.

She joined her father on the balcony, closed her eyes, and took in a deep, pleasing breath of fresh air. Zahra let it out slowly, feeling her pulse nearly pause. She hadn't been this relaxed in a long time. George pushed out a chair, and just as Zahra sat, there was a knock at the front door.

"Really?" Zahra complained. "Come on, man!"

George patted her on the knee and got up. "Stay put. I'll get it."

She didn't argue. Zahra took a long sip of her coffee and watched as another sail came into view. For now, it was just a bobbing blur, but if she waited long enough, she'd be able to see it for what it was. Zahra checked her watch. She'd love to do just that. Sit, and wait.

"Zahra?"

"Yeah, Dad?" she answered, not taking her eyes off the distant watercraft.

"We have a visitor."

Zahra didn't have her gun, or even her knife. They were both upstairs in her bag. She was completely defenseless. The only weapon she had was her bruised fists. She launched to her feet, feeling her lower back protest the sudden movement. But as soon as Zahra spun and had a look at their guest, she knew they weren't in any imminent danger.

"Zahra, this is Sofia, the owner of this place."

A woman around the same age as her father stepped in and looked around. The only way Zahra could describe the look on her face was *satisfied* — satisfied that she and her father didn't wreck her property overnight.

"I trust your stay was pleasant," her English was easy enough to understand, but Zahra could tell she was struggling with it.

Zahra smiled. "It was," she replied in Italian. "Thank you. It was very generous of you to let us stay, and on such short notice."

Sofia smiled wide, responding in her native tongue. "When Vincenzo called me, it was a blessing that I had the room available. What luck! I've been booked solid for months, except for last night. And about that..."

"Oh, yes." She looked at her father. "Get our stuff. We're leaving. She needs the room."

George sighed. "Talk about an early checkout."

Zahra returned her attention to Sofia. "What do I owe you?"

"Ninety euros."

Zahra nearly choked on her coffee as she went to take another sip. That equated to only one hundred and six U.S. dollars. It was the very definition of a bargain, considering the lady could have just as simply turned them away.

"You don't happen to take credit cards, do you?"

Sofia looked amused by the question and pulled out her cellphone, attaching a card reader to it in seconds. Apparently, the older woman was accustomed to dealing with plastic currency, rather than the paper variety.

Zahra happily tipped her an extra fifty bucks.

"How far in advance do we have to book for a return stay?"

Sofia smiled. "For you, I can make an exception. You can come back whenever you'd like. I will give you my personal email." Zahra smiled. Looks like she had just made a very useful friend and ally. She'd need to remember Levanzo the next time she was in the Mediterranean. George came clambering down the stairs. "Take your time getting ready," Sofia said. "My next guests aren't due to arrive until this afternoon."

Zahra shook the woman's hand. "Thank you for everything. We'll only be a few minutes."

# CHAPTER 46
# ZAHRA

The Kanes exited the cottage thirteen minutes later to the sound of a roaring engine. Cork and Vincenzo pulled up the short driveway just moments later. The Brit hopped out, leaving the local to himself behind the wheel.

"We good to go?" Zahra asked.

"Yeah," Cork replied. "Vincenzo is a wizard with his hands."

Zahra glanced at her father, who was similarly uncomfortable with Cork's phrasing. She was about to ask whether or not Cork had found, yet another, port-side lover, but refrained from asking the question with Sofia standing nearby.

"You get much sleep?" Zahra asked.

Cork shrugged. "Enough."

The Kanes waved their goodbyes to Sofia and headed for the tow truck.

"The only problem is fuel."

Zahra and George stopped dead.

"Fuel?" Zahra asked.

"Yeah," Cork replied. "Vincenzo doesn't have enough to give us."

"We'll happily pay him for it."

Cork shook her head. "I told him that, but some things aren't worth parting with. He needs the fuel more than the money. Shipments are few and far between out here."

"What does that mean?" George asked.

"It means — " Cork started.

Zahra butted in. "It means we're even further away from getting to Cairo."

The three of them climbed into the waiting truck. Cork blew out a long, annoyed breath. "Looks like we'll have to land somewhere in Sicily and refuel, then head out again."

*And again.*

Zahra had already done the math. Even after a stop in Sicily to refuel, they would need to stop one more time, probably somewhere in Greece, before finally arriving in Egypt. It was the frustrating part about using this kind of transportation. The freedom this method offered was priceless, however. Zahra could go anywhere she wanted, bring along anything she wanted, and leave whenever she wanted.

The biggest downfall was that it took a lot longer than it would on a 747.

*Still...*

Vincenzo chauffeured them to his property, giving Zahra her first glimpses at the man's operation. There was a large barn-like building with multiple additions at the plot's center. If Zahra had to guess, the add-ons had been done over time. It's where Vincenzo must have stored his helicopter. There was no other building large enough to contain it. The local's residence was, obviously, off in the distance. Next to the barn sat the *Puss E. Galore*. The plane looked like it was ready to go, as was Zahra.

They exited the mechanic's truck and headed toward the plane, but Zahra waited.

"*Signorina*?" the local asked.

"We really need that fuel, Vincenzo," Zahra said.

He shook his head. "As I explained to your friend, I cannot part with it."

Zahra was becoming angry but stayed calmed. Vincenzo wasn't being malicious or overly obtuse about the situation. He was just looking out for his own interests. He valued the fuel more than the money, which was actually quite admirable to Zahra. His future livelihood mattered more than the cash he would collect from them in the short term.

"What if we do something for you?" Cork asked. "You know, do something to pay off the debt?

"No, no, no... There is nothing you can — " his eyes lit up, "well, there is one thing... If you can help with this, I will give you all the fuel you require."

Zahra looked at Cork with a look that combined interest and concern. Whatever it was Vincenzo needed help with, it was something that would bring him more money than Zahra could offer him. It also meant it was going to be dangerous and, more than likely, illegal.

"What do you need help with, exactly?" Cork asked.

Instead of answering Cork, Vincenzo turned to Zahra and looked the archaeologist up and down. His eyes were focused on Zahra's body, mostly.

"Hey, *Sleezio*!" Cork yelled, noticing. She stepped toward the much smaller man. "Get your eyes off my girl's rump roast!"

Vincenzo stepped away from Cork and threw up his hands. "No, you have it all wrong, I — "

Cork growled. "I know exactly what you were doing!"

"No, please." The local was genuinely scared of Cork. "I was just thinking — of whether or not she would fit."

"Fit what?" Zahra asked, crossing her arms and leaning onto her left leg.

Vincenzo's eyes darted back and forth from Cork to Zahra. They settled on the more-threatening Cork, but he spoke to Zahra. "My ex-wife's dive suit."

Zahra was confused. "Dive suit? Did I miss something, why do we need dive suits??"

Vincenzo looked at Zahra and smiled. "You will see..."

# CHAPTER 47
# ZAHRA

Vincenzo drove Zahra out to the coast, leaving Cork and her father back at his property. Before leaving, he had announced that his fuel pump was locked down, and that there would be no fuel to be had. That meant Cork wouldn't be able to steal it while they were gone. Needless to say, Cork had been disappointed to hear that.

Vincenzo pulled over. The view, as it had been from the balcony of the cottage, was breathtaking. Zahra followed Vincenzo's lead and climbed out of the pickup truck. Before leaving for their very illegal mission, Vincenzo had opened the barn door. Inside was, indeed, his helicopter, but there was also a run-of-the-mill two-door pickup truck. The change in trucks was smart. The smaller vehicles would draw much less attention to anyone curious.

In the bed of the blue, 2005 Ford Ranger was their dive gear. The two had already changed into their wetsuits back at Vincenzo's place. And like he had guessed, the garb fit Zahra well. The only thing she didn't like about it was its color.

Hot pink.

"Doesn't go with my gun," she had said, half-kidding.

There would be no firearms here. There was no need. If they got caught, Zahra wasn't about to shoot her way out of custody. The only means of self-defense would be her SOG knife. It was currently strapped to her right thigh, right where her Glock typically sat. Vincenzo also carried a knife, but he carried one for a very different reason, especially when he went on dives.

"There are sharks."

"What kind?" Zahra had asked.

"Many varieties, including great whites."

Zahra sighed. "Just wonderful."

"Do not fear, *Signorina*. They are rarely ever spotted. We *should* be safe."

*Should be?* Zahra shoved the statement aside. "First of all, I never said I was scared. Secondly, great whites aren't what Hollywood says they are. They hardly ever attack people unless they get confused or startled." Vincenzo seemed pleased with Zahra's confidence, and her knowledge. "Bull sharks," she shuddered, "those are the *real* nasties."

"Quite true," Vincenzo nodded. "Luckily, we don't have them here."

*That* Zahra didn't know, and quite frankly, it was good to hear. She didn't like the ocean. She wasn't a fan of open water — period. Not knowing what swam directly below your kicking feet was nerve-wracking. Even a large, freshwater body bothered her deeply. It didn't mean that Zahra wasn't an accomplished diver. She just loathed doing it.

"I've been meaning to ask... Why are we doing this in broad daylight?"

Zahra figured they would have to wait until nightfall but hadn't pushed the point since she needed to leave as soon as possible. If Vincenzo was confident that they could pull this off, even though it would account to theft, then Zahra was willing to give it a go. The wreck was a protected site. Just touching it could land them in serious trouble with Italian authorities. Not even the nice people of Levanzo could turn a blind eye to it.

With his mask resting high on his forehead, Vincenzo threw his tank over one shoulder and collected his fins. Zahra stopped him.

"Okay, time to cut to the chase. What the hell am I doing out here? What does this wreck hold that is so important to you?"

Vincenzo had been very vague, and for good reason. If their roles were reversed, Zahra wouldn't have spilled the beans too early, either. Say she refused to help him, now she was a liability and knew of his plan.

"It is not for me."

"Who is it for?"

"A couple months ago, a man came to Levanzo — a man of great wealth. He said he was interested in the ship, but not for its historical value. He — "

"He wants its cargo," Zahra finished.

"Precisely."

"What is its cargo?"

Vincenzo almost looked embarrassed to divulge what he was holding back. But he did. "Wine."

"Wine? You're kidding me, right?"

He shook his head. "No. This man — he said his name was Giorgio, though I am not sure if it is his real name, or not. He offered me a great sum of money per amphora recovered."

Amphorae were terracotta containers used by ancient Greeks and Romans to hold various types of liquid — in this case — wine. They were tall with oval bodies and had two handles while also sporting a narrow neck. If the ones here were still properly sealed after hundreds of years of being submerged, then it was very likely that there would be liquid inside, though it wouldn't be drinkable wine. The contents would be closer to vinegar by now. It didn't make them any less valuable to the right people.

Whoever Giorgio was, he was obviously a collector with too much money. Stuff like this would prove to be more as a status symbol than anything else. Then again, he wouldn't be able to share it with anyone without bringing unwanted attention to himself. The wine jars would do nothing more than stroke his ego.

"How much did he offer?" Zahra asked, her interest piqued.

Vincenzo's eyes dipped to the earth, and he nonchalantly kicked at a small loose rock with his foot. "One million euros each."

Zahra nearly choked on her own air. "Holy shit..."

"Yes, that was my reaction as well."

Something still didn't add up. "Why wait until now to go after them?"

He tipped his head backward to the land behind him. "'Levanzo' is the problem. Everybody knows everybody. I was frightened to ask anyone here for help. What if they decide to turn me in to the authorities? I would lose everything!"

Zahra put the rest together. "So, in walks an outsider with the means and ability to get the job done, and you pounced on the opportunity to change your life."

"Precisely, yes. I had to wait for the right person. You, *Signorina*, are that person. I knew it from the first time I laid eyes on you." His eyes traced a line up and down her tight, hot pink form. "And it just so happens that the excavation crew is gone for a few days while their main pump is being repaired. Luck is truly on our — "

"Hey!" she interrupted. "I'm not your ex. Ogle me again, and I'll drown you."

He swallowed and laughed nervously. "Yes, well, shall we?"

To anyone that might be watching, Zahra and Vincenzo resembled a commonplace duo of divers — maybe even a romantic couple on vacation. They weren't the only ones in the area either. The 4th-century wreck was dead-center in Cala Minnola, surrounded on three sides by the picturesque shoreline. Groups of beachgoers were sprawled out on the warm sands, enjoying the gorgeous weather. Zahra couldn't imagine Levanzo being anything but beautiful.

Several boats were anchored in the waters, though they purposefully kept their distance from the ring of circular, orange buoys. The markers indicated which part of Cala Minnola you weren't allowed into — the spot Zahra and Vincenzo were headed to now. The pair kept close to the bottom, following it deeper and deeper. So far, the terrain had consisted of nothing but sand and a few rocks. It had been a while since Zahra had done something like this. The pressure building in her skull was uncomfortable, but not a nuisance. She knew she'd become more and more accustomed to it as the minutes passed.

*Still sucks,* she thought, blinking hard beneath her mask. She looked around. *Well, at least we have good visibility.* That calmed her some.

She blew out a long breath, cringing at the burst of bubbles floating toward the surface. The warbling swarm scattered a small school of fish as they rose. If there was anyone with half a clue watching the waters, all they would have to do was watch the trail of bubbles to know that someone was headed where they shouldn't be. They had scoped out the area with binoculars, pretending to be looking at the water. In reality, they had been looking for authority figures. After finding none nearby, Vincenzo had led Zahra to a shore further to the south and then quickly slipped into the surf. Luckily, the Mediterranean never got all that cold, especially around the shallower coastlines.

The wreck sat in ninety feet of water. Zahra had never dived that deep before. As far as she knew, their equipment was only meant to be used for depths of up to 130 feet. Hopefully, there wouldn't be a reason to test it. The sandy bottom dropped away sixty feet out, and Vincenzo kept near it, navigating around patches of seagrass. The growths were becoming more prevalent as they continued deeper. Zahra stayed close to him, doing her best not to think of drowning. Her gear seemed to be in top-notch shape, but still...

*Shut up, brain!*

Vincenzo looked over his shoulder and pointed straight ahead. Zahra followed his outstretched hand. She could just barely see a shape buried in the seabed. The shipwreck was just that — a wreck. It owned the classic oval body with pointed ends. The base of the center mast was present, but the rest of it wasn't anywhere to be seen. As she swam closer, she noticed that it was in decent shape, considering its age.

The entire keel was beneath the seabed. The cargo ship's contents might have been preserved by the packed sand, as long as the hull's integrity had held. The announcement of the amphorae gave Zahra hope that there was, indeed, something to find.

The increasing pressure was starting to get to Zahra. Her head felt like it was in the jaws of a vise. She slowed because of it. Vincenzo took notice and turned and swam back to her. Zahra tapped her temple and shook her head. Vincenzo shook his own head and held up his left wrist, tapping his dive watch. They didn't have time to surface. To do so meant they'd have to swim back the way they had come.

Zahra sucked in a deep breath of tank air and tried to calm herself. She agreed. This was their only shot. Zahra had experienced so much worse in her life than this. She was safe but was having trouble convincing herself of it. So, she didn't give herself the time to think it over. Zahra bit down on her regulator's mouthpiece, pushed onward, and started swimming again. Vincenzo fell in line beside her, and the two arrived on the scene minutes later.

# CHAPTER 48
# ZAHRA

For just a moment, the duo peacefully floated and admired the ancient remnant. The uppermost deck was a mess of sand, coral, and rotting wood. There was no way through it, not for Zahra and Vincenzo, anyway. They didn't have the tools or the time to bust their way in. Plus, Zahra wanted to do as little damage as possible. She was an adventurer, but she respected the stuff from the past as well.

Vincenzo looked over at her. Zahra lifted her right hand and pointed at her eyes with her middle and forefinger. Then she pointed down at the wreck and made a circular motion. They would survey the site before trying anything else. Zahra quickly slipped into her element — that of an experienced archaeologist. She zoned out and swam, never once taking her attention away from the cargo ship.

The port side offered them nothing. They headed around to the stern and found much of the same. The rear of the ship would have traditionally contained the tall looping sternpost that resembled the neck and head of a swan. But like the central mast, the decorative sternpost had been severed at its base, decapitated some time ago.

There, just around the corner of the stern, was a dark void in the rear section of the starboard side. Both divers headed for it. Zahra arrived first and pulled up to examine the hole. It would be a tight fit, but she was pretty certain she could squeeze through. As for Vincenzo... not so much. He was thicker than Zahra. The only way he could make it inside was if he were to remove his air tank.

Zahra turned to him and jabbed a finger into her own chest. Then, she pointed at the opening. Vincenzo had already done the math and nodded. He unclipped two folded nets from his belt and handed them over to Zahra. Her own belt held similar nets. The plan was to collect two amphorae each for a grand total of four million euros — a penny of which Zahra was certain she'd never see. Nor did she care. She was here for one reason, and she needed to remember that.

But she was enjoying herself — even with the crushing waters of the Mediterranean surrounding her.

Vincenzo gave her a thumbs-up and paddled backward, giving Zahra some room to work and maneuver. The entry point was nearly the size of a warped manhole cover. Zahra closed in and unclipped a small flashlight from her belt. The interior of the ship was much darker. The sunlight didn't reach here. Surprisingly, the hold looked to be void of most debris and sand. The latter still existed, but not in the amounts that Zahra would have thought. And it made sense because when Vincenzo had briefed her, told her that the excavation team's pump was broken. That would explain the lack of sand inside the cargo hold.

*In we go.*

Like a too-tight pair of denim jeans, Zahra wiggled back and forth, taking care not to sever her oxygen hose. Thankfully, the edges of the hole weren't jagged in the least. The worst thing she could imagine doing was snagging her hose and, momentarily, ripping the regulator out of her mouth. She doubted the hose would tear, though. Her hypothesis gave her confidence, and she planted her hands on the inside of the hull and pushed. After a second of non-movement, Zahra popped free, and she gently drifted into the hold of the centuries-old ship.

*Woah,* she thought, looking around.

It was amazing, but eery. She was terrified of getting stuck with whatever air she had left, a real-life possibility. The wreck was 1,700 years old, after all. Anything could happen. A shift in the tide could collapse the deck on top of her.

Something near the center of the large hold caught her attention. A row of dilapidated crates stuck out like a sore thumb in the otherwise empty space. Other treasures surrounded Zahra, however, none of them had been given the care of the containers she was headed toward now. It felt as if the vessel's crew had deemed these of ultra-importance.

*I wonder...*

She kicked for them, stopping in front of a fallen beam. The antiquated fragment sat diagonally across the breadth of the room. She would either have to swim over it, or duck beneath it. She played her light over the ceiling and cringed at what she saw. The deck above her head had started to cave in. There was no telling how long ago it had begun, or whether it was strong enough to last another thousand years. Zahra decided against getting too close, and she opted for the lower route.

She gave the heavy-looking beam a wide berth and hugged the starboard wall where the gap below was the widest. Even though she had plenty of space to make it through, it was still an unnerving couple of seconds. As soon as her hips cleared the beam, the cargo ship moaned. It was the first noise she had heard out of the sunken craft. Zahra instinctively tucked her legs into her chest, rolling into a slow-moving ball.

But nothing happened.

She sighed. *Must have been a wave or something.* The constant motion of the Mediterranean was one major factor in the erosive condition the ship was currently in. Eventually, Mother Nature would finish it off for good and turn it into little bits of Empirical kindling. All things on Earth were at Mother Nature's mercy, but none more than what was in her oceans and seas.

Zahra eyed the ceiling, once more, continuing to float through the hold. She was so focused on the deck coming down on top of her that she hadn't realized how far she had traveled. The back of her head ever-so-slightly bonked into something hard. Zahra spun and discovered that she had just accidentally floated into the nearest crate. She had just added another transgression to her already laundry list of infractions.

The sound caused her to smile behind her mouthpiece.

*There's something inside!* she thought. She used her hands and legs to steer herself upright and gazed upon the crate's lid. With practiced care, she clasped the edge of the lid and pulled, applying the tiniest of pressure. It didn't budge an inch.

*Huh, impressive.*

Zahra assumed it would come off with hardly any effort, yet, here she was, unsheathing her knife to use as a makeshift pry bar. With the same amount of methodical care, she searched for a gap between the lid and the top edge of the crate with the weapon's blade. Finding one, she slipped it in halfway and then adjusted her grip. With a little more *oomph* this time, she pushed down on the knife handle. The sodden rot splintered and fell apart, pluming in every direction. She replaced her knife and went about removing the rest of the decimated lid. Zahra felt awful about desecrating the find.

The act made her wince, but she quickly forgot all about it after spotting the crate's contents. Her gut had been right. It was loaded with the precious amphorae...but every single one was smashed and unable to be saved. She inspected each one, confirming their condition. Even though they had been packed tight, they had not survived the sinking. The Romans had used a technique not unlike one Zahra had seen inside the box containing her Christmas decorations. Each jar was placed into its own quarters inside the crate. Slats of wood had been used to separate the amphora to keep them from banging into one another during travel. Modern-day wine cases served the same purpose.

Zahra leaned around the ruin and counted the crates, stopping at twelve. She moved on to the next one, but saw that it, and its contents, were already in shambles. Long ago, something heavy had fallen atop the lid and smashed the container into pulp. She was 0-2, but fortunately, she still had another ten crates to go.

The scene outside the sunken cargo ship was serene. The world was cool and quiet, and it made Vincenzo all the more nervous. He was out of contact with Zahra — both verbal communication and hand signals. He was contemplating an attempt to enter the hold through the hole in the hull but thought better of it. The whale-like moan he had just heard emanating from the wreck had deterred him. Drowning was Vincenzo's worst fear. It had almost happened to him as a child while snorkeling on the northern side of the island. He had gone too deep, but lucky for him, his father had been close by. The event had scarred him.

He glanced down at his dive watch but was struggling to see its face. Their light source had been blotted out by something. So far, the sun had been unperturbed by anything. The weather reports had called for a nearly cloudless sky from sunrise until tomorrow morning.

*What then?* he asked himself, looking up.

Just as he craned his head skyward, the shroud moved off. The reignited bloom of light was strong enough to cause him to wince against it. He shut his eyes and turned away. As he did, the veil returned. Then, once more, it was gone. Vincenzo held up his hand and peered past it, seeing what was causing the disturbance.

His eyes went wide. *Oh, no.*

It was the ocean's most feared hunter, *Carcharodon carcharias*, the great white shark.

And he and Zahra had just had a conversation about how unlikely it was for a human to be attacked. Vincenzo was an intelligent man. He understood that if he remained calm, the apex predator would leave him alone and move on. All it was doing was searching the shallower water for food. Cala Minnola was a frequented swimming hole, and with the recent discovery of the cargo ship, it had seen a significant increase in visitors.

The shark was close enough for Vincenzo to get lost in its vacant stare. To Vincenzo, it was one of the animal's single most frightening features. Its jaws were at the top of his list, of course, as was the creature's immense size. This one wasn't any larger than the average great white, sitting at, what Vincenzo estimated to be, fifteen feet in length. The shark was virtually ten feet longer than Vincenzo was tall.

A dull clunking sound picked up from within the wreck. This was the worst possible time for Zahra to make any type of noise. But what could Vincenzo do? It's not like he could warn her.

The wraith-like aberration turned and glided back toward Vincenzo's location. Now more than ever, he wanted to be inside with his partner. But he didn't budge. The last place he wanted to be was stuck in a hole at the waist with his lower half in prime biting position. He shook and waited. The shark dipped its head and dove deeper. Vincenzo closed his eyes and prayed to God. He was someone Vincenzo had not talked to since his wife had left him. A *whoosh* of water pulled along like a precision rip current. The disturbance forced his eyes back open, and he did so just in time to see the belly of the beast pass by overhead. It had passed by with only feet to spare.

Then, with a trio of pumps from its powerful tail, it was gone.

# CHAPTER 50
# ZAHRA

Zahra bit down on her mouthpiece as hard as she could. It wasn't caused by an act of physical exertion. It was the result of anger and frustration. Eleven of the twelve crates had turned up nothing. Every one of them held the decimated remains of the wine amphorae. A few of the containers were in better shape than others, but none were in the condition the buyer was seeking.

She had just sheathed her knife. Both of her hands rested on the edge of the eleventh crate. Her eyes were closed, and her head was dipped. The rest of her body bobbed at a forty-five-degree angle. She opened her eyes and looked right. The twelfth and final crate awaited her.

*Come on,* she willed. *Please be there.*

Zahra unsheathed her knife and jammed it into a gap between the lid and the crate itself. She gritted her teeth and pushed the grip down, forcing the blade upward. The ancient wood gave way and broke apart. The effort was exhausting and met with a groan from both Zahra and the ship. She paused and looked up. The wreck had made a handful of noises since she had entered, but none louder than this.

*Oh, shit,* Zahra thought, watching as the deck above her head cracked inward. As luck would have it, after 1,700 years, the Roman cargo ship was about to fall apart, and with Zahra inside it. She removed the blade from beneath the crate lid and took a deep breath.

The wreck settled. The lid was now free.

Breathing easier now, Zahra sheathed her knife and removed the broken pieces from in between her and her prize. She leaned over the opening and impatiently waited for the cloud of particles to settle. When they did, Zahra grinned ear to ear.

*Yes!*

The majority of the crate's contents were smashed, but at its center, Zahra counted four very much, intact amphorae. She'd done it! Now, she had to remove the artifacts without damaging them, a feat she had never attempted while being underwater.

*This should be interesting.*

She used her knife blade to meticulously remove debris from around the tall wine jars. For a moment, Zahra pictured herself doing the same thing, but with a paintbrush from a dino dig site. She poked and picked at itsy bits of wood, and whatever-the-hell else was in the way. Once she was satisfied with her work, she detached one of the four nets folded on her dive belt. Zahra unraveled it and stuck it into place beside her, pinning it to the side of the crate with the tip of her knife.

She flexed her tired hands and shook them as fast as her surroundings allowed. Not only were they strained from the effort, but so was her mind. A nagging pressure had built up in the back of her head, exacerbated by the burden of being underwater. She floated higher until she was directly over the opening. She reached down and gently gripped the exposed handles. Zahra bit her lip and pulled, enthused to feel it slip free with very little resistance. Once it was completely free of its 1,700-year-old bondage, Zahra took a second to admire it. She frowned. There wasn't much to appreciate. The amphora was covered in hundreds of years' worth of grime and growth.

*Hey, there.*

A tiny shrimp scurried around to the top of the amphora and raised its pincers up at Zahra, giving her what could only be a double middle finger.

*Come on, little buddy.* She softly flicked it aside with the back of her hand. *Off with you.* The shrimp went tumbling before its tiny legs found purchase, kicking feverishly. Zahra watched it slow and drop down toward the floor of the hold before she continued with her illegal excavation. With the help of the water, she easily moved the two-foot-tall amphora into place and held open the net sack with one hand.

*One down, three to go.*

# CHAPTER 51
# BAAHIR

**The Pharaoh's Lounge** | Giza, Egypt

As the hours ticked by, Baahir was becoming more and more suspicious as to why he was actually here. The work had all, seemingly, been done before he had arrived. The only missing piece, it seemed, had been the canopic jar. He pondered all of this while sitting at the light table, staring blankly at *the* Book of the Dead. He still couldn't believe it.

*Mom would be proud.* The thought was short-lived, though. *Would she?* The discovery had led to some very bad people trying to do very bad things.

The stone tube that had housed the scroll for centuries laid on the table just a few inches from the relic found within it. Baahir could easily use the tube to destroy the glass pinning the scroll in place. Then, all he'd have to do was tear up the artifact. The idea had been short-lived. Baahir could never do such a thing. He didn't have the heart to destroy the scroll, no matter how foul the subject it contained was.

"Dr. Hassan?"

Baahir took his eyes off the scroll long enough to see a thin, hunched man standing off to this right. Salem was the oldest person here by several decades. While Baahir's conversations with the elder had been brief so far, he found the man to be kind and incredibly knowledgeable.

"You don't believe in all of this, do you, Salem?"

The other man's eyes narrowed. "I do."

"Really? You believe that this scroll," Baahir motioned to the Book of the

Dead, "contains directions to a place to help replicate the Biblical plague? The 'Temple of Anubis?'"

Salem's face was stoic and unemotional. "I believe in what Khaliq believes."

"But why?" Baahir asked, turning in his stool.

"Because the man terrifies me, and I find it better to be on his side than oppose it."

*Oh.* Baahir had thought it was because Salem shared the same radical beliefs. But, no, it wasn't that at all. He identified with Khaliq as a way to ensure his survival.

"How long have you been working for him?"

Salem's eyes fell. "Too long."

Baahir didn't push it. It was plain to see that the subject was a rough one to talk about. But maybe the old man could help Baahir understand something.

"What about me?"

Salem regained some composure. "What about you?"

"Why am I here?"

"Your sister — "

"Besides that," he interrupted. "There has to be more to it than just being a shield against my sister's sword. Khaliq doesn't like my family. That much is easy to see. Every time he says my last name, his voice is laced with disdain — Ifza too."

Baahir's eyes opened wide. "Is there any information, unrelated to the plague, that we have access to down here?"

"There might be something, yes." Salem thought it over. "We have looked into the Ayad family tree extensively. There could be something useful, I suppose."

*It's worth a shot.*

Baahir stood. "Show me."

Salem led him over to a computer that was in desperate need of an upgrade. The load time was slower than Salem's footspeed, which was hard to believe. Once it booted up, Salem walked Baahir through the process of pulling up the research that had been done over the years.

Decades of research.

"Woah," Baahir said, "you weren't kidding."

"Yes, we've been very thorough."

Baahir scrolled down to the origin — the first name listed.

"Anubis... Of course, it says Anubis."

"Why wouldn't it?"

Baahir sat back in the creaky folding chair. "*Because* Anubis wasn't real! Sure, maybe there was a person who believed he was a god, but it wasn't actually Anubis in the flesh. He," Baahir jabbed a finger at the screen, "was just another man."

"A man far more intelligent than anyone of his time."

Yes, that too. Baahir also believed that whoever this person was, he was far beyond the human understanding of science at that time in history. After "Anubis," Baahir didn't recognize a single name — and there were too many of them to sort through. Each person had a subfolder with in-depth information about who they were and what they did.

So, Baahir decided to start from the other end of history. He scrolled up to two names. Khaliq Ayad and Ifza Ayad. The modern descendants all possessed pictures next to their names too. Their father had been a man named Aaftab Iyaan Ayad. Aaftab had four siblings — one girl in the bunch — that were quite a distance apart from one another age-wise.

Baahir mentally did the math. *Twenty-two years.*

He recited the brothers' and lone sister's names in order from eldest to youngest. "Aaftab, Jabbar, Haamid, Galib, and Kamaria."

Baahir scrolled past the names and pictures, but paused, seeing something odd. He wheeled the mouse back up a bit. The one woman looked familiar, but he couldn't place her. Based on her age, she'd be in her sixties today. Baahir clicked on Kamaria's name, and it brought up her file. Baahir was hoping to see something about the woman he recognized. Maybe he had met her before in Egypt — at a conference perhaps?

"Who are you?" he asked himself.

Her file contained a bevy of information, but it concluded after her death. He was about to close her file but stopped. His right hand rapidly began to shake the mouse cursor all over the screen. The only tidbit of information Kamaria's file had that intrigued him, besides her familiar face, was the dates of her birth and death.

*Both are the same as Mom's.*

His face flashed back to the woman. It was grainy and in black and white. But there, forming at the corner of her mouth, was a smirk that he remembered to this day. It was one Zahra had inherited.

"Mom?"

Salem was confused. "Who?"

Baahir slumped down into his chair. Everything from her death rushed back and slapped him in the back of the head.

"Kamaria Ayad," Baahir explained, putting it together as he went. "When she disappeared, she went to America and enrolled at NYU to study archaeology. There, she met a man whom she would later marry and have two children with. Her name became Hanan Hassan."

"Hassan?"

Baahir nodded. "She was my mother." He looked up at Salem. "Khaliq and I are cousins. That's why I'm here. That's why I'm still alive. He needs me for something else—I know it!"

Salem's face darkened. He opened his mouth to say something but shut it and turned away.

"What is it?"

Salem's shoulders fell. "You are correct in assuming that he needs you for something other than labor."

"What do you know?"

The old man faced Baahir with sorrow in his eyes. "There has been a theory that the Ayads, being a part of Anubis' bloodline, are immune to the sickness in some way, but until now, they've had no way of testing that theory since only Khaliq and Ifza are accounted for."

"Where are their other relatives?"

"In hiding, or dead."

Baahir's hands went to his head. "And now they have me..."

"Yes," Salem agreed, "and I fear that what they have planned for you will not be a pleasant experience."

"Worse than the other man's fate?"

Salem nodded. "Yes. Much worse. His death will come in time, though. If the theories are correct, he will not know that he is dying, or even feel it. You," he continued, "they need your blood — all of it."

"So, they plan on testing my blood against whatever virus they cook up. Is that what you're telling me?" Salem nodded. "Wonderful. And when is this supposed to happen?"

"I am not sure."

It infuriated Baahir that someone who had been here as long as Salem knew very little. But it also didn't surprise him. Khaliq had no reason to share everything with his people, even if they were the ones doing most of the work.

"Is there a lab on-site?"

"Yes," he glanced at the floor, "right beneath our feet."

# CHAPTER 52
# ZAHRA

The next three amphorae took a little more effort to procure than the rest. Zahra had been forced to break apart a large portion of the crate in order to get to the bottom of it. The salt and sand had effectively glued the trio to the ship's hold. But she had gotten them — and all in one piece.

*Yeah, no damage done...* She refused to look at the decimated crates. Most of the destruction had been her doing.

One by one, she swam an amphora over to her original entry point, spotting an excited Vincenzo through it. He held out his hands as if he was a small child looking for "uppies" from an adult. Zahra gladly handed over the relics, easing them up and into the opening. They worked together to avoid the splintered hull, and quickly removed three of the four containers. The last one was a fraction wider than the rest, and it took a little more time and thought to free it.

Vincenzo must have been pumped, because he yanked it the rest of the way through, pulling Zahra along behind it. She hadn't expected the sudden surge and became awkwardly stuck, which jammed her in sideways. Her tank was pinned, as was her waist. Angered, she snapped her attention to Vincenzo, but the local wasn't looking back at her. His eyes were off in the distance, out into deeper water.

Both divers froze. The blur's rear end twitched from left to right in a perfectly timed rhythm. At first, it moved slowly, like it was out for a stroll.

Then, with a sudden pump of its crescent-shaped tail, it increased its speed and directed itself at Zahra and Vincenzo.

*Oh, damn,* Zahra thought, feeling Vincenzo panic. He pulled on the amphora, causing Zahra's air tank to grind against the wreck's hull. The noise spurred the great white shark into motion, and it shot off like a cannon.

And Zahra could do nothing to stop it.

She let go of the artifact and reached for her knife but couldn't find it. It was sheathed on her hip, on the other side of the hull. Zahra's top half was about to be removed from her bottom half in a gruesome display of savagery, and all for nothing more than some undrinkable wine.

Zahra closed her eyes and waited to die. But she didn't. A form propelled itself into her. She opened her eyes to find Vincenzo's back pressed up against her chest. He was floating between her and the great white.

The animal attacked and opened its mighty jaws. Vincenzo leaned away from them and thrust the fourth amphora into the predator's gullet, just barely retracting his hand before they were detached from his wrists. Thinking it got something tasty, the great white took off, thrashing wildly back and forth. Zahra and Vincenzo immediately went about removing her tank from her back.

Zahra took one last inhalation before spitting out her mouthpiece. Vincenzo handed one of the amphorae to her while he hefted the remaining pair. They then made the arduous journey back to the shore, buddy breathing the entire time. Zahra was saddled with the responsibility of passing Vincenzo's mouthpiece back and forth. She'd read about divers in their same circumstances killing one another over the prospect of drowning. Not everyone possessed the ability to stay calm and focused during deadly situations like this. In retrospect, perhaps they should have surfaced.

Unfortunately, they couldn't. They still needed to keep their theft a secret.

Zahra's head broke the surface first, and she took in half a dozen greedy lungfuls of the fresh sea air. Vincenzo spat out his mouthpiece and joined in. They sat in the shallows of Cala Minnola, safely keeping their treasured wears concealed beneath the ever-rolling surf.

Vincenzo lifted his dive mask away from his face. "You..." he said between breaths, "owe me... one million euros."

Zahra removed her own mask and patted her body as if searching for a wallet. "Apologies, but I'm a bit short." She looked back toward the location of the wreck. "Sorry about that, Vincenzo. And thank you."

He shrugged. "No life is less valuable." He stood in the waist-high water and helped Zahra to her feet. "You have delivered your half of our deal. Now, it is time for me to do my part. Let us get you and your friends on your way."

# GRANT

Somewhere deep beneath *The Pharaoh's Lounge*, Grant Upton awoke from a horrifying nightmare. He was head-to-toe, dripping in sweat, and nauseous to the point of vomiting. He tried to sit up but couldn't. Grant had been strapped down to whatever he was lying on. So, he turned his head and threw up right then and there. He felt particles slap against his bare shoulder.

It was then that Grant noticed that he had been relieved of all his clothes except of his boxers.

Through waves of nausea, he took in the space. If he didn't know any better, he figured it was some kind of observation room. The only thing in the empty square space beside him was a single, wall-mounted TV, and the table he was attached to.

No, that wasn't the only thing. He could hear the low hum of machinery somewhere out of sight and over his head.

In his hallucinogenic state, Grant spotted all manner of cables and hoses protruding from his body, arms, and legs. Even his scalp felt cold. Scalp? Grant panicked and noticed that the ceiling was mirrored. In it was his reflection. As he had suspected, his head had been shaved, and he was wearing some kind of monitoring device. The observation room was, in reality, a surgical suite.

And he was the patient.

The cables and tubes ran from his body to the machine responsible for the insistent humming. He attempted to crane his head in that direction but became too exhausted to execute the maneuver. He flopped his head back down to the hard metal table just as a door squeaked open somewhere over by the machinery. At this point, Grant didn't care who had just entered the room. He was so sick that he was forced to keep his eyes shut and concentrate on his breathing. The only thing he could take solace in was that his stomach was empty. There would be no more vomiting from him.

*Just dry heaves.*

"What...what are you doing to me?" he asked the unknown person. "Why...do I feel...so awful?"

Soft footfalls answered him, as did the squeak of wheels. Soon, A blur stepped into view off to his right. It took everything in him to focus on the person's face.

"You?"

It was Ifza Ayad, and she was holding a rolling IV pole in her left hand. Grant turned his head and followed a pair of IV tubes, starting from the bags down to his arms. One of each had been attached to each of his hands.

"What is in those?" he asked, slurring his speech.

Ifza gently caressed the first IV bag. "This one contains a standard saline-based IV fluid."

"And the other one?"

Ifza smiled. "Something special we created just for you."

Grant was too exhausted to ask for a deeper explanation. Ifza sensed as much and offered up the information willingly.

"This one," she stroked the second bag as if it were her lover's cheek, "is much of the same thing, but we've mixed in a heavy concentration of gluten."

To the average person, the news of gluten being blended into IV fluid would be nothing more than an oddity. But to someone with Celiac — like Grant — it was a potential death sentence.

"Gluten?" he asked, terrified. "You're poisoning me with gluten?"

Ifza nodded and stepped away from the rolling IV pole. "Yes, you have something special in common with our other test subjects."

"Others?"

"Yes, others. You all have illnesses caused by an autoimmune disorder." Grant couldn't fathom why. "And as a result," she continued, "it makes it very easy for you to contract nasty little viruses, yes?"

Grant's feverish skin went cold.

Ifza's face soured. "As it were, an individual with a typical, *un*compromised immune system can fight off sickness at a much higher success rate. That is what you and the others are here to confirm. We believe that the ancient plague is far deadlier to someone like you." She smiled. "We hope to correct that limitation."

"But," his mind swam, "why me? Out of all the people with Celiac, why me?"

"Oh," Ifza replied, failing to hide her smile, "that is a simple explanation." She leaned over Grant, lusting over his body. It wasn't his fit body, or good looks, that attracted her to him. She was getting off on seeing him in his current condition. "You can blame your involvement here on Zahra Kane." Ifza leaned away from Grant. "She killed some of my dearest friends back in London. The least I can do is return the favor." Ifza headed off. "Welcome to the cause, Mr. Upton. Your eventual sacrifice will not be in vain. We will learn much from you. You should count yourself lucky."

"Oh, yeah," he asked, his head clunking back down to the table, "why's that?"

Ifza gazed over her shoulder, her eyes alight with fire. "Because you have been kept alive for much longer than the others. If it were up to me, I would have already cut your head off and mailed it back to your family."

# CHAPTER 54
# ZAHRA

The Cessna's twin turbines came to life. Zahra shielded her eyes against the early afternoon sun, as well as the dirt rushing from the aircraft. She slipped on a pair of sunglasses and waited for Cork to give her the all-clear.

"Are we ready?" George asked, shouting over the noise.

Cork slid open her side window and stuck out a skyward pointing thumb.

Zahra patted her father's shoulder and hefted her bag. "We are!"

The concussive sound died down as Cork killed the engines and climbed out of her plane. She rejoined her team over by the entrance to Vincenzo's hangar. The local was smiling wide, and for good reason. He had just gotten off the phone with his buyer. The man, Giorgio, was supposed to be coming in by boat later in the day to collect his prize. In six or so hours, Vincenzo was going to become a millionaire.

Zahra, her father, and Cork packed up their gear, but still had one thing to take care of.

"What are we doing about a runway?" George asked.

Vincenzo climbed into his truck and started it up. His window slid down. "Stefano has taken care of it."

"He has?" Zahra asked.

"*Si, signorina.*"

There was no further explanation. The mechanic threw the vehicle into reverse and carefully moved it to within inches of the Cessna's front strut.

He and Cork then went about hooking up his winch and tow cable to the plane, just as they had the day before. Wherever they were about to lug the plane, apparently, it was an area they could use as a makeshift airstrip.

After taking a right out of Vincenzo's property, they drove for half a mile before taking a second right. Then, they took another right a mile after that. The rising sun was on Zahra's right, telling her they were headed north. The two-lane road was in good condition, and based on the absence of traffic, she guessed it was from its lack of use, and not due to recent refurbishment. Up ahead the roadway split, and sitting directly in the middle of the fork, was a squad car with its rooftop lights flashing. No siren accompanied them. The vehicle's owner was leaned up against the trunk lid, arms crossed.

Vincenzo rolled up to the officer and lowered the windows.

"Good morning, Stefano."

The two men shook hands. The police chief greeted everyone else with a quick wave.

"Hello, Vincenzo. Are we ready?"

The mechanic turned and looked back at Zahra. She nodded. "Yes."

Vincenzo opened his door and hopped out of his truck, closely followed by Cork. Zahra and George were last to exit the vehicle and joined Stefano over by his squad car with their gear.

"We've cleared the way for you until you are in the air," Stefano explained in heavily accented English. "Just follow this road to the north."

"That's our runway?" George asked, appalled.

Stefano shrugged. "It is the best we can do for you unless you are willing to load the plane onto a ferry and head to Trapani. That could take all day, though."

"No, this'll do." Zahra put a reassuring hand on her father's shoulder. "We'll be fine. Cork can handle it."

"I 'can handle' what?" the pilot asked, stepping over. She had not heard anything.

"The takeoff," George replied. He jabbed a finger to the left-hand road. "Down that."

Cork turned and faced the narrow roadway. Even Zahra could tell the Cessna's wings were barely going to stay clear of the trees growing off to either side.

The pilot shrugged. "Shouldn't be a problem."

"*Shouldn't*?" Stefano asked, standing straighter.

"She says that a lot," George muttered, keeping his eyeing off the pilot.

Cork sneered at him but didn't respond. "Nothing is certain until we're in the air," she said, turning back to the police officer. Now, it was Stefano's turn to look nervous, joining in with George. It was evident that the cop was beginning to regret his decision to help. "But don't worry your cheeks," Cork continued, "I'm damn confident I can do this."

Her reassurance didn't help the two men's mood. Zahra knew her friend well and was also confident in her abilities to get them safely off the ground.

"Let's go," Zahra said, picking up her stuff and heading for the Cessna. "We have no time to waste."

George, begrudgingly, followed his daughter over to the plane. As she tossed her bag in the door, George laid his hand on her back.

"This is crazy, Zahra."

She nodded. "I know, but we don't have a choice. Baahir is running out of time."

"You don't know that?"

She sighed and turned. Her eyes looked tired, and her shoulders were rolled inward. Zahra wasn't the beaming light of poise she typically was.

"Look, Dad, people like Khaliq Ayad are only going to keep valuable assets around for so long. Once Baahir does whatever he's been forced to do, there will be no reason to keep him around. He'll become nothing more than a loose end." She looked up at the clear blue sky. "One that will need to be cut free."

"She's right, Mr. Kane," Cork added. "I've personally dealt with people like this Khaliq guy, and it rarely ever turns out well for those in your son's position. We really do need to get moving. We also still have a few stops along the way." She patted the plane's hull. "My bird is reliable...ish, and I know I can get us there in one piece, but — "

"But it won't matter if we're still standing here talking about it next week."

Zahra waved her goodbyes and thanks to Vincenzo and Stefano and climbed inside.

Cork shrugged. "That wasn't exactly what I was going to say, but sure, whatever..."

The Kanes buckled in. Cork secured the door and then squeezed into the cockpit, swiftly going over things. She flicked switches and tapped on seemingly random gauges. Her fingertip struck one of the instruments, and it instantly came to life. Zahra cringed when she saw it was the altimeter.

She may have exaggerated the condition of the *Puss. E. Galore* a little to her father...and to herself.

The front and back props came to life, startling George. His fingers tightened around his armrests, and he nervously looked out the windshield and swallowed. Cork pulled them away from the fork and down the left-hand side of the road a bit before increasing their speed. Zahra watched as people stepped outside to gawk at the plane using their rural street as a runway.

"What are they doing?" George asked.

"They're here for the entertainment!" Cork called back. "I doubt they've ever seen anything like this before!"

Zahra was going to add a snarky comment but was too zoned-in on what she and Cork had said about Baahir's situation. They were both right. Once her brother's usefulness wore out, he'd die.

Cork applied consistent pressure on the thrust lever, pushing it, and the aircraft forward. The lightweight plane quickly got up to takeoff speed. Cork didn't waste any time. She eased the nose of the Cessna up, and they rapidly began their ascension into the cool Mediterranean sky.

"So," George asked, "where to?"

Zahra looked to Cork for a reply.

"Based on mileage, I'd say somewhere in Greece would work best...but I have a feeling Zahra is about to try and convince me to head straight for Port Said." She peered into her rearview mirror. "Am I right?"

"Um, well," Zahra stammered, "you did agree that getting to Baahir ASAP was a matter of life and death."

Cork sighed. "Yeah, I did." She growled. "Me and my big mouth."

Ifza quickly shut the door behind her. She was due to meet with her brother as soon as she was done checking on Grant. He was just across the hall from the surgical suite, preparing the sacred canopic jar for transition. It's what the Book of the Dead called the process of the hellstone changing to its life-taking form. It transitioned from the harmless to the harmful.

The Ayad siblings had grown up with this exact possibility in mind, though, if Ifza was being honest, she never thought she'd see the day that it would happen. So many others in their bloodline had failed before them. Why were they to be the ones to succeed? What made her and her brother so special? No one had been more devout to the cause than their grandfather.

*Until Khaliq was born.*

His beliefs were unshakeable, and above all else, were at the forefront of everything he did. Ifza wasn't too far behind. She wanted the plague to come about as much as anyone. Her desire to see it came from her need to cleanse the planet of the weak and unworthy.

The Ayads were worthy.

Ifza pushed off the surgical suite's door and closed the short distance between it and the adjacent examination room. It was where her brother had set up shop. He had spent the last day, since arriving from Cairo with Baahir, preparing for his part in the transition.

Ifza took a deep breath and turned the doorknob. It quietly opened to reveal a low-lit space beyond. The only light within the room was a ring of candles encircling her brother.

He was kneeling in the center of the circle, wearing nothing except a traditional shendyt. The kilt-like garment was standard attire for a wide variety of social classes from ancient times but was typically worn by nobles or those from the upper class.

Khaliq's was constructed out of the finest silk, instead of linen, as was the custom, and was incredibly soft to the touch. He wore a crown on his bald head that featured the jackal head of Anubis, and his neck and wrists were adorned with jewelry made of pure gold. He certainly did look like a Egyptian pharaoh.

And every king had an enforcer. That was Ifza's calling. When her brother needed something special done, she went out and did it personally. She loved being involved and getting her hands dirty. Ifza didn't know anything else. She had been trained in the art of warfare since the day she could walk.

"Ifza," Khaliq said, motioning to the floor next to him, "come, sit beside me."

The stoic killer straightened her posture and marched forward. The air in the room was unnerving. Heat radiated from a small, electric stovetop. Resting atop it was a familiar stone bowl. The two-thousand-year-old, hand-cut artifact had been the oldest heirloom in the Ayad family tree until the canopic jar resurfaced.

Ifza took her place on her brother's right hand and settled in on her knees like him. Khaliq raised a sack similar to the one she had used on Grant and handed it to her. But instead of it housing a man's head, this one contained something infinitely more valuable. Carefully, she procured the Anubian jar and admired it in the light. Just holding it gave her the chills, despite the warmth of the room.

"I give you the honors," Khaliq said, holding open the sack. "Tonight, we see if what our family has stood for is true, or not."

Ifza slipped the irreplaceable piece of antiquity back into the sack and stood. She tied the open end shut with a simple leather strap and looked to her brother for confirmation.

Khaliq nodded once.

She stepped away from the stove and lifted the jar above her head, picturing it in all its glory. Then, with a savage growl, she slammed the precious artifact onto the floor, picking it up and doing it again and again until it was damaged beyond repair. Eyes wide and out of breath, she presented the ruined jar back to her brother, who gleefully accepted the offer.

Khaliq set the bag down and untied it. He reached in and picked out a piece no larger than a Ping-Pong ball. The chunk went into a second, larger stone bowl, and the thickly built Scales of Anubis leader went about grinding it into a fine powder with nothing more than his strength and will and a cylindrical grinding stone. He placed the second bowl between his knees to hold it in place and then got to work.

Ifza was amazed by how quickly he got into a rhythm. She silently watched, biting her lip as he got closer and closer to completing the millennia-old task. Neither one of them knew exactly what would cause the transition to take place. To the naked eye, it was just another piece of volcanic rock. Even Anubis' teachings didn't properly describe it.

Dripping sweat and panting like a dog, Khaliq set down the grinding stone and lifted the larger of the two bowls above his head. In between heavy breaths, he said a prayer to Anubis and to their ancestors to guide them on their next journey. If this worked, it would only be the beginning.

Khaliq poured the powdered stone into the boiling water within the Ayad family bowl. The liquid within it instantly turned to an inky black, and it swirled with a shimmer that typically came from precious metals. There was definitely something else in the igneous rock besides solidified magma.

Khaliq lifted the bowl above his head and said one last prayer before bringing the steaming bowl to his lips. With wild, untamable eyes, Khaliq took a sip and closed his eyes. According to the legend, the deadly concoction would begin its work within seconds of entering the human body.

He offered the bowl to Ifza. She swallowed her rising fear and accepted it.

"Do not be afraid, sister," Khaliq said. "We were born for this."

Ifza always loved the idea of being immune to a deadly plague, but now, here, with it right in front of her... She shut up her mind and followed in her brother's footsteps and drank.

"Come." Khaliq stood. "We need more blood."

"I have the perfect test subject." She frowned and picked up a piece of the broken jar. "We also need more hellstone."

Khaliq smiled. "Yes, our subject will help with that too."

**The Lighthouse of Port Said** | Port Said, Egypt

Nestled up against the Mediterranean Sea and the Suez Canal is Egypt's fifth largest city. As its name suggested, Port Said's bustling harbor community houses over a half-million people. It was founded in 1859 and named after the country's ruler at the time, Mohamed Sa'id Pasha.

Uncle Wally had given Zahra insight into his hometown when she was a little girl. He always believed that Port Said had always been overlooked as one of the greatest cities in all of Egypt. Typically, travelers came to the country for the historical and archaeological wonders found in places like Cairo, Giza, Luxor, Alexandria, and Thebes.

*And he was right,* Zahra thought, staring out over the glimmering water.

Besides its noteworthy beaches, Port Said's other main feature was its now retired lighthouse, a landmark that was completed just one week prior to the Suez Canal's inauguration in 1869. As the years went by, the infrastructure surrounding the lighthouse changed drastically. Contemporary buildings sprouted out of the sand containing the likes of commercial businesses, restaurants, hotels, and homes. Even a modern shopping mall had been built next door to the architectural marvel. The three-story building looked incredibly odd, sitting directly across the street from the 153-year-old lighthouse.

Zahra glanced down at her watch hand and confirmed the time. Wally had texted her and told her to be at the top of the lighthouse at this time, on the dot. And yet, he wasn't here. There wasn't anything for her to do but wait. So, she leaned forward atop the rails of the octagonal tower and appreciated the view. Having some alone time was a blessing, in retrospect. Her father and Cork had, once again, stayed behind to let Zahra work. This time, they were holing up in a motel deeper into town.

Zahra had no idea what to expect from Wally. She also didn't know whether or not the Scales of Anubis had men on the ground. At this point, Zahra needed to assume they had agents placed in every major Egyptian city. She'd rather be overly paranoid than unprepared and caught off guard.

"That's probably what Wally is doing right now," she mumbled, getting a look from a man to her left. He and his kids were atop of the national monument with Zahra, gawking, enjoying the scenic backdrop. The breeze coming off the water wasn't bad either.

*Nothing like Levanzo, though.* The balcony view would be forever etched into her mind. Their arrival into Egypt had gone much smoother than she had expected. They had arrived on fumes but did so by using an actual runway this time, instead of a cramped, four-lane road.

Zahra dipped her head and closed her eyes, listening to the world around her. She wasn't sure how long she had zoned out. But a familiar voice broke the silence.

"Zahra?" She spun around and found herself alone with a very different-looking Waleed Badawi. "Is that really you?" He looked nothing like the man she once knew — but it was him. His eyes gave him away. Gone was his shoulder-length, dark hair and clean-cut face. Wally now sported a shaved head and a graying beard that reached down to his chest. He was also a good thirty pounds lighter than when Zahra had seen him last.

"Hey, Wally. Yeah, it...it's been a long time."

His eyes looked sad. "Yes, it has." He shifted his weight, looking uncomfortable. "Why are you here?"

Zahra had purposely kept the exact reason she had come from him. She wasn't sure if he would have agreed to meet her, or not, if he had known what was really going on.

Zahra dug into her jacket pocket and removed the picture her father had given her. She stepped forward and handed it over to him. Wally's eyes locked onto the image and, if it were possible, they became even sadder. This wasn't the funny, happy-go-lucky *uncle* from her past. He had obviously been through a lot since Zahra had last seen him.

They all had.

"I know everything about my mother." Wally snapped his attention back to Zahra. He kept silent and waited for Zahra to say whatever she was about to say. "Khaliq Ayad has her canopic jar."

If Zahra could describe Wally's reaction, it would have been one of agony. It looked as if the man's heart had just been torn out of his chest.

"That is unfortunate to hear," he replied, handing the photo back to Zahra. She shook her head.

"I want you to have it."

He nodded his thanks. "Is that all you've come to tell me? You could have saved yourself some trouble and called."

Now, it was really time to bear the *real* bad news.

"The Scales of Anubis also have the original Book of the Dead."

"What?" Wally took a step back. "No! How?"

"You, uh, can thank Baahir for that."

Wally turned and gripped the railing with both hands, squeezing it until the blood drained from his fingers. He took a deep breath and let go.

"Where did he find it?"

"Beneath a golf course in Giza, of all places. The road got taken out by a storm and in the destruction, a hidden temple that houses the scroll was revealed." Zahra dropped her eyes. "That's when all hell broke loose. A lot of people have died since then."

She recited everything that had happened so far.

Wally took it all in and mentally worked it all out. He knew more about this stuff than Zahra — possibly even her father.

"Did you come alone?"

Zahra shook her head. "Dad is with me — not here — but he's in Port Said."

"George came along with you? That surprises me."

Zahra blushed. She had forgotten to mention how her father had joined her. "I sorta dragged him along."

Wally grinned. "How'd he take it?"

Zahra smiled. "Not well. He's getting a crash course in how I do things." The delight faded. "I think he has finally realized that I'm not his little girl anymore." She crossed her arms. "Will you help us?"

He turned back toward the water, lost in thought. "I don't have much of a choice, do I?" He stood tall. "If we don't stop the Scales of Anubis, millions will die." Wally locked eyes with Zahra. "Potentially many more."

Wally pushed away from the rail, crossed the balcony, and opened the door leading back down to the ground floor. Zahra entered and descended the first set of stairs, pausing at the landing. She turned to check on Wally and noticed the limp in his right leg. She had known that he had a limp, but this seemed more extensive. She'd never seem him cringe so much while he was walking. Wally noticed the attention.

"How's the knee?" Zahra asked.

"Like the rest of me, older. It has good days and bad days." He snorted. "More bad days as of late." They kept moving, nearly halfway back to the bottommost level. "Were you ever told how I injured it in the first place?"

Zahra did remember. "A soccer match, right?"

Wally snickered. "I guess you don't know..." They paused at the middlemost platform, and Zahra placed her hands on her hips. The stance told Wally that they wouldn't be moving again until he came clean. "It happened the night we got your mother out of the country."

Both of Zahra's eyebrows hit the ceiling. "What?"

He nodded. "As soon as my men and I got her loaded up, we were ambushed by Ayad's men — Khaliq's father's people." He flexed the joint. "I was the only survivor, though the bullet left its mark."

"You were shot?"

"First and only time." He winced and descended another step. "At the end of the day, we did a good thing — the right thing." Zahra turned but was stopped. "And yet, here we are, in the same mess that we attempted to prevent all those years ago." He sighed. "Fate can be cruel, yes?"

Zahra agreed, thinking of everything her family had been through. "It sure can."

# BAAHIR

**The Pharaoh's Lounge** | Giza, Egypt

The elevator door slid open to reveal Ifza and the two large men from her brother's private bar. Baahir watched them pound down the ancient steps and make a beeline straight toward him. At this point, he wasn't afraid of what they could do to him. Even in the short time being held captive, he was already numb to their threats. He was a realist about death. If Baahir was to die at the hands of these animals, then so be it.

Ifza held up her hand, pausing the two men from ten feet back. She continued forward and waltzed up to Baahir, who was still lying down on this cot, ankles crossed, hands behind his head. If Ifza expected him to jump to his feet so that he could drop on his knees and kiss hers, then she could kiss another part of his anatomy.

"Hi there," he said, nonchalantly greeting her.

"Come with me," she said, getting right to it.

Baahir sighed and sat up, and swung his feet over the side of the bed. He looked up into her intense eyes. "What for?"

"I need to show you something," she grinned. "Trust me."

Baahir burst out in laughter.

Ifza raised a clenched fist, but held back the punch. Still, Baahir got quiet as soon as the threat had arisen. The fanatic looked amused by Baahir's reaction, then took a step back to allow Baahir to get to his feet. As soon as he did, Ifza spun away and headed back toward the lift. The two guards didn't budge an inch until Baahir got moving.

With the pair of hulking men in tow, Baahir swiftly caught up with Ifza, entered the elevator, and watched her press the button to close the door. It was just Baahir and Ifza now. If he wanted to make a break for it, now was the time.

Not that he had a remote chance in hell of defeating the woman in a fight. Even beneath her black thermal, it was plain to see Ifza was well-built. She could easily kick the crap out of Baahir with her eyes closed.

*What I wouldn't give to see her go toe-to-toe with Zahra.*

The thought of his sister refilled his emptying gas tank of hope. Grant believed that she was alive, and Baahir needed to trust the young man.

The elevator door slid open. Ifza didn't move to leave. Instead, she motioned for Baahir to go first.

"First window on the left," she said.

Baahir took two steps toward the window but stopped when Khaliq joined them from an empty doorway to the right.

And he looked like an Egyptian pharaoh.

"Why are you dressed like that?" Baahir asked, honestly confused by the man's choice in apparel.

"It is the clothing of a king," Khaliq replied, deadpan.

"A king?" Baahir asked, confused. "You believe you're of royal blood?"

Khaliq opened his hands, motioning to the three of them. "We all are. Our lineage proclaims it."

Baahir shook his head, and placed his hands on his hips, exhausted. "You guys really are something, aren't you?" He squeezed his fists tight and shouted. "Anubis is a myth! We are not related to him, because he wasn't real."

Baahir's outburst got no reaction out of Khaliq. Ifza, on the other hand, stepped toward him, drawing a pistol as she did.

"Sister, no," Khaliq turned to face her and held up a hand. "He needs to see." He faced Baahir. "He needs to believe."

Baahir refrained from rolling his eyes, but he did as the siblings requested and stepped over to the first window on the left. It was long and rectangular. Baahir felt like a detective on the hidden side of a one-way mirror. But instead of building a case against some two-bit car thief or even a perverted Peeping Tom, Baahir searched for a wastebasket to vomit into. Grant's condition was unbearable to look at.

But he couldn't turn away.

Ifza's phone vibrated. She lifted it, angling the screen so that it could only be read by her and Khaliq. Whatever the message was, it made both of the Ayads smile.

"Proceed," Khaliq said.

Ifza replied to the sender and then pocketed the device. After a moment of silence and inaction, footsteps from further down the subterranean corridor picked up. Motion-sensitive lights winked to life every ten feet, guiding the way for the new arrival. Baahir didn't recognize the individual, but his scrubs gave him away as a doctor of some kind. In his hands was a single black, rectangular box, not unlike what a celebratory fountain pen would be presented in.

The newcomer stopped in front of Khaliq and bowed his head slightly, presenting the box to him. The Scales of Anubis leader gently accepted the container and lifted its lid. Baahir couldn't spot its contents, but whatever the box contained, it was satisfying to the elder Ayad. Ifza placed a reassuring hand on her brother's shoulder and squeezed. The gesture moved them along.

"Do it," Khaliq ordered, closing and handing the box back to the doctor.

The other man backed away.

Baahir watched him enter the surgical suite. When he did, he finally spoke up.

"Who is that?"

"A dear friend," Khaliq replied, keeping the explanation short.

The way the man moved gave away his training. He really was a doctor of some sort. He placed the box atop a rolling cart and pushed it up next to the table holding the motionless Grant Upton. The doctor lifted Grant's left wrist and held it while checking his watch.

*Looking for a pulse,* Baahir thought.

The doctor gave no indication that he had found one, and when he replaced Grant's arm by his side, it flopped off the table before the doctor moved it back into place.

It was the first time that Baahir contemplated that he was staring at a dead man.

"You killed him?" he asked, sidestepping away from Ifza.

Khaliq kept his eyes glued to the scene on the other side while his sister turned and faced Baahir.

"No, he is only in an induced coma. "We saved his life, actually."

Baahir tried to laugh heartily, but it came out as nothing more than an exhausted gasp for air. "You saved him? How? You poisoned him!" Baahir's eyes flicked back to Grant. "You're all monsters."

Ifza's eyes narrowed. "Watch your words, Dr. Hassan, or you'll end up just like him." She pointed into the room — to Grant.

Baahir knew he should do as she said and watch his words carefully, but he couldn't.

"Better than becoming anything like you."

Ifza smiled. "You already are." She shared a soft laugh with her brother. The Ayads thought they were enjoying an inside joke at Baahir's expense, and he was more than happy to spoil the moment.

Baahir faced the window. "Just because we share the same blood *does not* make us the same." He snapped his head to the right and glared at the surprised siblings. Both were looking at him, confused. "Yes, I know about our family history, and it means absolutely nothing to me." Lost in his emotional outburst, Baahir spun and stepped toward his captors, banging the base of his fist on the glass. "The Ayad name means nothing!"

Ifza lashed out and slammed her fist into Baahir's face, dropping him to the floor with the single punch.

Baahir prodded his bloodied lip and then wiggled a newly loosened tooth with his tongue. He didn't care. It had been worth getting what he said off his chest. Plus, he was still alive.

Ifza loomed over him.

"Sister, stop." Khaliq spoke softly. "He spits insults because he is helpless and afraid."

Baahir climbed to his feet. He peeked into the suite and stopped where he was. On one knee, he watched the doctor plunge a syringe full of black liquid into Grant's neck. He applied consistent pressure to the plunger until the last drop was gone. Baahir was appalled. Never in his life would he have thought he'd be watching an innocent man be experimented on. He stood and waited, unsure of what would happen next. He doubted the Ayads knew what to expect either. This was uncharted territory for everyone.

"What's the black stuff?"

"That is powdered hellstone," Khaliq explained. "Once it is hydrated, it transforms into something amazing."

"Don't you mean something appalling?"

Khaliq ignored him and took his sister's hand. They appeared nervous. It was an uncommon characteristic for the killers.

Nothing happened.

# CHAPTER 58
# ZAHRA

**The Lighthouse at Port Said** | Port Said, Egypt

Zahra made it to the bottom first. This time, she opened the door and held it open for her *uncle*. It was still hard to accept the fact that Wally wasn't really a member of the family. But did he have to be to still be something more to Zahra? He had put his own life on the line all those years ago to protect her mother. That had to count for something, right?

She pushed open the door and was immediately hit by the incoming breeze coming off the water. She could smell the saltiness of the air and the natural calmness the seaside flow brought her. Zahra loved the coast, no matter where she was in the world.

Patiently, she waited for the elder man. If she had to guess, Wally must have been in his late sixties by now, though the heavy limp portrayed him as much older than that. He was halfway down the steps when Zahra turned and peeked back out over the water. A commotion had picked up in the area surrounding the lighthouse's eastern entrance. The shadows of a dozen pine and palm trees made it difficult to make out exactly what the disturbance was. Port Said had seen its share of violence. Every place in Egypt had at some point.

A cloud moved away to unveil the uproar's origin, and the party responsible for it. Locals and out-of-towners, alike, ran amuck, veering around a trio of men standing fifty feet from Zahra and the base of the lighthouse. The guy in the middle knelt and lugged a heavy-looking metal tube onto his shoulder.

*Oh, shit.*

Zahra let go of the door and ran back the other way, grabbing Wally by the arm as she began to reascend the stairs.

"RPG!" she shouted, pulling the stumbling man along with all her might.

They reached the first landing, hooked a right, but didn't move any higher. At this angle, if they squeezed against the far wall, the entrance was hidden behind the next step of concrete stairs.

*Hopefully, they're solid enough.*

The door to the Port Said lighthouse disintegrated as it, and the surrounding support structure, was decimated by the rocket-propelled grenade. Debris was tossed everywhere, some of it deflecting around the tight confines of the stairwell and hitting its occupants. Wally had thought fast and had covered Zahra and himself with his cloak, keeping most of the shrapnel out. However, some did hit them. As he removed his cloak, both he and Zahra realized they were bleeding from tiny cuts to their exposed skin. Zahra felt the sting of filth socializing with an open wound on her chin.

Shouts arose, and two men entered the cloud of dirt and dust, brandishing twin AK-103 rifles. Zahra drew her gun from beneath her jacket and opened fire.

Wally did as well, pulling a pistol from a hidden holster Zahra hadn't known he had been wearing.

Each pursuer went down, sporting a pair of gunshot wounds before they could even get a shot off. Thankfully, the bodies weren't that of local law enforcement or the military. Their civilian clothes and masked faces identified them as what Zahra figured were mercenaries, or, more than likely, members of the Ayad cabal.

Additional voices announced the arrival of more men. Zahra and Wally were outnumbered and outgunned. Being attacked, out in the open, at the most famous landmark in Port Said was not something either of them had taken into account. A wave of automatic gunfire got Zahra and Wally moving. With nowhere else to go, they headed back up the way they had come.

"We can't go this way!" Wally yelled.

Zahra heard him, even past the ringing in her ears. "Like hell, we can't!"

Wally squeezed her wrist, but they kept moving higher. "There's no exit!"

She didn't care. Anywhere was better than sitting idly by where they were. If anything, they could get to the top, and back outside, and call for help. The concrete walls of the lighthouse tower were surely blocking all cell service, not that Zahra had the time to check. She kept her Glock trained on the route behind her and climbed higher.

Wally slowed and allowed Zahra to pass him. He was tiring and in need of a break. The break came in the form of a crack in the landing beneath his feet. The fault grew quickly, suddenly giving way and depositing Wally onto the landing, a floor below.

"Wally!" Zahra shouted, leaning over the gap in the staircase.

"Go!" he shouted, holding his bad knee. He slowly got back to his feet and waved her off. "I will find another way out!"

She couldn't believe her eyes. Wally had just fallen over ten feet and had somehow been spared a devastating injury. One by one, the stairs beneath Zahra's feet fell away, chasing her up to the next landing. She didn't stop there. Zahra kept going, round and round, until she reached the outside observation platform.

Zahra took a moment to catch her breath and gripped the rail, setting her forehead on her hands. A series of unnerving quakes interrupted her respite. She looked over the edge at the grounds just outside the ruined entry point. The asshole armed with the RPG swung it back up to his shoulder and swiftly fired a second explosive at the base of the lighthouse. The subsequent detonation was enough to get a groan and an ear-splitting crack out of the monument. Massive chunks of concrete broke away from the tower and fell to earth. The thunderclaps continued, as did the upward moving crack.

Zahra was nearly two hundred feet in the air with nowhere to go but straight down. She desperately surveyed the area around her for an escape plan but found nothing. Even from where she was, her grappling hook wouldn't reach anything useful. With one last shudder, the lighthouse separated a third of the way up. The top portion, and Zahra, slowly tilted northeast. She hung onto the railing for dear life and reflexively closed her eyes and locked her jaw.

*No!* she thought, snapping them open. *This isn't over!*

People scattered, getting as far away as possible. Zahra did a double take when she spotted a cloaked figure leap from a hole in the side of the lighthouse. Wally launched himself out of the crumbling structure, landing somewhere within the bushy canopy of a pine tree. Zahra couldn't tell if he made it to safety or fell to his death. She couldn't concentrate on Wally's circumstances. Zahra had her own shit to deal with first. *If* she survived, then she'd check on the older man.

The lighthouse leaned back to the north, directly into the newer three-story building. It was the mall that Zahra had spotted earlier. And based on the current rate of descent, she and the lighthouse were about to squish it like a bug. For good measure, Zahra unclipped her grappling hook from her belt and snapped its clawed head open. She wasn't sure when or how she was going to use it, but she needed to be prepared.

The last of the compromised tower gave way, and it fell like a cut redwood. Zahra laced her hook into the railing and coiled the cord around her right wrist. The lighthouse smashed through the mall's roof but didn't completely obliterate the much smaller building. The modern construction held its own and absorbed most of the impact. The abrupt stop jarred the railing, and Zahra, free and they both went tumbling through a hole where a twenty-by-twenty skylight used to be. Zahra covered her head with her hands and was surprised when she didn't go *splat!*

Instead, she bounced off a, now-ruined, mattress set and thanked her lucky stars she had entered directly above the retailer's bedding supplies.

But she didn't stick around to gawk.

Another section of the ceiling broke free.

The overwhelming girth of the lighthouse was going to eventually win the battle. Zahra needed to not be around when it happened. She untangled herself from the bed's comforter and turned and planted a hand atop a dresser, and vaulted over it, heading for the center of the department store. Up ahead, a sign dangled dangerously from the ceiling, showing her where the nearest escalator was. Multiple escalators were situated on the outskirts of a wide opening at the center of the department store. Here, Zahra would be able to clearly see the floors beneath her. She ran for the exit as the sign fell. It nearly clipped her heels as she passed beneath it.

An enormous section of ceiling caved in directly in front of her, and she quickly changed course. As Zahra had done with the dresser, she planted her hand on the railing next to the escalator and jumped. She fell six feet and landed gracelessly on the still mobile stairway. Zahra was stunned to see that it was operational. Between the suddenness of the landing, the forward momentum of the moving staircase, and the rumbling of the room, Zahra went down, falling sideways. She rolled and bounced down the unforgiving metal stairs and landed on her chest.

"Ouch…"

Zahra flopped onto her back and stared up through the open hole in the ceiling. She could just barely see the clear blue sky through the ever-widening gap. And through that hole, Zahra witnessed the entire uppermost section of the lighthouse — the lantern room — tear away from the rest of the tower and plummet directly toward her, smashing through the remains of the ruined skylight with ease.

Eyes wide, she rolled onto her hands and knees and dove forward, curling into a ball and covering her head with her arms. As the living room-sized wrecking ball passed by, a mangled section of the observation platform's railing snared her open grappling hook. Zahra didn't notice it in time and was unable to unwind the cord from her wrist, and she was swiftly yanked along with it.

"Shit!" she cried, disappearing below.

# CHAPTER 59
# BAAHIR

Baahir wanted nothing more than to leave, return to his station, and put this grotesque show behind him. He went to step away but stopped when he saw movement from someone other than the doctor. Grant's hand twitched once. Then, again.

"It's working," Ifza whispered. She grabbed Khaliq's arm and squeezed. "It's working!"

Grant's movements appeared to worry the doctor. Baahir thought he saw fear in the guy's eyes. He backed away from the *subject* and headed for the door but was unable to leave. Khaliq calmly pressed his thumb against another door pad, locking the man inside. The doctor tried several times to unlock the door. When he discovered that he couldn't, his confusion quickly morphed into terror. He rushed to the examination window and banged on it. The thick glass quieted his frantic impacts down to nothing. It felt like Baahir was watching an old-timey, silent movie.

*A horrifying one.*

Miraculously, Grant sat up. He lifted his hands to his head, squeezing it hard, going as far as to beat his own skull with his closed fists. Whatever was happening to him, Baahir got the impression that Grant wanted it to stop.

Then, he stopped, slowly lowering his hands and looking them over as if he was seeing them for the first time. Baahir couldn't describe it in any other way. His attention turned to the rest of his body. He ran his hands across his chest and poked at his right biceps. He slowly swung his legs over the edge of the table, and for the first time, Grant noticed that he wasn't alone.

He lifted his eyes away from his own body. The sight made all four people take a giant step back.

"I..." Baahir muttered, voice shaking, "I don't think *this* was in the Bible."

"No," Ifza said, swallowing hard, "this... this is something else."

"Something magnificent."

Both Baahir and Ifza turned toward Khaliq, a man who was wholly enthralled by what he saw. There was joy in his eyes. He looked like a child on Christmas morning.

Grant's eyes were completely black. They contained none of the separations of color. The pupils, irises, and whites were all an inky black.

The doctor pressed his back against the glass as if anticipating what was about to transpire.

Grant Upton slid down from the table and attacked.

The doctor didn't stand a chance.

Ifza turned away first, raising a shaking hand to her mouth.

Baahir wasn't far behind her, seeing blood spray into the air in his periphery. It slathered the window in a healthy layer. He held back the contents of his stomach and stumbled back toward the elevator.

"Wha — " he gagged, "What happened to him?"

"Grandfather said that our sacred bloodline keeps us protected from the effects the hellstone has on the unworthy."

"And those that don't share our lineage?" Baahir asked.

Ifza looked at him. Her hard eyes had been softened by the carnal display. "They become something worse than death."

Fear. It was the first emotion Baahir had seen out of the killer other than rage.

The elevator door slid open, and out stepped one of the large guards from upstairs. He pushed past Baahir, slowing when he took in the gruesome scene. Still, he continued forward and swiftly conversed with his superiors.

Baahir didn't hear much, but what he did hear lifted his spirits.

*Zahra?*

Ifza stepped around the guard and bore holes into Baahir. "It seems that your dear sister has survived. She's been spotted in Port Said and is traveling with a man who has long been a thorn in our side."

Khaliq growled and headed back into the room across the hall from the surgical suite. The man's change in demeanor hinted that he knew who Ifza was talking about.

"Oh, yeah?" Baahir asked, blowing out a long breath. "Who is it I should thank?"

Ifza regained her composure and said, "Waleed Badawi."

Baahir burst out in laughter. "Uncle Wally? That's the guy you've been having trouble with?" This news also called into question Wally's relationship with the Kane family. Knowing what he knew now meant that Wally, plainly, was not his uncle.

*So, who is Waleed Badawi, really?*

Ifza's phone vibrated again. She procured it from her pocket and shouted for her brother. Khaliq reappeared, no longer wearing his Anubian crown. His gold jewelry was gone, as well. The shendyt-kilt was the only covering Khaliq had on from his kingly wardrobe.

"We have our location," she said. "And it is...familiar."

Baahir didn't know what that meant, nor did he have the opportunity to ask.

A strong hand slapped against the window, startling almost everyone. Of the four people in the hallway, Khaliq had been the only one showing no emotion, whatsoever. He stared at the figure moving behind the crimson smear, an intrigued look on his face.

"What will happen to him?" Baahir asked.

A wave of sadness and regret suddenly washed over Khaliq. "Mr. Upton has served his purpose. He will now be terminated and studied." Khaliq didn't look away. "Ifza, intercept Ms. Kane." He finally took his eyes off the carnage and gave the woman a look that Baahir figured he typically used on his enemies. "Don't fail me again."

Ifza shrank away. Fear crept into her eyes. "My men are closing in as we speak." She glanced at Baahir. "I've given them the order to do whatever is necessary to stop her. I will join them shortly."

Khaliq nodded. "Good. I will lead a team into the desert and face my destiny." His eyes moved from Ifza to Baahir. "And you, *cousin*, are coming with me."

# CHAPTER 60
# ZAHRA

The world was fuzzy and muffled. Zahra couldn't make out what she was seeing, only that she was currently still indoors — inside the shopping mall. There were a few people rushing about, but the place was mostly deserted now. A security guard was across the way, trying to usher an older couple outside.

She tried to sit up but couldn't muster the strength, not yet. So, she just laid there — somewhere. Her head flopped to the right, and she spotted a familiar face. It was painted white and had big, red lips and an equally red, poofy wig.

*Ronald McDonald?* She blinked and shook her head. *Am I in hell?*

As her vision cleared, Zahra realized that, no, she wasn't in hell, though her stomach would beg to differ based on where she had found herself. Zahra had landed atop the front counter of an Egyptian McDonald's food court eatery.

Footsteps announced someone's arrival. Zahra had no idea whether that someone was a friend or foe. The sound of a pistol's hammer being locked back gave her the answer to her question. They were not friendly. She turned away from the kitchen area and looked out over the quick serve. A masked figure dressed in all black paused when he was spotted.

"Hello," Zahra said, exhausted. She slowly sat up. "Can I take your order?"

"No," the assailant replied, "but you *can* die."

Before Zahra could respond, the man was shot from behind. When he fell, she saw the man's killer, and her savior.

She gazed down at the dead man. "Would you like fries with that?" Zahra tentatively slid down from the counter. "Thanks, Wally." It should have surprised her to see Wally take another man's life so dispassionately, but she was rapidly understanding that the man wasn't what he seemed.

*Nothing* in Zahra's personal life was what it seemed.

He rushed over to her, limping worse than ever. "In the name of Allah, how are you still alive?"

She snickered and grabbed her side. "I... I sometimes ask myself the same question."

Screams could still be heard everywhere around them as they neared the closest exit point. Wally led Zahra over to a crumbled section of wall and helped her down to street level. He disappeared back inside before following her. For her part, Zahra stumbled over to a light post and leaned against it, and waited. Wally reappeared moments later with a pair of dark shawls. He shimmied down to her and carefully outfitted her head and shoulders in the garment. He also adorned the other shawl.

"We must be careful," he explained.

She understood. If the Scales of Anubis still had people in the vicinity, he and Zahra needed to conceal their identities before heading out.

The filthy, dust-covered duo entered the throng of equally grimy onlookers and emergency workers and disappeared without additional confrontation. No one within earshot of the demolition had been spared by the advancing plume of white and gray. The chorus of sirens diminished as Zahra and Wally distanced themselves from what would surely be labeled as a terror attack — which it was. The oldest concrete lighthouse in the world was no more.

And once again, Zahra was at the center of the confrontation.

*First, the museum. Now, this.*

"Come," Wally said, ushering her along. "Over here."

They slipped into an alley and kept moving. Zahra had no idea where they were going, but Wally did. This was his stomping grounds, after all. He knew the streets of Port Said better than anyone. He had spent his entire life living within the city limits. It also meant that the lighthouse's destruction had surely hit him hard, personally. It had been his people's crown jewel.

All of Port Said would be mourning its loss for years to come.

"I'm sorry," Zahra said, feeling the need to apologize. "If I hadn't come here, I — "

"Stop." She did. Wally turned, fire in his eyes. "You are not at fault for this defilement." A killer look washed onto his face. "Khaliq Ayad is to blame." He turned and started off again. "He will not get away with this."

"Where are we going?"

"To my place of business."

"Your business?"

He nodded. "Yes, the Suez Shipping Company. I have some people I'd like you to meet."

"The Suez Shipping Company? How can your shipping company help us?"

He slowed and glanced over his shoulder, and picked his words carefully. "The SSC is not what it seems."

Zahra was certain she knew exactly what Wally meant. While he did operate a legitimate shipping company out of Port Said, it also sounded like he had a good-sized under-the-table operation, as well. Zahra was curious as to precisely what Wally moved through the shadows. He pulled out his phone and dialed. Whoever he was calling picked up immediately. The call ended after a few short words.

"We're almost there." He directed her, heading left around a corner. "Our ride awaits us."

# CHAPTER 61
# ADNAN

**The Pharaoh's Lounge** | Giza, Egypt

After Khaliq and the others had left, a three-man cleanup crew was ordered to the labs. The trio was armed and thickly built. They weren't there to sanitize the gore within the exam room. These men had come to sanitize the individual responsible for it — a man named Grant Upton, apparently.

*Find him, and eliminate him.*

Then, the body would go on ice until it was time to dissect him.

Adnan stood tall, waiting for the elevator door to open. When it did, he stepped out with his team in tow. Haydar and Naeem weren't as experienced as Adnan was with the job, but they were, nonetheless, effective.

"What happened?" Naeem asked. His eyes were glued to the smeared glass.

"It doesn't matter," Adnan replied.

Haydar opened his mouth to speak but didn't get the chance.

His boss snapped his attention to him. "Open the door."

It took him a moment to respond, but Haydar did so with just a nod of his head. He stepped around Adnan and drew his sidearm. He held up a shaky hand and pressed his thumb up against the biometric scanner. A click announced the doorlock's disengagement. Adnan and Naeem fell in line behind Haydar, and all three men swiftly entered the destroyed medical suite.

It was empty, save for the body parts littering the floor.

"Adnan?" Naeem asked, gagging and swallowing his rising bile. "The door...it was locked."

Adnan glared at Naeem. "Which means he is still here."

"Or not," Haydar said, getting both men's attention. He gazed up at the ceiling, right where a section of the ceiling was missing.

"Where does that go?" Naeem asked.

"Ventilation," Adnan replied. "The system is networked to every suite. Check them!"

Haydar and Naeem rushed out of the exam room, darting left and unlocking and entering the neighboring room. Even though his men's voices were slightly muffled, Adnan could hear their screams, plain as day. Khaliq's experiment had set a trap, and Adnan and his team had fallen for it.

Adnan stood his ground and waited, leveling his pistol at the doorway. There was no other way inside except for the hole in the ceiling. He sidestepped away from the opening above his head, keeping his eyes on the door. A noise similar to an angry dog halted his movements. Once more, Adnan stood his ground and waited. He wouldn't be caught off guard as easily as Haydar and Naeem had been.

"Are you there?" he asked, hoping to entice Khaliq's pet. "Are you unhappy with your stay?"

The growling intensified.

Adnan grinned. "Down, dog."

Silence.

"You still there?"

No reply.

Adnan stepped lightly, heel to toe, keeping his footfalls quiet. He paused midway to the doorway and waited. He was a patient person, but he needed to exit the exam room before he was locked inside. At the very least, he needed to call in reinforcements.

He stopped just inside the door and launched himself around the corner, intent on shooting the man responsible for all the bloodshed here. Adnan leveled his firearm at the other open doorway but saw nothing. The hallway was entirely void of life. Adnan took a step backward and immediately bumped into something. He spun on a dime and had his chest caved in by a single, crushing blow.

He felt nothing, and his body suddenly stopped working. His eyes fell to the impact point, and he was stunned to see nothing but a crimson-colored fist pulling away from it. He followed it to its owner, coughing up blood as he met face-to-face with the man who used to be Grant Upton.

*What...the hell?*

The man's exposed upper body rippled with dense musculature. Adnan didn't remember the Brit being so well-built. His body mass resembled that of a steroided wrestler from the eighties and nineties.

*And those eyes...*

*How?* His mind faded. *The... the virus?*

The demon uttered one word. "Ayad." But Adnan was too far-gone to formulate words, and his eyes rolled back.

Upton roared in anger, reached out, and tore Adnan to pieces.

# CHAPTER 62
# IFZA

**Cairo, Egypt**

It would typically take three hours to drive from Giza to Port Said. Ifza didn't have that kind of time. She was currently airborne in her brother's private helicopter, traveling directly to the area in question, and would arrive shortly. She had already received notice of her men's failure to kill Zahra Kane. Even Waleed Badawi was still alive. Their bodies were not among the dead. Authorities had reported gunfire shortly after the lighthouse's decimation. The only people that would be shooting back at her people would be Zahra and Waleed.

"Should I notify Khaliq?" one of her men asked.

"No!" Ifza blurted. "No... I will contact him myself."

Ifza had no plans to tell him, either. His earlier threat still had its fangs dug into her throat.

*"Don't fail me again."*

If he did ask about the mission, Ifza would counter with an explanation that the operation was still in progress — which was true. She knew she could probably pawn off the failed op on the incompetence of her men — men that wouldn't be alive much longer. She was going to personally end their wretched existences once she landed.

She rubbed the sleep from her eyes. *I need better men.* It had been nearly twenty-four hours since Ifza had last slept.

And she wouldn't be getting any sleep anytime soon.

# CHAPTER 63
# ZAHRA

**Suez Shipping Company** | Port Said, Egypt

Wally's operation, the SSC, was seriously impressive. All manner of heavy machinery was present, including three of the largest cranes Zahra had ever seen. The dockside gantry cranes were used to load and unload intermodal containers from container ships. The operator sat in an unsettling, glass-bottomed pilothouse directly above a mechanism called a *spreader*.

Machines like this had always caught Zahra's attention. It wasn't just mankind's past that she was impressed with. She also enjoyed the planet's modern ingenuities. At one time, all the things she studied from ancient times *were* modern ingenuities.

"We've come a long way, huh?" she said, staring up at the cranes in motion.

Wally stepped up next to her. "Yes, we have. And yet..." Zahra unlocked her gaze and glanced at Wally, "we still have no concrete ideas as to how the pyramids were built."

"Sure, we do," Zahra said, turning and heading inside.

"We do?" Wally asked.

She stopped and placed her hands out, palms open, hovering around her head. "Aliens," she said, imitating the well-known meme.

Wally rolled his eyes and stepped around Zahra, leading the way. The two had only just arrived and had yet to go indoors. Upon their arrival,

Zahra had been too absorbed in the trio of gantry cranes. Wally's property only sat two miles down the coast from the lighthouse and could easily be seen from the shoreline. Zahra still couldn't believe the monument had been erased from history, only minutes ago.

The driver had taken a circuitous path back to the SSC.

"What are you doing?" Zahra had asked. "I thought your place was in the other direction?"

"It is," Wally replied, "though I'd rather not have us drive straight to it. We will come in from the south and hopefully throw off the scent of Ayad's dogs."

The plan had worked. They had not been followed.

Before they exited the car, Zahra called her father and instructed him and Cork to join her and Wally.

"Yeah, Dad, we're fine. Just get here as soon as you can. I have a feeling we'll be leaving again soon."

He opened the door to the gray, utilitarian warehouse. They passed by a series of offices where people chatted on phones and clacked away on keyboards. The business was just that, a business. Interestingly enough, no one paid Zahra or Wally any attention, even in their current state of filthiness.

*Hmmm...* Zahra wondered how knowledgeable the people here were of his other dealings.

A door led them into the heart of the SSC. Forklifts zipped around everywhere, carrying anything you could think of. Not only did Wally move entire containers for companies, but it looked as if he also did some local shipping and storing too.

A man around Zahra's age came hustling over to his boss and delivered another gut punch.

"Ayad has mobilized."

Zahra and Wally exchanged worried looks.

"Where are they headed?" Wally asked.

"Southwest — across the desert."

Wally ran a hand over his bald head. "They must have identified the temple's coordinates."

"Dammit!" Zahra slammed her right fist into her left palm. She took a deep breath and calmed. "We're screwed, aren't we?"

Wally scratched his chin. "Maybe... maybe not. Come. I have something else to show you —"

The door to the offices opened again. George and Cork stepped through, accompanied by another of Wally's men. Their eyes scanned the warehouse, eventually landing on Zahra and the operation's owner.

"Waleed," George said, stepping over to him. "It's been too long."

Wally accepted George's outstretched hand.

George looked his daughter up and down and frowned but didn't ask what had happened.

But Cork did.

"Oi, Zahra, you look like *shit*! What happened?"

"The thingy fell down, and I was in it."

Cork frowned, and Wally gazed up at the tall woman.

Zahra turned and performed a brief introduction. "Waleed Badawi, this is Cork. She's... a friend."

The two shook hands, and the cocky Brit elaborated. "I'm her *pilot,* and, if necessary, her pain-tolerant muscle."

"I bet," Wally said, eyes darting back to Zahra. He cleared his throat. "I was about to show Zahra another part of my operation, if you'd care to join us?"

Everyone fell in line behind Wally. One by one, four men added themselves to their group, including the younger guy from earlier. They kept their distance, though. It was plain to see that Wally was being careful. At least a few of the workers inside were more than *just* employees of the SSC.

*Probably the people he wanted me to meet,* Zahra thought, happy she hadn't been relieved of her gun. She didn't think anyone here would try anything stupid, but if they did, she'd be ready to respond.

Cork would be, as well. There was no mistaking that she'd be armed too.

The group headed across the main floor of the warehouse, weaving through rows of conveyor belts and sorting machines. Two additional men joined the rear of the party, making Zahra's anxiety peak. She was about to stop and voice her worries but didn't get the chance.

"We are here," Wally announced, turning around in front of the wall of containers. These were heavily worn, even rustled in some spots. Zahra figured that their condition had put them out of commission.

The younger man stepped up and unlocked a stout padlock from the centermost container. He and Wally pulled open the heavy doors to reveal something odd.

More doors.

These looked new and contained a pair of biometric devices. Both Wally and the other guy placed a palm on a pad, and a blue light activated and scanned their hands. A soft clunk followed their efforts. Unlike the older doors, these slid apart into what Zahra realized were false walls. She leaned around the open container doors and saw nothing out of the ordinary. The modern doors were perfectly hidden behind what the average person would think were unusable shipping containers.

*Impressive,* Zahra thought, eyes wide at what was on the other side of the second set of doors.

Stairs.

The younger man spoke up. "Please, follow me." Wally winked and tipped his head toward the entrance.

Zahra and George stepped up next to Wally. "So," Zahra asked, "who's he?"

"That is Ali," he smiled, "my son."

"Your son?" her father asked. "You have a son?" Apparently, Wally had kept *that* tidbit of information from George over the years.

"Yes, I do, and what lays beyond is his domain."

Cork leaned in close to Zahra as the group moved toward the stairs. "I don't like the sound of that."

"Yeah," Zahra said, "me either."

**Western Desert, Egypt**

The trek along El Wahat Road was long and consisted of nothing except shades of brown. There was nothing to see in any direction other than sand and more sand. The sky held a haze that mutated it from a beautiful blue tapestry to a yellowish murk. But even in the harshest environments, the land would occasionally offer a blemish within the, otherwise, dominating sandscape. Oases weren't just a fictional paradise devised by a writer to torture his sun-stroked protagonist. One such sanctuary protruded from the Western Desert a hundred miles west of the Nile River.

Baahir sat behind the driver, and Khaliq's personal bodyguard, Ajmal, eyes glued to the landscape. Baahir's ears, however, were intently listening to the conversations emanating from the front seats. Khaliq was shouting orders and directions to his personal driver and those navigating the two large SUVs behind them. In Khaliq's hand were photocopies of the last few pages of the Book of the Dead. If Baahir had to wager a guess, he'd say that Khaliq had probably read them a hundred times by now.

Khaliq's men had triangulated the supposed location of the Temple of Anubis using topographical maps and charts from hundreds of years ago, as well as modern-day satellite imaging and even grainy pictures obtained from Google Earth. The trouble was that out here, the earth itself moved — the dunes constantly shifted, changing the topography and landscape, making any reasonable attempt at locating something lost to time nearly impossible, even with modern technology.

But it wasn't these images that scared Baahir. It was the LIDAR — the 'light detection and ranging' — images. These high-resolution images weren't just run-of-the-mill images — they had been created with technology that was prohibitively expensive, then rendered on machines that most individuals couldn't dream of using, much less owning.

It told him that Khaliq had friends in high places. Someone had supplied this madman with images that *no one* — outside of the Egyptian government itself — should have.

*Probably one of his benefactors,* Baahir thought, recalling some of the things that Khaliq had told him. He had comrades with money who had helped him build the Scales of Anubis headquarters beneath *The Pharaoh's Lounge*.

Baahir leaned around the driver and spotted a sign for Bawiti — a town of 30,000 inhabitants nestled within the lush, fertile lands of the Bahariya Oasis. A handful of historical discoveries had been made in Bawiti over the centuries. Tourism was now a major source of income for those living in the town, supplementing jobs that were typically only viable in the iron ore industry.

Khaliq pointed off to their left, and their driver clicked on his blinker to notify the vehicles behind them that they were pulling off. The destination: A gas station.

"What are we doing?" Baahir asked, speaking up for the first time since being loaded into the back of the SUV.

No one replied. They just turned into the station and stopped. Once all three vehicles regrouped, Khaliq turned and faced Baahir.

"What do you know about the tombs discovered in Bawiti?"

Baahir was forced to pull the answer from the far reaches of his memory. "Qarat Qasr Salim... It is of the Twenty-sixth Dynasty, the last native dynasty to rule Egypt before the Persian conquest of 525 B.C."

"Correct, and what of the people entombed here?"

Baahir opened his mouth to answer but balked. He didn't know. He knew of the discovery here, but his depth of knowledge was vague as to who it belonged to.

His non-answer made Khaliq smile. "It belonged to a very wealthy Saite merchant who also happened to be a family member of ours."

Baahir wasn't going to argue the whole 'blood doesn't always make family' thing again. He had accepted that the Ayads were his relatives. The quicker he moved on from the revelation, the better his mental health would be.

"And you think this is where our entrance is?" Baahir asked.

"I do," Khaliq replied.

"You do?"

"Yes," Khaliq nudged the driver, and he got them moving, "it is said that our ancestor was close to finding Anubis' temple, but — "

Baahir put it together. "But the Persian invasion halted his search. You think our predecessor buried his findings with his body, don't you?"

Khaliq smiled and faced forward. "I do."

Baahir looked out his window. Another question — a potential obstacle came to him. "If that's true, wouldn't it have been found by now?"

Khaliq laughed softly. "No, future scholars did not look hard enough."

"How do you know that?"

"Because men like that proceed with caution and preserve the find." Khaliq gazed over his shoulder. His eyes were alight. "I would have flattened the landscape to find it."

# CHAPTER 65
# ZAHRA

The ominous wording Wally had used to hint at what lay beneath the SSC had spooked Zahra, big time. As they descended the stairs within the faux containers, she casually slid her right hand into her jacket, just beneath her shoulder holster, pretending to hold her, truthfully, sore ribs. That wasn't what she was doing, however. Zahra was keeping her hand close to her Glock.

*Come on, Wally,* Zahra mentally willed, *don't do anything stupid.*

Wally had helped them, and seemed admirable and trustworthy, but even some heroes had ulterior motives.

It was confusing to Zahra, too, why people were that way. Wally didn't *feel* like the Deadpool-Venom antihero type, but then again, some people were willing to get their hands very dirty in the name of what was good.

*What they* believed *was good.*

Some people, like Zahra, had their limits. She could never take an innocent life. The people she had killed over the years deserved it, or at the very least, had it coming, eventually. Human life was something to cherish. It crushed Zahra to have to resort to violence. Unfortunately, there were people that could only be stopped through deadly force. The Scales of Anubis, for instance. None of them were going to just lay down their arms because Zahra asked nicely. Fanatics like that would happily die for their cause. It's what made extremist organizations so dangerous. It wasn't the way that they operated. It was the fact that they had zero problems dying to do what they believed was right, no matter how many innocent people died in the process.

Zahra could never be so coldhearted. She looked at her father, then Wally and Ali. She pictured what she would be like if she had been raised in a place like this instead of the United States or England. Her influences had been much different, even with her mother being murdered at such a young age. She still had her father to teach her what was right and wrong. George had done his best with both Zahra and Baahir, but hadn't been the loving, consoling parent.

*Mom was.*

"Are you seeing this?"

Cork's question caught Zahra off guard. She looked up at the taller woman, confused by what she said. Cork glanced back and forth between Zahra and the room they had just entered.

"Earth to Zahra." Cork softly patted Zahra's cheek. When she didn't reply, the pilot grabbed her face between her thumb and forefinger and turned it to the left. "Look."

At the bottom of the hidden staircase was a second bustling shipping and storage facility, only this one handled goods of an illegal variety. Everything weapons related was represented below the Suez Shipping Company. What really caught Zahra's eye were the RPGs hanging along the right-hand wall. They were a match to the one that had been used to take down the Port Said lighthouse.

"Geez..." Zahra said, turning and staring at Wally. "So, *this* is how you got all your money?"

He shrugged. "If you want to make a living selling weapons, I suggest you do so in the Middle East." Wally glanced at his son. "Lots of clients here."

Ali nodded, then started shouting at the group of men standing around doing nothing. The younger man's mousy demeanor had flipped on its head once they had entered the underground sanctum. As Wally had said, this was his son's domain.

George didn't have anything to say. He just stood there dumbfounded.

"You okay, Dad?"

He didn't answer.

Zahra was worried that all of this was going to mentally break her father. This was a world he had never really been a part of. Her mother's past was something George had accepted, but not one he had participated in all that much. Once she had faked her death and come stateside, all George needed to do was love the woman.

"I'm sorry you have to be here."

He closed his eyes and turned his face up. He released his tightly clenched fists and blew out a long breath.

George turned and faced his firstborn. "Well, that makes one of us."

Zahra didn't know what to say. So, she stayed silent and allowed her father to explain.

"Zahra, this is our family's history, regardless of if we choose to accept it or not." He looked out over the facility. "I was too late to the party, but I'm here now. I didn't trust you at first — I thought you were being reckless."

Zahra swallowed, tears in her eyes.

"But you're right. This is *our* fight now. We owe it to your mother to finish this. It's what she would do if she were here."

Cork pretended to gag. "You guys are barmy!"

Zahra looked at her dad and shrugged. George didn't know what the word meant, either.

"It means *crazy*!" Cork shouted, frustrated beyond belief. "You two are fuckin' nuts!"

"That we are." Zahra joined her father and watched the workers move about. She grinned. "That we are..."

Luckily for Baahir and the others, the tombs of Qarat Qasr Salim weren't hard to locate. The often-visited archaeological site had been built into a low plateau and owned a somewhat manicured pathway up to the top. Signs pointed the way, ushering Baahir, Khaliq, Ajmal, and one other man, Feroz, higher. No guns were visible, but the three captors each carried imposing pistols beneath their jackets.

The tomb was smack-dab at the center of a neighborhood. The entrance had been cut directly down into the rock. A single man greeted them, wearing the sweat-stained uniform of a park ranger.

"Hello," he said, waving, "and welcome to the tombs of Qarat Qasr Salim! My name is Daniyal, and I will be your guide!"

Baahir wiped the sweat from his forehead. *He's awfully chipper.* The desert heat was something Baahir was used to, but nothing he liked.

Khaliq mumbled something to Ajmal, and he took Daniyal aside and began explaining something very carefully. Daniyal glanced back and forth between the goon and Baahir before nodding and accepting an envelope. Baahir watched as Daniyal opened it to find a stack of cash.

"You're paying him off?" Baahir asked.

Khaliq nodded. "Occasionally, subtlety works. Lots of eyes here." He motioned to the homes surrounding the site. "We need this man to forget we were here."

"And if he doesn't forget?"

The larger man shrugged. "He dies. Ajmal is also explaining that."

On cue, Daniyal's eyes widened. Ajmal placed a thick hand on the park ranger's shoulder and squeezed. Daniyal fervently nodded, gripping the wad of money tightly. He backed away and then scurried down the entrance, disappearing from sight.

"We can begin," Khaliq announced, tipping his head toward the entry point. "After you."

Baahir headed off, unsure of what he was looking for. This site had been ransacked by graverobbers during Roman times, though the tomb contained well-preserved vibrant wall paintings. Baahir had seen pictures of the excavation but had never visited it until now.

The four men descended a hand-cut stairway with an incredibly low ceiling. Baahir was happy to see there was artificial lighting below. The burial was a popular tourist attraction and had been given an update over the years for its visitors to enjoy. No one would need their flashlights.

The steps continued into a circular chamber of an impressive size. The man that had originally been entombed here must have been fabulously wealthy. Usually, places like this were reserved for royalty, and, as it were, the filthy rich. Baahir was curious if any of that wealth had been passed down to the Ayads.

*Doesn't matter.*

He inspected the room, floor to ceiling, and found nothing of note.

"There has to be something," Baahir said to himself.

Khaliq was a madman, yes, but he was also smart and well-studied. He wouldn't have dragged a team this far without a solid conviction. Plus, Baahir needed to stay relevant.

He turned and rubbed his eyes, uncaring that his hands were dirty. Baahir was already a mess, and he had barely done anything of note.

"Trouble?"

It was Khaliq. Baahir's hands fell away, and he faced the man. When he did, his eyes found the wall on the other side of the room. He stared at it, looking past his captor. Khaliq noticed that his attention was somewhere else, and he looked where Baahir was focusing his attention.

"Good eye."

Both men headed over to a painting depicting what Baahir recognized as the Bahariya Oasis. Stone structures dotted the landscape, giving Baahir and Khaliq a bird's eye view of the ancient world. There were recognizable places, but not where Baahir would have expected them to be. It was as if he was looking through a time machine.

Both men leaned in and tried to make out exactly what they were looking at.

"It's a map!" Baahir exclaimed, leaning away. "Or... it *was* a map."

Sections of it had been lost to time, but much of it was still discernible. They located Qarat Qasr Salim, which was highlighted by a brilliant, yellow sun. Other than that, Baahir saw very little else of note. The map, while impressive considering its age, wasn't much help to them. Baahir was about to give up but noticed a black smudge to the north of the oasis.

"What is that?" Baahir asked, pointing at the conical formation.

Khaliq scratched his chin. "Gebel Dist. It sits just to the north of the oasis. Some say it was what inspired our people to use pyramidal designs."

"Yes, I know the formation is Gebel Dist — but what is *that?*" Baahir hovered a finger over the smudge sitting on top of the oasis landmark. "It kind of looks like..."

He and Khaliq came to the same conclusion in unison. "Anubis!"

Baahir could just make out the jackal's pointed ears. It wasn't a smudge, either. It was a clearly delineated pictograph of the god of death that had been partially eroded away. Unfortunately, Khaliq was a smart man as well, and he swiftly put the two and two together.

"We've found it," Khaliq's voice was low, but it was loud enough for Ajmal and Feroz to hear. They stepped over and joined their leader in a moment of silent reverence. All three men were enveloped by the faded image.

Baahir stepped away and saw that his captors weren't following him. So, he stepped lightly and kept moving. He made it back to the stairs before he was finally noticed.

"And where do you think you're going?"

*Damn.*

Baahir turned and found three pistols pointed at him. He played it cool and thumbed over his shoulder. "Heading for Gebel Dist. We have a lot of work to do."

He was plainly lying, and Khaliq figured as much, but the trio holstered their weapons and joined Baahir at the exit.

"Ajmal." The brute stood at attention. "Make sure our distinguished Egyptologist doesn't find himself lost, will you?"

Ajmal grabbed Baahir by the shirt collar and forced him up the steps.

*Great,* Baahir thought, *now I — ouch — have a babysitter.*

He needed to come up with an escape plan soon. Once Khaliq and his team found an entrance into the pyramidal rock formation, he would officially be expendable. Not even Zahra would be able to save him.

The cities that made up the Bahariya Oasis were large enough for one man to disappear into. That was now Baahir's goal. He was going to do the opposite of what Khaliq had said and attempt to "get lost."

# CHAPTER 67
# BAAHIR

**Gebel Dist** | Bahariya Oasis, Egypt

The climb to the top of the Gebel Dist rock formation was an infuriating one — one full of sandy gusts and near-death falls. Baahir's rage was aided by two other sources. The first was the oppressive heat combined with the unbearable sun shining down from above. On multiple occasions, Baahir had looked up and raised a hand to block out the fiery ball. Each time, he swore he thought the damn thing had grown brighter and gotten closer.

The second origin of his anger was his present company. There wasn't an archaeologist in their ranks, which meant they didn't plan on doing any exploratory research.

This was a demolitions team.

Baahir hated the fact that these men were content with destroying whatever it was they were about to find up there. He was also interested in exactly what it would be. The area was typically rife with hikers. Baahir couldn't imagine the entry point was an exquisite one. If it had been, it would have been found long ago.

"Spread out!" Khaliq ordered. "Feroz, with me. Search everywhere. I want that entrance found." He turned to Baahir. "You too...and take Ajmal with you."

Baahir's shoulders dropped. He, once more, was provided with a babysitter. Escaping would be all but impossible now. Patience would be vital. The key to his bondage would come in the way of oversight. Khaliq's men were under a great deal of pressure, and soon, even a man like Ajmal, would screw up. Baahir turned to the southeast and shielded his eyes. There were farms, campsites, and what passed for hotels less than a mile off. If he could make it there, without getting shot in the back, he was confident he could disappear for good.

Well, *confident* may have been overstating it a little, but Baahir was definitely hopeful.

Khaliq had made another decision was in Baahir's favor. Two of the men were left at the outskirts of town to keep watch. That left six people in total, including Baahir, left to climb to the top of Gebel Dist.

He and Ajmal headed west. Baahir took his time, looking for anything out of the ordinary. The summit wasn't all that large and would be easy to comb before the sun began to dip. As much as Baahir didn't want to help Khaliq find what he was looking for, he needed to do his part to stay alive.

Assorted rock piles took up most of the area atop the pyramid mountain. Baahir did his best to mentally trace his steps, but quickly became lost. Every new angle presented the same pile with a new look. One such group to the east caught his eye. He squinted at it, trying to figure out what seemed off about it. Normally, he would never have stopped scanning the horizon — this divot, in his view, seemed to be just like all the others.

But now that he was here, actually *looking* for something, it seemed odd.

But he didn't waste much time investigating. He wasn't about to give Khaliq and his team the satisfaction — not yet. But this one did look forced, as if it were constructed with purpose. It would make sense that the entrance was sealed.

"Or, I'm just seeing things," Baahir mumbled to himself.

"What?" Ajmal asked, hearing him.

Baahir stopped and glanced over his shoulder. "You say something?"

Ajmal didn't reply. He just stood there, as stiff as one of the boulders. Baahir stepped away, but not before giving the rock pile a second look.

"Come on. There's nothing here."

Ajmal eyed the same mound and stared at it for a moment, eventually falling in line behind Baahir. They searched for some time before they were summoned across the plateau. Two of Khaliq's other men waved frantically and shouted for everyone to come. Baahir was tired and sauntered over, but Ajmal made him move faster. The larger man shoved Baahir along. He abided to the big man's will and sped up, more to stay out of arm's reach than anything else.

He didn't speak up, instead he allowed Khaliq to waste more time. The smaller stones were moved by hand. Even Baahir assisted. The only one who didn't help was Khaliq. His glare had intensified — borderline manic.

Baahir wished to stay out of his crosshairs. He figured helping to move the rocks would be a good way to do that.

It took forty minutes and an untold number of water bottles to finish the task. That it was a waste of time was obvious to Baahir, and that only made the mindless work that much harder.

Finally, the only thing left to do was blast through the bigger, unmovable boulders.

Ajmal did just that.

He set the explosives, something Baahir knew little about. He just watched and took it all in. Even now, Baahir knew they weren't going to find anything. It was obvious to him, and he was pretty sure Khaliq knew it too. The SOA leader had a look on his face that said as much.

"We're ready," Ajmal announced.

Khaliq didn't take his eyes off the semi-cleared piece of land. He only nodded and backed up behind a nearby pile. Ajmal forced Baahir to follow. He knelt between the two men and covered his head with his filthy, blistered hands.

The detonation was mostly contained, but it did toss a few stones into the air. Baahir and the others were pelted with debris, but nothing larger than a gumball. As the dust settled, Baahir stood and inspected the damage. Everyone did. Baahir hung back with Khaliq and Ajmal while the others moved in to clear the area of the, now, smaller stones. It took some time, but once everything was cleared, Baahir's suspicions were confirmed.

There was nothing here.

Khaliq took a deep breath and closed his eyes. He released it and dipped his chin to his chest, and chuckled softly. Then, he turned and drew his pistol, shooting Haider, the man who had made the "discovery," in the chest. The display of violence was plain as day. Fail Khaliq here, and you die.

Baahir's nerves had unknowingly got the best of him. He fidgeted in place. His right leg shook like crazy, and he, all of a sudden, didn't know what to do with his hands. It didn't go unnoticed.

"Do you have something to say, Dr. Hassan?"

Baahir didn't meet Khaliq's hard stare. "N — no. Why do you say that?"

Khaliq stepped up next to him. "I've seen this look before — I've seen it in my own men's eyes." Baahir finally met his gaze. "You have something to say, but you are too frightened to reveal it."

Khaliq smiled. "Let me help you..." He raised his sidearm and pointed it directly at Baahir's face. "Tell me, Dr. Hassan, or share in the same fate as him." He motioned to the dead man.

Baahir swallowed his terror. "There isn't anything to — "

"Over there," Ajmal interrupted. He motioned east. "He reacted to something over there."

Khaliq's attention shifted to his trusted colleague. Ajmal nodded his assurance. He lowered his gun. It was now aimed at Baahir's chest.

"Show me."

Ajmal grabbed Baahir by the shirt collar and dragged him back to the spot he had mentioned. Once there, the Egyptologist was tossed into it. Hands out, Baahir caught himself before he bounced off the rubble. His breathing was fast, anxious. The coarse surface of the rocks stung his abused hands. Baahir paid the discomfort no attention, though. He pushed himself off and turned to meet his maker.

"Is this it?" Khaliq asked. His pistol was back in the holster on his hip.

Baahir didn't reply.

Khaliq stepped forward and went for his gun.

"Yes!" Baahir blurted out. "I mean, maybe. I don't know for certain." Khaliq gently rested his hand on the grip of his sidearm but didn't draw it. That didn't mean the threat wasn't just as powerful. Baahir slowly raised his hands, pleading with the man. "I'll need time."

"You have one hour."

Baahir didn't argue. It wouldn't have mattered anyway. Khaliq could kill him whenever he wanted, regardless of the agreed-upon timeframe.

Baahir nodded and turned back toward the rocks. "Okay," he said, talking it out, "when I first saw these, they looked different to me. Does anyone else see it, too?"

Khaliq and Ajmal joined Baahir, but still kept their distance.

"I do," Khaliq agreed. "These look as if they were placed here."

Ajmal grunted. "Unnatural."

"Yes!" Baahir exclaimed, imagining what lay beneath. "We need to clear as much off as we can — by hand." He met Khaliq's eyes. "If this is it, then we need to be careful not to cause a major collapse." Khaliq didn't seem pleased. "You've waited this long. A mistake like that could bury it for another lifetime."

"And if you're wrong?" Khaliq asked.

Baahir shrugged. "Then I will no longer be your pet."

Starting from the top, Baahir, Ajmal, and two other men began pushing stone after stone aside, allowing them to crash to the earth below. It wasn't a very long drop, only fifteen feet or so, and when they landed, two other men, assisted by Khaliq himself, cleared the debris away the best they could. The Scales of Anubis leader had decided to get his hands dirty, which was good. They needed the extra set of hands. In a fit of rage, he had gunned down one of his men and depleted the team of a valuable asset.

The one-hour death threat was long overdue by the time they got to the bottommost boulders. And like before, these were heavy and unmovable. They'd need to use something besides brute strength to move them.

Ajmal dropped his pack and dug in. He produced an identical block of plastic explosives and charger set and got to work rigging the blockade.

"Please be careful," Baahir begged, cringing at the thought of damaging the entrance.

*If there is an entrance,* he thought, praying there would be.

"Ready," Ajmal announced, handing the remote detonator to Khaliq.

Khaliq refused it with a shake of his head. "Give it to him." He pointed at Baahir.

"Me?"

"Yes," Khaliq replied. "We will see if your guess is correct, and it will be by your hand if it is or isn't."

Baahir swallowed and held out a shaky hand.

"It's all set," Khaliq explained. "All you have to do is press the red button, and then, we'll see if what we came for is here." He sighed and looked off to the horizon. "At long last."

*Yeah, no pressure.* Baahir closed his eyes and attempted to calm himself. He'd been through a lot in the last few days, but *this* was it. This was the most nerve-wracking experience of his life. This was the moment that would ultimately decide his fate.

Life, or death.

Khaliq and Ajmal led him away from the site and, once more, ducked down behind the cover of a mound of stones.

Khaliq nodded, giving him the all-clear to act.

Baahir held up the detonator, pictured his sister's face in his mind's eye one last time, and depressed the remote's little red button.

The explosion rocked Baahir's molars. It had been much larger than the last one. He cringed at the thought of destroying what lay beneath — if anything did. Taking a breath, he instantly regretted it as the wind shifted toward their position. Baahir hacked and wheezed for air, jumping to his feet and shambling away.

No one followed him. If Baahir was going to make a break for it, now was the time.

"Khaliq — Khaliq!"

One of the other men had ventured into the dust cloud and was frantically calling out his boss' name. Baahir took one more step away before sighing and turning. His curiosity had overpowered his reasoning. He needed to see what had gotten the goon so worked up. So, he fell in line behind Khaliq and Ajmal and waded through the billowing haze. As he neared, the breeze picked up and pulled the remainder of the disturbance away. When it did, Baahir saw *him.*

"Oh, my god," he said, stunned.

"Yes," Khaliq agreed. "Yes, *he* is..."

At the center of the circular blast zone, and carved directly into the rock, was the jackal-headed god, Anubis. He was positioned in the classic style, kneeling beside an oversized scale depicting a feather on one side and a human heart on the other.

"Clear it off!"

Everyone, including Baahir, got to work. Khaliq joined in, and they hurriedly moved every piece of debris out of the way. A sharp gale-force wind assisted them too, swiftly sweeping the still settling dust from the find’s surface. It was as if something wanted them to find this place. As a result, Baahir's skin broke out in goosebumps.

Khaliq stood before his god, staring down at Anubis. “Find me a way in.”

“It...it’ll take some time,” Baahir replied quietly. “We don’t know what’s on the other side.”

Khaliq faced the Egyptologist and smiled wildly. “I do.”

**Suez Shipping Company** | Port Said, Egypt

Ali's underground lair was alive with activity. Everyone, man and woman, were arming themselves to the teeth. Wally hadn't been kidding when he had said that his people were capable individuals. George had voiced his apprehension about going up against a faction as old, and well-put-together, as the Scales of Anubis. The Badawi men had laughed off his concerns, scoffing at the notion.

"Let them try," Ali had said, looking very confident. "We will be fighting on our own turf. No one knows Port Said better than we do."

Zahra felt as if she was back in the military. She sported a lightly used, black Kevlar vest and a brand-new AK-103 rifle. There were several crates of weapons nearby. The more Zahra examined Ali's base of operations, the more she noticed the armaments. They were everywhere — in all shapes and sizes.

"Did you know Wally was into stuff like this?" Zahra asked her father, keeping his voice low.

George shrugged and pulled at his own vest's straps. He wasn't used to wearing body armor. Until now, he'd never worn it in his life. "I've always been aware that he was involved in *some* things, but nothing to *this* level. Your mother had described him as a tight-lipped, honorable man — the perfect person to get her out of the country."

"Seems she was right," Zahra added, exhaling hard.

Cork was similarly outfitted, though she had an expensive-looking Bellini shotgun slung around her back instead of a rifle. They were known to be the best 12-gauges in the world. Upon seeing the black beauty, Zahra had watched Cork's mouth water, and she uttered a soft ''ello, love' before snatching it up.

The local she had taken it from was upset after being relieved of the Bellini, but he did not attempt to take it back. Hopefully, it wouldn't matter which weapon any of them had. Zahra prayed none of them would have the need to use them.

*Although with my luck...*

Another battle was right around the corner — Zahra could feel it. If the Temple of Anubis really did exist, it would surely be the toughest test yet.

Ali and Cork joined Zahra and her father.

"Are we ready?" Zahra asked.

Ali and Cork both nodded.

"Yes," Ali replied. "I have sent a team ahead of us to Cork's plane to load the majority of our gear. He glanced down at his watch. "I suggest that we join them shortly."

"Agreed," Zahra replied. She didn't meet George's eyes. She didn't want to see his worried face right now. She needed to stay focused. Everyone was counting on her to lead them.

"We know exactly where Khaliq is?"

"More or less," Cork replied. "Ali's people have narrowed down the coordinates enough. I can get us in the general area — no problem."

"The Bahariya Oasis," Wally announced, stepping around his son. "We have long suspected it to be of significance to them."

"And based on the haste with which the Scales of Anubis are moving toward it," Ali added, "we think we finally understand why. Whatever information the Anubian scroll had to offer has mobilized Khaliq in a way we have not seen in years."

"So," Zahra said, "the Temple of Anubis, huh? This is it."

Wally nodded. "I believe so, yes."

"Okay, then," she looked at Ali, "let's go."

As if on cue, three other armed individuals joined Ali, two male and one female. Even though the woman was much smaller than her counterparts, Zahra knew she must have been a fierce combatant to be included in a mission as dangerous as this one. The rifle she cradled was nearly as long as she was tall.

Ali finished the introductions.

"And this is Rabia."

Zahra recognized the weapon she held. "McMillan TAC-338, right? You any good with it?"

"She's the best," Ali replied. "No one's hands are steadier, and no one's eyes are keener."

"How do you know what kind of rifle that is?" George asked.

"It's what Chris Kyle used — the famous American sniper."

"Ah, yes!" one of Ali's men shouted cheerfully. "Bradley Cooper!" He smiled, happy with himself. "Doug? Where is Doug?"

Zahra didn't know where to start. The local had smashed two of Cooper's iconic movies together, and Zahra was too tired to correct him. "Yeah, him..."

Rabia didn't comment. She didn't utter a single word, in fact. Zahra wasn't even sure the woman was breathing. Her face was indifferent, like stone, in fact. The precision shooter's eyes were ice — cold and calculating. Zahra had known several people like Rabia. They lived and breathed their craft. Zahra did too, but she also knew that you needed to have a little fun along the way, or you would turn into, well, Rabia.

Even though this was technically Zahra's operation, she allowed Ali to lead the way. He was the real expert here — in this world. Zahra was more of the supervisor here. She was well-rounded in many facets of life, but guerilla warfare wasn't one of those areas. Once they were on location, Zahra would take over.

They clopped up the stairs of the hidden entryway and returned through the false container's doors. George and Wally brought up the rear of the group, and when they each set foot on the concrete floor, a massive explosion rocked the grounds outside of the compound.

Pandemonium ensued.

Alarms blared, nearly drowning out the sounds of additional explosions and the sudden roar of gunfire. The battle that Zahra had felt coming was here. As one, everyone lifted their various weapons and charged forward *toward* the conflict. Even George was rushing onward, though keeping back a little. The academic was only armed with a nine-millimeter pistol, refusing to carry anything else.

*Not that it would have done him much good,* Zahra thought. Her father was a liability, as it were. Giving the man an assault rifle would have been a horrible idea.

She pointed at him but looked and shouted at Wally. The elder Badawi snapped his attention to her. "Take care of Dad!"

He nodded and grabbed George's arm, dragging him away. Three of Wally's men followed the pair closely, keeping a vigil watch for intruders.

"Zahra!"

She skidded to a halt. "Go, Dad! I'll be fine!"

Wally nearly yanked her father out of his shoes before pulling him toward the bunker storehouse. It would act as the two men's fallout shelter. The description was fitting too. The world outside resembled that of life itself coming to an end. Even while still inside the core SSC building, Zahra could hear the groan of metal. It slowed everyone to a light jog — but not Zahra. She picked up her pace and swiftly rejoined the others near the front door. She had fallen behind them while checking on her father. Ali gripped the metal sliding door handle with two hands, but hesitated. Like Zahra, he was unsure of what he'd see on the other side.

He drew it open. The heavy door moved to the right. It was just in time to see one of the enormous gantry cranes lean out toward the Suez. One of its support legs was smoldering and badly damaged. Then, they all watched as it buckled and gave out like that of a prize fighter who'd taken one-too-many headshots.

The multi-million dollar display of mechanical ingenuity tilted out over the Suez and crashed into the water with authority. Two good-sized container ships were annihilated in the process, and a third was upturned. Zahra spotted men leaping from the trio of ill-fated watercrafts, just moments before they were sunk.

Bullets whizzed by Zahra, compelling her and the others not to dawdle. She shadowed Ali and Rabia, taking comfort in knowing the entire team was still intact. Cork and two others were bringing up the rear, letting loose with sporadic gunfire. Zahra had yet to pull the trigger, but she figured that moment would come soon.

"Down!" Ali yelled, diving behind a row of double-stacked steel barrels.

The gong-like impacts of bullets on metal alluded to their contents. Nothing. The barrels were empty but would still provide them with ample cover.

*For now.*

# CHAPTER 70
# ZAHRA

"We need to move!" Rabia yelled. It was the first time Zahra had heard the woman speak.

"Cover us," Ali ordered. The sniper nodded, and hefted her immense rifle, jamming its stock deep into her shoulder. She quickly lined up her target through a long black scope with *Razor HD* printed on its side. Zahra spied Rabia's shoulders relaxing as if what she was doing was child's play. Then, she took the shot.

The three-and-a-half-inch long .338 Lapua Magnum round exited the rifle's elongated barrel, traveling at nearly three times the speed of sound. It meant that the guy who received the .338 in the chest was dead — as well as missing a sizable chunk of his sternum — long before anyone near him heard the shot.

"Go!" Rabia shouted, moving off to the right.

Ali motioned for everyone to follow him around the opposite side.

"What about her?" Zahra asked.

"Who, Rabia?" Ali asked. "Never mind her! She can take care of herself!" He ran across a void of emptiness before concealing himself behind a pair of parked vans. Zahra slid in beside him, banging into the rear quarter panel harder than she intended. It didn't matter, though. There was too much noise for anyone to have heard it.

Ali leaned in close to her so she could hear what he was about to say. "You should feel sorry for the people shooting at her instead!"

A second and third shot rang out. Zahra couldn't see their victims. She couldn't she Rabia either. She'd have to trust in the sniper's abilities. Ali had faith that the woman would be fine on her own. And Zahra didn't have time to worry about it. Ali didn't stay put for long. He slithered out of cover, forcing Zahra to turn away from the action and run along behind him.

Another bone-jarring explosion rocked the SSC. This time, it belonged to the second gantry crane. The Scales of Anubis had come to play. Instead of the crane leaning out toward the water, like the other one had, this behemoth teetered backward toward the facility...and the people within its walls. Zahra slowed and quickly deduced that the central building was too far away to meet the fate of the ships from earlier, but a lot of people were still in its landing zone.

Including Zahra and her team.

"Must... run... faster!" Zahra called out between breaths.

"What? I..." Ali didn't finish. His line of sight continued up and past Zahra's head. She spun and saw what he was gawking at.

The gantry crane was already beginning its descent.

Zahra pulled Ali along. "Everyone, move!"

As she started to move, Zahra spied the sniper. Rabia was following them, but was further back. A trio of men was plinking her cover from across the compound. The archaeologist shrugged out of Ali's grip and shouldered her AK-103. She sent a handful of rounds toward Rabia's pursuers, happy to see them duck away as a result. Rabia used it as a chance to move up and sprint off behind a row of containers. Then, Zahra lost sight of her.

"Keep going, Zahra!" Ali yelled.

"What about Rabia?" Zahra countered. It was probably a stupid thing to do, but Zahra bit her lip and ran...back into the fire. She barely knew the local, but Zahra needed to help Rabia out, however she could. The sniper was willing to sacrifice herself to see that the others survived. Zahra owed her the same.

"Zahra, no!" It was Cork shouting this time.

Zahra covered her head and ran as fast as she could. Debris rained down from above. The gantry crane blotted out the sun, its shadow looming dangerously overhead.

And Zahra was directly beneath it.

She was clipped by something sharp as it fell past her. The unknown object cut her head — her right temple — opening a gash beneath her hairline. Blood ran down the side of her face, making it to her neck and chest in no time flat. Her shirt was already drenched. The billowing dust and dirt latched onto the crimson, stinging sharply as it snuck its way through her matted hair and into the fresh wound.

A silver SUV came squealing around the corner. It fishtailed before straightening itself out and continued toward Zahra. At the last second, and on wobbly legs, Zahra rolled right and dodged the SUV. It zipped past her, leaving her in the dust.

Gritting her teeth, she got up and pushed forward, pouring on the speed until she couldn't run anymore. Zahra dove forward and tucked her feet into her chest and rolled. The massive crane landed with a *boom,* crushing the row of barrels she had just used as cover. The truck, likewise, met the same flattening fate. It was crushed beyond recognition, and so was its driver.

*Good riddance*, she thought, climbing to her feet. The guy had been so hellbent on running Zahra down that he had lost sight of the crane.

Zahra backed away from the flaming heap. She spotted Ali and Cork through the entanglement of steel, fire, and smoke, and waved them off. "Go! Get the plane ready! We'll meet you at the airfield!"

Ali seemed satisfied, but the pilot obviously wasn't. Still, Cork waved back and allowed the local to guide her away from the wreckage. Zahra bent over and groaned, picking up her rifle. She checked it over. Everything was in working order. She then turned and shouldered the weapon, and began the search for her missing comrade.

*Dammit, Rabia, where are you?*

The telltale report of a large caliber rifle gave Zahra the answer she was looking for. She headed left and listened intently. A second, echoing gunshot got her moving faster. Rabia was somewhere nearby. The second shot had been louder than the first. It meant Zahra was getting closer.

A sound, like a giant bee, buzzed by her right ear. Zahra flinched and dropped to one knee and looked over her shoulder. Fifty feet behind her, a previously unseen assailant had climbed atop a rusted, blue container before he got knocked off his feet in a spray of blood. Zahra traced the bullet back to its origin and discovered where it had come from.

She discovered *her*.

Rabia was lying prone beneath a dusty, red, four-door truck. She was still two hundred feet away. Even at this distance, Zahra was pretty sure she could see the woman smiling from ear to ear. Rabia had enjoyed that shot.

The sniper's cover got turned to Swiss cheese right before Zahra's eyes. Luckily, the shooters were so focused on Rabia that they didn't see Zahra approaching. The archaeologist unloaded her magazine into a duo of gunmen, giving Rabia enough time to gather herself and join in. The sniper slid out from beneath the truck and drew a pistol. Rabia displayed the same steady aim and sent a pair of nine-millimeter bullets into the third and final attacker's chest before finishing him off with a headshot.

Both women were breathing hard. Rabia silently thanked Zahra for her efforts with a curt nod of her head. While Zahra reloaded her AK-103 and watched the immediate area, the sniper ducked beneath the truck to retrieve her prized firearm.

"Bleeding already?" Rabia asked, motioning to Zahra's flowing blood. The precision shooter had avoided injury thus far. The only sign of any kind of exertion was the beads of sweat rolling down her face and the smear of dirt and grime on her clothes from crawling around beneath the truck.

Zahra shrugged. "Yeah, I mean, it's not a contest... We need to find the others."

"Yes," Rabia agreed. Her face morphed back into that of an emotionless assassin. "Follow me."

Ali Badawi grabbed Cork's right bicep and attempted to haul her away. She resisted him, applying the brakes, and refusing to move until Zahra was gone from her sight. Her friend was about to risk her life to save someone she hardly knew, just because it was the right thing to do. Zahra was as selfless a human being as Cork had ever met. She secretly wanted a sliver of that mindset for herself. As per usual, people in Cork's line of work tended to exclusively look out for *numero uno*. It's what kept you alive the longest.

But it was also a lonely way to exist.

*Alright, alright... Cut out the pity party shit.*

She stepped away from the downed gantry crane and yanked free from Ali's grip. Cork was a few inches taller than him and was nearly the same weight as him. If she had to, she knew she could take him in a fight.

Cork sighed. *Really, girl?*

Ali had proven himself to be an ally, and yet, her mind immediately went to the possibility of having to harm him. Losing sight of Zahra just now had knocked something loose. For Zahra's sake, Cork needed to push aside her typical survival instincts and try to be more like her remarkable friend, though Cork really was a fish out of water here. These were Zahra and George's people, not hers. Waleed and Ali held no allegiance to her.

Cork was led away from the action. For now, the gunfire was wholly near the water, on the eastern side of the compound. It meant that she, Ali, and his two men — whatever their names — were in the clear. Still, they moved fast, jogging to a foursome of identical automobiles. Ali's people continued past Cork and him, claiming the forwardmost white SUV for themselves.

Cork headed for the vehicle behind that one, specifically the SUV's driver's side door.

But so did Ali.

"What are you doing?" Ali asked.

Cork jammed a thumb into her own chest. "Duh, I'm driving."

"But I usually drive."

Cork snorted out a laugh. "No chance. I always do the driving when I'm with Zahra."

Ali crossed his arms in front of his chest. "But you aren't with Zahra, are you?"

"Semantics." The muscular Brit waved him off. "You don't have to come then."

Another explosion rocked the SSC.

"We do not have time for this!" Ali shouted. Cork didn't budge. Finally, he gave in and threw up his hands in frustration. "Fine, you win! I will navigate. We better get moving." He rounded the front of the SUV and popped open the front passenger side door. "Also, I thought you were a pilot, not a driver?"

"I am." She grinned. "I *drive* the plane." Cork reached for the ignition but stopped. "What about Zahra and Rabia?"

"I suspect they won't be too far behind us."

Cork was curious. "What makes you so sure?"

"Because, if Zahra is as good as I think she is, then she and Rabia will make short work of these Scales of Anubis pigs."

Cork smiled. "Oh, you better believe she is. Zahra is a special kind of something, for sure. She's the most determined person I've ever met. I'm even starting to think she's bulletproof!"

Ali turned and looked deeper into the SUV, gazing through the rear window. "Yes, well, for everyone's sake, I hope she is."

Cork pressed the push-start ignition and turned over the engine. She quickly threw the SUV into gear and pulled away. Ali reached up to his seat's sunshade and tapped a small white button. It looked like a garage door clicker. Up ahead, a gate slowly began to open. Cork aimed for it, biting her lip as she glanced into her rearview mirror.

*Come on, Zahra. You've got this.*

Cork added more speed, matching that of the lead vehicle. Both barely made it through the still-opening gate. The other men went right, much to the dismay of Ali.

"Left!" Ali yelled, pointing south. "Go left!"

"What about — grrr!" Cork growled.

Cork followed his instructions and cranked hard on the steering wheel. She sent the SUV into powerslide fit for a big-budget Hollywood movie. As soon as they exited the property, a threesome of blacked-out vehicles, two sedans, and one hulking four-door truck, appeared behind them. Upon seeing the new arrivals, Cork stomped her foot on the gas. She and Ali shot off like a rocket, weaving in and out of slower-moving traffic.

# CHAPTER 72
# ZAHRA

Up ahead sat a trio of cookie-cut white SUVs. Rabia led, with Zahra close behind. They passed the rearmost vehicle and were enveloped by another barrage of gunfire. Thinking quickly, Zahra snagged the driver's side door handle and pulled as she hurried by it. Her quick thinking saved her and Rabia's lives. The door was immediately walloped by a half-dozen projectiles. Each one of them had been, more or less, lined up with the pair of fleeing women's backs.

Zahra thanked her lucky stars that the door had been unlocked.

"Looks like they made it!" Rabia shouted.

She was already opening the door to the lead car by the time Zahra arrived, and instead of skirting around to the passenger side, she slid past Rabia and leaped in.

"How do you know that?" Zahra asked, covering her ears with her hands.

"Because..." A hail of automatic gunfire shredded the other two SUVs. Rabia yelped in surprise and shoved Zahra in the ass, forcing her headfirst into the passenger seat's footwell.

"There should be four cars, not three."

Zahra landed with a "Gah!" and looked up to witness her headrest get turned to stuffing as a pair of bullets impacted it from behind. The back window shattered as a result. Rabia ducked her head to the level of the steering wheel and gritted her teeth. She fumbled for the gear shift before finally gripping it and throwing it into *drive*.

Zahra tucked her legs and awkwardly worked herself into a seated position. She grabbed whatever she could and pushed away from the floor, and slid into the seat behind her. She saw that the front gate was already open.

*Must have been Cork and Ali,* she deduced.

Additional projectiles whizzed by their accelerating getaway vehicle, and as soon as they exited the Suez Shipping Company's grounds, Rabia yanked on the steering wheel, sending the pair right — to the north. Zahra half-expected to see her compatriots further up the road, or at the very least, the remnants of their own escape. But there were no turned-over vehicles or fires. No innocent bystanders huddled for cover. The way was clear except for the humdrum local traffic — of which Rabia zigged and zagged through like a seasoned pro.

Rabia hit the steering wheel. "They didn't come this way," she muttered. She shook her head, glancing in her mirrors.

"How do you know?" Zahra asked, looking in the side mirror just outside her window.

"Because..." Rabia's eyes flicked to Zahra. "There would be much more commotion than there is."

"Where'd they go, then?"

Rabia thumbed over her shoulder. "South. Ali likes the southern route — thinks it's quicker." The sniper shook her head. "But he knows it's foolish this time of day."

"Why do you say that?" Zahra asked, grabbing at the overhead handle.

Rabia smashed her palm down on the steering wheel, blaring the white SUV's horn. She even went as far as nudging the car in front of them with the front fender, coaxing it to move out of the way after two such *love taps*. With an opening directly ahead of them, Rabia applied more pressure to the gas pedal, and they sped away.

"Yes," she replied, "there are fewer traffic signals to the south, but there's also more congestion there too." Rabia tapped the brakes before zooming through a red light. "I don't plan on abiding to those signals."

It all meant that Cork and Ali were going to, more than likely, get in a trickling logjam of afternoon drivers.

"We have company," Rabia said, gazing into the rearview mirror.

Zahra spun in her seat and watched as a trio of black sedans came screaming up the street behind them. Besides announcing their arrival,

Rabia didn't look all that concerned about the prospects of being in a car chase. She was fixated on the immediate here and now — the road ahead and other cars.

Zahra got an awful idea.

"Wreck the other cars." Rabia pulled her eyes away from the road and stared Zahra down. "It'll buy us some time. Just...don't kill anyone, if you can help it."

Rabia rolled her eyes and sped up. She poked at the rear bumper of the pickup in front of them. It wobbled but didn't spin out. Rabia gritted her teeth and slid left, pulling forward some. Then, she gently spun the wheel right and bumped the left rear quarter panel of the truck. The force was enough to make the driver panic and overcorrect as the vehicle's rear wheels jerked to the side.

The sniper backed off and veered right, missing the swerving pickup by inches. It nicked a neighboring minivan, which caused every other automobile on the roadway to slam on their brakes. Three or four of them ended up being involved in a fender-bender, but the plan had worked. Zahra and Rabia's pursuers were stuck at the back of the pack.

That was...until one of them went left and mounted the sidewalk. Zahra watched in horror as bodies were launched skyward. The car responsible just plowed straight through the pedestrians with no regard for their safety.

*Bastards!*

And it was Zahra's fault.

She growled and climbed into the backseat of the SUV, dragging her AK-103 with her. Zahra planted her left knee into the seat cushion, loaded in a fresh thirty-round magazine, and took a deep breath.

She lowered the window. "Let this one get in close."

Rabia didn't argue. The SUV slowed, allowing the lead sedan to do as Zahra had wanted. It dismounted the concrete sidewalk and got in close.

As it did, Rabia banked right and allowed it to pull up alongside their left flank. Once its front wheels were even with their back wheels, Zahra made her move. She stabbed the barrel of her rifle out the window and took aim at the driver. He was the first to die. Between him and his two passengers, Zahra unloaded the weapon's entire thirty-round payload. She was satisfied to watch the bullet-riddled, blood-splattered sedan list to the left, cross four lanes of traffic, and careen into a telephone pole.

Zahra took a second to catch her breath before fully re-entering the SUV. She plopped in the rear seat and let the empty, smoking rifle fall to the floorboards, settling in next to Rabia's large-caliber variant. It took her a moment to realize that Rabia was eyeing her, using the rearview mirror to spy on her.

"What?" Zahra asked, annoyed by the attention.

"I like you."

"Thanks..." she replied. "But — and don't take this the wrong way — that doesn't make me feel better."

Rabia shrugged. "You do what has to be done, no matter the cost."

"*That?*" Zahra asked. "That was nothing more than petty revenge! I wanted to pay them back for what they did to those people back there."

Rabia nodded. "I would have done the same thing, but with fewer bullets. Your emotions are your strength, Zahra. Use that strength when the time comes."

Zahra gave an exhausted laugh. "And you? The 'Emotionless Ice Queen?'"

Rabia's eyes narrowed. "Just because I'm better at hiding my feelings doesn't mean I don't *feel* them. Here, if you show weakness, you *are* that weakness." She sighed and patted the front seat. "Come. Let's find our friends before more of Ayad's men arrive."

Zahra climbed back into the front, leaving the AK-103 behind. "You think they're doing okay?"

Rabia shrugged again. "I'm not sure. Let's hope so."

# CHAPTER 73
# CORK

**Port Said, Egypt**

"Ali, you fucking bastard. I'm going to kill you!"

Cork was not pleased with her navigator. Ali had claimed to know Port Said inside and out, boasting that Ayad's men would soon lose them. Instead, he led them directly into a bumper-to-bumper traffic jam reminiscent of those in major metropolitan cities like London and Los Angeles. Still, Ali wasn't about to admit defeat.

"You are the so-called *expert* driver, yes?" He held out his hand, motioning to the congestion of vehicles. "Time for you to get us out of this mess, if you can..."

"The mess *you* got us into!"

He grinned. "Semantics."

That pissed Cork off. He was mocking her, using her own words against her. She smashed down on the horn and hopped the curb. They continued south along the eastern sidewalk. Cork was careful not to hit anyone, allowing people to clear the footpath before pushing forward. Ayad's men followed closely behind them, not giving the pedestrians the same courtesy. Luckily, everyone had already moved off, squeezing into nearby storefronts, and even leaping out into traffic.

"I swear," Cork shouted. "If we get out of this, I'm going to kick you in your tiny little pecker!"

She meant it, too.

Ali leaned away from the irate woman, doing what was best for him and keeping his mouth shut. For now, it was up to Cork to keep them alive.

A car rolled forward, stopping directly atop the crosswalk up ahead. The driver looked both ways, snapping his attention back to Cork and her white SUV as they zoomed down the sidewalk. The man threw his car into reverse and tried to back up but instantly met resistance in the form of another automobile.

*Holy shit!* Cork thought. There was nowhere to go except straight through him.

Thankfully, Ali had already spotted a way out. "There!"

Cork saw it a second later. Up ahead, mere feet from the impending collision, traffic was thinning out enough for her to conceivably re-enter the roadway. It wouldn't be pretty, however. To pull off the gutsy maneuver, she'd have to slow and squeeze their bulbous SUV through a gap no bigger than it. And on either side of the opening stood a concrete telephone pole and a fire hydrant.

She bit her lip and drifted the SUV to the left, skimming the blur of storefronts. Cork planted both of her feet on the brake and yanked the steering wheel right. The passenger side mirror was sheared off by the telephone pole and the SUV's left rear quarter panel clipped the fire hydrant, sending a geyser of water high into the sky.

"Bloody hell!" Cork yelped, swerving around a massive garbage truck.

In her overhead mirror, she spied the big four-door truck directly behind them, attempting to complete the same move. Somehow, it successfully passed through the tight pathway but was hit with a wash of water as gravity took hold of the newly created fountain. It obstructed the driver's view just enough for him not to see the garbage truck. The much heavier vehicle t-boned the truck, causing it to barrel roll into the middle of the intersection, coming to a rest on its roof.

Cork pried her eyes away from the joyous carnage, smiling wide. She glared at Ali. Her jubilant expression vanished in an instant.

"Just so you know, I wear a men's size eleven."

# CHAPTER 74
# ZAHRA

Even after ridding themselves of their lead pursuer, Rabia couldn't shake off the next one. The smaller sedan was quicker and constantly vanished in and out of the larger SUV's blind spots. Zahra only spoke when pointing out the vehicle's location, allowing Rabia to concentrate on not getting them killed. Traffic was beginning to thin out, and their speeds increased. She turned and spotted her rifle.

*No dice,* she thought, biting her lip, and thinking. It was out of ammo. The only thing they had was her pistol. They still had Rabia's massive sniper rifle, but Zahra quickly pushed aside that option. You couldn't have paid her enough money to attempt to use that thing while inside a moving vehicle.

So, she gazed past the four-door, and the pair of men within, and was happy to see that it was alone. Its buddy had yet to unclog itself from the traffic jam further behind them.

*Good...* All they needed to do was lose this guy, and they'd be home free.

Rabia was on the same wavelength.

"We need to say goodbye to our friend before meeting the others," she said. "Any ideas?"

Zahra drew her sidearm.

Rabia shook her head. "That won't do. We need something that hits harder."

Now, it was Zahra's turn to shake her head. "My gun is spent."

"Mine is not."

Zahra sat and stared at the woman. "You're kidding me, right? You want me to use that 'monster' inside a moving vehicle."

"One that will be swerving back and forth while also rapidly braking and accelerating, yes."

Zahra laughed. "You're crazy. You know that?"

Rabia shrugged. "I'm still alive, aren't I?"

So was Zahra. She was still alive after so many daring escapes *because* she did what she had to do to survive. As much as Zahra didn't want to admit it, she and the sniper were very similar to one another.

"I'll walk you through it, okay?"

Zahra sighed and nodded. Next, she went about the arduous task of working the four-foot-long McMillan TAC-338 precision rifle into position. What made matters worse was that Zahra had to kneel in her seat while facing the rear of the SUV. If she didn't get shot during the attempt, she'd surely get car sick.

"Okie-dokie," Zahra muttered. "Here we go."

She lifted the weapon, setting the barrel across the back bench seat. Rabia pulled the steering wheel hard to the left, sending them sliding around a corner. When their tires caught, she shot off, but the sudden jerking motion, combined with Zahra's awkward positioning, spilled her backward into Rabia's lap.

"Zahra!" Rabia shouted, unable to get her hands back on the steering wheel. "Get off!"

"I can't! I'm stuck!"

Reacting quickly, Zahra grabbed the wheel and held it in place.

"Left!" Rabia instructed, trying to yank her arms free.

But she couldn't. Zahra was stuck, and the side-to-side rocking was working her deeper and deeper into place.

Zahra edged left.

"Back right — right!"

Following Rabia's orders, Zahra moved them right. As she did, she left herself up into a crunch, leaning forward enough for Rabia to slip her left arm out from beneath her back. Back in control, Rabia steadied the SUV long enough for Zahra to wiggle back into her own seat. Neither woman reacted to the ridiculousness of the past couple of seconds. Zahra refused to meet the sniper's gaze and, instead, went about realigning her shot.

She had used bolt-action rifles before, so getting everything in order wasn't a problem. Holding the heavy weapon in place while moving was the issue, as was her diminished strength. Zahra was tired, and her arms shook.

"Take a deep breath before taking the shot," Rabia coached. She then lowered all of the windows. Even with the large suppressor attached to the barrel, the report was going to be deafening. The open windows would help lessen the beating Zahra and Rabia's brains were about to endure.

"Aim for the front grill," Rabia said softly.

Zahra didn't hear her and took the shot, putting the .338 Lapua Magnum round through the driver's chest instead. As expected, the concussive force was unbearable, punching Zahra in the skull like a jackhammer.

Rabia felt it, too. She winced and flinched, tossing Zahra to the side as her hands flowed her head to the side. "Or," she said, cringing, "you can do *that*."

The result was instantaneous. The sedan's passenger freaked out and grabbed the steering wheel away from his deceased compatriot, but he unsuccessfully de-escalated the situation. If anything, Zahra was pretty sure the car sped up before plowing into the rear end of a street-side parked truck. There was still no sign of the third, and final, car.

Zahra set the rifle down across the backseat and fell back into her place beside Rabia.

The sniper patted Zahra's thigh. "You did well."

"What?" Zahra asked, her ears ringing.

"You did well!" Rabia shouted.

But Zahra was faking her deafness, and it was too late by the time Rabia had noticed. She just rolled her eyes and sped up, clunking the side of Zahra's head on the passenger side window as she swiftly tugged on the wheel.

Zahra rubbed the fresh knock. "Thanks..."

Attempting to prevent another mishap, Zahra buckled in, surprised when she and Rabia were rear-ended. Both women snuck a look behind them and found the third and final sedan riding their ass. Somehow, it had snuck up close without either of them noticing.

The driver hit them again.

The steering wheel was ripped out of Rabia's hands, but she quickly reacquired it before she lost control. They were hit again — then again. Zahra thought about peppering the tailgater with nine-millimeter bullets but decided against it. It would be a waste of ammo at this point. Rabia would have to take care of it herself.

Or not...

An exact duplicate to their silver SUV came sliding through the next intersection, just barely missing Zahra and Rabia by inches. The new arrival sideswiped the sedan out from behind its twin with a crunch of metal and fiberglass, sending the smaller vehicle directly into oncoming traffic. Cork had caught up to them faster than Zahra had expected. She knew Cork would be driving as if her hair was on fire—if she had any—so it really shouldn't have surprised her. Rabia hit the gas and further distanced them from the resulting collision.

Cork sped up and pulled alongside Zahra and Rabia. She was excited and looked a bit wired.

Ali's expression was that of sheer terror.

*Poor guy,* Zahra thought, knowing exactly what he had just been put through.

Rabia pointed at Cork and then motioned to the rear of her and Zahra's SUV. Cork got the message. She slowed and fell in line. The sniper would lead the pilot the rest of the way. Both vehicles had seen better days, especially the one carrying Cork and Ali. Rabia continued west, staying parallel with the coast. Every now and again, Zahra could just barely make out the blue water at the end of the roadways pointing north and south. Her mind, once more, returned to the gorgeous Levanzo view.

"What are you thinking about?"

Zahra blinked out of the blissful memory. "Nothing."

Rabia glanced at her. "That wasn't a 'nothing' kind of look."

Zahra stuttered, "I... was thinking of a better place." She stayed vague, not giving Rabia any more information than that. It didn't feel right to blab to the world about Levanzo. It was her little sliver of paradise and no one else's.

They rode in silence the rest of the way. Both women would occasionally check behind them and make sure their friends were still following close. Zahra and Rabia were also on the lookout for more of Ayad's men. They traveled faster and faster the more they moved away from the hubbub of the Suez Canal. Eventually, they left the city behind and rode directly along the shore, Saad Zaghloul. The only things standing between them, and the Mediterranean, were a beach and the businesses that dotted its surface.

Zahra was so close to telling Rabia to pull over so she could get out and feel the cool incoming breeze. But she didn't. Up ahead, Zahra read a sign that reminded her of what was coming up next on their mission to save her brother and all of humanity.

“The airport is just up ahead,” Rabia said. Her eyes darted all over the place. To Zahra, she reminded her of someone with way too much caffeine in her system, though she knew the professional was always just on high alert.

A radio attached to Rabia’s hip squawked to life. It was Ali, but he wasn’t talking to her. He was speaking to someone at the airport.

“We are nearly there,” Ali said. “Prepare to open the gate.”

Two minutes later, the side gate to the Port Said International Airport opened. It hit Zahra that this was the second discreet entrance into an airport that she had taken in just a few days’ time. But unlike the one she and her father used back in Cambridge, this one wasn’t being manned by some random employee at the orders of one of Cork’s lovers. The three people eyeing them each owned stone-cold stares. These were Ali’s men. There wasn’t an airport employee in sight. The amount of freedom Ali was being given both impressed and unnerved Zahra. It felt very mob-like, in a way.

She pictured Wally. *You own this town, don’t you?*

The front tires bumped some unseen threshold between the roadway and the airport grounds. It jarred Zahra free of her thoughts. Luckily, Rabia was too lost in her own world to notice and, therefore, question Zahra.

Rabia slowly rolled through the gate with Cork and Ali following close behind. She veered left, away from the main buildings, and headed toward a group of hangars. Planes took off as scheduled using the east-to-west constructed tarmac, roaring loudly off to Zahra’s right.

A single building sat further away from the others, and it didn’t shock Zahra that it was the one Rabia steered them towards. When they were a hundred yards away, the front doors parted, creeping away from one another to reveal a familiar aircraft, the *Puss E. Galore.* Zahra had to admit, she was quite happy to see the old bird again. It brought some comfort to her disheveled mind, like seeing a close friend after a hard day at work. It was usually Dina that she would see. Zahra missed her.

The doors closed only after both battered SUV's had made it inside the hangar. Everyone exited and quickly went about loading and unloading gear.

Cork didn’t pay Zahra and Rabia any attention. She rounded the front of the vehicle and wound up her right foot to kick Ali but stopped and smiled when he flinched. Then, she growled and pushed between Zahra and Rabia and headed straight to her plane, shouting at the men moving in and around it.

Ali sauntered up to the ladies, looking shook.

"What was that all about?" Zahra asked, thumbing over at her pilot.

"N — nothing," Ali said, shaking his head. "She's an intense one, isn't she?"

Zahra grinned. "You did something to piss her off, didn't you?" She snickered. "Whatever it was, you should consider yourself lucky. Cork has a really big foot."

Ali swallowed. "Yes, so she tells me."

# CHAPTER 75
# IFZA

**Suez Shipping Company**

High above the Suez Canal, a lone helicopter hovered in place. Its occupants watched as a full-fledged war broke out. One of the gantry cranes toppled to the ground, crushing everything in its path. Muzzle flashes ignited everywhere like tiny fireflies. The only way Ifza could tell the sides apart was what direction the scurrying ants were traveling. Those moving toward the central building were her men.

From the initial onslaught, Ifza could tell her people were struggling to push forward. Like Zahra Kane, the Scales of Anubis had greatly underestimated Waleed Badawi — namely, the size and skill of his force.

Khaliq's words, once more, bounced around inside Ifza's skull.

*Don't fail me again.*

If she did, in fact, fail Khaliq again, would her brother — her own flesh and blood — follow through with his implied threat and kill her?

She wasn't planning on finding out.

A column of ants poured out from a side exit and rushed away from the conflict. Ifza knew it was her prey. She frantically looked for her people, hoping — willing — them to see what she saw. A handful did, but they were swiftly gunned down where they stood. Her team's muzzle flashes died down as the seconds ticked by.

"Take me down."

The pilot protested. "But ma'am, I — "

She drew her pistol and pushed it into the insolent man's temple. She spoke, gritting her teeth hard. "I said, 'take me down.'"

The pilot nodded and immediately began their descent into the still brewing, though quieting, conflict. If Ifza could get down there and, at the very least, interrupt Zahra's escape, it might just be enough to watch the woman bleed.

And Ifza Ayad would be the one to make her bleed.

Bullets pinged off the underbelly of the helicopter but did little else besides make an annoying noise. As they neared the ground, Ifza unbuckled. The men sitting across from her did the same.

"Man the door," she ordered.

They responded in silence, nodding curtly. Both men shouldered their matching rifles, gripping them tightly.

Ifza picked up her own rifle and checked it over. Her weapon was different than the others. Hers had a grenade launcher attachment mounted directly beneath the barrel.

*Open with the grenade, then shoot anything that moves.*

And she meant *anything*. Ifza didn't care if the victims were Waleed's men or hers. She wouldn't take the chance of misidentifying anyone and giving them an opening to kill her first.

With ten feet to touch down, Ifza gripped the door handle and pulled. The locking mechanism released, and she slid it open. The helicopter's interior was met with a cool breeze laced heavily with smoke. Ifza squinted against the noxious haze. It stung her nose and throat, and it made her eyes water. She took aim and applied slight pressure to her rifle's secondary trigger. But Ifza wasn't given a chance to enact phase one of her personal assault plan.

A projectile exploded from somewhere within the open doors of the central structure. It was followed by a trail of smoke and was headed straight for Ifza and the helicopter.

"RPG!" the pilot shouted, attempting to climb.

Ifza made the decision to jump, and she did. She fell ten feet and hit the ground, rolling forward as soon as she landed. She made it four strides before the helicopter, as well as the three men aboard it, were obliterated. The Rocket Propelled Grenade had done its job perfectly, exploding dead center inside the rear cargo hold. The impact and detonation tore the aircraft apart bit by bit. Somehow, the rotors functioned long enough to pull the helicopter back toward the water. It only made it halfway before its skids clipped the top of a steel container, sending it rolling onto the ground on the other side in a screech of metal.

Ifza's left ankle was on fire from the fall. She turned back toward the RPG's origin and watched as a group of seven armed men poured outside and quickly surrounded her. Her rifle was gone. It laid on the ground where she had landed. All she was armed with was her sidearm and a knife.

She raised her hands in surrender and sneered when a bald, bearded man approached her. It had been years since Ifza had seen him, but she instantly recognized him as Waleed Badawi. He had been a thorn in the Scales of Anubis' side for years.

Ifza closed her eyes, ready to die.

But she didn't.

After ten excruciating long seconds, she reopened them, and found Waleed staring at her with the slightest of smiles on his face.

"Bring her!" he shouted.

Four of the seven men rushed Ifza and swiftly apprehended her. She was zip cuffed relieved of her remaining weapons.

Waleed stepped up to Ifza, stopping within a foot of her.

"Unlike you, I am not a cold-blooded killer."

And with that, Ifza had a thick wool sack slid over her head. She allowed Waleed's men to march her away to God-knows-where, manhandling her like the prisoner she was. Ifza could have easily tried to fight back, thrashing against her bonds like a feral beast. She didn't, though. As Waleed had shown her, he wasn't a cold-blooded killer. *That* intrigued Ifza, but it also concerned her.

*What else do you have planned for me?* she silently asked.

Based on the echoing sound of footfalls, Ifza could tell she was led inside a large room. She guessed it was the central building of Waleed's operation. She'd never been inside, so she had no idea where she was being taken. They stopped and waited. A clunk preceded the sting of protesting metal as a door, in need of oil, swung open. Ifza was, again, dragged along, finding steps beneath her feet. Her captors slowed and allowed her to keep her feet underneath her.

Ifza had not expected to be treated with such care. If it were her and her people, they would have simply pushed Ifza along, and if she fell, that would have been that. Ifza would be picked up off the ground, or forced to stand on her own, regardless of any injury sustained from the fall, and forcibly shoved forward to meet some terrible fate.

This didn't remind Ifza of that.

Several voices spoke up as she was guided along. The cloak and their hushed tones made it impossible to discern what was said, but Ifza figured they were talking about her. A door opened somewhere in front of her. The men on either arm led her in, spun her around, and sat her down on a chair. Through the sack, Ifza could just make out a lone light overhead. The rest of the space was as dark as night, from what she could tell. Her ankles were then shackled to the legs of the chair.

The door shut. She sat in total silence for sixty seconds.

*Why leave me alone?*

She suddenly realized. It's because she *wasn't* alone...

"I know you are there," she said, listening carefully.

Soft footsteps picked up somewhere in front of Ifza. They stopped just in front of her. If her legs hadn't been restrained, she would have been able to lash out with her feet.

The wool sack was torn from Ifza's head, taking some of her hair along with it. She tried to look up at the man standing over her but was met with a blinding light instead. Ifza had looked directly into the single bulb dangling overhead.

She blinked away the spots in her vision.

"It's been a long time, Ifza."

## CHAPTER 76
# BAAHIR

**Gebel Dist** | Bahariya Oasis, Egypt

Baahir couldn't believe what he was seeing. They had only just finished clearing off what he now knew to be a seal around a doorway.

As of now, he had displayed nothing more than indifference. He was hoping Khaliq hadn't discovered it yet. But Baahir could only play dumb for so long.

The seal depicted Anubis and his scales, though instead of the god holding them aloft, he was seated in an oversized, throne-like chair. In one hand were the scales. In the other was the fabled Anubian canopic jar.

*Mom's canopic jar...*

The epiphany hit him hard, and it was too hard not to react.

"What is it?" Khaliq asked, eyeing him.

Baahir swallowed. "Do you think the temple really exists?" He hoped the question would distract the psychopath.

It worked.

"Yes, I do." He tipped his chin at the seal. "What do you make of this?"

Baahir needed to give the man some information. If he delayed for too long, Khaliq would order Ajmal to blow a hole through the priceless remnant. It was bound to happen.

*Not yet!*

Baahir attempted to explain his hypothesis, trying to stay as vague as possible. "We obviously have Anubis sitting in what could only be a throne, right?" Khaliq nodded. "And he's holding his scales, as well as our family's prized canopic jar, the one you destroyed and used to infect an innocent man with a centuries-old virus."

Khaliq turned his attention from the seal to Baahir. The Egyptologist cleared his throat.

"What else do you have, Dr. Hassan?" Khaliq asked. "A child could decipher that much."

Baahir's pulse quicken. "Yes... yes, I was just trying to — "

"To *delay*."

Baahir shook his head. "Why would I do that?" Now it was Baahir's turn to stare down someone. "It's not like I have anyone rushing here to rescue me, right? I mean, you did say that my sister was dead, after all."

For a moment, Khaliq's stoic expression faltered, cracking enough for Baahir to realize that he didn't know for sure if Zahra was really dead. His eyes returned to the circular seal, and he stepped out onto its face.

It was nearly ten feet across, and hieroglyphs accompanied the striking artwork. The ancient language had been engraved along the edge of the relic, telling of a danger that would meet anyone who ventured too far into the underworld.

Khaliq spoke up next. "*Death awaits those who cross this threshold*." He gazed at Baahir. "Or did you forget that I could read hieroglyphs?"

"No, I didn't forget." He shrugged. "I just didn't feel like telling you."

Ajmal grabbed Baahir by the shirt and jammed a pistol into the underside of his chin. Baahir swallowed, his Adam's apple bumping the weapon's muzzle as it rose and fell.

Baahir was past being intimidated. "If you're going to kill me — just do it already!" He glanced over to Khaliq while still being held. "Your threats mean very little to me."

But Khaliq didn't order his execution, which made Baahir smile. "Oh, I see." He chuckled, gagging a little when Ajmal pushed the pistol's muzzle deeper. "You're afraid."

Khaliq violently ripped Baahir away from Ajmal and threw him into the center of the seal. Baahir hit the seal and rolled a few feet, feeling yet another wound open. This one was a small cut on his ear. It bled slightly and stung but was superficial at best.

"Watch your — "

"Tongue?" Baahir finished. He groaned and dusted himself off as he stood. "How about we blast this thing to pieces, and see if you don't bring the entire mountain down on your precious temple?" He held out his arms. "Until then, I'm going to go sit down."

Baahir was over it. He turned and walked away from his captors, hoping he didn't get shot in the back for his outburst. He doubted Khaliq had ever experienced having anyone speak to him like that before. Khaliq deserved so much more too. But for now, Baahir straightened his posture and marched forward, going as far as pushing through two other men. He decided that he was far enough and sat facing the east, spotting the town he had seen earlier.

*Less than a mile away.*

"Blow it," Khaliq said, heading off in the opposite direction.

The two men that Baahir had just pushed his way through joined Ajmal. The trio dug into their respective bags and began setting charges, forgetting about their captor. Baahir looked around and realized that there were no eyes on him.

So, he did the only reasonable thing, and attempted his escape.

# CHAPTER 77
# IFZA

"Waleed Badawi, in the flesh," Ifza said, her voice tinged with malice. "I can't say I've lost sleep over it."

"Nor have I." Waleed's eyes her dark and brooding, but tired.

The two stared one another down, refusing to allow the other to win the battle of wits.

Waleed broke first, but he did so with a sly smile. "Still the fighter, I see. You are very much like your mother, you know?"

"Please," Ifza scoffed. "You didn't drag me down here to talk about my family, did you? Because, if you had — "

"You'd already be dead," Waleed interrupted.

"You said you weren't a cold-blooded killer."

Waleed nodded and began to pace back and forth. "I'm not, but you've murdered quite a few of my people over the years, some of which have family on my staff. *They* would love to speak with you after I'm done here."

"So, you threaten me, and for what? What do you need from me?"

Waleed slowed and turned away from her. "I need you to understand. I need you to look inside of yourself and see that what you and your brother are doing is wrong." He turned, looking Ifza right in the eyes. "It's evil."

"Because we will succeed."

"Says the woman shackled to a chair."

"My brother will come for me."

Waleed's right eyebrow raised. "Will he?" Ifza didn't reply. "I know him well, remember. He isn't the type of man to look back. I'm afraid he has already forgotten you, Ifza. His goal has always been the plague, and you were just a means to that end."

"Shut up!" Ifza shouted. Her eyes welled with tears. She hadn't felt an emotion other than rage in a long time.

"You know I am right. I can see it in your eyes. It's etched on your face."

She seethed, gritting her teeth. "And what does my face say now?"

Waleed's hard gaze softened. "Regret, sadness," he stepped forward. "A life wasted attempting to destroy humanity, and all for what, your demented brother's quest for chaos and ruin." Ifza pulled at her bonds. "And what happens if you succeed? What happens, Ifza, when you and Khaliq kill off more than half of the world's population? Will he be satisfied? Or will he have you hunt down every last person — men, women, children — and make them beg for their lives before he has you slit their throats."

"We...we do what we must."

Ifza's voice faltered. This was the first time in years that she had felt unsure of her and her brother's motives. The care with which she was being shown confused her greatly. These weren't murderous monsters — Waleed seemed to be quite the opposite.

*No!* She knew it was a game, a trap.

Ifza sneered and bore daggers into Waleed's eyes. The older man didn't waver. His face was still soft and caring. He really did feel sorry for Ifza — for her life — her upbringing.

Waleed turned and slowly walked over to the left-hand wall of the bare room, though, Ifza now saw that it wasn't as empty as she had originally thought. A small square table sat pushed up against the wall, and resting atop it were a corded phone attached to a landline, and a tiny rectangular box. It was hard to make out, but Ifza deduced that the object was some kind of speaker.

Waleed picked up the receiver.

"Who are you calling?" Ifza asked.

"Your brother. I want to ask him a question."

Ifza's eyes were wide. "What? How?"

Waleed gave her a small grin. "You don't think you're the only one with connections, do you?" He began to dial. "Let's just say that not everyone inside the Scales of Anubis agrees, wholeheartedly, with Khaliq's vision of death."

"And my brother?" Ifza asked. "What are you going to ask him?"

Waleed brought the receiver to his ear and gazed at Ifza. "I'm going to ask Khaliq how much you mean to him."

The door burst open, and in marched a pair of thickly built men. One reached forward and latched onto Ifza's head, gripping it tightly. Ifza shouted, but quickly had something jammed into her mouth by the second newcomer. The gag had one specific purpose. She wouldn't be able to alert her brother of her situation.

Her brother answered the call, his voice booming through the small speaker. "What!" It was obvious to see that he was in the middle of something.

It made Waleed smile. "Hello, Khaliq."

"Waleed..." Khaliq's gravelly voice was overflowing with anger, and slightly tinged with annoyance. "How did you get this number?"

Waleed chuckled softly. "Oh, you know, I have my ways. Let's just say that not everyone in your cabal is as loyal to you as you think."

"What do you want?"

Waleed leaned against the wall next to the phone. "Isn't it obvious? I want to negotiate."

Khaliq laughed. "You have nothing to offer me, Waleed."

Waleed eyed Ifza. "How about your sister?" The elder Ayad sibling didn't reply. Waleed used Khaliq's silence to his advantage and pushed the man more. "Your team failed in their attempt to destroy my operation, as did Ifza. And the reason she was left alive was — "

"Because you are weak."

Ifza's eyes left Waleed's and locked in on the speaker.

"You couldn't do what needed to be done."

Waleed made sure Ifza was paying attention, and he stepped in between the speaker and the understandably confused woman. When he spoke, he did so deliberately and calmly.

"Sparing someone's life is not weakness, Khaliq. Even a person, such as your sister, doesn't deserve to die like a stray in the street." He took a deep breath, already knowing the answer to his upcoming question. "Will you give up your quest to save your sister's life?"

Khaliq didn't hesitate. "I will not."

Ifza turned away from Waleed, tears streaming down her face. He could, quite literally, see her world come undone. Everything she had believed in — killed for — was wholly based on her loyalty to her brother. It seemed the dedication had only gone one way, though.

It broke Waleed's heart.

He stepped back over to the corded phone and hovered his hand above the speaker button. "See, Khaliq, I am not the weak one here. You are."

Waleed hung up.

He walked over to Ifza and gently removed her gag. "I am sorry." Without another word, Waleed left the room, closing the door behind him.

# CHAPTER 78
# BAAHIR

Baahir slipped away, moving quickly but quietly. Once he was out of direct sight, he picked up his pace and slid down the steep side of the natural pyramidal formation. He was lost in his adrenaline-enhanced escape, and before he knew it, he was back on flat ground.

Baahir didn't know how far he'd get before anyone noticed that he was missing, but he was hoping it'd be far enough. He ran for the edge of town, pumping his arms hard. His legs burned like crazy.

The explosion at the peak of Gebel Dist wasn't all that loud from where Baahir currently was. He looked over his shoulder and watched as a smoke plume shot into the sky.

Baahir pictured the ruined seal. *Bastards.*

He felt an impact of a small object on the ground around him, then another.

*What the hell?*

His reaction was met with realization. They were *shooting* at him. Baahir began moving in serpentine patterns, never heading in one direction for too long. A half a mile from town, the gunfire stopped. With the pause, Baahir slowed and straightened out his trajectory. He fell into a steady jog, trying to decide on his next course of action. He had no phone, and no ID of any kind. Baahir had been relieved of his possessions shortly after arriving at The Pharaoh's Lounge.

*Need... to find one,* he thought, breathing hard.

Baahir stumbled, pausing against a lone boulder protruding from the sand. He turned to face Gebel Dist and spotted something he dreaded. A lone figure was nearly to the bottom of the formation, and if he had to guess who it was, he reckoned it was Ajmal. Though, the real question wasn't who had been sent, it was whether or not the person had been instructed to bring Baahir back to the temple seal or silence him.

At this point, given everything Baahir had just said to Khaliq, he wouldn't be surprised if the man hunting him was doing so with a kill order in his back pocket.

*Knowing my luck, yes. Yes, he does.*

# CHAPTER 79
# ZAHRA

**Port Said International Airport** | Port Said, Egypt

Weight issues delayed Zahra and the others longer than expected. The *Puss E. Galore* wasn't built to handle six grown adults, plus their gear. Cork was confident she could get them airborne but wasn't sure how high or for how long.

Ali had supplied Zahra, himself, and two additional men with parachutes. Zahra's was already secured to her body, fitting tighter than she remembered. She had clocked a decent number of hours skydiving, but it had been quite a while. Since her army days, in fact. Her nerves weren't buzzing from the prospect of jumping out of a perfectly good aircraft — but from jumping out of a sixty-year-old, overloaded Cessna.

*What could go wrong?* she thought. Then, she visualized herself pancaking into the desert.

"Okay," Cork called out from the cockpit. "It's now or never!"

Ali glanced at his men before turning to Zahra. She nodded.

"Take us up."

The pilot groaned. "I was afraid you'd say that." She powered up the engines and slowly pushed the Cessna's thrust lever forward.

They chugged along the runway, getting to takeoff speed in the nick of time. The nose lifted, then the rest of the plane. Cork needed to continue to apply more speed while also pulling back on the yoke. If the *Puss E. Galore* didn't properly respond, Cork would have to make a tough decision, and either push the Cessna harder, or find a nice, sandy spot to put her down.

Zahra gripped her armrest harder. The whine of the twin props grew louder. Cork wasn't in the business of giving up.

Luckily for them, the old bird didn't fail them.

Cork visibly relaxed. The tension in her shoulders subsided, as did her grip on the yoke.

"How high are you taking us?" Ali asked, shouting over the noise.

Cork shrugged. "High enough so we don't bonk a pyramid."

Ali's eyes darted to Zahra. "It would be suicidal to jump from that altitude."

The archaeologist smiled, implying that Cork had been joking. She faced the window and look out over the landscape.

*At least, I hope she's joking.*

# CHAPTER 80
# KHALIQ

**Gebel Dist** | Bahariya Oasis, Egypt

The beautifully carved seal over the doorway was now gone, obliterated by plastic explosives. There were stairs beyond the smoldering opening, and Khaliq was anxious to start exploring inside.

But the seal wasn't the only thing missing from the ancient space.

"Where is Hassan?" Khaliq was furious, and as usual, he blamed someone else.

Ajmal stood his ground, not allowing his employer to intimidate him. His obsession with the Temple of Anubis had clouded his judgment. If it were up to Ajmal, Baahir Hassan would have been dead long ago.

"He slipped away while we tended to the seal, per your orders."

Ajmal threw the last bit in for good measure. It was Khaliq's fault Baahir had gotten away. While Ajmal, Feroz, and Junaid took the time to properly set the charges, Khaliq had recessed into his own head, and lost track of Baahir. The man's entrenched psychosis was making him sloppy. He was also too used to getting his own way and having others do things for him.

His only job had been to keep an eye on *one* person while the others had worked.

Ajmal was fed up with his superior, and instead of fighting with him, he did the best thing for himself and walked away.

"Bring him back, Ajmal!" Khaliq called after him.

Ajmal growled and stopped. He looked over his shoulder. “And if he refuses to comply?”

Khaliq’s phone buzzed. He turned back toward the entrance and hovered his thumb over the screen. “Then bring me his corpse. I still want his blood.”

# CHAPTER 81
# AJMAL

The town of Bawiti was the largest settlement in the Bahariya Oasis, and the closest destination from Gebel Dist when traveling on foot. Ajmal had a feeling that it was where Baahir would go. His gut had rewarded him too. Down below, he could see a figure heading southeast, shambling along on what must have been tired legs.

He raised his pistol.

*I see you...*

But Baahir was too far away to hit with the small caliber. After a half dozen tries, Ajmal holstered his weapon and continued down the slopping face of Gebel Dist, fumbling with his phone while he did. He quickly notified Lahan and Qadim, the pair they dropped off at the southern edge of town, that the Egyptologist had escaped.

"Move a half a mile to the southeast and await further instruction."

Ajmal kept to a steady jog until he stepped onto a paved road. Directly in front of him were acres of farmland but nestled in between it all was a cream-colored wort in an otherwise green landscape. Ajmal had heard of the lavish resort. It had once been a mansion belonging to a European philanthropist. Now, it was a destination hotel for the rich.

He crossed the battered, two-lane street and continued along the narrow dirt path. It led up a soft sloping incline, winding itself back and forth to the resort. If he were Baahir, that's where he would go. The first thing Ajmal would have done was find a phone and call for help.

*Can't let that happen,* Ajmal thought.

It wasn't just Khaliq's life on the line if news got out.

It was also his.

## CHAPTER 82
# ZAHRA

**Egyptian Airspace**

The overloaded Cessna cruised at an altitude of 800 feet, nearly twice the height of the Great Pyramid of Giza, the monolith that Cork had joking said she was going to try and avoid hitting with her plane. Cork guided their plane over the Giza Necropolis only because she thought it would be cool.

She was right. It really was cool.

Zahra could still see the three pyramids in her mind. She'd visited them several times in her life but had never seen them from this vantage point.

"Incredible," she said to herself. *This* was her heritage. *This* was Egypt.

Ali screamed into a satellite phone, and before Zahra could pull herself from the memory and listen in, he hung up. He slid the device back into his pack and delivered the news.

"My men on the ground say that Khaliq's convoy stopped near Bawiti."

"Bawiti?" Zahra asked. "The Bahariya Oasis?"

"The same."

Cork turned around. "That could be a problem, Zahra."

"It is?"

The pilot nodded. "Bawiti isn't exactly a big place, but it isn't all that small, either. Searching it on foot could take days."

"We don't have days," Rabia said.

Zahra shrugged. "But we don't have a choice."

Cork didn't look hopeful. She plopped back down in her seat. "We're nearly there. Where do you want to be dropped off?"

Zahra rolled her eyes. They weren't being "dropped off" anywhere.

"The main road into town is to the south," Ali chimed in. "I suggest we begin our search there. Hopefully, one of the locals stopped them."

Cork eyed Zahra in her overhead mirror.

Zahra nodded. "Do it."

# CHAPTER 83
# KHALIQ

**Gebel Dist** | Bahariya Oasis, Egypt

*"See, Khaliq, I am not the weak one here. You are."*

The line went dead.

Khaliq nearly crushed his phone with his bare hand. Waleed Badawi had captured his sister alive, and was attempting to use her as a bargaining chip.

It would not work, though. There was *nothing* more valuable than this mission — not even his dear sister's life.

Ifza's life was now her own responsibility.

He pocketed the device and raised his hands to his head. Khaliq would have ripped his hair out of his scalp if he had any. He clawed at his exposed skin and roared at the destroyed seal. His voice echoed down the newly unearthed stairway.

Khaliq knew what he had to do.

"Feroz," he said, getting the man to snap to attention, "with me. Junaid, stay here and guard the way in."

Feroz and Junaid glanced at one another. The second man shrugged and stepped back from the opening. Feroz blinked hard and attempted to swallow his fear.

Khaliq knelt atop Gebel Dist, in front of the cracked top step of a path that had not been used in thousands of years. He flicked on his flashlight, and pointed it into the pitch darkness to reveal a fairly ordinary corridor of stone. The corridor looked like it had been formed as a natural fissure that had been modified. The rounded ceiling had been smoothed out, and stairs were cut. It was impossible to tell which had been done first, not that it mattered to Khaliq. All he cared about was what would come at the end.

"The Temple of Anubis," he muttered.

"Sir?" Feroz asked. "What about Ajmal?"

Craning his head up and to the right, Khaliq melted his subordinate with his gaze.

Feroz dipped his head. "My apologies, Khaliq. Lead the way."

Khaliq stood and lifted his foot, holding it aloft for just a moment. He was relishing the fact that he was the first man to cross into Anubis' lair since the god's time on Earth. It felt fitting, too, that he was the one to do so.

He closed his eyes and lowered his foot. When it connected, he didn't stop again. Khaliq ducked his head and slinked into the low-cut path. He wondered if there had once been a grand entryway surrounding this spot. He figured there was, picturing it in his mind as he eyed his steps. The steps had been shallowly constructed, carved right out of Gebel Dist. As he and Feroz continued down the steep grade, the way spiraled to their right, and the ceiling rose, relieving the stress on the men's backs.

*Four times?* Khaliq thought, estimating the number of times they went around. It was hard to tell how deep they were going.

The path ended at an opening as big and as wide as the stairwell itself. Khaliq showed his light through it and found flat ground on the other side. He stepped through and played the beam across the walls. Feroz entered the space and added his own light. The circular chamber was forty feet squared and sported a low, eight-foot-high ceiling.

"Incredible..." Khaliq was entranced by what he saw. It was the first sign of anything noteworthy since the seal.

Classic Egyptian artwork greeted the two men. There were hundreds of humans depicted sideways, kneeling, and pointing in the same direction — toward a doorway cut into the opposite wall.

"Worshippers," Khaliq said.

Feroz aimed his light into the next corridor. "Anubis?"

Khaliq didn't reply. He crossed the chamber with purpose. Halfway there, he stopped, hearing a *click* under his foot. It was followed shortly by a low, reverberating *clunk.*

"Move!" Khaliq shouted, sprinting for the chamber exit.

Feroz made it to the hallway first.

The two men practically dove through it just as a dozen slots opened in the ceiling.

Khaliq was immediately mesmerized by the sight, but the slots didn't stay empty for long. A second later, *things* began dropping from them.

And the things were alive.

Black, wriggling creatures poured out of the open holes. Khaliq backed away, pulled along by Feroz before either man could study the living payload enough to identify it.

*A trap,* Khaliq thought, amazed. *And it's still working.*

This place had been constructed centuries ago, and had been lying in wait after all this time. Not only was Khaliq astonished — he felt a well of fear rise up in him, as well.

He shuddered. These creatures — bugs, or beetles, he couldn't be sure — must be cannibalistic, eating each other to stay alive. The hidden compartments were their home, and they had, most likely, never ventured out of the darkness of the cavern.

"Slowly," he ordered. "Watch your step."

Feroz nodded and did as he was instructed and eased up on his pace. Both men directed their lights exclusively to the steps. If there was one trap, there was bound to be another.

As soon as Khaliq made contact with the top step, the impact sank the step an inch, setting off another *clunk* back in the chamber. He lifted his foot, and the step rose back into place. He attempted to sink the step again, but it didn't move.

The trap had been reset. He'd need to remember that...

They continued down and around in circles again. Khaliq estimated they had traveled the same depth as before. A second opening swallowed Feroz's light. He slowed to a crawl and edged out into the void. This space was infinitely larger than the last one. A sound like running water greeted them, but Khaliq didn't see anything in the illumination that hinted there was water nearby. The walls of the cavern were sixty feet from one another.

"It sounds like radio static," Feroz said.

Khaliq agreed. The noise unnerved him.

The ground beneath them narrowed to three feet in width and extended through the nothingness. Khaliq followed it with his light, realizing what it was.

"It's a landbridge." He stepped onto it. "We cross here."

He turned in time to see Feroz swallow down his fear and warily shuffle forward. The bridge was cracked and crumbling in places. If it broke underfoot, they'd fall into...what?

Khaliq needed to know.

He faced the abyss and directed his light into it. Surprisingly, it wasn't as far of a drop as he was expecting. But what it lacked in depth, it made up for in nastiness. The pit was some twenty feet down...and it moved.

"What is it?" Feroz asked.

But Khaliq already knew. His hands trembled. He had never seen so many in one place.

He removed his light from the godawful pit and faced his cohort, looking through the man and not at him.

"What are they, Khaliq?"

Feroz's question focused Khaliq's attention, and he met the man's fear-filled eyes.

"Man-killers... Tens of thousands of them."

Translating from the Greek *Androctomus*, 'man-killers' venom produced one of the deadliest neurotoxins in the world. The black, fattail scorpion was feared by everyone in the desert communities of North Africa and the Middle East. They sported a long, agonizing history of killing healthy, grown men quite easily.

"Man-killers?" Feroz asked, leaning over the edge. His light found the sea of creatures. His face went white, and he stammered backward. Khaliq caught his arm before he could walk himself off the landbridge and into the throng below.

But Khaliq's efforts weren't enough.

A section of the pathway broke away beneath Feroz's foot, and he dropped, ripping out of Khaliq's flat-footed grasp. In a last-ditch effort to save his subordinate, Khaliq latched onto the man's backpack, but only came away with the pack itself. Feroz slipped free and fell for over two stories before landing flat on his back.

He screamed in pain and was almost instantly overwhelmed by thousands of man-killers.

Feroz's cries only lasted a few seconds.

Khaliq waited for Feroz's body to finish convulsing before he pulled his attention away. He was alone now. It was fitting too. Khaliq wanted to be the first to see Anubis' lair. Feroz's death had all but guaranteed that.

He shook with anticipation. The muscles in his body and face spasmed slightly. Something in him broke. He no longer had any interest in pushing forward *slowly*.

With his flashlight gripped tightly in one hand and Feroz's backpack in the other, Khaliq took off at a sprint, needing to see what was at the other end before more time passed.

# CHAPTER 84
# BAAHIR

**Big House** | Bawiti, Egypt

*The Big House* was, in essence, a big house. And it was hosting a community event for the residents of Bawiti. Dozens of vendors had set up tents on the grounds outside the estate's gates. It reminded Baahir of the markets he had seen around the world. People hawked their goods, shouting as loud as they could at every single passerby.

This was Baahir's chance to evade his pursuer. He needed a place to hide. His first choice was the Big House itself, but he doubted a man in his current, filthy state would even be allowed on the premises. So, he decided to keep as many tents in between him and Ajmal as possible. He stationed himself at the center of the market, spying Gebel Dist in the distance. There, he watched and waited, eventually spotting a hulking mass hiking up the long, winding drive.

The other option had been to keep running and head for the middle of town, but it was a few miles off, and Baahir was too tired. This was his best option. Baahir peeked out from behind a booth selling handmade trinkets constructed of bits of junk. They were impressive, resembling miniature sarcophagi and pyramids.

Ajmal stopped and swept his head from left to right slowly, scanning the area for his prize. Baahir inhaled and squeaked when Ajmal snapped his eyes directly toward him.

*Did he see me?* Baahir asked himself. He didn't think so, but nor was he going to take the chance.

He scurried behind three more tents and parked himself behind the fourth. He leaned out around the hastily built structure and was forced to peer through a haze of deliciousness.

Everything in front of him was some sort of food item.

Baahir hadn't enjoyed a proper meal in some time. The lamb looked incredible, and the spices wafted into his nose.

*Dammit!*

Ajmal had vanished. Baahir had lost the goon somewhere between hiding behind the tent and pining over the sights and smells of this food.

"You want something?" a voice asked.

He looked up. "No, I — "

But the vendor wasn't speaking to Baahir — he was talking to Ajmal. Baahir shuffled backward, bumping into a table directly behind him.

"Watch it!" cried a young woman.

Before Baahir could apologize, he planted a hand on her table, leaping over it. He crashed to the ground beside her. She attempted to berating Baahir, but was quickly silenced.

"Shhh!" He held a finger to his lips. "If you stay quiet, I will buy *everything* you have!" That quieted her, but she frowned down at him.

He suddenly realized something else about the woman.

She was absolutely *gorgeous.* Her skin reminded him of delicious cocoa.

He swallowed. "Please..."

She glared down at him, then back up to the crowd in the market. "He with you?"

The young woman's inflection was similar to the dialects Baahir had heard in Kenya. Her English was flawless but accented. Baahir figured she was talking about Ajmal, but he didn't know for sure. "What does he look like?"

"Big and angry."

He belly-crawled under the front table. "Yep, that's him." A heavy cloth was draped over the front of it so no one on the outside of her booth could see what laid beneath. The contents now consisted of this woman's personal belongings.

And Baahir.

"What does he want?"

Baahir snickered. "To kill me."

She looked appalled. "And this is funny?"

Baahir shrugged. "If you knew what I have been through, I— "

"Can I help you?" she asked, stepping forward, talking to someone else Baahir couldn't see.

Her foot landed on Baahir's pinky finger. He squeaked, but thankfully his protector coughed to cover up the sound. She subtly lifted her foot while continuing to speak to the newcomer, allowing Baahir to remove his trapped digit.

"I said — *can I help you*?"

A shadow blotted out the light on the vendor's face, and Baahir knew, in that instant, that it was Ajmal. His pursuer was leaning in close to the merchant now, and Baahir could hear his breath falling out over her face. Baahir wouldn't forgive himself if he got this nice woman hurt.

"I'm looking for my friend," Ajmal said, "have you seen him?"

Baahir's blood went cold. The woman could just as easily sell him out and save her own skin. He had given her no reason to trust him. No reason to think *he* was the good guy.

*Please don't, please don't, please don't...*

"That depends on what this friend looks like."

Ajmal described Baahir perfectly.

An awkward silence hung over them as the vendor contemplated his question.

"No, I'm sorry — I haven't seen anyone who fits that description."

Baahir looked up and watched her eyes go wide. He couldn't see Ajmal, but Baahir guessed he was giving the woman a look that could rust iron. He was attempting to intimidate her without the use of force.

Thankfully, there were too many people around from him to *actually* use force.

Then the shadow on her face vanished. Baahir could hear heavy footsteps fade as Ajmal left.

She waved him off but spoke to Baahir through gritted teeth. "You owe me, big time."

"Name's Baahir."

"I don't care what — "

"And you are?" he asked, wearing the cheesiest grin he could muster. He hoped it was coming across as a 'cute, harmless gentleman.'

Her nostrils flared. "Durah, but — "

"Well, Durah," he said. "How about a fancy dinner and a movie?"

She paused, then snorted out a laugh and crossed her arms. "You are unbelievable."

"*Two* dinners, then. Drinks too!"

She didn't speak.

Durah simply held out an open hand that he took to mean 'stay down.' It was low enough on her leg that only Baahir would be able to see it. Crunching footfalls announced the arrival of someone familiar, but as soon as they started towards him, they faded away again. Ajmal was still on the prowl.

The Kenyan glared down at Baahir, once again looking furious for being put in a position such as this.

Baahir could do nothing else except stay hidden beneath her table. For good measure, he held up three fingers, silently increasing his offer.

To his delight, Durah didn't kick him in the ribs or stomp on his hand. Instead, the corner of her mouth curled into a smile, and she shook her head and rolled her eyes. Then, the vendor got back to work, and left Baahir to himself.

She coaxed him out of hiding sometime later.

"I believe your friend is gone. I have not seen him in a while."

Slowly, Baahir poked his head out from below the table and scanned the surrounding area. He waited and watched, not seeing Ajmal anywhere, either. He groaned, and crawled out on his hands and knees. Durah helped him up, then handed him a bottle of water. Baahir was struggling physically, and was tired and thirsty.

"About our deal..." she began.

Baahir took a long pull from the bottle and nodded. He swallowed and recapped the drink. "I don't have any money."

The Kenyan let loose with a string of what Baahir guessed were curses in her native tongue. He held up his hands. "But... I *will* uphold my end of the bargain, Durah. Scouts' honor."

"You were scout?"

"Actually, no—but I promise to keep my word."

The vendor huffed out an annoyed breath. "Fine. Two dinners. With drinks." She started to turn away but was stopped.

"Make it three." He grinned.

Durah could only roll her eyes.

"One more thing," he said sheepishly.

She locked eyes with Baahir, but didn't speak.

"Do you have a phone I could borrow?"

She looked like she was about to hit him over the head with one of her wares, but finally relented. "Baahir..." she handed him a phone. "Did I mention that I am *not* a cheap date."

**Suez Shipping Company** | Port Said, Egypt

There was no way of telling how much time had passed, and Ifza didn't, honestly, care. Her brother had betrayed her and left her to die at the hand of their enemy. She had been loyal and had killed so many in the name of Anubis.

What did it bring her now?

Her head dipped as stared at the concrete floor.

Suddenly, two men rushed inside and forced a sack onto her head before she could identify who they were. One unshackled her while the other held her in place while pressing the muzzle of a gun to her temple. She was re-cuffed behind her back and dragged forward. Ifza wasn't given the option to walk.

They brought her to a flight of stairs and hauled her up them. The tips of her shoes bounced off every single one. A heavy door shut somewhere behind her, and she was tossed to the ground.

"Don't move, or you'll be shot!" a man yelled. She did as she was told, and laid still, listening as a pair of feet faded into the distance of the grand room. The high ceilings and hard floors echoed every movement, clueing her into the extensiveness of the space around her.

As soon as the pair's footfalls disappeared, a new sound emerged from straight ahead. More footsteps, but not the same people who had just left her. Those men had gone off to the left.

There were more of them, too. They yelled and ordered each other to spread out and secure the suspect — Ifza.

If she had to guess, she was about to be arrested by local police. She was lifted to her knees and was freed of the heavy head covering, squinting against the light. Ifza found herself inside the main warehouse of the Suez Shipping Company, and she was alone except for the ten police officers that now surrounded her.

Ifza allowed a grin to form on her face. If there was ever a situation that Ifza was confident that she could escape, it was this one. These men weren't trained to hold someone like her. She'd be patient and wait for her opportunity.

Then, she'd strike.

# CHAPTER 86
# ZAHRA

The LALO jump that Zahra had just completed might have been the single most dangerous thing she'd ever attempted. Typically, a Low-Altitude, Low-Opening jump was designed to insert military personnel underneath the lower altitude limit of the enemy's radar. And unlike the static line variation, where the parachuter's ripcord was attached to a cable running along the inside of the aircraft, Zahra and company had been put in charge of popping their own chutes. Luckily, none of the quintet had pancaked into the Egyptian desert.

Cork would circle the area for as long as possible before heading back to Cairo to refuel. She'd wait at the airport until she was contacted.

"Later, Zahra!" Cork had yelled, waving over her shoulder. "Keep me posted, will ya?"

"Will do." Zahra had grinned and waved back. "See you around, Gwen."

The last thing that Zahra had witnessed before she leaped from the Cessna was Cork's face morphing into that of a primal beast. In retrospect, poking the bear, when that bear was your ride, probably wasn't a good idea.

"That was really stupid," Zahra said, feeling her entire body shaking from the massive adrenaline spike. No matter what she did, her hands wouldn't quit trembling.

The one positive was that the jump had been so quick that it was over before Zahra could process it.

Ali didn't acknowledge her. She could tell by the way he was struggling to unclip his harness that he was also suffering the same effects as her. Sometimes the high or rush an extreme athlete experienced was exactly what was needed to complete the maneuver, but in this case, it had only delayed them. They were forced to take a few minutes to get themselves under control before heading off.

Unsurprisingly, Rabia had recovered first, and had quickly unfolded the stock of her rifle. Then, she slipped the suppressor out of her bag and screwed it into place onto the tip of the barrel. The sniper was currently laying prone atop a rise to the north, doing a bit of reconnaissance through her weapon's high-powered scope. Her position overlooked the main street into the Bahariya Oasis, El Wahat Road.

"See anything?" Zahra shouted, cupping her hands around her mouth. The rest of the team was camped at the base of Rabia's perch.

The sniper didn't respond, but she did pack up her gear and made her way down to the rest of her team. When she was back at ground level, Zahra repeated the question.

"Anything?"

Rabia shook her head. "They're too far ahead of us."

Zahra figured as much. "Where should we start looking?"

"Ask the locals," Ali replied, speaking for the first time since landing. "Knowing Khaliq, he more than likely made a memorable entrance."

Zahra nodded her agreement and followed Rabia as she led them north. They skirted around the rise and took a moment to survey the roadway. Zahra realized something she didn't like. She and her people were dressed for war. They'd stick out like a sore thumb and alert the wrong kind of people.

She relayed her concerns. "We need a low-viz approach for this to work."

"Zahra's right," Rabia said, frowning.

So, the team removed their combat gear, hiding it below the rise. Now, they all still looked out of place, but now they didn't look like a small, militarized unit either. Rabia was forced to disassemble her beloved rifle and pack it into a large satchel. Happily, everyone's rifles sported folding stocks, same as Rabia's weapon. They slid into backpacks and were hidden from sight.

Ali, Elyas, and Tajj edged onto the side of the elevated roadway and tried to flag down a passing vehicle for a ride to town. Smartly, no one dared stop for three seemingly random, tough-looking men. After ten minutes of fail after fail after fail, Zahra slapped Ali on the shoulder.

"What?" Ali asked, not understanding the gesture.

"Have you ever seen professional wrestling before?"

Ali shook his head. He glanced at Elyas and Tajj. They also shook their heads, no.

"I just tagged you guys out." They didn't budge an inch. "It means get off the road!"

Elyas shrugged, and they did as they were told. Rabia started to follow them but was pulled back the other way by Zahra.

"Why don't you guys let the ladies handle this one?" Zahra gave the trio a playful wink and threw her arm over Rabia's shoulder, and stuck out her thumb.

Two minutes later, they had a ride. A scruffy-looking man pulled a 1970s Chevy pickup onto the shoulder and rolled down his window. He was a local and sported a thick head of black hair and the bushiest beard Zahra had ever seen. With her arm still draped around Rabia's shoulder, she gave the driver a wide smile.

"Don't suppose you can give us a ride to town, could you?"

The local grinned. Zahra doubted he saw very many women hanging out on the side of the road over the years.

"Where's your car?" he asked, looking around.

Zahra thumbed behind her. "In the ditch."

He tried to look past Zahra and Rabia but didn't get far. Zahra forced Rabia to move with her, and they sidestepped back into the local's line of sight. He was rightfully suspicious, and was doubting the real reason the two women had been "stranded" on the outskirts of town.

Rabia shrugged out of Zahra's arm. "We'll pay you."

The local smiled. They agreed upon a fee, and the local looked tickled.

...Until Zahra signaled for Ali, Elyas, and Tajj to join them.

"I thought it was just the two of you?"

Zahra glanced at Rabia. "I never said that... did I?"

Rabia shook her head, hand in her pocket.

"Is this a problem?" Rabia asked.

The local growled. "Your friends must sit in the back." The bed of the truck was thickly lined with hay and would keep their asses from becoming too sore during the ride to town.

Zahra eyed Ali, Elyas, and Tajj. She winked. "Sorry, boys."

Ali stepped up to the bed and stopped, seeing something within it she didn't like.

"What's wrong?" Zahra asked.

"Come and see."

Zahra left Rabia and went to see what had Ali's feathers so ruffled. Even before she got there, she knew. Zahra could smell it.

She cooed. "How sweet."

Zahra counted nine Baladi goats of all shapes and sizes. They were a prevalent breed in the region and provided a good source of meat and milk. A few of the truck-dwellers were quite old, some no more than a couple of months old.

All of them were covered in their own filth. One of the younglings popped its head up and playfully bleated, allowing Zahra to scratch its chin. She smiled, much to the disdain of Ali and the others.

She retracted her hand and cleared her throat. "Yes, well, have fun."

Ali didn't budge. His face sported a deep scowl.

"Look," Zahra said. "It's either this or you walk. You choose."

Zahra rejoined Rabia, and the pair circled around the front of the truck and climbed in. Their chauffeur eyed their big, overstuffed packs.

"What's in the bags?"

Rabia looked forward. "Tools."

"Tools?"

She calmly turned her attention to the local. "Yes, tools." Her tone was direct and laced with a warning.

Stop asking.

Smartly, he did, moving on to something else.

"So, your friends, are they — "

Rabia held up her hand and silenced the local. The bed of the truck shook and bent as the three men climbed in.

"Now, we can go," Rabia said, handing over the cash.

He accepted the money, counted twice, then threw the vehicle into drive and puttered off.

Zahra cleared her throat. "We're looking for a friend."

"No! No more friends!" the local snapped, turning and staring at her.

"Hang on, hang on..." Zahra lifted a hand up in defense. "He doesn't need a ride, or anything. We're just... *looking* for him, that's all."

He calmed and faced the road.

"Can you think of anywhere an out-of-towner would go?" Rabia asked. Her voice was steady and in control.

"If you came for the nightlife, you came to the wrong place."

"What's the right place?" she asked. "Somewhere that will have a lot of people?"

The driver didn't answer.

"He's not really into nightlife, per se," Zahra continued. "But he did get into some... trouble."

The driver swallowed.

"Please," Zahra said. "We're just trying to prevent *more* trouble. Last we heard, he was heading in this direction. Is there somewhere busy? Like a shopping center?"

"The Big House."

"The Big House?" she asked.

He nodded. "Yes. There is a big event there today."

"Can you take us there?" Zahra asked.

"Yes." He thumbed over his shoulder. "I hope to sell my goats there today."

**The Big House**

The trek through the Bahariya Oasis wasn't a long one, but it took longer than she would have liked. The roads weren't in great shape, and neither was Zahra's mode of transportation. She felt terrible for the boys in the back. She and Rabia held back their commentary every time their driver hit a divot in the ground. The shockwave pounded Zahra's lower back. She imagined the truck bed looking like the inside of a clothes dryer, albeit one with goats and goat shit inside.

Zahra wasn't looking forward to smelling her associates — not that she smelled of roses, either. Right now, she couldn't tell whether it was her own body odor she smelled, or Rabia's, or even the local's stink.

*Probably all three,* she thought. Even riding with the windows down did very little to satisfy their need for fresh air.

Zahra leaned forward and peered up at the structure at the summit of the property.

"Geez, you weren't kidding."

*The Big House* was enormous and stood out against everything they had seen so far in Bawiti. The surrounding area was made up of, mostly, farms and shops with a dusting of modern industry.

"How many rooms do you think it has?"

Rabia shrugged.

Zahra repeated the question in Arabic.

"Forty-nine," the driver replied.

They rode in silence the rest of the way. Two minutes later, the local pulled off and announced that this was where they would be getting out. Zahra thanked him for his help, and she and Rabia waved their goodbyes. Ali, Elyas, and Tajj did not acknowledge the local in any way. They were too busy rubbing their aching backs and asses.

Zahra curled her nose.

"Don't say a word!" Ali stopped her with a pointed finger.

She and Rabia shared a look, but neither one of them laughed. It wasn't their fault they now smelled like a barn. She knew that if the situation was reversed, Ali would have kept his mouth shut too.

As the local pulled away, the baby goat popped his head up and bleated at Zahra. She smiled and waved, getting a second bleat out of him.

"You make friends fast," Rabia said, stepping up next to her.

"Yea." She sighed. "Enemies too."

The group headed into the throng of tents and stands. The market seemed to be part of a bigger celebration, and from the looks of it, these people weren't leaving anytime soon.

"What is all this?" Rabia asked, getting the attention of a nearby vendor.

"We celebrate!" the man shouted.

Zahra looked around. "What are you celebrating?"

"The day the first owners of Big House died."

*That* wasn't what Zahra was expecting to hear. "And that's worthy of celebrating?"

"Yes," the vendor replied. "They were very bad people."

And with that, he turned to a group of patrons, holding up his wears.

Zahra's front pocket buzzed. She removed the device and saw a number she didn't recognize.

"Um, hello?"

*"Zahra?"*

She knew the voice in an instant. "Baahir!" Zahra's hand went to her mouth, and her eyes welled with tears. "Thank *God*!" Zahra yelled, grabbing Rabia's shoulder and stopping her. The sniper waved for Ali and the others to do the same. "Where are you?"

The response came back immediately. *"Turn around."*

# CHAPTER 88
# ZAHRA

Zahra spun on a dime and frantically looked around. She saw a lone, unmoving individual gazing at her from only one-hundred feet from where she was standing. Without looking away, she ended the call and pocketed her phone. She moved off, walking slowly, at first. The crowd was thickest here. She shoved through, unapologetically, keying in on one thing and one thing only.

Her brother.

Baahir matched her stride for stride. Soon, the siblings were speed-walking, then sprinting toward one another. At the very last moment, an elderly couple walked out in front of them, making the pair skid awkwardly to a halt. Once they had safely passed them, Zahra threw herself in Baahir's arms, and sobbed uncontrollably.

Baahir whispered to her. "It's okay, Zahra, I'm here. I'm fine." They separated, and Zahra wiped her eyes as he continued. "They told me you were dead."

"She *should* be," Rabia said, coming up behind Zahra. "This one has a death wish, for sure."

Baahir grinned. "Zahra has always been a little reckless... yet here she is — alive and well." He took in the state of his big sister. "Maybe not *so* well, huh?"

Zahra laughed softly, nodding. "I've been better."

Baahir slipped his arm around Zahra's shoulder. "Who are your friends?"

She ticked off the names of her companions one at a time. "This is Rabia, and the two big guys are Elyas and Tajj."

"And him?" Baahir asked, tipping her chin at the third man.

He held out his hand. "I am Ali Badawi." Baahir shook it. "You may know my father."

"Wally?"

Ali nodded. "Yes, but no one here calls him that."

"Speaking of fathers..." Baahir said.

"Dad is fine," Zahra replied. "He's in Port Said with Wally."

"He's here?"

"He is, though it wasn't by choice." Baahir went to say something but was stopped by Zahra. "We'll catch up on all that in a second."

"Baahir?"

A stunning, dark-skinned woman approached Zahra's brother from behind. She wasn't at all happy with the attention she was getting. Whoever she was, she seemed to know Baahir.

"Everyone, this is Durah." He held out his phone and gave it to the woman. It was easy to see that the device belonged to her and not Baahir. "She helped me escape — hid me from Ajmal."

"Ajmal?" Rabia asked, tensing as she gripped her bag. "Is he still here?"

Baahir shook his head. "I don't think so. That doesn't mean he isn't still close by, though."

"We need to take care," Ali said, looking around. "He's a very dangerous man."

"Tell me about it," Baahir said, scratching his head. He winced when he touched some unseen wound.

Durah eyed Zahra. "What your brother tells me, it is true?"

"I'm afraid so, yes."

She bit her lip and nodded. "Well then, go with God. May he protect you." She looked at Baahir. "Don't forget our deal..."

The group found a quieter place to continue their reunion. Baahir led them to a low stone wall to the right of the front gates of *The Big House.* He sat and let out a long breath. Zahra sat next to him. Rabia sat next to her, cradling a large duffel bag between her knees.

"What's in the bag?" he asked.

Rabia leaned around Zahra, eyeing Baahir. "A very big gun."

His eyes widened, and he glanced at his sister. Zahra smiled sheepishly.

The siblings recounted everything they had been through so far, skipping the less important details. Those would come later.

When Zahra got to the part of Grant being kidnapped from the museum, Baahir placed his hand on top of hers. "I'm sorry. I know you too were close."

"Can we do anything?" she asked. "He's suffering because of me."

He shrugged. "I'm not sure, but we need to stop them, either way."

She wiped away a drying tear and nodded. "We do, but I'm honestly a little shocked to hear you say it. I figured you'd want the first ticket back to Cairo?"

Baahir gazed out over the bustling market. "A lot has changed."

Zahra put her hand on his shoulder. "Yeah... A lot has."

Baahir stood, gaining the attention of everyone. "I've seen what they have planned. I've been in the proverbial 'belly of the beast,' Zahra. *Millions* will die if we do nothing. Grant..." his voice caught. "What I saw him become... That can't happen again."

"And not to the extent that Khaliq strives for," Ali said, speaking for the first time since their introductions. "If he completes his goal, and he gets his plague, there will be no stopping it."

"Are we sure about that?" Zahra asked. "This is a centuries-old virus, after all. There could be something simple out there to counter it."

"There could be, yes," Ali agreed. "But we don't have the luxury of time, nor do we have a sample to test."

Zahra stood. "Where is he? Where is Khaliq?"

Her brother turned and pointed to the northwest. "Gebel Dist. We found an entrance into the mountain a few hours ago, just before I made a run for it."

Zahra met the eyes of everyone involved. All of them, including Baahir, gave her a curt nod. They were ready to go.

"Right... Gebel Dist it is."

# CHAPTER 89
# BAAHIR

Baahir stepped away. "Hang on." Zahra dug her phone out of her pocket and held it out. "You still have one more call to make."

It took Baahir a second to figure it out. When he did, he hesitated in taking the phone, but ultimately did. He dialed the appropriate number and turned away from the others, pulling the phone up to his ear.

*"Zahra?"* George Kane asked from the other end.

Baahir had not heard his father's voice in some time. "No, it's — "

*"Baahir? Thank the heavens. It's great to hear your voice, son!"* He sounded choked up. *"Are you okay — is Zahra there too?"*

"Yeah, she's here too. We're both fine... Dad."

That was the first time Baahir had called his father anything but "George" since his mother had died. The gesture didn't go unnoticed.

*"I love you, son."*

Baahir looked over his shoulder at Zahra. "Yeah," he let out a shaky breath, "I love you too... and, uh... sorry for everything. I—"

*"It's okay, Baahir. We'll sort everything out later, okay?"* Baahir closed his tear-filled eyes and nodded, feeling years of guilt and anger lift off his shoulders. *"Can your sister talk?"*

"Yeah, she's right here."

Baahir handed the phone back to Zahra. The group headed off, aiming for the lump in the sand off to the northwest. They weaved in and out of congested crowds, all the while Zahra chatted with their father. Baahir was still trying to process the short, but sweet, conversation he just had with his estranged parent. It filled him with regret. He had avoided the man for years because of something he now knew, for an absolute fact, wasn't his fault.

It was Khaliq's doing.

That enraged him.

Zahra hung up and looked grim.

"What's wrong?" Baahir asked.

"So, apparently, they captured Ifza Ayad during a failed raid on the SSC."

"Why is that bad?" Ali asked.

"Because she escaped police custody."

Oh, Baahir thought, that is bad.

"Nothing we can do about it from here," Rabia said. "I suggest we keep our focus on stopping Khaliq."

She was right.

Since Baahir was the only one of the six-man team to have been there so far, he took the lead and guided the assault team along. Soon, the shouting vendors and "oohing and aahing" patrons vanished, and the human centipede snaked its way down the dirt road, back to the edge of the city.

"Hang on," Rabia said. She cycled through a series of hand gestures, and Ali, Elyas, and Tajj each ran off in different directions, disappearing from view. Rabia stayed put and dove into her oversized duffel. In no time at all, she hefted a monstrous rifle, her "very big gun," as she had put it.

"What are you — "

The sniper silenced Baahir with a raised hand. Seconds later, the *thwap* of two suppressed shots softly echoed through the landscape. Baahir hit the dirt, earning a grin out of Rabia.

"What the hell was that?" Baahir asked, standing in time with Rabia and Zahra.

"We weren't alone," Rabia replied.

Baahir looked around, seeing nothing. "You sure about that?"

"Yes."

Elyas and Tajj rejoined them, each of them now sporting assault rifles slung around their backs. Ali came up from behind them, having not fired a shot. He was also carrying a weapon of the same assortment.

The gunmen nodded to Rabia, confirming their findings. They had just killed Lahan and Qadim in the blink of an eye — and thank goodness they did. If not, Baahir and the others would have been gunned down from behind.

"Wait, you said 'four,' right?"

"Ajmal..." Ali said, gritting his teeth. "He's still out here somewhere. We need to be careful."

Baahir agreed. "Definitely." He gave Rabia a slight bow and held out his hand. "So, um, ladies first?"

Zahra's hands found her hips, and she sighed and shook her head. Baahir was way out of his league right now. Asking Rabia and Zahra to lead the pack was the smart thing to do. He fell in line behind them, with Ali, Elyas, and Tajj bringing up the rear. They swiftly crossed the road and found cover within a thicket of dried-out shrubs.

# CHAPTER 90
# KHALIQ

**Beneath Gebel Dist**

Khaliq roared in anger. The next room he found himself in wasn't the long-sought temple he was after. The burning desire to find Anubis' stronghold was still inside, but the desire to get there immediately had subsided some. Khaliq now walked instead of running into the unknown. The rising mania had slithered itself from being deeply rooted in every inch of his body to being mostly in his head.

Khaliq mumbled to himself as he progressed, his eyes darting left and right, taking everything in.

Khaliq paused mid-stride, seeing something on the floor ahead. Even from here, in the dim aura of his flashlight, he could tell what it was.

A foot.

Then, another.

He swept his flashlight back and forth, taking in the scene. The large space was naturally formed, and it featured a series of stalactites hanging from the domed ceiling. Interestingly, there were no stalagmites reaching up to greet them. Khaliq decided that they had been removed some time ago and moved on with his exploration.

Bodies littered the room. Very few were whole. Khaliq thought back to when Grant Upton tore one of his scientists apart with his bare hands.

*Is that what happened here?*

Stone slabs spread throughout this section of the cave, each standing vertically about eight feet tall. They were clearly manmade, and Khaliq stepped up to the first one.

It wasn't just stone that met him.

The remains of a human had been fashioned to the rock.

...with spikes.

The poor soul hadn't exactly been *crucified,* but the means of attachment had been similar, and it had likely been no less painful. This person had been held down and nailed to a block of stone.

And then what had happened here? Why had someone nailed this person to the stone while still alive?

Khaliq's mind raced, then his eyes grew to saucers. He whispered in the darkness.

"It's a laboratory..."

# CHAPTER 91
# ZAHRA

**Gebel Dist**

Zahra and the others stopped at the base of the large pyramidal formation. Rabia took the extra time to piece her Macmillan Tac-338 back together, and thankfully, everyone was able to catch their breath.

Zahra felt exhausted already, and she knew they hadn't even *done* anything yet.

Unfortunately, Rabia was finished assembling the rifle long before Zahra felt sufficiently rested. She hefted it up and peered through its powerful scope, doing a little recon while Zahra and Baahir watched on.

"Anything?" Zahra asked, removing her war belt from her backpack. She sat next to the sniper but faced the opposite direction while buckling the belt in place. At the moment, she was more worried about what could be behind them versus what was on top of Gebel Dist.

*Ajmal.*

"Nothing I can see from here." She pulled her face away from the scope. "We need to get closer."

And so, they did.

Zahra stood and slipped her Glock from her bag, holstering it on her right hip. Her trusty grappling hook went into place on her left hip, as did her handheld flashlight. She also had her blade sheathed at the small of her back. Zahra breathed easier, knowing her gear was within reach.

Baahir led them this time, showing them the way Khaliq and his crew had taken. The hike wasn't as bad as Zahra thought it would be, though she did hurt worse because of it. Her back, knees, and feet were already in rough shape. Now she could add ankles and hips to the list of injuries. The uneven incline was doing a number on her.

"Ugh," she groaned, pausing and kneading the base of her spine — just above her butt. "Gonna hurt for a month after this."

Rabia continued past her. "Better than being dead."

*True,* she thought. *Or is it?* Zahra had never hurt in so many places at one time.

She put one foot in front of the other and caught up with her new friend. Rabia kept surprising her. At first, the woman was an enigma. She was stoic and unreadable. But since they had first met, the local had opened up a bit and shown Zahra a piece of herself — her personality. She didn't think people like Rabia possessed a disposition other than being a stone-cold killer twenty-four-seven, so she was pleasantly surprised to discover more about who the woman behind the sniper was.

And she was already starting to think she'd make a good, long-term friend.

"Hang on," Ali said suddenly, pointing. They all stopped. "I see something." He was looking through a pair of sleek binoculars. "Down!" he hissed, dropping to his stomach. Everyone followed his lead.

"Rabia," he said.

"On it," she replied.

Zahra was only a couple of feet behind her, and she watched the professional intently, keen on learning something useful. There was one thing that Rabia didn't do, and that was flinch. She never displayed any nervous jitters. Even Zahra still got the shakes on occasion.

"See him?" Ali asked.

"No, where did you — " The pause told Zahra that her target had just come into view. And the sound that followed, like a pair of two-by-fours slapping each other — said that she saw enough of him to take the shot. She got up onto her knees. "Threat neutralized."

Baahir got to his feet and helped Rabia up. "That was impressive."

She shook her head. "Killing is never something to marvel over."

"I didn't mean — "

"I know what you meant. Just don't do it."

Rabia headed off.

Baahir leaned in close to his sister. "Is she always this intense?"

Zahra's hands found her hips. "Want her number?"

Everybody was breathing hard by the time they made it to the top. Once there, Rabia confirmed her kill — easy to do considering the amount of blood and brain matter that had been scattered all over the Saharan landmark. No one else paid the gruesome scene any attention, however. Everyone else was staring at the hole in the top of Gebel Dist.

"It exists," Ali said, letting his words trail off.

A breeze whipped by just as he uttered the words. It crawled up Zahra's spine and pushed her forward. She knelt in front of the narrow, steep stairwell and contemplated what to do next.

"I think it would be wise for Elyas and Tajj to stay here and keep watch," Ali suggested. Both men looked at their boss and nodded. "There are still enemies nearby."

*Ajmal,* Zahra thought.

"I agree," Rabia said. "I assume there is only one way in or out, and we would be at a serious disadvantage if this entry point was overtaken by unfriendly forces."

Zahra nodded and bit her lip, thinking hard.

"What's wrong?" Baahir asked, eyeing the opening.

Zahra chuckled. "What *isn't* wrong?"

Baahir scratched his hair, causing sand to fall from it. Zahra stood and brushed it off.

"You sure it's just Khaliq and one other guy down there?"

Her brother nodded. "One hundred percent."

"Four against two," Ali said. "I'm comfortable with those odds."

"Plus, whatever else is down there," Zahra added. "I have a feeling there will be some nasty surprises along the way."

"What makes you say that?" Ali asked.

She looked at him, then turned away. "Experience."

Zahra pulled her flashlight free, clicked it on, and began her descent.

# CHAPTER 92
# BAAHIR

**Beneath Gebel Dist**

After struggling down a spiraling stone staircase, the group came upon a circular chamber roughly forty feet in diameter. Zahra stepped aside and allowed Baahir through. He became entranced by the artwork put on display, jerking his own flashlight around the room. In doing so, he unconsciously wandered into the center of the room before it could be cleared of any dangers.

Zahra, Rabia, and Ali stayed close, lights aglow, but held back near the entrance.

"Baahir!" Zahra hissed. "We need to be care — "

He took another step backward, and something clicked beneath his foot. He spun, raising his fists, but didn't find anything to fight. The others fanned out, closely inspecting the ceiling and walls. Even they didn't find anything.

Baahir picked up his foot, revealing a cylindrical notch in the floor.

The sound of grinding stone picked up overhead, and a dozen or so palm-sized objects fell from newly agape openings.

One of them fell onto Baahir's right shoulder, and he shuddered as he felt it start to move. He tried to see it, but it was too close. Just a blur.

*An evil-looking blur.*

He was about to scream out, his eyes widening as the huge black orb began walking over his shoulder, but suddenly a flash of metal flew across his vision. He flinched, but the weapon *whooshed* past him, inches away from his face, carrying the bug with it.

And the knife had sliced a small wound into the meat of his shoulder.

He pulled back. The injury stung, but it was better than dying at the hands of — whatever the insect had been.

"Um, thanks?" Baahir said, unsure of what to say.

Ali passed by the Egyptologist to retrieve his blade and slapped him on the shoulder. Baahir cringed.

"Did I get you?" Ali asked, looking at his hand. He found blood.

"Yeah, but it's fine — I'm fine."

Ali wiped it off on his pants. "You need to work on your reflexes."

"*You* need to work on your aim," Baahir mumbled.

"What was it?" Zahra asked, checking on her brother.

Ali paused where his knife had come to rest. "You, my friend, should count yourself lucky." He picked up both the blade and the creature.

"What *is* that?" Baahir asked, squinting in the low light. From this distance, he couldn't identify the thing that Ali had impaled.

"*Androctonus*... very dangerous."

"Andro-what-now?" Baahir asked. He didn't recognize the name.

"*Androctonus*," Rabia repeated. "They're also known as 'man-killers.' They're one of the deadliest species of scorpions on the planet."

"Scorpions?" Baahir felt the blood drain from his face. He knew how deadly the ones in this region were. "How — how are they still here?"

Zahra answered. "Very likely that the builders of this place put a nest inside the walls. It offered enough protection for the little creatures, so they stayed. Their whole colony is here, feeding off their dead comrades, waiting for someone to come."

"So, they could rain down on my head," Baahir said.

Rabia nodded. "You should consider yourself fortunate. I doubt anyone besides Ali could have made that throw."

Baahir swallowed back his fear. "What about you?"

She patted her rifle. "I prefer guns."

Baahir faced Ali and raised a shaky hand. "Uh, thanks again."

He gave Baahir a playful wink. "Any time."

The others continued to look around, marveling at the artistry of the pictographs. Baahir, on the other hand, didn't give a damn about artistry. He was still shaken up by the scorpion incident, and what it meant.

*That was certainly not the only booby trap we're going to come across.*

He stood by the exit, applying pressure to his shoulder wound, and when he became too antsy, he voiced his discomfort.

“Can we go, please?” he said, eyeing the ceiling.

He was answered by soft laughter and approaching feet. Soon, the foursome was on the move again, descending another spiraling set of steps. It too wound around like a corkscrew, but instead of ending at a second circular chamber, they exited into a long narrow cavern.

“Woah,” Baahir said. The grandness of the space devoured his voice.

Zahra and Rabia stepped around Baahir, joining him on either side.

His sister craned her neck back. “Definitely, ‘woah.’”

# CHAPTER 93
# ZAHRA

The ceiling above the space Zahra was standing in now was made up of countless crags and stalactites. The latter had formed thousands of years ago, back when water was plentiful in northern Africa. Ground-penetrating radar confirmed that much of the Sahara had been flooded for thousands of years. There was even evidence of riverbeds beneath the sand, and she had heard a theory that Atlantis had once been in that same body of water.

Some believed that Thoth, the Egyptian god of science, mathematics, and writing, had come from a majestic empire located there.

*A kingdom to the west of the lands of Egypt,* Zahra thought, recalling something her mother had said.

Zahra had always thought it was interesting that most ancient civilizations talked of a great teacher coming from a kingdom in the middle of an ocean. Their technological advancements and progressions were similar, yet they had never had contact with other civilizations.

"You hear that?" Baahir asked.

Zahra had not. She had been too lost in her own head.

But she did now, and the constant white noise disturbed her.

Then, it was gone.

"It's not water," Ali said from the rear of the group. He had stayed back near the base of the stairs.

"Agreed," Zahra said, inching forward.

She swept her light back and forth, but found nothing except for a long, thin landbridge. On either side of it was nothing. The ground just disappeared into the abyss. So, she focused on what she *could* see. The bridge.

"We need to cross."

Baahir snorted out a laugh. "Yeah, okay..." Zahra turned and looked at him. "Oh, you're serious?"

"There's no other way," Rabia added. "If Khaliq came this way, he would have crossed here too."

"He did."

Everyone followed Zahra's flashlight beam, seeing what she had spotted in the dusty stone pathway. Two sets of footprints beckoned them along.

"Khaliq and... Feroz... I think," Baahir said, sounding unsure of the second man's name.

She cautiously took another step out onto the bridge. It held her weight fine, so she kept going. The others followed her, but wisely kept their distance from one another. If someone should fall, they could inadvertently drag someone else along for the ride. Zahra's light struck the bottom of the pit, but there was only blackness to greet it. She paid it no attention and returned her light to the bridge. They were a third of the way across when Zahra stopped.

"That can't be good."

Everyone leaned around her to see what she was looking at. A piece of the bridge had broken and collapsed into the pit on the left side of the chamber.

She lifted her foot but placed it right back down. Her light had shifted back to the path, and she noticed something. Only one set of prints continued past the breakage.

"Someone fell in," she announced softly.

Zahra edged right and shuffled forward, thinking lightweight thoughts. The bridge was still two feet wide where it had failed, giving the group plenty of room to pass. Their speed was good — slow and steady.

And with the next step she took, the bridge crumbled beneath Zahra's feet.

She worked her arms as she lost her balance, but it was no use.

Zahra fell.

# CHAPTER 94
# ZAHRA

Zahra flailed wildly as she entered the abyss. She was close enough to the bridge that she hit the side of it, then noticed it began to slope outward as it met the floor of the cave. She tumbled end over end, but it was like falling down the edge of a half-pipe.

She'd get a few more bruises, but at least she would live.

Twenty feet later, Zahra's feet touched down, then her ass. Her momentum sent her tumbling down the embankment. She landed on her stomach, covered in dust and grime. She just laid there and silently assessed the damage. Nothing felt broken, though she was definitely bleeding from several new spots.

"Zahra!" Baahir yelled, finding her with his light. Two more beams landed on her, and she turned over onto her back and lifted a feeble hand, and waved. "Oh my God, you're alive!"

"Yeah..." she mumbled. "I'm still here."

A sound like sizzling electricity filled the cavern, echoing all around Zahra. She sat up fast and discovered that she wasn't alone. There were other bodies with her, and one was fresh and had been picked apart.

*Feroz?* she asked herself.

She climbed to her feet as the noise grew. She spun and played her light over every surface of the pit but didn't see anything except dust and bones.

"Zahra, the wall!"

She stopped and directed her light to the outside wall of the pit. It was pocked with hundreds of fist-sized holes.

*Oh, shit.*

She knew in an instant how the other man had *really* died.

Just as her beam passed one of the openings, the first of the man-killer scorpions started pouring free from them. She scrambled back to the base of the landbridge, but knew it would be impossible to climb.

She unraveled her grappling hook. Rabia immediately got the gist of what Zahra was planning, and the woman handed Baahir her flashlight. Zahra gave the folded tip of her hook some slack and held it out to her side, spinning it half a dozen times before launching it skyward.

It fell short by five feet. Zahra's shoulder ached. It wasn't letting her get as much behind her toss.

The sea of scorpions was throbbing, growing larger now and starting to advance toward her, looking for space to fill.

Zahra tried again. She spun it faster, then glanced behind her again. This was her last chance. Zahra eyed Rabia and released the nylon cord. The head sailed into the air, right on target.

Rabia caught it!

She shouldered the weight, and together Baahir and Ali secured their hands around the hook and braced themselves, ready to accept Zahra's weight as well.

Zahra gripped the cord and planted her feet on the curved, half-piped base of the landbridge, and began her ascent. Unfortunately, she didn't get far.

Her hands slipped, and she fell once more to the floor.

"Zahra!"

On her knees, she looked up, breathing hard. All three of her friends were pointing farther into the cavern.

The incoming scorpion horde was gathering numbers — and speed.

So she ran, trusting Rabia — or anyone above — to look after the grappling hook.

They might just get another chance.

She darted left, avoiding a mass of man-killers.

Zahra leaped over another swarm, barely clearing it with her heels, quickly sidestepping to the right. She jumped, planted a foot on the curved sidewall of the landbridge and vaulted over more of the creatures. She was home free.

...For now. As she moved, Zahra could see more of the scorpions emerging from their underground realm.

*How many of these bastards are there?*

Zahra could hear the others running along with her. The plan was... well, there *was* no plan. She needed to come up with one *before* she made it to the end. Zahra spotted it in the haze up ahead.

She had nothing. She was too tired to think *and* run.

She tried to catch her breath. Her heart was racing. She was exhausted and dehydrated. She grabbed two handfuls of hair and screamed in frustration. Her cry dwindled down to a drawn-out squeak when she noticed the wall at the end of the pit.

There were no scorpions pouring out. They were only collecting around her here, and there was just enough of a path for her to make it to the opposite wall.

*Maybe...*

She leaped onto the wall, using the fist-sized holes as hand and footholds. She hoped there weren't any stragglers — any scorpions waiting for an easy snack.

If any were inside the holes, she didn't want to give them time to rush forward and stab her. She moved as fast as she dared — falling back to the floor now would mean *certain* death.

She scaled the wall.

About halfway up, she stopped, hearing something odd.

Something skittered toward her.

It was coming from the hole directly in front of her face. As she listened, she heard more skittering. More sounds of rushing little legs, scrabbling to get out of their dark holes in search of a meal...

"*Shit...*"

She turned and looked up at her brother. The look on his face told her he had heard it too.

"Zahra — *jump*!"

She did, aiming for the nylon cord of her grappling hook. It dangled beneath his feet, beckoning her along. As soon as she completed the move, a stream of man-killers came spewing out of the hole where her head had just been. All the holes were now teeming with scorpions.

Zahra caught the line and gripped it as hard as she could. She was immediately yanked skyward by Baahir, Rabia, and Ali. Their combined strength was enough to get her up to the edge.

One by one, they released their hold on the cord and grabbed Zahra.

Baahir gripped her jacket near her shoulders, Ali snagged a sleeve, and Rabia reached around and latched onto the back of her belt.

The group, Zahra included, fell onto the landbridge after one final pull.

Zahra didn't move. She did nothing but lay there, staring at the ceiling and trying to catch her breath.

"I found... Feroz," she said, huffing hard.

"You did?" Baahir asked, sitting up.

"Yeah," Zahra replied. She lifted a shaky hand and pointed back into the pit. "He was down there."

Baahir's nose wrinkled up in disgust. "What a way to go."

"Yeah, that'd be pretty awful."

She sat up, and accepted Rabia and Ali's offered hands. They slowly helped her up. Rabia didn't let go until Zahra proved she could support her own weight. She gave the sniper a nod and tested her legs. Like everything else, they were sore and felt like gelatin.

Zahra prodded her lower back and thrust her hips left and right, audibly realigning the vertebrae. She took a deep breath and looked over her team.

"Thank you," she said, making eye contact with each of them, "all of you."

Rabia stepped up next to her and placed her hand on Zahra's shoulder. "You aren't getting out of this *that* easy."

The trio headed for the exit tunnel.

Zahra spun and lifted her arms. "Who said that was easy?"

Everyone shared in a laugh. It felt good to laugh.

Zahra stepped over to her grappling hook and began to reel it in. Something felt off. *It feels heavier than usual.* With twenty-five feet left, she spied movement. She leaned over the edge and spotted a dozen scorpions making their way up to them via the heavy-duty nylon cord.

"Dammit!" she yelled, vigorously whipping the cord back and forth. Once all the man-killers were knocked free, she quickly pulled in the rest of the rope. Then, she gave herself a moment to catch her breath, and her hands found her knees.

"What was that all about?" It was Baahir.

She unfolded her spine and turned. Everyone was staring at her like she was a crazy person. Apparently, they hadn't seen what was coming.

"If I didn't hate bugs before, I *definitely* do now!"

## CHAPTER 95

# KHALIQ

The path beyond the archaic laboratory was long and winding, and the walls enclosing it sported the same kneeling figures as the trap room. There must have been tens of thousands of them. Whether it was Anubis himself who had decreed the art be made, or not, it was an impressive sight. Maybe the craftsmen were even members of the Ayad clan? Was this where his bloodline began?

That intrigued Khaliq. Hopefully, there would be answers up ahead.

His flashlight flickered, stopping him in his tracks. Without the aid of artificial light, Khaliq's mission would be nearly impossible. He waited for the beam to dim again, but it didn't. Satisfied that it had been nothing more than a blip, Khaliq continued his search.

He spotted an opening in the right and left-hand walls up ahead. He slowed and aimed his light into the room. It was small, maybe half the size of the room with the traps in it. Khaliq ducked inside the low opening and discovered the space to have once been living quarters. There was ancient furniture scattered around, most of which was broken and long rotted away.

He exited and quickly examined the adjacent room from the corridor, finding it essentially the same as the previous one. More rooms dotted the path, leaving Khaliq with more questions than answers.

He had never heard that Anubis' followers had lived beneath the surface. If that had been the case, it was all news to him.

*And what does it mean?*

A chill ran up his back. He recalled the bodies back in the laboratory. Were they the ones that had once inhabited these rooms? If so, why did they succumb to a fate that amounted to torture?

*More questions,* he thought, stopping when his light dimmed and went out.

He growled in frustration but noticed something odd. The tunnel wasn't entirely dark. There, up ahead, was a pinprick of orange and red light. The aura of his flashlight had been drowning it out, until now.

*Could it be?*

Khaliq discarded his dead flashlight and ran, dragging a hand across the wall as he moved.

He could feel it.

This was it.

# CHAPTER 96
# ZAHRA

"Oh my God," Baahir said. "We're in a torture chamber."

But Zahra wasn't sure he was right. Sure, everything about the scene before them was vile and hard to look at, but there was something... clinical about it.

She didn't argue. It was a strange room, either way, so she kept her eyes moving as she led the way into the high-roofed room. It seemed that this room had also been naturally formed by time and then later retrofitted for use.

Zahra gave the nearest body a thorough inspection. Based on the narrowness of its build and thickness of its hip bones, *it* was actually a *she*. The woman had her hands and feet nailed to the stone slab. Zahra didn't think this person had been punished, or even tortured by some maniac.

It just didn't... fit.

Though a maniac had been responsible for this place, for sure. Still, Zahra believed that the spikes had been used to merely restrain the subject — much like the straps on a hospital bed in a mental health facility.

*For their own safety...*

"They were experimented on," she said, gaining everyone's attention.

"How can you tell?" Ali asked, standing on the opposite side of the slab.

Rabia moved into position above the woman's head, while Baahir stepped up to her feet.

"Think about who we're dealing with," she started. "Let's say that

Anubis really *did* cook up some plague. That makes him sound an awful lot like a scientist or doctor, right?" Nods all around. "My guess is that these people," she motioned to the multitude of bodies, "were Anubis' test subjects, not just his victims."

"It's still disgusting," Baahir said.

Zahra nodded. "Absolutely."

"*What* was he testing?" Rabia asked. It was the next obvious question.

"His plague," Ali replied, sneering.

Zahra stepped in. "Which means we're about to find the origin of his infamous hellstone."

The death-filled chamber fell into an eerie silence.

"Come on," Zahra said, stepping away, "let's find Khaliq, and then get the hell out of here."

They looked around at the rooms connected by corridors to this larger space. It appeared as if people had lived in some of the rooms.

It surprised her, of course — she hadn't known of any Egyptian population that had lived underground — but what she was really interested in was *why*?

She stopped short, in front of another room, then snapped her fingers.

"This is it," she said, putting it all together.

"This is what?" Baahir asked from behind her.

She shined her light into the room. "This is where the Scales of Anubis began." She eyed her brother. "Think about it. A secret society of Anubis followers... where would they gather? Where would they live?"

Until now, Zahra hadn't spent much time thinking about it.

"When do you think they abandoned it?" Ali asked.

Zahra shrugged. "No idea."

"The bodies," Baahir said. "The Scales of Anubis did that."

*Maybe.*

"Or," Rabia said, her voice low, "*Anubis* did that to *them*."

Zahra squinted. "Hang on. Turn out your lights, will ya?"

They did, and the sudden darkness was infinite.

But slowly, a *new* light source started playing tricks with her eyes. A hellish glow from farther into the cavern caught her eye.

Zahra sighed. "I think we're about to get the answers we seek."

# CHAPTER 97
# KHALIQ

**The Temple of Anubis**

Walking through the Temple of Anubis should have been an exhilarating feeling for Khaliq Ayad. After all, this is what he'd been dreaming of his entire life. This was where his bloodline had started. The Scales of Anubis — his ancestry — had been Anubis' first disciples. He didn't feel any joy, however. Khaliq was scared.

Something about the place was off. Initially, he had thought it was a lost kingdom. Now, as he walked its streets, seeing the structures up close and personal, Khaliq thought the appropriate description of the subterranean cavity was that of a labor camp. It looked like an archaic detention center. The only way in or out was the stairs he had just descended.

Of course, the river of magma would also be a proper exit, if one was so inclined.

*An exit from life,* he thought.

The shadows seemed to move independently of the glow radiating from his right. The lava flow wasn't far. He could feel its heat. The shadows didn't bend as they should have.

*You're tired.* He had come down from his euphoric state. The adrenaline spike had dissipated enough for a little of the old Khaliq to reappear. That was the only part of him that still possessed reason. His mind was split, and he knew it could slip away again at the drop of a hat.

That terrified him the most. If he was too foolish, he wouldn't survive long enough to know if what he had come here for was *actually* here.

He wanted evidence that Anubis had really existed — human or not.

Khaliq came upon the fiery river, and was forced to shield his eyes. From what he could see, the only way to get to the enormous statue at the back of the cavern was to cross the serpent-shaped bridge, just to Khaliq's left. He headed for it, putting a healthy distance between himself and the river. It was impossible for him to tell what kind of shape the overpass would be in. He'd have to get in close to properly inspect it.

*And possibly die doing so.*

He turned, perfectly lined up with the bridge, and walked toward it. It was twenty feet wide, built of solid igneous rock, and still looked solid enough.

As he neared it, he realized something else. The hellstone around the bridge seemed to block a huge amount of the deadly heat. Khaliq didn't even have to block his eyes, though he was forced to squint. Not taking any chances, he quickened his pace, making it up to the middle of the bridge.

He saw the damage now — half of the left side of the bridge was missing, a chunk of stone had previously fallen into the fiery river.

But it would have to do.

Khaliq didn't think. He ran, sprinting over the immense tower of heat radiating from below. He shut his eyes for a moment and prayed that he didn't simply run off the edge. Once he felt the searing temperature lessen, he opened his eyes and slowed again. Khaliq took the slope in stride and jogged down to the other side. After leaving the bridge, he placed his hands on his knees, taking deep breaths. He looked up and stopped, holding in his air.

*The shadows.*

They moved.

Once again, he swore he caught sight of movement from far away.

*No,* he decided. *It's just the light playing tricks on you.*

# CHAPTER 98
# ZAHRA

**The Temple of Anubis**

The light emanating from the tunnel was blinding, growing brighter as they neared it. Zahra was shocked at just how bright it was. Their eyes had adjusted to their near-black world some time ago, and their flashlights had barely helped to light their progress.

Now, they could see clearly *without* artificial light. This form of illumination from the next hallway wasn't stagnant, either. It moved, shifting between yellow and red.

Something else emanated from the entrance ahead, too.

*Heat.*

And the smell of rotten eggs.

Blinking against both waves of light and heat, Zahra shielded her face with a hand and stepped through the opening. Her eyes immediately teared up in response to the smell. Still, she kept moving, hearing Baahir shuffling along behind her.

His hand suddenly grabbed at her jacket, and gripped it tightly. It was a garment Zahra was going to have to remove as soon as possible, as she was already drenched with sweat.

She gazed back at her brother, who was already staring off into the void past Zahra. His eyes had evidently already adjusted. The look on his face said it all.

Zahra fought through it and dropped her hand away from her face.

"Woah."

This wasn't just some subterranean place of worship, or even an extension of the laboratory they had found earlier. The cavern — the largest one she had ever seen — was an entire, underground city.

*We're in the Kingdom of Anubis,* she thought, spying a network of pathways that ran up the walls and connected to more of the hidden corridors and rooms off of the great hall in front of her.

Roads and buildings had been carved out of the black earth as well. Everything — all of it — had been constructed from the igneous rock.

And right in the center of the space, along the far wall, was a massive statue of Anubis. It had been carved directly into the rear wall of the cave.

*From hellstone.*

"Hellstone," she repeated, this time out loud. "This place is made *entirely* of hellstone."

Baahir placed his hand on her shoulder. "This is it, Zahra."

She nodded. It was the source of their mother's vase.

*The source of so much death.*

It was easy to see what was responsible for the light. Snaking its way through the center of the kingdom was a river of magma. The empire had been designed around it. Zahra could even see bridges built over it in some areas. She'd been around lava flows in the past and knew the heat they could generate. Apparently, that heat was also able to incubate a nasty little virus too.

"Are we sure this air is safe to breathe?" Rabia asked.

Baahir nodded. "It should be. Khaliq said the virus is only active after it's been hydrated. Water works well. So does—"

"Blood?" Ali asked.

"Yeah, blood works best."

To their left was a staircase cut from the wall of the cavern. It descended sharply, coming to an end nearly sixty feet beneath the team's boots. Even from here, Zahra could see that there were sections missing from the steps, having crumbled long ago. She rested her left hand on the top of her grappling hook. Zahra couldn't fathom not needing it again soon.

"I still don't get something. Where did it *come* from?" Zahra asked no one in particular. "How does something so sinister just... naturally form?"

"How does any virus or disease come to be?" Ali asked in response. Zahra turned and faced the man. He shrugged, continuing. "Sometimes things just happen. And it's a natural phenomenon, something Anubis must have discovered."

Rabia lifted her rifle and looked through its scope. She panned back and forth twice before lowering it. "The way is clear."

"I would assume so," Baahir said.

She gazed at him. "You should never assume things like that."

He held out his arms. "We're in a place that no living man has stepped foot in for centuries. I think it's safe to think we won't run into anything hostile...except for Khaliq, of course."

Rabia began their descent. "An even better reason to choose caution."

Zahra waited for Rabia to get six steps away before falling in line behind the sniper. But before she did that, she slipped out of her well-loved leather jacket. With nowhere else to put it, Zahra tossed it aside, relishing in the immediate temperature shift. Her black tank top wouldn't offer her much in the way of protection, but at least she wouldn't succumb to heatstroke.

Baahir was next to move, and Ali brought up the rear.

The stairs were in bad shape. The first of the handful of compromised sections came only ten steps into their journey. Rabia stopped and knelt, examining a ruined step.

Zahra cringed when Rabia suddenly went airborne, leaping over the busted step. She landed effortlessly on the other side, caught her balance, and gave Zahra a swift nod before heading off again.

Zahra said a quick prayer to her mother, then followed suit. She landed — a bit harder than Rabia had — but she was still alive.

Zahra blew out a long breath. She descended two more steps and turned just in time to see Baahir attempting the same move. Zahra could immediately tell that Baahir had timed it wrong, and she went up to meet him. The Egyptologist had overshot, nearly missing his landing point altogether. Zahra braced herself, reached out, and grabbed her brother by the shoulders. She pushed against his momentum, steadying him.

"Thanks," he said, looking slightly embarrassed.

Zahra patted his shoulder. "Maybe you should take a page out of Rabia's book and be a little more careful?"

Before Baahir could react, she gave him a sly smile and turned around. Rabia had gotten farther ahead of them, and Zahra hurried to catch up. It was only when she was back within their six-step buffer that she slowed and got back into time with the sniper. Rabia paused to examine the next broken section of stairs that curved down toward the floor.

"How does it look?" Zahra asked, already seeing that, now, *two* of the massive steps were missing.

"Not good," Rabia called back. She stood and faced Zahra. "The third step is cracked too, and will need to be skipped."

"So," Zahra said, hands on hips, "it's a three-step jump?"

Rabia nodded. "Yes, I'm afraid so."

"Did she just say, 'three steps?'" Baahir asked.

"Yep," Zahra replied, looking over her shoulder. "Three steps."

Baahir's head fell back, and he looked skyward, closing his eyes. He was nervous — they all were — even Rabia. Zahra didn't care whether she showed it, but there was no way the sniper didn't feel even a pinch of trepidation.

Rabia threw her rifle around her back and tightened the sling as much as she could. She jiggled it and did a couple of in-place test jumps. The weapon sloshed around but seemed to be manageable. She met Zahra's eyes. All Zahra could do was give her a thumbs up. Rabia returned the thumbs up and set her feet, one foot behind the other.

Then, she leaped.

For a moment, Zahra had thought Rabia, like her brother, had misjudged the distance. It looked as if Rabia would fall short. Her heels barely made it to the fourth step, but she wheeled her arms around and kept her balance.

Unfortunately, half of the landing zone broke apart from the impact. She hopped forward as the third and fourth steps fell away.

Now, the gap was four *entire* steps, not two.

*Shit...*

"Screw this..." Zahra unclipped her collapsed hook and tossed it to Rabia. The sniper caught it. "Just in case."

Rabia gripped it in her free hand. Zahra climbed back up a step, then got somewhat of a running start. She bounded forward and jumped, doing as Baahir had done and overshot her target. Still, it meant she wasn't going to fall short and plummet to her death. She collided with Rabia, and the two women went down, but they were both cognizant enough to prevent themselves from rolling uncontrollably.

Zahra scraped her left shoulder and palm in the process, opening two new wounds. She climbed off Rabia and felt a stinging sensation in her right knee as well.

*Make that* three *new wounds.*

The rough igneous rock had not only torn through her flesh, but it had also ripped through her heavy-duty pants. Rabia was also bleeding from a cut to her chin.

Both women stood and faced Baahir. He looked terrified of what was to come.

"I'm not so sure about this."

"I'm not, either." Zahra tossed the head of the hook up to him. He caught it. "But we don't have much of a choice."

Baahir snuck a peek over the edge and cringed. Even though they were only forty feet up, the drop was a guaranteed death. Baahir understood that. Like Zahra, Baahir backed away to give himself some space to speed up, then launched forward over the gap.

This time, there were two people to catch him. They wrapped their arms around him and dug their boots into the grainy surface. Thankfully, Baahir wasn't heavy. His lean frame allowed the two petite women to effectively stop his momentum. Rabia went high. Zahra went low, accidentally jamming her shoulder into his solar plexus.

Baahir was driven back onto his ass. He plopped down with both women in his lap.

"That was... um, thanks."

They silently nodded, and picked themselves up. Baahir pushed himself to his feet, and the three turned and faced Ali, the last one to make the jump.

He didn't look at all pleased.

Zahra brought the grappling hook up and tossed the head to him. With three adults on this side, the grappling hook would be a safer method for Ali to get across.

*Hopefully, he's not ten percent heavier than me...*

Ali fumbled with the line, causing him to lose his balance. He leaned right, toward the drop, then overcorrected and dove back into the cavern wall.

He hit his head on the rocks.

"You okay?" Zahra asked.

"Yes. I... it has been a long day."

"Come on," she said. "Not too much more."

*And let's hope there's an* exit *as well,* she thought. The last thing they needed was to get stuck in Anubis' lair without a way out.

Baahir slid in between Zahra and Rabia. The three of them held the cord, ready to accept the man's weight if he toppled off the side of the cliff.

Ali squeezed the grappling hook, then jumped. Just at the edge of the stair, a piece of stone broke beneath his foot.

He lost nearly all his lift. There was no way Ali was going to make it.

"Hold the line!" Zahra shouted, leaning back.

Baahir and Rabia did as Zahra did and held on tight.

Ali hit the bottom step chest-first...

...And then disappeared.

Zahra screamed, but was thrilled to then feel the rope go taught. All her muscles tensed, and she felt the line yanking her over the step.

But Ali was still hanging in there — literally. He floundered around, kicking, and wrestling for control of himself.

"Down!" Zahra screamed, getting an idea. "Lower him down!"

Inch by excruciating inch, the trio of Zahra, Baahir, and Rabia lowered Ali down. He let go with a few feet to go and crashed to the cavern floor, rolling to a stop a few feet later.

Zahra's hands stung like hell. Still, Ali was alive, and so was everyone else. After a moment of catching their breath, they continued down the remainder of the stairs with no issue.

Ali met them at the foot of the staircase and hugged them one after another.

"Thank you," he said.

Zahra waved him off. She was already focused on the edge of Anubis' infernal kingdom. It was the closest thing to hell that Zahra had ever seen. She could only imagine the mentality of the people that had once called this place home. Were they faithful devotees, or tormented souls with nowhere else to go?

*Hang on...*

Zahra spun and looked up toward the opening, picturing the lived-in rooms. Then, her mind went further back — to the crucified bodies. Lastly, she, once again, took in the glowing city, closely examining the structures. They weren't beautifully ornate or designed with lavish comfort in mind.

It came to her.

"The bodies," she said, working it out.

"What about them?" Baahir asked.

She faced him. "I don't think he performed tests on his own people."

"How do you know?" Ali asked.

"This place. Look at it. Does it look like any kingdom you've ever seen?"

Baahir shook his head. "No, and now that you mention it, it kind of looks like a — "

"A prison," Rabia finished, coming to the same conclusion. "Anubis imprisoned people here. Then, he conducted his awful experiments on them."

"And the rooms upstairs?" Ali asked.

Zahra shrugged. "I don't know, his guards — the Scales of Anubis?" All three of them stared down Zahra. She felt uneasy. "It's just a theory..."

# CHAPTER 99
# ZAHRA

"You see that?" Baahir asked.

"See what?" Zahra asked, resting her palm on her holstered pistol. They had reached the extreme edge of the city after having descended the stairs. She was exhausted, but knew their journey wasn't over yet.

"Over there," he said, pointing down the road. "I think I saw something move."

"Khaliq?"

Baahir squinted, but didn't say anything.

"I think you are tired, my friend," Ali said. "We are all seeing things."

Even Rabia's eyes looked heavy.

Zahra was scared, too, unsure of what might happen next. She was leading this expedition into hell.

And if any of her present company died, their blood would be on her hands.

The shadows did seem to dance in the wavering light produced by the river of fire. The radiating heat was intense, but it was a comforting blanket to Zahra. She felt exposed without her jacket, and the warmth reminded her of home. Of anything besides this place.

*The Prison Camp of Anubis.*

"There's a bridge up ahead," Rabia announced.

She had moved further up the road, leaving the rest of the group behind. If it was anyone else, Zahra would have suggested they stay with the pack, but the sniper knew what she was doing.

Ali must have been thinking the same thing. "Rabia, you — "

She turned and held up a hand, silencing him quickly. Then, she pointed at her right ear. It was the universal sign for "listen, numbnuts!" Zahra didn't hear anything, but she trusted Rabia's instincts. But after twenty seconds of inaction, much of which Zahra had spent holding her breath, Rabia signaled for them to keep moving. The sniper threw her rifle around her back, tightening the sling as she did. She opted for her sidearm instead, drawing it and keeping it at the low ready.

Zahra drew her pistol free too.

Next, Rabia silently moved off to the nearest building, and ducked her head inside. A light bloomed to life and swept back and forth. No shots were fired, and Rabia exited and headed for the next structure. Something had spooked the woman, and she now found it necessary to clear the buildings of a dead city.

*It can't hurt, I guess*, Zahra thought.

She decided to help and crossed the road. The closest structure was a low-roofed, brick-shaped building. The door was nothing more than a rectangular opening, barely wide enough for a human to slip through. Zahra clicked on her Glock's rail-mounted light and leaned inside, keeping her lower body outside. Panning from left to right, the first pass revealed a single room, and very little else. She gave the room another look, this time, slower...and lower.

*More bones.*

The floor was sprinkled with them.

The sight gave her the chills. Seeing enough, she leaned back out into the city and was, once more, hit with the sulfurous stench. Rabia was two houses ahead of Zahra and still on the opposite side of the road.

Zahra was about to continue her own search. Curiosity drove her now. If there had been people living here in the past, then there would be evidence of their living habits. Artifacts.

And there were other dangerous things lurking about — in the form of Khaliq Ayad, and maybe even Ajmal — but this was still a *groundbreaking* archaeological discovery, and she did not want to rush.

A crossroads was up ahead. Zahra watched Rabia turn right and disappear behind the last structure. Zahra, Baahir, and Ali picked up their pace and swiftly caught up with the sniper.

They took the right turn, as well, around the house, nearly banging into the back of Rabia. Zahra saw what had caused her to stop — there was no way to miss it.

They stood in awe of the ancient stone bridge... and the infernal glow emanating from beneath it. Without the cover of the buildings, the heat was much more intense here.

"We're supposed to cross *that*?" Baahir asked.

Rabia nodded. "Yes."

She didn't remember spotting another way across, and it could take the rest of the day to search for an alternate route. As amazing as this place was from a historical standpoint, they still had a job to do.

They needed to find Khaliq.

They needed to stop him.

Zahra looked at the others. "We, uh, need to get moving."

No one moved. Not even Rabia. So, Zahra led the way. She took the centermost path up to the foot of the bridge, going as far as ducking her head down. This was the moment that she missed her jacket the most. It would have made an incredible heat shield. Luckily, the bridge was wide enough to block some of the heat. She took the incline in stride, never once stopping.

If she had, she might not have been able to start again.

Zahra turned and saw that her brother was struggling with the climb. He looked exhausted, and rightfully so. He'd been out in the desert heat longer than the rest of them. Zahra slowed and allowed Rabia to move ahead of her. When she was within reach, she held out her hand. Baahir didn't verbally respond to the gesture. He simply took her hand and kept going. Zahra pulled him along the best she could. The companionship seemed to give Baahir the energy he was missing, and he picked up his pace, slightly.

Rabia made it to the peak of the bridge first and stopped. Zahra wouldn't have stopped, but she understood why a few seconds later. The left side of the bridge was missing, cutting the width in half. Zahra knew what it meant. They'd be more exposed to the searing heat, while also having to trust the integrity of the already faulty construction.

"Um, my friends..." Ali said from behind.

"What?" Zahra asked, squeezing her eyes closed. They needed a break from the heat and fumes.

"I fear that Baahir may have been... correct."

Everyone spun around, and Zahra's eyes opened again — then widened — as they saw dozens of shadows moving below.

And they looked human.

There had been no evidence of anything *alive* down here, but these shadows suggested otherwise.

Rabia pointed to the crossroads. "Look..."

And there, from within the smoky gloom, stepped a single person.

Zahra swallowed. *What the* hell *is this place?*

And then another, and another. More and more people filled her vision.

The people — if they could still be called that — were all in varying stages of decomposition and decay. A few were missing limbs and chunks of flesh altogether. They were mostly nude, with skin that was dry and leathery, and each of them was caked in dust.

And blood. Centuries-old blood.

*How are they moving?*

"Are they — "

Zahra sighed, finishing her brother's thought. "Zombies... they're *zombies*. Right? They have to be."

"I think we should run away," Ali said, turning back to the broken section of the bridge. "*Then* we can discuss it."

Baahir backed away. "I second that."

Zahra leveled her pistol at the nearest '*person,*' but then lowered it. She didn't know if they would respond to the sound, or if they would even be affected by the blast.

"Go."

All four of them bolted into action, running over the bridge, paying the heat and the broken section no attention. They cleared the ruined section in no time, and allowed the decline to aid in their escape.

*Zombies...* Zahra thought, breathing hard. *It* can't *be.* As fun as they were in fiction, this was real life — and something like that *couldn't* exist.

*Right?*

Suddenly, the group stopped, and Zahra nearly plowed through them all. The collision was a hefty one, and Ali was knocked to the ground. Rabia and Baahir picked him up.

Not that Zahra noticed. Her eyes were glued on the shadows moving about before them.

"Shit..." she hissed.

The others froze in place and watched as dozens more of the decrepit army came into view. They began pouring out of buildings — not unlike the way the scorpions had seemed to multiply and press forward constantly — and appeared out of the obscure haze of the city streets.

"How is this *possible*?" Ali asked.

"It... it's not," Zahra replied.

"It doesn't matter," Rabia said, reequipping her rifle. She shouldered it, gazed down the scope, and pulled the trigger.

The closest of the bunch lost his head. The skull exploded in a puff of goop and dust — not at all what Zahra expected to see.

*No blood?*

"What the..."

"What is *that*?" Zahra asked as she lined up another man's head in her pistol's irons. But she was focusing on what she saw now coming *out* of the headless corpse Rabia had just shot.

She fingered the trigger but didn't pull it. Rabia's description stopped her in place.

It was the same description Zahra would have used, but it could not possibly be accurate.

"I see... *worms*?"

"Worms?" Ali asked, looking sick to his stomach. Even in the firelight and caked in dust, Ali's skin visibly changed color.

Rabia lowered her weapon and eyed Zahra. "Yes, worms."

Zahra nodded. "And a *lot* of them."

# CHAPTER 100
# ZAHRA

Oddly, it was Baahir who stepped forward. Zahra could see that he was deep in thought. Zahra knew the look. She wore it often.

"What is it, Baahir?"

"The hellstone... it's the cause of the plague that Khaliq is trying to recreate, right?"

No one said a word. They all agreed with the statement. It's why they were here, after all.

"What's your point?" Rabia asked.

Zahra spoke up. "Our father had a colleague of his test the hellstone many years ago, and he discovered that it carried a species of microscopic organism. The stone itself is nothing more than igneous rock. It's what's *inside* it that's interesting."

"Interesting?" Ali retorted. "It could be the end of the world, Zahra. Those... *things*. *That's* what hellstone creates, right?"

Zahra, Rabia, and eventually Ali unloaded a burst of gunfire into the first four humanoids that made it up the base of the bridge. Every gunshot wound just produced more of the same — a burst of wriggling, inch-long worms that fell from open necks, chest cavities, and missing limbs.

As soon as the worms hit the ground, however, they stopped moving. Each one instantly shriveled up, dried out, and died.

"The organism," Rabia said, reloading. "What are — "

Baahir answered, cutting her off. "It's a pathogenic parasite."

Everyone paused and faced Baahir, waiting for him to explain. "I know this," he started, waiting for Zahra to blast another round through the nearest oncoming life form. "I studied this. It's called *cordyceps.* It's a *fungus,* actually — one that invades a host like a caterpillar or a worm — and actually uses the host's own bodies for ambulation."

"Ambulation?" Rabia asked.

"To move," Zahra said.

"And it's infecting the humans? The... people?"

Baahir shook his head. "It's infecting the worms, but it seems to have created localized hive minds through them, as well. Perhaps with the help of the hellstone. Or the hellstone's reactive property *is* the fungus. But the worms use humans as hosts, and the fungus control the worms. Altogether, it seems like the fungus are controlling the people."

"I'd say they *are* controlling the people," Ali said. "Which is impossible."

Baahir shrugged. "You have a better explanation?"

"Not at the moment," Zahra answered, pulling the Glock's trigger three more times. The trio of rounds hit a shambling woman in the chest, knocking her down but not killing her. "How do you know all this, by the way?" Zahra watched in horror as the woman picked herself up off the ground and rejoined the swarm.

"I went down the rabbit hole for a course I did on ancient Egyptian mythology and legend. Everyone knows about scarabs, cats, and sacred symbols that show up in pop culture, but this course was about the truth behind those things — where they came from."

"Behind us!" Ali shouted, turning and firing. He clipped one in the shoulder and sent him toppling off the bridge and into the river.

The people — the *Damned,* as she was coming to think of them — on the opposite side of the bridge had pushed the team's position from behind. Zahra and the others were now the inside of an ancient, rotting, shit sandwich.

"Move!" Rabia shouted. She switched back to her pistol and began punching holes in the zombified people's heads with well-placed shots. Each shot put the walking corpse down for good. "Aim for their heads!"

Everyone followed her instructions. Thankfully, the Damned were slow, rocking back and forth, similar to the way penguins moved. The team cleared a section of the enemy away and took a moment to reload. Zahra didn't have enough ammunition for open conflict — no one did. She had one more magazine — fifteen rounds in all, with one already in the chamber.

"More to the right!" Rabia shouted, kicking a shorter man in the chest.

*No... not a man.*

Zahra's heart sank. *It's a boy.*

Anubis had apparently experimented on everyone — no one had been safe. These people, a tribe or village — whoever they had once been — were all fair game to him.

It reminded her of the atrocities committed by the likes of the Nazi's *Schutzstaffel* and Imperial Japan's *Unit 731.* All the atrocities perpetrated in the name of 'science.' Anubis was now on her list of tyrants who had thought the ends justified the means, no matter the cost.

Zahra lined up a shot to a woman's forehead, gazed into her gray, lifeless eyes, and pulled the trigger. The round struck the woman at point-blank range. The bullet entered and exited with such authority that it blew out the back of the lady's enfeebled skull and immediately penetrated the head of the next person. It was the most repulsive BOGO deal Zahra had ever experienced. A third Damned was showered in an explosion of muck and worms.

*Ugh.*

Zahra turned and physically pushed the group along. They slipped through, and sprinted past, wherever an opening popped up. They could run all they wanted, though. Anubis' dead army wasn't lacking in numbers. Every building they neared regurgitated another half-dozen people. Baahir coughed. The fumes were getting thicker, and more noxious.

"The... sulfur!" he yelled while catching his breath. He stumbled. Zahra caught his arm, keeping him upright.

"Sulfur?" Zahra asked. "What are you talking about?"

"Some species have been known to thrive on nothing more than sulfur produced by hydrothermal vents." He met Zahra's eyes. "These guys must have adapted to survive on only the sulfur down here."

"Well, there's plenty of it," Zahra said.

They made it past the thickest pocket of the Damned and broke into a somewhat pitiful pace, barely resembling a jog. More of the Damned cut them off at the next intersection.

Zahra's side suddenly exploded in pain, and she was forced to slow as a result. She tried keeping up, but the Damned were everywhere, and the sounds of their scraping, sliding bodies as they moved — as well as the gunshots from her group — made it too hard to hear anything else.

She tried calling out, but it was too late. A group of Damned moved in front of her.

She was cut off and separated from the group now, and only then did Rabia and Ali notice, stopping and turning to find Zahra.

They shot two of the Damned creeping toward her before they were waved off. "Don't!" Zahra shouted. "Conserve your ammo! I'll find another way!"

There were already two dozen Damned between her and the group, with more joining the ranks every second.

She got backed up to one of the buildings. She unclipped her grappling hook and gave the head some slack, then twirled it at her side. Luckily, her shoulder had loosened up a touch since her fall into the man-killer pit. She kept it close to her body. It took very little energy to get it going, but sustaining the high speed would eventually become a problem.

It wasn't intended to be used this way, but it was the best idea she had.

A woman broke away from the group, moving faster than the others. Zahra pivoted and released the hook. Fifteen feet later, it connected with her face, and she crumbled in on herself.

Zahra didn't hang around to celebrate the victory. She turned and ducked into the structure, flicking on her flashlight as soon as she entered. A single Damned was indoors. She paid the man no attention. Zahra found what she was looking for.

A crude set of stairs led Zahra up to a low-ceilinged, loft-like, second level. She reached the lone window and leaned outside. Directly below her perch was the road. Three Damned slipped inside. They'd soon trap her here unless she figured something else out.

Zahra brought in her hook and cord and climbed halfway out of the narrow rectangular window, and noticed that the roof was only a few feet above her head. With no other option, she stepped onto the knee-high sill and reached up and out. Her fingertips just barely found the edge of the building.

*Good enough.*

Zahra slipped her other shoulder out and snagged the roof's edge with her other hand. She kicked away from the opening and planted her feet on the rough stone façade. Her fingers protested the coarseness. One of the digits split and bled.

A hand swiped at her leg. Zahra looked between her legs and saw that one of the Damned had made it up to her in record time. She repositioned her feet and pulled with all her might. Her upper body climbed high enough to get an arm over the edge. She flexed the muscles around her armpit and in her shoulder to keep herself in place while she readjusted her grip. Then, she slid over and onto the roof and rolled onto her back, gasping for air.

She held up her raw and bleeding hands. Zahra tried to find a clean place to wipe them off but failed.

Gunshots rang out in the distance. Zahra was confident that none of the Damned could reach her here — she hadn't seen them climb, and the stairs would force them to come at her one by one — but the others weren't as protected. She rolled onto her belly and pushed herself onto her knees. The effort stung her hands. She paid the discomfort little attention and tried to locate the source of the gunfire.

More shots echoed around the cavern, but these had originated from near the Anubian monument. The base of it was only a couple of streets over. Baahir, Rabia, and Ali had either run into another collection of Damned, or they were fighting something else.

*Khaliq.*

# CHAPTER 101
# KHALIQ

He had successfully evaded Anubis' test subjects so far, but only by running for his life. Khaliq couldn't count the times he had almost died, cut off and surrounded. By sheer luck, he had stumbled into the shadows, hidden, and figured something out about the creatures. The shambling creatures couldn't see well in the dark.

*If they see anything at all.* Their opaque, lifeless eyes haunted his mind. Their empty stares unnerved Khaliq.

His hands shook uncontrollably.

He was curious how they communicated, or if they did at all. He could see zero evidence of any vocalization, or even hand signals, yet they seemed to move as one. Khaliq had heard of the "hive-mind" theory, where a group of individuals could operate through a shared consciousness. Until a day ago, Khaliq would have thought that to be preposterous. Now, he wasn't so sure.

He slid in behind a ten-foot-tall wall, just outside the entrance to what appeared to be a common area — a courtyard. The monument to Anubis was on the other side, waiting to be glorified. Khaliq planned to kneel beneath it and silently praise his ancestor for paving the way. Khaliq felt a bond with Anubis. They weren't so different. Both would do anything to get what they wanted. Though thousands of years apart, their methodology was nearly identical in practice. Perfection demanded experimentation.

Khaliq tried catching his breath before moving again. The air was thick with sulfurous gas, and it was becoming increasingly difficult to breathe. His head swam. Khaliq snapped his head back and bashed his own skull into the igneous barricade. The sharp pain of his skin breaking, and the leaking plasma refocused him. The sting of the wound took his attention off that which clouded his mind.

He stood, and entered the courtyard, smiling manically. His eyes opened, and he saw something he had not expected. There, built directly into the foot of the edifice, was a throne. It sat on a stepped, half-moon platform. The throne itself was easily fifteen feet tall. But the seat of power was only a small piece of what held his attention. What truly awed Khaliq was the fact that there was a ragged corpse sitting within it.

Khaliq's face fell. "Anubis?"

He sprinted toward the foot of the grand monument. A clearing of a hundred feet separated the throne from the city behind him. Khaliq's mind raced faster than his feet could move. His trek to Anubis slowed as the body count rose. Similar to the ancient laboratory, there were also hundreds of bodies lying about.

*No, not lying about.*

All of them had died on their knees in adoration to their king. Khaliq slid to a stop and pictured the intricately cut artwork in the trap room. The people there had been shown in the same posture. They, too, had been worshipping Anubis. He had been right to assume that Anubis had experimented on his own people.

Khaliq zeroed in on one of the dead men, or rather, his skin. It was dry and leathery, though still somewhat preserved by the arid atmosphere. Khaliq needed to know for sure. He knelt and examined the man's left arm and saw what he dreaded. There, tattooed into the corpse's forearm, was the symbol for the Scales of Anubis. It perfectly matched the one on Khaliq's own arm. Not only were these people his test subjects, and prisoners, but they had also been his most loyal followers.

They had been Anubian disciples, just like Khaliq and his family before him.

"Why would you want this?" Khaliq asked, picturing his ancestors. "Why would you want this after what he did to us?"

He knew why. Khaliq and Anubis were truly one and the same. Khaliq had done exactly the same thing to so many people over the years. His lineage had been raised to believe that they were born to complete what Anubis had failed to do, to wipe out the unworthy.

But he had succeeded, though the plague was not what anyone had thought. Khaliq imagined his father seeing this — seeing what had become of Anubis' most loyal followers. Much of them would have been related to the Ayads.

The bile in Khaliq's stomach rose, and he vomited where he stood.

The act helped clear his mind some, bringing an all-important thought to the forefront of his faltering, cracking mind. If Anubis was still here — and dead — then it meant one thing.

*Anubis was never a* true *god. Gods don't die.*

Khaliq coughed, heaving for air as his vision narrowed and his world crumbled. *Gods don't die!* Khaliq spun around and took in the death, recalling what Baahir had supposed. *Gods... don't die. Just a man.*

He fell to his knees, joining his brethren.

*Gods don't die. Just a man*. Khaliq looked up at the seated corpse. *No, 'not' a man.*

Anubis had just been a genocidal maniac.

Through tear-filled eyes, Khaliq spotted something on the ground next to Anubis' feet. The thin cylindrical shape matched that of the Book of the Dead. Was it, yet another, version of the scroll, or maybe the one Khaliq possessed was, in reality, a copy of this one?

*His personal Book of the Dead?*

Khaliq growled and pushed himself to his feet. Whatever it was, he would be the one to see what the false god had left behind.

# CHAPTER 102
# ZAHRA

The crowd below began to clear. The Damned were showing more interest in the noise further ahead. Zahra had been as quiet as a church mouse since scaling the structure, hoping her inaction would confuse — and eventually bore — her mindless attackers.

*What had Baahir called it? A pathogenic parasite?*

Zahra unclipped her grappling hook.

*Gonna have to look that up when we get home.*

She kept her movements silent and checked all four sides of the building. A mass of Damned was gathered along the main road. There were more along every side, but it was a much thinner herd. If she could get down to ground level and make a run for it, she was pretty sure she could find the others. The city was laid out with everything funneling in toward the monument. Eventually, she'd find her way there.

Zahra decided on a course of action, one that would swing her rather than drop her. She ran along what she guessed was the southern edge of the building, aiming for the southwest corner. She snapped open her hook's clawed head. When she jumped, Zahra dug the claw into the rock, giving the cord enough play to make the plan work. She estimated she'd need to give the cord fifteen feet before gripping back onto it. The next part was going to hurt. Her hands were already raw, and this was bound to make things worse.

Her forward momentum took her away from the building, due west.

Then, her weight took over, pulling the nylon cord tight. She swung around to the north down a tight alleyway. She took the landing in stride, hitting and rolling once before popping back up to her feet and sprinting away from the Damned. The handful that had been gathered along the rear of the building reacted too slowly, and Zahra quickly left them in the dust.

There were much fewer of them here. In fact, Zahra hardly saw any of them.

*Weird.*

She didn't overanalyze why the darker path was devoid of life. Zahra just kept moving as fast as she could until she came up to another crossroad. Here, there were more.

*Much* more.

She skidded to a stop, cringing at the sound of loose pebble grinding beneath her feet. Ten of the Damned snapped their attention her way in a horrible display of choreography. They turned in unison.

They didn't advance, though. Zahra had tucked herself into the recesses and hidden in the shadows. Her black clothing and filth-covered arms and face hid her well. Still, she wasn't hiding behind anything. At least one of them should have been able to see her.

*No eyes, right.*

And the sulfurous stench was incredibly thick here too. If they couldn't see, *and* they couldn't smell her, then it meant they'd be listening for her. Zahra didn't have time to play scientist. She needed to keep moving. Standing slowly, Zahra took each step with the utmost care. She hugged the building without scraping against its coarse surface and slinked around to the northern face.

The Damned didn't change their focus away from the alley. None of them had noticed her escape.

*Yet.*

Zahra figured it was only a matter of time before she was spotted. It was going to happen too. The next section of the road and building contained little to no shadow. This is where her tired legs couldn't fail.

She ran and reeled in her trusty hook.

Her first step alerted the army, and they turned to greet her. There were more up ahead, as well. Zahra unclipped her grappling hook again and used it as a club for anything that might get too close. If the blows didn't kill them, the hook would at least knock them away long enough for her to evade capture.

She took a left, and within the growing haze, she spied a low wall to the north. Gunfire announced the presence of her team. With every muzzle flash, a body dropped. The Damned were here, too.

"Zahra!" Baahir shouted, waving frantically.

She drew her pistol but waited to get closer. She didn't have many rounds left and needed to make them count. When she was within twenty yards, she let the rest of her magazine fly, connecting with ninety percent efficiency. Not all of them were 'kill' shots, but she cleared the area of the immediate threat.

Rabia stepped out and crushed the skull of one of the Damned with the stock of her heavy rifle. Then, she dropped her prized weapon at her feet.

She was out of ammo.

Zahra was, too.

She holstered her Glock and embraced her brother, getting nods from Rabia and Ali. They all looked terrible, but they were alive.

"He's here," Baahir said.

"Khaliq?"

"Yeah, and he's alone."

Zahra shrugged, thinking back to Feroz's body in the scorpion pit. "I kinda figured that."

"No, Zahra," Baahir said. "He's alone. Oddly, there aren't any of the zombies in there with him."

"Call them 'the Damned,'" Zahra said. "I refuse to call them 'zombies.'"

"Fine," Baahir shrugged, "I suggest we move into the courtyard. The *Damned* won't enter it for some reason." Everyone turned and looked.

"It's because they remember."

They all jumped at the voice.

It belonged to Khaliq.

# CHAPTER 103
# ZAHRA

Zahra drew her gun, but remembered it was empty.

"Ayad!" Ali shouted. "This is all because of you!"

Khaliq seemed docile. "You're right."

"Wait," Zahra said. "What?"

Khaliq held out his hands and turned completely around. "We *are* here because of me."

Rabia's eyes darted to Khaliq's waist. He still had a pistol holstered there. He seemed to notice the attention the firearm was getting.

"It is loaded, but with only one bullet." He gazed past the foursome. "I'd hate to waste it on any of you."

"Bullshit," Baahir countered.

"If you'll humor me, I'll show you why."

At first, no one moved. But Zahra sensed he wasn't bluffing. Khaliq was alone, and the status quo had changed. The four of them could easily overrun Khaliq and kill him with their bare hands.

And they were all, save for Baahir, armed with a knife.

No one advanced on the man.

"Tell us," Zahra said, holding her ground. She was curious about what the man had to offer. Khaliq wasn't an idiot — whatever was going on, it was bigger than she could imagine.

His entire attitude had softened as if his entire world had been deflated.

"What happened to you?" she asked.

He faced her. His eyes said it all. Khaliq Ayad was scared. "I see now that I've been misguided ever since I was a boy." He sighed. "My family... My father and grandfather believed in something that I now know is false."

The cavern went silent — all except the sound of hundreds of footsteps. Zahra turned and saw what was coming.

"Come," Khaliq said, "they will not follow."

Rabia spoke up. "How do you — "

"Because he said so," Khaliq replied.

"Who did?" Zahra asked.

Khaliq turned but looked over his shoulder before stepping away. "Anubis."

Zahra wanted nothing more than to shoot the man where he stood, but they required answers, and if Khaliq did have a change of heart, even if it was only to save his own skin, then they needed to hear him out. Any information about what was going on here was vital to their survival.

Zahra was the first to move. She was quickly followed by Baahir and Rabia. Ali hung back for a moment, but eventually scampered off as the Damned closed in. Zahra looked back several times and was flabbergasted to see that Khaliq had been right. The Damned did not enter the courtyard at the foot of the giant statue of Anubis.

"What did you mean when you said, 'they remember?'"

They all slowed down, and then Zahra entered the strangest mass grave she had ever seen.

"The infected retained their memories," Khaliq replied, "though, their personalities were lost forever. This will all make sense soon."

Rabia glanced at Zahra. "I seriously doubt that..."

Fewer things in her life had made Zahra more uneasy than the sea of corpses. They were eerily similar to the ones she encountered up in the trap room. That realization sent a chill down her sweaty spine. Zahra reckoned that they had been placed there, postmortem, as sort of a strange totem.

*No, that doesn't make much sense. Why would someone go through all the trouble of lining up hundreds of bodies like this?*

Then, she saw him.

Zahra had been so focused on the morbid phenomena that was the kneeling bodies that she hadn't yet noticed the dead man sitting on the black throne. His crown said it all. It was gold and held a pair of iconic jackal ears aloft. He wore very little in the way of clothing. The only garb Zahra spotted was a gilded shendyt. She knew why. It was too damn hot down here to wear anything, other than something like a shendyt, for long periods of time.

"Anubis." Zahra couldn't hide her shock. "He was real..."

"Yes, he was," Khaliq said, turning, "and he was so much worse than any of us could have ever imagined."

Based on the looks on everyone's faces, none of them quite understood what Khaliq meant. Thankfully, he was in the mood to share intel. He stepped aside and motioned to something laying at the foot of the dead god-king.

"I give you...the diary of Anubis."

Like everything else here, the scroll had been impressively preserved. Two stone tubes pinned either end of the unrolled parchment down. It was identical to the *Book of the Dead* based on the way Baahir had so vividly described it. Still, his in-depth account of the relic hadn't done it justice. The casing was magnificent to look at, as was the scroll itself.

The latter contained both written words and crudely sketched drawings. Zahra was too far away, and honestly way too tired, to read what had been penned. But they had Khaliq to communicate what he had already read.

"We — my family — were mistaken." They listened and waited. "I had been taught from a young age that we, the Ayad clan, were *special* — that we had been born for a very specific purpose. Yes, we are immune to the effects of the hellstone, but that didn't stop Anubis from using us in his early trials." Khaliq looked off into the void. "We were supposed to cleanse this world of the unworthy. I grew up believing it. Why else would we be immune?"

"What does the diary say?" Zahra asked, voice soft.

Khaliq looked at her, unblinking. "Anubis admits what he was *really* planning. Anubis, or whoever he truly was, first discovered the virus after it killed his wife. After that, he dedicated the rest of his life to finding a *cure* for what had taken her."

"The plague?" Rabia asked, speaking for the first time in a while.

Khaliq shook his head. "No. He hoped to cure death itself. Whatever this is — the hellstone — he thought he could use it to become immortal. He thought it would turn him into a god." He looked away from the group. "I looked up to him as a child, but now... now, I see him for what he truly was." He looked at Zahra. "A broken man with nothing to live for."

"The Damned... the people here," Zahra said, "who were they?"

Real-life tears fell down Khaliq's dirty face. Zahra didn't think the man was capable of emotions on that side of the spectrum. He seemed genuinely hurt, broken. He placed a hand on his chest. "They were *me*. When Anubis ran out of test subjects — the bodies upstairs — he turned his sights on his most loyal disciples."

"The Scales of Anubis," Ali said, unapologetic. "They followed him until it cost them their own lives." He jabbed a finger at Khaliq. "After all these years, how many people have shared the same fate as a result of blindly following you?"

Khaliq turned away, facing the throne. "Many."

He ruffled through his front pants pocket and pulled out something small and cylindrical. He faced Zahra and the others and held the object up. "Which is why I intend to right my wrongs with *this*. I *will* cleanse the world of everything here."

Zahra took a few steps back.

Khaliq was holding a remote detonator.

# CHAPTER 104
# ZAHRA

The cave was still. No one breathed. Zahra waited for Khaliq to blast them all into oblivion, which was still the better option. It was either that or dying horrifically at the hands of the Damned. Everyone lifted their hands simultaneously as if Khaliq were pointing a gun at them. He was, in reality. He was holding a very big gun.

"Easy there," Zahra said, keeping her words smooth and soft. "There are other ways to handle this."

Khaliq's face portrayed an array of emotions and expressions: anger, guilt, excitement, shock, awe. There was no stopping him. He, honestly, seemed to believe that this was the only way he could fix everything. There was no redemption on the horizon for Khaliq. His fate had been sealed with every death caused by his disjointed moral compass.

And now, he was willing to kill everyone — Zahra, Baahir, Rabia, Ali, and himself — in an attempt to set things right.

Zahra clutched her brother's shirt, not intending to leave his side again. After all this, she would make sure Baahir was coming home... alive.

She slowly backpedaled away from Khaliq, palms up. "Easy, cousin."

His tear-streaked face fell, and his eyes closed.

Then he turned back toward Anubis.

"Khaliq, no!"

Everyone took off running as the earth shook.

A fireball ignited at the base of the Anubis statue, throwing the fleeing group to the courtyard floor. The concussive blast made Zahra sick to her stomach, but it was the impact with the ground as she rolled over that made her want to die.

Khaliq had used enough explosives to remove the lower half of the hundred-foot-tall monument. Anubis' throne had simply ceased to exist.

As did Khaliq. The stepped platform was reduced to chunks of igneous rock, and the first few rows of kneeling corpses had been wiped away.

Zahra came to a stop, dust and debris falling around her head. She held her arms over her face, protecting it, and waited for it to end.

Finally, she tested her scrapes and cuts, bones, and body. Everything seemed to be in working order. Exhausted, and bruised to the core, but working.

"Everyone okay?" Zahra asked, barely able to hear herself speak. Her ears rang, and her head pounded. The best way to describe the way she felt was *hungover*.

Rabia sat up and gave Zahra a half-hearted wave.

Zahra moved in slow motion, and stood on wobbly legs. Baahir got to his feet, and the siblings held on to one another for support. Rabia helped Ali up, and the team regrouped.

*Crack!*

No longer was Zahra solely focused on their wellbeing. The noise sent a chill down her spine, and her concern shifted to that of the structural integrity of the cavern itself. She craned her head up and watched as an *enormous* crack spread its way skyward, further decimating the ten-story-tall Anubis carving. Chunks broke off and fell like car-sized bombs.

A piece the size of a single-family home came free from Anubis' chest. Zahra dragged her awestruck brother back, Rabia and Ali followed closely behind.

When the boulder hit the cavern floor, it flattened what remained of the stepped platform, bursting through what Zahra now saw was just a thin layer of rock. A wave of intense heat immediately washed over Zahra, stinging her eyes. The others had the same reaction and shielded their faces with their hands.

She looked back and saw that the Damned had completely surrounded the courtyard.

The floor succumbed to the newfound stress of the fracturing rock, and began to plummet into the ever-growing pool of magma. Zahra led the retreat, pausing when she was within fifty feet of the exit. There was no way through the throng of the Damned. They were about to die terrible deaths of one form or another.

"So, which is it?" she asked, glancing at the expanding subterranean shoreline. "Door Number One," she shifted her gaze over to the empty stares of hundreds of Anubian creations, "or Door Number Two?"

Baahir and Ali stepped over to her, sharing in a heartfelt, apologetic goodbye. The only one not participating in the farewell was Rabia. She was too busy staring at the wall separating the courtyard from the neighboring city.

"How about a third option?" She looked back and smiled.

Zahra didn't see it at first.

*Yes. The wall!*

Then she bolted for it with Rabia right beside her.

"Come on!" she shouted. "Move your *asses*!"

Baahir and Ali leaped into motion, arriving at the divider wall just as the two women put their backs against the wall. They clasped hands. Zahra tipped her chin up.

"Ali, you're up first. Baahir, you're next."

"Up there?" Baahir asked, backing up to give Ali room.

Ali stepped into the women's hands and was launched up high enough to grip the top edge of the wall. The women then ducked lower and shoved up as hard as their tired bodies would let them. Finally, Ali pulled himself up the rest of the way and relieved Zahra and Rabia of his weight.

"Come on, brother..." Zahra said, gasping for air.

"Zahra, I — "

"Will *die* if you don't listen to me."

He glanced back at the advancing sea of red and orange and nodded. He lifted his right foot up and slipped it into the stirrup that was made up of two pairs of bleeding hands.

"Ready?" Zahra asked.

Rabia actually shook her head, getting an exhausted laugh out of Zahra. Nevertheless, the ladies heaved the lighter Baahir up. Ali reached down and promptly relieved them of Baahir's weight and pulled him up the rest of the way. With picture-perfect synchronization, Zahra and Rabia slid down the wall and onto their butts.

"What's this?"

They looked up and found Baahir staring down at them. "No time for that crap." He knelt and reached a hand down to them. Ali mirrored him, offering a hand of his own.

"Go," Zahra said. "I…" she swallowed what saliva she had, "I'll be right behind you."

Rabia gave her an unsure look, but she heeded Zahra's request and stood. Zahra stood next and cupped her hands, placing her back flat against the wall.

"See you soon," Zahra said, winking as Rabia stepped onto her improvised lift.

She grunted and pushed upward, allowing Rabia to get high enough for the sniper to step onto her shoulders. Then Baahir and Ali grasped Rabia's wrists, and they pulled.

Now, the only one left was Zahra. She leaned against Door Number Three, beyond exhaustion, numb to the Damned's breathy chorus. Within the glow of the molten rock, Zahra slowly slunk to the floor and closed her eyes.

# CHAPTER 105
# ZAHRA

"Dammit, Zahra, move!"

She snapped awake and popped up to her feet, drowsy and confused. The magma pool was gaining ground fast. She knew what she had to do, but was unsure if she had the strength to do it. She unclipped her hook, snapped it open, and tossed it up. It caught on the top of the wall, but that wasn't the challenge.

The real question was whether Zahra had the upper body strength to climb, and if the grappling hook line was still strong enough after all it had been through.

*Seeing as I don't have a choice...*

She gripped the nylon cord and cringed as she felt it dig into her bleeding hands. Both her palms and several of her fingers sported open, flowing wounds. The blood made it difficult for Zahra to hold onto the cord. She failed in her first attempt, but Zahra wasn't a quitter. She clutched the cord again and gained some steam. Then, all of a sudden, she shot upward, yelping in surprise and pain. The trio of Baahir, Rabia, and Ali had each grabbed the hook and lifted it, aiding in Zahra's attempt.

"Grab her!" Ali said, bracing himself. He was in the middle of the three of them and got into a stance much like a powerlifter attempting a heavy deadlift. He stuck his chest out and squatted slightly. Then, with a nod, he signaled the others to let go and help Zahra.

They did, diving chest-first onto the top of the divider wall. Zahra's hands slipped off just as they secured her wrists. Ali placed the hook down, knelt, and beckoned Rabia to give him Zahra's hand. The sniper acquiesced and allowed Ali to take the burden.

"Help Baahir."

Rabia slinked around Ali, taking care not to fall off the three-foot-wide partition. Her leverage was better. Baahir had no leverage since he was flat on his stomach. She took Zahra's hand, which got Baahir to his feet. The trio pulled one last time.

Zahra slipped her elbows over the edge and held herself in place long enough for one of them to grab her belt. Next, Zahra got her left knee up and was rolled atop the wall where she took a much-needed breather. They all needed one.

"Um... yeah... thanks."

No one answered her. They just waved her off, each one of them huffing and puffing. Ali was favoring his left shoulder, which wasn't good. A rotator cuff tear at a time like this would absolutely constitute as piss poor timing.

"You good?" Zahra asked, still on her back. Ali was bent at the waist, rotating the bad joint slowly. Something must have pinched and caused the man a good amount of pain. He sneered but didn't whimper.

"I'm... fine."

Rabia offered him some support and helped Ali to his feet. "You've always been a *terrible* liar," she said. Then she gave Ali a soft kiss on the lips, "But I am happy to hear it."

Zahra almost laughed from the look of surprise on Baahir's face. She had been taken aback as well — apparently, there was *much* more to this woman than she had initially thought.

Chunks of the wall broke away, reminding Zahra of the imminent danger and urging all four of them to their feet. Zahra was at the front of the pack, pointing to something she had seen earlier. One of the buildings was close enough to the wall for them to jump.

"Come on," she said, moving at a brisk pace.

They traveled to the left for sixty feet along the top where the main entrance into the courtyard vanished. Zahra skidded to a halt and watched dozens of the Damned tumble into the molten void.

Then, section by section, the foundation buckled and the entire wall fell. Its demise quickly followed them.

Zahra ran, keeping her hands out wide to balance over the shifting floor. The wall shook with every undulation.

They were nearly free.

And then more of the cavern's back wall broke apart.

The pieces of massive stone hit the floor, and Zahra leaped onto a nearby rooftop. She landed and rolled to one knee. Baahir was next. Rabia and Ali jumped at the exact same time.

The wall disappeared just as their feet left it. Zahra scrambled to her feet and headed for the other end of the roof when it too fell away. The entire building was coming down beneath them. They were thrown off their feet. Zahra rode the collapsing structure and landed flat on her ass as it became more of a slide than a Tower of Terror-esque vertical drop.

They were all deposited onto a buckled road that was also wrenched to a steep angle. Zahra kept sliding, taking the legs out of a random Damned as she slid. He smacked his head on the hard ground, cracking his skull like an egg. Parasites spilled everywhere.

No one stuck around to see if he was dead. They all got up and ran, darting in and out of buildings of all sizes all while pointing themselves at the dilapidated stairway. This time, they stayed close, refusing to separate from one another. Zahra was armed with her grappling hook, swinging it around like an amateur Japanese *kyoketsu-shoge* fighter, and she did so with the hooks wide open.

One of the blades impaled itself in the temple of a Damned woman and was grotesquely torn free with the flick of Zahra's wrist. Even worse was the pressurized geyser of inch-long worms that spurt from the wound. She didn't care. At this point, Zahra's revulsion had been dulled by her tiredness, and the heat and smoke of the cavern. She doubted she'd ever be truly disgusted by anything ever again.

A slight woman limped out from behind a squat, square structure. The top half of her skull was missing, giving the world a glimpse into exactly what was going on inside her head.

Literally.

*Ugh,* she thought, *spoke too soon.*

The exposed innards of her brain were the worst thing yet. It was as if someone had glued a dust mop head to the top of the woman's skull and then somehow brought it to life with electricity. The worms wriggled and moved in sync with each other, and with every coordinated pulse, she moved.

Baahir covered his mouth with his hand. "I think I'm gonna be — "

Zahra grabbed his shirt and pulled him left. "Me too, brother. Me too."

# CHAPTER 106
# ZAHRA

The Damned thinned out as they moved farther away from the courtyard, but that didn't mean they weren't still in trouble. The crumbling ground sped up, chasing them. Zahra could barely breathe. Baahir was wheezing worse than she was. Ali's shoulder was giving him fits, and having to run wasn't helping. Rabia was tired, but otherwise fine, annoyingly so. Zahra loved her to death, but she was sick of that woman never looking miserable.

Zahra couldn't imagine how terrible she looked right now.

The ground shook, causing Baahir and her to lose their footing and careen into one another. Baahir went down hard, smacking his chin on a chunk of rock. He cursed and clutched his face with both his hands. Zahra was frightened that he was seriously hurt — and so close to the end too. His hands came away slathered in blood, and when he looked up at her, she sighed in relief.

Baahir held up his open hand. Inside was a tiny white square.

"My tooth!" he said, whistling slightly. Blood ran down his chin.

If Zahra had been in better spirits, she would have died laughing. Now, she might die from the lack of breathable air.

"I'll buy you a new one," Ali said, hauling him to his feet. "Come. We are nearly there!"

Zahra recognized the part of the city they were in. They had just stumbled upon the main road — the one they had used when they had first arrived. That meant that the entry stairs were on the other end and were a straight shot from here.

Just the thought of seeing the sun again was all the motivation she needed, but instead of pouring on the speed, she laid back and helped Rabia with Ali. He was struggling with his shoulder, mightily. The bouncing motion of having to run was jostling the injured joint to the point of him whimpering with every step.

"That bad?" she asked.

Ali could only nod, locking his jaw as he moved.

*And he did it because of me.*

Zahra gave herself some credit. It had been a life-or-death situation and she would have absolutely done the same thing if the roles had been reversed. They had all saved one another so many times that it would have been impossible to keep track if they had tried to do so.

A thicker, tall, Damned man stood in the middle of the road. He was all that stood in the way of their freedom. Him, and a crumbling staircase. Zahra unclipped her hook and handed it to her brother, allowing ten feet of cord to unspool. Baahir understood her thinking, and the siblings separated themselves far enough to stretch the cord out taut. They shouted like mad and ran at the larger man with the cord dipped low, taking out his ankles. He faceplanted into the road with a thud.

Baahir handed the hook head back to his sister and gladly mounted the first step. Rabia and Ali skimmed past him and climbed higher. Zahra didn't. She came to a stop just before the first step and looked out over the "Lost City of the Damned." This was the second lost civilization she had found recently, yet oh-so different than the one prior. Her previous find had been a living, breathing ancient society of people untouched by modernism. This was a true hell on earth and something that needed to be buried from the world above. Zahra did not plan on telling anyone about this place, and she was pretty damn sure the others felt the same way.

"Nothing good can come from this place," she muttered to herself.

"What was that?" Baahir asked, joining her below.

She turned and confirmed her hypothesis. "We can't tell anyone what we found down here, correct?"

Rabia and Ali shared a look but nodded.

Zahra turned and stared at her little brother. Baahir was a talker, but even he threw his hands up. "Fine, fine... But if anyone asks, the bruises came from a passionate lover."

Two separate hordes of the Damned appeared through the haze, but they didn't advance past the city limits. Baahir was the first to put it all together.

"The sulfur," he said, taking in a large lungful of air.

"What about it?" Zahra asked.

"It's thinner here. They can't follow us. If they do, they'll suffocate—like a fish out of water."

Ali patted him on the shoulder. "Best news I've heard all day."

The entire city rumbled, and the majority of it plummeted into the roiling pool of magma. Zahra clumsily pushed Baahir up the steps, and the quartet of exhausted explorers began the arduous climb to freedom. The busted sections of steps were an issue, but luckily there were four brains working together to find a solution.

Zahra tossed her grappling hook up the steps with the hope of hooking it onto a jagged outcropping of rock. She got a hold, then handed the line to the others. They held it tight, allowing Zahra to use it as well as the crags in the wall to her right to scale her way up.

Once Rabia had completed the parkour move and was standing next to Zahra, she lobbed the head of the hook to her brother, and he used it hook one of the lower steps. The two women drew it taught and held tight. Baahir scrambled up to them next. Ali struggled to get a foothold on the wall while also pulling himself along with one hand — his movements kept pushing himself away from the rock, like a rappelling exercise.

He gave up. "Just go," he said, staring up at Rabia.

Baahir snorted from down below. "Not a chance. We'll think of something."

Zahra was impressed with her brother's determination.

She thought for a moment. "Throw me the hook."

Ali did.

Zahra tossed the end of the cord back to him. "Tie this off to your belt. We'll pull you up."

Ali was about to argue.

Baahir butted in. "Just do it, dammit."

Ali grinned and did as he was told. "Now what?"

"Now," Zahra said, bracing herself. She smiled down at Ali. "Pray we don't drop you." She winked. "It's been a long day."

Ali rolled his eyes, but allowed the others to get into position. Naturally, Rabia was up front for this one. Baahir stood two steps up and was behind her. Zahra wrapped the line around her waist several times and gave her brother a three-step buffer. She wasn't going to let go, no matter what happened.

The gap in the steps was the largest of what they'd need to scale. Once they passed this final test, they'd be home free.

*Don't forget the man-killers, dummy.*

The cavern itself cried out with the shaking earth, and it spurred Ali into motion. He took two steps and leaped out into nothing, stretching his right arm out. Rabia, knelt and their fingertips touched. She locked wrists with him and somehow held him aloft long enough for Zahra and Baahir to pull the cord tight and backpedal up the steps. Rabia bore the rest of Ali's weight by herself and, quite literally, dragged him onto the staircase.

Once she had both hands locked around his wrist, Zahra and Baahir dove forward and grabbed whatever they could, and continued pulling him up. He fell into Rabia's arms, and she squeezed him tight, and they rode the wave of shaking earth together. Once it subsided, the duo gingerly climbed to their feet.

"Geez," Zahra said.

"Yeah, guys. Get a room," Baahir finished.

It was the first time that Zahra had seen the woman look embarrassed, but she didn't let go of Ali. They moved apart while Zahra reeled in her line, watching building after building, and Damned after Damned, disappear into the molten earth.

The thought made her shudder, and she turned and hurried to catch up to the others. If the cavern's structure completely collapsed, they'd be royally screwed — dying by asphyxiation or getting squeezed like a lemon.

Or just swiftly charbroiled.

They eventually found themselves on the landing that overlooked the Temple of Anubis. From here, it looked like lake of liquid fire. Zahra watched as the last of the buildings, roadways, and the long-dead Anubis victims were swallowed.

"That's it," Zahra said, turning back and looking over her friends. "They're all dead..." she shrugged. "For good, this time."

# CHAPTER 107
# ZAHRA

They took the hike to the surface at a steady pace. All of them wanted out as soon as possible, but Zahra finally felt that they were no longer in danger, unless the magma continued to rise.

Zahra prayed it wouldn't. She wasn't sure she could move any faster than she was now.

"I'm not running for a month after this," Baahir said, getting a chortle out of everyone.

Zahra agreed. "Two months for me."

"I could go for a beer."

They stopped and turned their attention to Ali. He shrank back. "What?"

Rabia wrapped her arm around Ali's waist, earning a grimace from him. "I'll buy the first round."

*Deal,* Zahra thought. She looked forward to seeing a different side of Rabia after the woman got a few drinks in her.

They marched past the rooms of the main corridor, paying them no attention. The next room was the space they had proclaimed as a 'torture chamber.' Zahra refused to even look at any of the bodies. Her nerves were frayed, and she needed to stay strong until they made it outside. Then, she'd allow her emotions to burst forth, and flood like the Nile in the summer.

They walked through and reached the man-killer pit room, taking the dilapidated landbridge slowly. She didn't know if the scorpions were back in their holes, or if the collapsing cavern down below had scared them off.

No one wanted to find out.

Zahra had been beyond lucky to survive the fall she had taken the first time, and no one wanted to run it back for a second chance.

"Watch your footing," Zahra reminded the group. She bounded over the break in the bridge.

The group took turns leaping the small gap, then stopped for a moment just outside the next tunnel.

"Um," Baahir said, pointing back the way they had come, "what's that?"

Zahra felt the heat hit her face as she turned to look. The lake of magma had, indeed, risen.

"Time to pick up the pace again!" she shouted.

The first set of spiraling stairs passed by in a blur, but whatever momentum they had gained came to a screeching halt once they entered the trap room. Thankfully, all they had to do was avoid the central floor's trigger Baahir had stepped on earlier, and they would be scot-free.

Zahra lifted her foot to begin the next phase of their ascent and felt her leg turn to mush and then cramp up. She pushed through it — it wasn't a good time for her body to fail her.

Everyone struggled up the topmost spiral staircase. They trudged along, looking over their shoulders every few steps for the incoming sulphuric glow.

It moved toward them ominously, but slowly.

And suddenly she saw something else.

"Guys, look."

*Daylight.*

The others let out a collective sigh and finished the climb in silence. The low sun was there waiting for them, as were Elyas and Tajj. They were leaning against a boulder, looking downright bored — which was good. Hopefully, it meant they hadn't seen any action.

Still, she was a bit jealous — she wished they could split the action *she'd* experienced between the two groups.

Neither man said a word. They saw the state of the team and immediately rushed forward, tossing out bottles of water and protein bars.

Ali waved them off when they asked how injured he was, but he did accept a handful of painkillers.

Everyone else easily gulped down their bottles of water, and then sat or laid down.

"What about Ayad?" Tajj asked.

Zahra sat up on her elbows, having opted to lay on her back. "He's gone. The Scales of Anubis are no more."

# CHAPTER 108
# ZAHRA

The climb down the pyramidal mountain was a rough one. They followed the path they had used earlier that day. Zahra couldn't believe she hadn't pass out from exhaustion. The water had helped immensely, keeping her upright and conscious. As did the snack. It was enough sustenance to get them back to solid ground.

Ali and Rabia gave Elyas and Tajj the short version of what they had discovered down below, including Anubis and the Damned. The full truth would be kept secret from the rest of the world, at least for now, but Ali's men deserved to know more than most.

They came upon an abandoned four-door SUV that must have belonged to Khaliq and his men. Zahra grumbled a string of expletives when she remembered that they didn't have a car of their own. Cork had *dropped* them off.

"Anyone know how to hot-wire this thing?"

"It's new," Rabia said. "Won't work."

*Damn.*

"And we need to get our things from where we hitchhiked into town."

She was right, but it was going to be a long, *long* walk. And then what? She wasn't sure Cork would even be able to land on these roads, and Zahra was damned sure the pilot wouldn't be able to carry everyone back with her. They had an extra body with them now.

"Oh," Elyas said as if reading her mind, digging into his pocket, "I found this on the man that Rabia shot."

He held up the grandest thing Zahra had ever seen.

A car key.

She sighed in relief, and the six of them piled into the vehicle, happy to see that it sported three rows of seats. Zahra and Baahir slid into the rearmost seat, while Rabia helped Ali into the center seats. Elyas sat up front, and Tajj drove.

Minutes after grabbing their discarded gear, Zahra, Baahir, Rabia, and Ali were fast asleep.

Thankfully, Zahra's subconscious decided to spare her the nightmares of what she had seen down below in favor of a more peaceful slideshow.

She dreamt of Levanzo, Italy. She dreamt of the cottage, and the view it offered.

She dreamt of a peaceful paradise.

# CHAPTER 109
# AJMAL

**The Pharaoh's Lounge** | Giza, Egypt

For the first time in his life, Ajmal had no purpose. Like Khaliq, he had been born into the Scales of Anubis. His late father had been a scholar, and someone that had been held in high esteem within the organization. But Ajmal was not academic at all — he had been an athlete, the biggest kid in his class. When his middle-school growth spurt hit, he had grown taller and thicker than most of his teachers.

*I have no purpose now,* he thought, kneeling.

Ajmal had abandoned his mission in Bawiti. With keys in his pocket, he stole away back to Giza, where he'd attempt to come up with a plan — an excuse — in case Khaliq showed up and questioned his whereabouts. But if he was being honest with himself, Ajmal would rather Khaliq not come back at all. He was tired of being the man's muscle, his "do boy." His voice had been silenced long ago when he was given to the Ayad clan as a kind of trophy.

"My son will serve you well, Aaftab." Ajmal's father had said. "He will protect what you value most."

The valuable commodity was Aaftab's own son, Khaliq.

The gesture spoke volumes as to how the two fathers admired their boys. Aaftab genuinely loved his son. Ajmal was seen as nothing more than an asset used to gain favor within the Scales of Anubis, and for the last thirty-one years, he had done what he was told.

Until now.

*I have no purpose.*

He pulled the sewer manhole cover free and plodded down the steps, covering the entry point before he made his descent. Few people knew of this path. Even fewer had ever taken it. It was actually Ajmal's suggestion that Khaliq have it built as a way out, just in case something awful happened. Owning an underground base of operations had its benefits, but it was also a liability if your only way out was compromised.

There was no light to speak of besides what the moon offered from overhead.

He looked west into the darkness and waited, holding his breath, and listening. Ajmal knew better than to assume he was alone, but after thirty seconds, he moved off and marched east, and counted his steps. He was halfway beneath the parking lot of *The Pharaoh's Lounge* before stopping again. To his right, and concealed within the stone-and-mortar wall, was an access panel. He reached for it, knowing exactly where it was without looking. Ajmal dug his finger into a false crack in the mortar and pulled, popping the camouflaged lid free. It swung open on a maintained hinge to reveal a single red button.

Ajmal pushed it.

The ground in front of him clunked open with a hiss of hydraulics, and another set of stairs was unveiled. He mounted them, and descended, and with every three feet that he traveled, another motion-activated light blinked to life. Once again, Ajmal counted his steps, finishing precisely when he knew he would.

He had arrived.

The same technology was in place here that had been used in the labs. Ajmal placed his thumb against a nondescript pad and held it in place for two seconds. A soft clunk announced that he had successfully gained entry into the Scales of Anubis' underground lair.

He pushed through the door and stopped.

The space on the other side reeked of blood. He kept his eyes on the lit corridor and drew his pistol without a sound. Even from here, he could see the lump in the floor. Someone had died here, for sure, and it was near the exam room holding Grant Upton.

And the door was open.

Ajmal knew the protocols. He had written most of them. A three-man cleaning crew had been sent down to remove Upton from the exam room by any means necessary.

Ajmal leveled his gun at the open doorway and silently, and smoothly, continued down the hall. A second lab had been opened, and it, too, was in a state of carnal disarray. Two men lay dead in a combined pool of blood, tissue, and organs. Ajmal didn't recognize either of them, but knew it would be one of Adnan, Haydar, or Naeem. They had been good men, and like Ajmal, loyal to a fault.

Now, they were dead, torn to pieces by something inhuman.

*Khaliq.*

All of this was his doing. More good people gone as a result of his ambition.

He snapped the pistol into the open doorway, finger resting atop the trigger, but nothing attacked him. Ajmal sidestepped left and repeated the motions in Upton's room. Again, there was nothing.

Satisfied he was alone down here, Ajmal knelt and inspected the body out in the hallway. It was Adnan. He was mostly intact, and his face had been frozen in death.

"Upton," Ajmal said under his breath.

With nothing more to do here, he stood and cleared the room across the hall. Khaliq had ground up the Anubian vase here, catapulting these events into motion. Upton would still be in his cage if it hadn't been for Khaliq, and the cleaning crew would still be alive.

He gritted his teeth and drove his meaty fist into the elevator call button. When the lift arrived, the door slid open to reveal a mess. Blood streaked every surface of the metal box. Ajmal cautiously stepped inside, weary of an attack from above. The hatch in the roof of the elevator cabin would be the only way in or out once it was in motion and not parked on its intended floor.

Ajmal selected the button for the research floor, and he was whisked away. Seconds later, he arrived. The room was still, and in much worse shape than the labs, mostly because there were more people here, on average. With his gun down by his leg, Ajmal waited to exit. He wanted to see if anything in the natural cave was still alive.

He took in the room, shocked to see that it was completely devoid of life. It was usually the busiest department within the Scales of Anubis. That's when he noticed the blood — he smelled it too. The reason the research floor was devoid of life was because everyone in it had been slaughtered.

Something near the light table moved, but Ajmal held his ground. He'd wait longer.

A noise that reminded Ajmal of sliding hay across the floor of his barn caught his ears.

Then just as quickly, it stopped.

"I hear you," he said, stepping forward and lifting his pistol. The door slid shut as he descended the ancient stone steps. If he could entice Upton to —

A hunched figure stood, holding a man by his throat. The victim had been here for years. Salem had been one of the gentlest souls Ajmal had ever met. It was plain to see that Ajmal had been too late. Salem's lifeless eyes could be seen from here.

This was the first time Ajmal had been afraid. The creature standing before him was no longer Grant Upton. His eyes had turned an awful milky white, and they stared straight through Ajmal, causing his very spirit to stir.

"What's wrong?" Upton said. His voice was low and gravelly. He dropped Salem and held out his hands. "Is this not what you desired?"

Ajmal couldn't speak. So, he pulled the trigger of his gun. The bullet struck Upton in the abdomen but did little else than enrage the demon further. He flung a heavy steel table as if it were made of balsa wood. His body rippled with muscle, and his skin was pulled taut, and looked rough, even leathery.

*What's happening to him?* This was most definitely not what Ajmal had wanted.

He pulled the trigger again, but the result was the same as before. The round struck with little effect, other than angering Upton further. This time, Ajmal aimed higher and clipped Upton in the neck, just below his lower jaw. The impact paused Upton's advance, and his hand went to the wound. Had Ajmal mortally injured the man?

Upton looked confused as his hand came away holding a small, white, wiggling creature. To Ajmal, it looked like a worm of some kind. Upton held the insect as if it were a near and dear friend. He gently poked and prodded it until it went still, and quickly grayed in color.

His next emotional outburst wasn't one of sadness.

It was one of unbridled rage.

Ajmal backpedaled, but his heel caught on the ancient entry's lowermost step. He fell and let another four rounds fly. The shots were wild, uncontrolled, and only one of them found their mark, striking Upton in the side. He took the impact in stride and reached up and crushed Ajmal's right wrist as if it were a grape.

The man howled in pain, much to the satisfaction of Upton.

He leaned in close. His breath smelled of rot and copper.

"Is this not what you wanted?"

Ajmal was so close to the man's face. He watched the inside of Upton's eyes undulate with worms. It was sickening.

"No!" Ajmal cried. "I wanted none of this! This was Khaliq's dream!"

Upton sneered. "Ayad... Where is Ayad!"

The elevator door slid open.

"You looking for me?" Ifza asked, stepping out.

"Ifza!" Ajmal shouted, wailing when Upton crushed his mangled wrist more. "Help me!"

"You?" Upton said. "Yes, I know you. You're — "

Ifza raised her steady hand, aimed her pistol at Upton's head, and pulled the trigger. The nine-millimeter jacketed hollow point did as it was designed to do and punched a hole in the man's forehead. It entered and spread, shredding everything it touched until it busted through the back of his skull.

Worms exploded outward from the gory wound. Upton fell backward, dying. He writhed for a moment on the floor, but eventually went still. Ajmal leaped to his feet, swatting the creatures off of his body and face. Ifza descended the steps and took in the room, leveling her gaze at Ajmal when she was done.

Ajmal cradled his broken wrist in his other hand and nodded his thanks to her.

"Ifza, your brother — "

"Is dead, most likely."

Ajmal was taken aback by the ease with which she had said it.

Ajmal sat back down to rest. "This place... it is *ours* for the taking, Ifza. We can mold it into something else — something better."

Ifza nodded softly and turned and faced Ajmal. "You're right, my friend. We could transform the Scales of Anubis into something amazing."

She lifted her gun and shot Ajmal in the chest twice.

"Or... I could do what I should have done years ago, and I can burn this place to the ground."

# EPILOGUE

**Levanzo, Italy**

Zahra sat back with her eyes closed and got lost in the cool breeze coming off the Mediterranean. She cradled a freshly made coffee in her hands, allowing its warmth to offset the crisp temperature. She sat in the same chair as she had done with her father, though he wasn't here this time.

George had returned to Cambridge with the intention of staying in touch with *both* of his kids, regularly. Wally had done what he said he'd do and taken care of him. Besides a few scrapes, and a headful of unanswered questions, her father had fared well.

Baahir was back in Cairo, digging further into the myths surrounding the gods of Egypt. He needed to confirm that there wasn't anything else to fear. If Anubis had been real, man or not, what about the other gods? He was also working with George and looking deeper into their family history. Baahir was still talking to Durah, the woman he met at the Big House market. He had kept his end of their deal and taken her out. Now, they were something of an item.

Rabia and Ali rejoined Wally back at the SSC but were doing so with the idea of shutting down the weapons trafficking portion of their operation. With the Scales of Anubis gone, Ali didn't seem to think it was necessary anymore.

"There are still a lot of bad people out there," Zahra had argued.

Rabia nodded. "Many of which have benefited from our business." She laced her finger within Ali's, showing more outward emotion than she had ever shown before.

"At the very least," Ali added, "we will be more selective on who we do business with."

Zahra was happy to hear that. She wasn't sure what her future held, but could always use someone in their field of work to have in her back pocket.

The breeze kicked up, jettisoning Zahra from her thoughts. She opened her eyes, spotting a sailboat gently rocking back and forth further out to sea.

*I could sit here all day.*

And that was the plan. Zahra was on a permanent leave of absence from the museum. It was going to be under construction for months. Plus, everyone that was killed there... It was just too painful to go back to. Dina had been sad to hear that Zahra wouldn't be returning, but she understood. She was even trying to decide whether or not to stay.

It took Zahra some time, but she was eventually cleared of any wrongdoing when it came to the deadly events at the British Museum. Dina had helped with that. She had told the police that Zahra had spent the night with her and her girlfriend, even going as far as recording videos of a house party that never happened and then backdating the videos to during the time of the museum's attack.

"You sure Josie can handle this?" Zahra had asked, rightfully skeptical. She knew the woman was good with computers and coding, and dabbled in some less-than-legal hacking and tampering, but to this level?

"Josie is a wiz with stuff like this, Z. Don't worry about a thing."

Investigators didn't take much longer to declare that Zahra had nothing to do with what happened. Explaining Grant's disappearance was something else altogether. What could she honestly say? The only positive was that he didn't have any close family nearby. As of now, there was still a missing person's case centered around him.

And as for Cork...

The front door opened. "Hey, girl, how's it hangin'?"

Zahra leaped to her feet and rushed inside from the porch to embrace her good friend. Cork and Dina had gotten together to collect Zahra's things from her London flat.

"You get everything?" Zahra asked.

"Sure did," Cork replied, sticking her thumb over her shoulder. "Have it all in Vincenzo's truck." She grinned. "You have some nice toys, you know?"

Zahra winked and slapped Cork's shoulder. "I know. Give me a hand?"

The two women headed out front, and with the help of Vincenzo, the newly made millionaire, they brought in the rest of Zahra's personals.

"Put them anywhere," Zahra said, moving to the fridge. "I'll go through everything as the days pass." She procured three cold beers from the door and handed them out. "Drinks?"

Cork and Vincenzo happily accepted the beverages.

"It really is a nice place, huh?" Cork asked, getting a grin out of the local. "It was ace of you to buy it for Zahra, Vincenzo."

He gave the women a small bow. "Yes, well, I wouldn't have anything without her help." He smiled. "It was the least I could do."

Zahra lifted her bottle toward him and then drank.

"So," Cork said in between sips, "I don't suppose you'd, um, want a roommate?"

Zahra looked around. As amazing as her new home was, it was small, and wouldn't comfortably sleep more than just Zahra unless she shared her upstairs bed with Cork. But what could she say? None of this would have been possible without the pilot's aid.

"I mean, I can't have my hero pilot sleeping on the streets, can I?"

Cork dove at Zahra and gave her a huge bearhug. Luckily, both women had set their beers down before they embraced. The wood floorboards were beautifully stained and decades old, and Zahra wasn't about to ruin them so soon after moving in.

"Ugh," Zahra groaned, gasping for air. "Down, girl."

"Or," Vincenzo said, getting Zahra and Cork's attention, "Cork could stay in the next-door cottage." He flashed a big smile. "I bought that one too."

Cork released Zahra and dropped her to the floor like a sack of potatoes. She pounded over to Vincenzo, picked up the shorter man, and planted the biggest, wettest kiss on his lips. When they parted, the local looked dazed and concussed.

He shook the cobwebs loose and blushed. "Yes, well, you are very welcome."

Cork seductively rubbed his arm. "There's more where that came from." She gave him a playful wink and brushed by him. "All you have to do is call — you too, Zahra."

"Cork," Zahra said, getting up, "I'm not — "

She waved Zahra off. "You know what I mean!" She headed out. "See you later, *neighbor!*"

**It took Zahra** three days to figure things out. She ended up donating a lot of her stuff, deciding to try a fresh approach to life. The cottage's amenities were enough for her. She kept most of her clothes and, of course, her gear — weapons included. Chief Stefano had invited her and Cork to dinner at his home as a sort of welcome to the community. Zahra still couldn't believe how nice everyone here was.

She climbed the steps to her front door and inserted the key but stopped. Something felt off. It was the first time that Levanzo hadn't felt like paradise. Zahra drew her Glock from beneath her jacket, keeping it hidden from prying eyes. Not that there was anyone to see it. The property was such that no one could see the front door, except from the road. A narrow, wooded area acted as a natural boundary between her and Cork's places.

Zahra slowly turned the key, throwing open the door, and lifting her pistol all in one motion. As she had suspected, Zahra found that she wasn't alone. The light out back was on, and a bald, well-built black man stood beneath it, looking out over the water.

*My water.* Zahra felt violated.

He noticed Zahra's presence and turned to face her, opening his mouth to say something.

Zahra growled, leaving the interior lights off and opting for the shadows. "Who are you?" she barked. "Why are you in my home?"

The stranger looked around, glancing casually over his shoulder. He didn't look at all threatened. He flashed her a sly smirk. "Technically, I'm not inside *your* home, am I?"

She stepped closer, keeping her gun aimed at his face. "Don't play games with me, smartass. You're on my property, unannounced. I have every right to — "

"Easy, Ms. Kane," he said, raising his hands. One of them held a steaming cup of coffee. Zahra had been so locked in that she had missed the alluring aroma.

Her eyes darted into her kitchen. "Did you make coffee?"

His smirk turned into a full-fledged smile. "It's kind of my thing."

Zahra was confused. "Your *thing* is to break into people's homes and make coffee?" She snickered. "You need a new hobby, pal."

"The reason I'm here is — "

"I don't care why you're here," Zahra interrupted. "I'm gonna give you till the count of three to — "

"To get my lousy, lyin', low-down, four-flushing carcass out your door?"

Zahra's jaw dropped. "Did you just quote *Home Alone 2* while at gunpoint?"

He shrugged. "There isn't much that scares me anymore. And I'm sort of a movie buff."

This wasn't the intruder Zahra had expected to deal with.

"This is interesting," he said, picking up Zahra's grappling hook from the table. Zahra hadn't left it there. "You wouldn't happen to know a Tom Colombo, would you?" Zahra couldn't hide her surprise. "You do? Oh, very interesting, indeed."

"Why?"

"He and I worked together a lifetime ago."

"You were with DARPA?"

He shook his head. "No, but I worked alongside them for years."

"Who are you?" Zahra asked, needing to know.

The stranger raised his hands slightly, and then gently set the coffee mug down. He stood tall, demanding, confirming Zahra's rising suspicion. He was military, possibly someone with real authority. *A colonel?* Judging by his age, he might even be a general.

Either way, this guy was used to commanding the attention of the room.

"My name is Solomon Raegor, and I oversee a little outfit called the *Tactical Archaeological Command*. We're under the DOD, but it's a pretty... loose 'under.'" He stepped inside and flicked on the house lights. "And I'd like to offer you a job."

Zahra lowered her aim. "What kind of job?"

CONUNDRUM
PUBLISHING
THE
BEST
IN
THRILLERS
PERIOD.
3 FREE BOOKS:
CONUNDRUMPUB.COM/FREE

# PRAISE FOR THE AUTHORS

Two of the genre's best writers team up!

— ERNEST DEMPSEY, *USA TODAY* BESTSELLING AUTHOR OF WHERE HORIZONS END

Matt James and Nick Thacker teaming together is like mixing nitroglycerin and C4—a high energy, explosive mix that is sure to be a blast. Bring it on!

— GREIG BECK, BESTSELLING AUTHOR OF THE ALEX HUNTER SERIES

You will not find a more dynamic duo than Nick Thacker and Matt James!

— RICK JONES, INTERNATIONAL BESTSELLING AUTHOR OF THE VATICAN KNIGHTS

Imagine a collaboration between James Rollins and Clive Cussler, and you've only scratched the surface of what Matt James and Nick Thacker have accomplished!

— MICHAEL MCBRIDE, INTERNATIONAL BESTSELLING AUTHOR OF SUBHUMAN

Thacker and James are two of the very best!

— ANDREW CLAWSON, BESTSELLING AUTHOR OF THE ARTHURIAN RELIC

Copyright © 2022 by Matt James & Nick Thacker

All rights reserved.

No part of this book may be reproduced in any form or by any electronic or mechanical means, including information storage and retrieval systems, without written permission from the author, except for the use of brief quotations in a book review.

# About Matt James

Hi, my name is Matt. I'm the international bestselling author of the electrifying JACK REILLY ADVENTURES, as well as two dozen other titles, including DARK ISLAND, and the intense UNSEEN action-horror novels. Moreover, I've been fortunate enough to partner with USA Today bestselling author Nick Thacker to create the wildly popular ZAHRA KANE archaeological thriller series. I'm also the Managing Editor for Conundrum Publishing, and I host REAL-LIFE FICTION on YouTube, a video podcast that features the book industry's finest talents.

My work is heavily influenced by the likes of Indiana Jones, Uncharted, Tomb Raider, The Mummy (1999), National Treasure, and The Goonies. As you can see, I'm a little obsessed with tales of daring adventure. When I was growing up, other kids went nuts for Star Wars or Star Trek. But not me. I fell in love with the globetrotting antics of Dr. Henry Jones, Jr., and the rest, as they say, was history. From that moment on, I was hooked. Though I dabble in other genres from time to time, my heart will always belong to ADVENTURE.

I live twenty minutes from the beach in sunny South Florida with my amazing wife, our two beautiful daughters, a lovable pitty, and an overly dramatic black cat.

YOU CAN VISIT MATT AT:

Website: MattJamesAuthor.com

Podcast: Real-Life Fiction

ConundrumPub.com

facebook.com/MattJamesAuthor

instagram.com/MattJames_Author

# ABOUT NICK THACKER

Nick Thacker is a thriller author from Texas who lives in Hawaii and Colorado. In his free time, he enjoys reading in a hammock on the beach, skiing, drinking whiskey, and hanging out with his beautiful wife, two dogs, and two daughters.

*For more information and a list of Nick's other work, visit Nick online:*
www.nickthacker.com

Made in United States
North Haven, CT
04 December 2024